42

42

a novel

M. Thomas Cooper

Ooligan Press
Portland State University
Portland, Oregon

Cover photo by Gary Cowles

Ooligan Press
Department of English
Portland State University
P.O. Box 751
Portland, OR 97207-0751
www.ooliganpress.pdx.edu

ISBN: 978-1-932010-24-4

Printed in the United States of America by
United Graphics, Inc.

Ooligan Press wishes to acknowledge and thank
Tin House Books for their sponsorship of
this book. For information on Tin House Books,
visit them at www.tinhouse.com.

To my parents,
John and **Helen**, for their
unwavering support
over the years. And,
of course, to **Carrie**—the
truest muse.

Acknowledgments

Writing and reading are solitary endeavors. However, the creation of a book requires a group of dedicated individuals and I would like to thank them for their effort and invaluable assistance. Chris Baty and the Nanowrimo crew for envisioning and implementing such an outlandish idea. Bill Johnson for his insightful comments on the early draft and the art of writing. Stan Ridgeway for his inspiring music. Portland State University and Dennis Stovall for Ooligan Press. The magnificent acquisitions editors of the press, Katrina Hill and Karli Clift. The most insightful and thorough editor ever, Kylin Larsson. Those devout souls in marketing, particularly Amanda Taylor. Professor Karen Kirtley and her exceedingly observant editing class. And also Penny Lyden, Karin Magaldi, William Tate, and Roger Weaver. As well as Kathleen and the Fantastic Five (Tim, Tammy, Jacob, Kaitlyn, and Zac). And finally, thank you, the reader, for spending a few moments with us and this beautiful item called a book.

"The **past** is never what it was
when it was the **present**."

—James Quincey O'Keefe
The Ballad of Low Tide

Prologue:

Truth and Honesty

I've seen the answer through the smoke, heard it on the wind, and accepted its scar on my skin. And though I don't know who is asking, or why, I do know the answer: the answer to the riddle of my life.

I know, declare, claim, and swear the answer is forty-two.

Curious words to write to one's self? Perhaps. Though is it not more curious to attempt to write a recollection, a recounting, of the past so the present may be understood enough to have a future? Perhaps even a future disengaged from whence the past was taking me, guiding me.

Does that make sense? I think it does. I hope it does.

First, let me begin by committing myself to honesty: I do hereby swear to tell the truth, the whole truth, and nothing but the truth. I will not waver when I must write about myself, "George Thomas Olson has once again claimed another lunch at Carafe with Charles as a business expense." Or, "Is it possible to differentiate sanity from insanity if one is insane?" Or, more to the point, "I am in great fear of not being a better husband, a better father, than I was."

Though this recollection is sure to be a daunting task, I have a memento, a lone one, taped to one of the surrounding whitewashed walls. I plan on using it, using it for inspiration.

It's an old photo of me as a child. I must be two-ish. My parents took me on a road trip through the southwest, even into Mexico. In the picture, I'm as dirty and unkempt as a beggar's child. I seem to be holding something small, precious, and magical, at least based on the reverent curve of my hands. You can't see the object. And I, unfortunately, don't remember what it was. But there's some talisman, distinctly there. The look on my face is an odd mixture of guilt and elation. Behind me, taking up the entire background, is my parents' car, a dusty, lime-green Volkswagen bug. The license plate, YHW 423, like a curious halo, shimmers above my head.

I also hope to use that curious gleam in the child's eyes to illuminate the path I took to reach these coordinates in space and time. And, honestly, how do I know that was me, when I am what I am now?

And who am I now? Where am I now?

Easy questions if I wanted easy answers. For I would simply say: I am on an island, in a white room overlooking the sea, writing and ignoring the mesmerizing voices of the Sirens. I'm not looking for easy answers, though. In this recollection I quest for something more ephemeral—the truth. Perhaps that's what the child once held? Perhaps. Perhaps not.

Are you ready to begin? I think I am. I hope I am.

As the sage Lao Tzu once said, "A journey of a thousand miles must begin with a single step." So, I assume the longest story, and for that matter the shortest, begins with the first word. And the first word to this story, my story, our story, is "bougainvillea."

No, actually, it's something much more disturbing than that. It's "destiny."

The First Incident:

Saturday, March 20, 2004

"Destiny?" I ask my daughter quizzically. Not because I wasn't familiar with the concept. I was; I was simply curious why an eight-year-old would be asking, particularly at the end of a frozen food aisle in a Portland, Oregon, Costco.

"Yes," Mirabella says, nodding her dark tresses, "destiny."

"Why?" I ask suspiciously, sure she's got some wicked eight-year-old subterfuge hidden behind her mother's brilliant brown eyes.

"Because Momma said you and she were destined to be together. So, it's destiny to be here." She, I think, means "born" and not "at the end of a frozen food aisle in a Portland, Oregon, Costco."

"Oh, I see." I glance down the crowded aisle to where a woman dressed in running shoes, black sweat pants and top, dark hair pulled through a baseball cap, searches for salmon fillets. Francesca, my wife, Mirabella's mother, turns her dark eyes toward us and smiles. She gives a thumbs-up and dives between two carts to grip the silver handle of a freezer door. Quickly she opens it, withdraws two packages of salmon fillets, and ducks back into the chaotic flow of seething shoppers.

I watch her gradually make her way toward us.

"Papa?"

"Destiny, Mirabella, is...." Already my explanation tastes sour and stale. I'm sure it has everything to do with my clandestine meeting that morning with ██████.

"Honey, I'm heading off to work for an hour or two," I hollered, almost through the door of our museum-immaculate home. "Going to try and get caught up on the shareholders' brochure. Okay?" I work in the Black Box, a building downtown at the corner of Third and Market. The insurance company I work for is on the seventeenth floor. We cover everything, from homeowners to life to health to travel to pets. We like to say, "God won't, but we will." An inside joke about assurances in life—the only two supposedly being death and taxes. My company will insure anything between those two, between death and taxes.

I run the publications department for the entire company, nationwide. The overseas branches take care of their own materials. Too much can be lost in translation, particularly between British and English, or, as they say, "Americane." That's another stupid little joke we have. Anyway, I had my car key in hand and Francesca was de-hairing the couch with one of those hair-removal–roller-things.

"Honey? Okay?"

"Okay," she said from the living room, running the roller over and over the couch. She peeled a hair-covered strip off. "But you can be back by one to watch Mirabella? ¿Sí? The ladies, we are going for a little run. Okay?"

"Sure. Oh, are we still going to Costco?"

"Later. After the run."

"Right. I'll be back by one." And I left. And instead of going to work, instead of working on the preliminary proofs for the shareholders' brochure, I went to ███████'s loft.

"Papa?" Mirabella tugs my sleeve and pulls me back into the present.

"Oh, right. Sorry." I notice that Francesca, halfway through her migration, has scooped up four packets of frozen fish sticks. "Destiny is the idea, the concept, that certain things—actually most things—are preordained."

"Papa?"

"What?"

"Smaller words. Remember?"

"What?"

"Pre—or.. or—"

"Preordained, it's a synonym for destiny." Mirabella scrunches her brow accusingly at me. "Sorry, sweetie. Preordained means basically the same thing as destiny."

"Oh. But what's *that* mean?"

Breathless, Francesca arrives and unceremoniously drops the salmon fillets and fish sticks atop the miscellany crowding the cart.

"Your daughter has a question for you," I say in an attempt to extricate myself from between the bull's horns.

"Does she?" Mirabella nods and smiles. "Well?" Francesca asks.

I push and follow, while Francesca, explaining destiny, gathers and places items in the cart. As she does so, I attempt to ignore the glare of the ruddy captain on the packets of fish sticks.

Francesca, I must admit, does an admirable job with her explanation, even though her statement, "Destiny is Life's way of giving hope," leaves me perplexed. I'd like to ask for clarification, but the captain's stare bores into me. It's as if he knows (all four of him) of my morning's indiscretion.

"George?!"

I look up. Francesca is ten feet away, hovering on the edge of the wine and bakery section. Mirabella holds a bag of spinach that's as big as she is.

"What are you doing?"

I push the cart to them. Mirabella muscles the bag of spinach into the cart.

"Maybe you should go get some wine?" Francesca knows my predilection for the grape, which she occasionally guides me toward as a general panacea.

I shake my head. I'd much prefer stabbing the captains blind.

"I'll wait for you out front."

"George?" I stop and turn. People mill about. A chubby, elderly man carrying a giant picture book of World War II walks between us. "Are you alright?"

It's as if I'm in the café scene from one of Francesca's favorite movies, *Abre los Ojos*. Everyone is looking, staring, peering at me. Knowing something I don't, but should.

"George? Are you alright?"

"Yes. Yes, I think so." It's just one more lie. I think—hope—this one will matter less than the others.

I give Francesca a quick kiss on the cheek as she takes over the controls and makes a beeline for soups and pastas.

As I head for the exit I overhear Mirabella say, "Papa needs a unicorn." I, unfortunately, don't hear Francesca's reply, though I do know exactly what Mirabella means.

I contemplate sitting in the car and listening to the radio, letting the car's dull warmth, like an Easy-Bake Oven, slowly cook me clean. Or maybe I'll read a few pages from Francesca's traffic book. She always has some trite pulp book under her seat in case she's caught in traffic or has to wait for Mirabella at school. I believe her current selection is *Ghost Lights*, a sordid tale of murder and mayhem in a big city theatre.

Exiting into fresh air, I realize I've only a vague and shadowy recollection of where we parked. A doll of Mirabella's had lost an arm; while Francesca parked, I attempted to return the limb to its designated socket. Thus distracted, I only remember that she parked the car somewhere on the east side of the building, probably in quadrant F, G, or H. Maybe even as far as I.

Rather than aimlessly wander the parking lot, which I'll admit I've done once or thrice before, I sit.

I prop myself against a pillar near the exit, where I can't miss the ladies leaving. The exiting crowd flows past me as the sun's spring rays seep into me, slow and steady.

Rivers and streams have always fascinated me, particularly on the hottest summer days. Especially mountain streams. Watching them flow ceaselessly without end perplexes me. It seems at some juncture they should stop flowing. Rationally, after a few weeks without rain, the rivers, the streams, should slowly dry up, and then disappear.

Sitting, watching the masses move in, move out, I'm struck with the same fascination, though somehow more so. First, I'm struck by the amount of people, all seemingly identical and faceless, flowing in. It doesn't cease. There's one after the other after the other. Second, I'm struck by the amount of products (which also seems to be endless) being removed from the warehouse by the identical faceless masses.

It seems logical that at some point along the chain of supply there'd be a gap, which would affect things here. That the store would eventually run out of products, of things, of stuff, and be forced to close. When I consider the number of people going in and coming out, this eventuality seems inevitable. And then, to think about all the other Costco's and big-box stores, it boggles the mind, at least mine.

Waiting for the ladies, I ponder. And while pondering, I intently watch the masses go in and come out. Come out and go in. Niagara Falls pours over seven hundred and fifty thousand gallons of water over its cliffs every second. Though the numbers aren't as large here, I swear it's just as staggering watching the people come and go. Go and come.

I'm as diligent as I possibly can be in watching for Francesca and Mirabella, but after nearly twenty minutes I begin to wonder if I missed them. I might miss them, but I should think they'd see me sitting in the sun, smiling benevolently as Buddha.

Another ten, fifteen minutes pass. Okay, assuming they've escaped the building, I missed them. They missed me. Somehow we missed one another.

Another ten minutes pass. Maybe I should go ask someone to make an announcement over the intercom? No, that would be ridiculous. How could a grown man lose his family? No, that's ridiculous. Another ten minutes go by.

Something nearby begins to ring and ring. Something so close it's practically inside me—my cell phone.

"Where are you?" I ask.

"Where are *you*?" she asks. Her tone is as cold and annoyed as mine.

"Exactly where I've always been. Right by the exit," I say, looking around, confirming that's exactly where I am. Francesca doesn't say anything. "Where are you?" I ask, almost afraid of the answer.

"Turn left."

Through the flowing throng I see a dark-haired, dark-eyed woman in a black jogging suit. She is not smiling.

During our walk to the car, she's adamant that I'd gone somewhere.

"Nowhere. I went nowhere. I stayed right there." I stop and point to the exact spot. "In the sun. Waiting."

She shakes her head.

"Mirabella looked. I looked. You were not there." She begins to add something, but stops. I believe she wants to say something about my not being here, in the marriage, for years—thankfully she doesn't.

"Where would I go?" I ask.

"I do not know. We waited."

"So, why didn't you call sooner?" I hear her Spanish Inquisition sigh. The one she uses when I'm being obviously, blatantly stupid and won't, for my own salvation, confess to my failings and shortcomings.

"I did. And I left a message."

I look at the blank face of the phone. There's no blinking message indicator. I pull a packet of yellow sticky notes out of my pocket and scribble,

Contact cell
company re:
messages

on one. The yellow sticky notes are my external hard drive, a place for miscellaneous information, tasks, and questions to be compiled.

"Well, I didn't get it."

She sighs again. Again she gently turns the thumbscrews. "We even went home and unpacked. And, for some reason, we've returned. It's been over an hour, George."

"What? You went home?"

"Yes. And back." I notice Mirabella in the backseat of the Eurovan, waving, smiling. I do the same in return.

"Francesca, I was right there the whole time." I too am insistent and adamant. "Besides," I say, hoping repetition will sway the jury, "where would I go?"

She replies slowly for emphasis, "I do not know."

"Nor do I. But...." We realize we're simply lighting matches in a wind tunnel, getting nowhere. "I can go home with you, right?"

Inquisition eyes, stern, disappointed, stare at the poor, lost soul strapped in the chair.

Finally she sighs a yes, knowing there's time enough to coerce a confession.

The Second Incident:

Wednesday, March 24, 2004

As per usual, Zeus and I escape to the park after dinner. Zeus is the middle-aged Rottweiler and bastard mix we saved from the gas chamber. For the most part he's a good dog. He does have a penchant for chasing cats and farting, but that's all the more reason to love him, isn't it? He's got a patch of white, supposedly the brand of shame for a Rottweiler, on his chest. A breeder suggested making a slit up his chest and sewing together the edges to hide this shameful, disgusting patch. I thanked the gentleman for his concern and told him, "No." Three steps later I told Zeus, "Go for the throat if he says anything else." Zeus, without missing a step, looked up, nodded, and grinned hungrily.

Traditionally, Zeus takes a dump a few blocks from the house. At this juncture it's impractical for me to return home with the plastic bag full of smoldering poo. I honestly believe he knows what he's doing. Basically, the knotted bag of steamy poo is my collar—Zeus claiming dominion over me. It's just a simple and gentle reminder to myself and the world of who, exactly, is in charge.

So, Wednesday, March 24, is like any other night. After an unenthusiastic dinner of salmon, salad, and bread, Francesca and I noncommittally chat about anything except what matters—our relationship. We chat about work, about where we might go for summer vacation, what to do with the unused and neglected raised beds in the "garden." The "garden" is actually two pathetic eight-foot by four-foot beds of amended soil I spent a weekend creating. They grow mainly weeds, though occasionally a few heirloom tomato plants or sunflowers struggle into the light of day.

We talk, or attempt to talk, to Mirabella about school.

"How is—" It doesn't matter what we ask. It could be about "the Martian cheese pie," or "sleeping on shredded glass," or "juggling chainsaws." Regardless of the topic, Mirabella's answer is the same: "Fine." Mirabella seems to be exchanging precocious for dark and depressed. Teen angst at eight is exactly what I was looking forward to and had hoped for.

"Is she okay?" I assume Francesca knows more than I do about what's troubling Mirabella, if not everything else.

"She is fine." Like mother, like daughter. Maybe that's where Mirabella picks up her ambivalence? Or, maybe Francesca picks it up from me, and it gets passed to Mirabella?

Quickly, lest blame actually be associated with me, I ask, "You're sure?"

"Sí."

"Okay."

"What is the problem for you?"

Gazing into Francesca's eyes, a sadness wells up inside me. Where did we get lost? Where exactly did we get off track? Sure, there were times I wondered why we stayed together. But that, I think, is the case for most couples. Maybe we should've accepted her father's offer to work for him in Milan those many years ago? Maybe a condo instead of a house? Maybe a country wagon in lieu of a Eurovan? Maybe roses rather than azaleas? Maybe. Maybe. Maybe. I can only look around and see what I have now. It's far too late to ponder the "what-ifs" and "maybes," isn't it?

Francesca smiles. She stands, picks up the leftover dishes, and marches to the sink with purpose.

In the awkward silence that lags between us, I ignore myself and wonder what if it'd been '89 instead of '88 I'd decided to flee the expectations of my parents and the gaping maw of "the real world"? Or if I'd taken the 11:15 via Chicago on TWA, instead of the 10:30 on Delta? And instead of Dublin to Killarney to Cork, I'd gone Tokyo to Kyoto to Okinawa? What if I'd missed the ferry to France? What if that severed hand hadn't surfaced in the soup and the horde of French schoolgirls hadn't subsequently vomited everywhere? What if we'd not fled (separate trajectories, but the same destination) the rising intestinal fumes to a remote corner of the lurching ferry? Would we be here? A forlorn husband wondering how long he has to remain until he can leave? A manic mother, the dishes now scrubbed and placed appropriately in the dishwasher, appraising the cleanliness of a pathetic coffeemaker?

Of course these are moot and futile questions, but aren't they relevant? Am I hacking a narrow track out of an overgrown forest? Or simply following a well-defined path that seems to be haphazard?

What if Francesca, now vigorously shaking the coffeemaker over the sink, hadn't found the same remote corner on the ferry? Or if neither of us had had a bottle of wine stowed in our backpacks? And if it'd been deep summer, instead of early spring, giving us much less reason to huddle together against the night's chill, to notice the curves and bends of our bodies, the rise and fall of attraction.

Francesca inspects the undercarriage of the coffeemaker as if it were the Rosetta Stone. A few black grounds accompanied by a brown liquid seep from a corner and mar the pristine countertop. I hide a wan smile behind the towel I hand her.

And whose idea was it to trek to Le Mont St. Michel? Francesca's, or mine? Yes, absolutely, a worthy adventure, particularly her straddling me one afternoon in the deep, cold shadows of a looming building. But, my God, what a maze and labyrinth to have escaped, only to spend the next few days falling, remorseful, through the twisted confines of Paris.

Francesca takes a spray bottle out and squirts the coffeemaker profusely. The kitchen fills with the fragrant stench of oranges—one of the only benefits of her obsession. Occasionally, if I close my eyes, I don't know if I'm in an orchard or a house.

What if while pregnant she'd had a glass of wine, a piece of chocolate? Was that when she stopped painting? Maybe I should've been more emphatic about her painting, my writing, or our lives? What about a house in the country, instead of the city? Carpet instead of hardwoods? Stopped drinking coffee, eating red meat, or watching Disney movies?

God, all these questions—were there answers, once, long ago? Or, have they too been lost, like Francesca and me?

Francesca, the coffeemaker nestled in her lap, is scrubbing furiously. The scent of oranges has dissipated, and something vaguely burnt and sour has taken its place. I wait a long moment, afraid she, and it, will burst into flames. Nothing happens, but still I stare in anticipation.

"What is wrong?" she asks, looking up from her reflection, the burning metal.

Again I smile and stand, the appropriate amount of time and consideration seemingly having passed for a forlorn husband. I kiss her on the cheek, and say, "Nothing. It's perfect."

"You are sure?" she asks, dubious, turning the coffeemaker this way and that.

"For the moment, yes." This seems to satisfy me, but not her.

Mirabella has disappeared somewhere. She's probably figuring out which tattoo she wants where, how to get a twenty-year-old meth addict for a boyfriend, and be pregnant by twelve. Or she's watching *SpongeBob*.

I leave Francesca sitting in the chair, scrubbing and scrubbing and scrubbing, and attempt to ignore the growing, thickening clouds of "what ifs" and "maybes."

So, I've rattled Zeus's leash, he's bounded over, and we've escaped on our walk.

Dutifully, four blocks from the house, he takes his dump. I thank him for his consistency and use a plastic bag to pick up the warm, steamy mound. He smiles up at me.

"Fuck you, Zeus. Fuck you," I say with a friendly and playful tone. He stares up at me, as if trying to apologize. As if saying, "Sorry, I'm just a dog. Taking big, steamy dumps is part of my business. Just like editing insurance brochures is yours."

"Good point," I say, tying the bag securely closed, "They approximate the same thing, don't they?" He looks up, smiling in agreement. I make a loop in the leash, cinch it tightly, and so the bag now dangles between us. "Okay. Let's go." Zeus bounds off down the sidewalk, pulling the leash taut and me behind him. The bag sways rhythmically as we go.

The days are staying lighter later, and spring, once again, begins staining the air with hope. With the warming weather a few extra people and pooches mill around the park, which causes us to linger longer than normal. Zeus has a slight crush on a black Lab named Tuesday, who happens to be here. I give the Zeuser a little extra playtime. Besides, the weather is too nice to exchange for a house cramped with subtext, scrubbing, and "fine."

Tuesday's owner is a young woman named June. Perhaps Zeus isn't that infatuated with Tuesday. Maybe I have a slight fixation on June. June is maybe thirty—but more likely twenty-five—with the most beautifully sad, Icelandic blue eyes.

June tends to talk about this and that. "This" tends to be esoteric dogma from the ages—how many angels (if they exist) could fit on a pin's head; where, physically, does heaven reside; what's the color of thunder; what's the sound of one hand clapping? "That" leans toward concrete extrapolations pertinent to social and biological existence—why does the Mayan calendar end on the winter solstice in 2012; is mass destruction of the world's ecosystem inevitable; how long until we begin processing Soylent Green?

Honestly, her "this" and "that" seem to be one and the same, but, regardless, she sure can entice me into believing anything is possible, if not probable. Usually I nod and smile, pretending I know what she's talking about, while actually attempting to decipher something of myself in her blue orbs.

Tonight is no different. June is going on about a phenomenon where the dead supposedly communicate from the grave. Some new technology registers and translates the electrical emissions from the deceased into recognizable speech patterns. She gets a lot of this nonsense from some radio show. As she mentions a movie exploring this phenomenon I imagine us on a bright and brilliant summer day lying beneath an ancient and well-pruned rhododendron. Hidden in the speckled shadows, we neck and grope passionately. Eyes closed, we begin discovering places we didn't know existed. Suddenly her grip is cold, jagged, precise. I open my eyes and in my arms I discover a skeleton.

Thankfully June doesn't notice the odd look on my face as she continues her diatribe on how the dead can, or can't, communicate from the grave and beyond.

Eventually, after a long discussion about whether the dead all speak a common language or retain their mortal languages, we both agree it's getting late. She and Tuesday make their way out of the park. I watch her perfect, Levi's-clad bum saunter off, wondering about the bones clacking within the thin, taut fabric.

Before sinking into a tepid melancholy, I call Zeus over. "Ready Zeusy?" He saunters over and takes the proffered snack. I put his leash on and we walk slowly home, away from June and Tuesday.

It's well into twilight now and the houses glow and cast small pools of light onto the sidewalk. I glimpse miscellaneous people living their miscellaneous lives—actors performing in dollhouses. I wonder if, and rather fear that, I look like them when I'm in mine, performing.

Hesitating to join the other cast members of my play, I contemplate the well-proportioned, two-story Victorian with an arbor-covered driveway. I want to watch me. I want to see the man I am from the outside. I want to see if he looks as tired, as forlorn, as rundown from the outside as I feel from the inside. I want to see if it's visible, this tugging, this sluggish pull into tomorrow and the repetition and subsequent boredom.

I wait and watch for the man. For the man who has seemingly everything, the wife, the daughter, the dog and cat, the house, the classic car, cigars and aged wine. Who has everything except hope, except understanding and salvation.

I wait and watch for this man. I wait to see if he'll take a book from one of the shelves and sit with a glass of red wine to read. I wait to glimpse his daughter, his wife. I wait, but no one walks by a window. The house, like the man's heart, seems to be empty.

Zeus, sensing my impending stumble into a self-imposed gloom, tugs me up the steps.

We enter into a strange and curious stillness.

The living room television is not blaring *Cartoon Network* blather above the banshee wail of the vacuum. Zeus looks up at me. I shrug and let him off the leash. He pads off down the hall as I ponder where the ladies might be. Perhaps in the basement doing laundry, rubbing vile spots from delicate fabric? Maybe they're in the backyard planting bright seeds in the dark earth? Or maybe, hopefully, they're upstairs in the attic unpacking and clearing a space for Francesca's easel and chair? However, that's improbable. It's been ages since Francesca has painted, has done anything except the drudgery of daily chores, as though she is purposefully cementing over her creativity with the quick-drying cement of grocery shopping, laundry, vacuuming, cleaning, organizing, and dusting....

The day Mirabella sprang forth, the Bohemian artist I'd fallen in love with became possessed by the tormented spirit of Martha Stewart. Nothing was ever clean enough, straight enough, pretty enough, or new enough. There was always something bigger, better, brighter needed to make Mirabella happier, our lives more efficient, more fulfilling. She began purchasing videos, cookbooks, self-help books, subscribing to magazine after magazine, and watching endless hours of *Trading Spaces*. Except she never made crafts, she never cooked King Lao's Shrimp or Spicy Polynesian Spareribs, or practiced meditation, yoga, tai chi, flower arranging, or knitting. She did, however, clean and vacuum and clean, endlessly. There were times in the middle of the night when I'd find the bed empty and her detailing the television or Cuisinart. I missed my Bohemian artist, because I sure as hell hadn't married Martha.

Lying in bed, staring at the ceiling as her scrubbing slowly lulled me to sleep, I'd think Francesca, too, missed something. Exactly what, I couldn't say.

A few times, usually after we'd shared a bottle of wine, when the illusion of camaraderie had been reestablished, I'd ask, as delicately as possible, as she polished the toaster, or stood under an autumn tree waiting for a leaf to fall, rake in hand and at the ready, "What about painting? Don't you miss it?"

"It is a phase," she'd reply cryptically, jabbing at the leaf with the rake.

"Yes, but for four/five/six/seven/eight years?"

She'd then turn her deep brown eyes on me, sigh ("Silly, stupid man"), and say, "Honestly, George, why you think I ever paint anyway?"

When I'd mention perhaps getting an easel, brushes and paints for a birthday, or Christmas, or Valentine's, or Easter, or.... "Honestly, George, why you think I ever paint anyway?"

Last Christmas I'd remained as silent as a mouse, alive or dead. I said nothing about paints or brushes. I hadn't even hinted at canvases. I did nothing except become an accomplice in the illusion that she'd always been a fanatical, motherly woman obsessed with cleaning. It somehow seemed to help.

So, struggling with acres of shiny gold paper I'd wrapped a mini-vacuum designed for computers and tight, tight spaces; a super-sized box of cleaning rags from Costco; a super-sized bottle of degreaser, also from Costco; a new and improved wood floor broom; and a pair of overalls with knee pads. She'd been as happy as a clam. I write,

Where did the expression "happy as a clam" come from /originate?

on a yellow sticky note. She'd been so happy, in fact she'd neglected the television, the toaster, the couch, the Cuisinart, everything, and detailed me, in a manner of speaking. It was as if we were still young, as if we'd just met.

The house feels tense, like it's waiting for something to happen, or as if something already has. Holding its breath, waiting to exhale.

It seems Francesca and Mirabella aren't home. There's always something distinctly different in the air when they're home and when they're not. Can't say exactly what, there just is.

I can't remember if they're off running errands, or something, but I'm pretty sure not. They hadn't mentioned anything. At least I don't think they did. Maybe they had and I forgot. Like where the car had been parked the other day at Costco.

Placing my keys on the hallway bureau, I notice a letter in Francesca's flowing hand. Her handwriting always reminds me of ancient proclamations. Her grocery lists look like edicts from Cortez or Pizarro annexing Costco and placing it under Spanish rule. Thus would the two conquistadors return to their beloved homeland with the requisite amount of toilet paper, chicken breasts, salmon fillets, and diet soda for the king and queen.

The letter is simple and direct. It's in keeping with Francesca's clean, minimalist style. However, like her style, it's also dark, vague, and cryptic.

George—

Terribly sorry. Wish I could explain though can not. Someday. Maybe. Please don't try to find us. For every purpose we've disappeared (à la Murakami) "like smoke." Please know I loved you. Ciao.

—Francesca

Good-bye? Disappeared? Terribly sorry? What the hell is she talking about? And I don't know who this Murakami is but I sure as hell am going to find out. I mean, what the fuck is she talking about?

Next to the letter is her set of keys, as well as her cell phone. What the hell is she talking about? What the hell is she up to?

From the kitchen I hear Zeus sloshing around in his water bowl. I reread the note. I then, dutifully, reread it again.

She'd done this before—duck and cover, run and hide. Usually, though, it was after we'd fought. For some reason, we tended to climb into the ring during the weekend. Usually it amounted to her screaming and yelling, while I calmly, logically, rationally continued explaining the fallacies of her argument as she drove off.

I'd then turn to the gathered witnesses Mirabella, Zeus, and Tyler the cat, saying, "Well, the place is ours! Let's party!"

We'd get Family Combo #2 from Hung Far Lee's, and pick up ice cream and movies. Eat out of the boxes, use our sleeves for napkins, put our feet up on the coffee table, walk around the house with our shoes on, and stay up far too late watching dwarves and princesses defeating evil witches.

Upon Francesca's return we'd clean the house beneath a deep, pensive silence. That night, over a dinner saturated with Omega-3s, beta carotene, and leafy greens, we'd begin talking, begin laughing again. By morning everything would be back to normal. Exactly how "normal" that may've been was open for interpretation and discussion.

However, she'd never written a note before. It was always face-to-face, *mano a mano*; Francesca's exits had always been spontaneous. And if she'd happened to take Mirabella, it was when the malls were open, when the most damage could be done, when the brainwashing would be most effective.

I call upstairs, "Francesca?! Hellooo?! Francesca?!" A heavy, oppressive silence replies. I look again at the note. Yes, it's written in her hand. The paper looks like it was ripped from a notebook of mine.

"Mirabella?! Francesca?! Hellooo?!"

Zeus pads back in and promptly drools backwash on my foot.

"Zeus, come on. Please," I plead, attempting to shake the slobbery wetness off.

On a normal day, Zeus dutifully follows me around until I sit down to read and have my glass of wine. Usually that's about ten minutes after we were done with the walk. Presently I'm reading *Surreal: The Biography of Gabriel Garcia Marquez*. After my read, Zeus would be well into REM time. I would stretch and then check on Mirabella. Occasionally, I'd help her with homework before she got herself ready for bed. Once I was again assured she didn't need my help, I'd organize myself for the next day: pay bills, brush teeth, return to read for a moment or two, then lock the house down, turning the lights off as I went. Everything was a smooth matter of routine. Even the moment or two standing in the dark downstairs, the light gently streaming from above, listening to the sounds around me. Then, before slipping in next to Francesca, I'd check on Mirabella. I liked to believe that last little check made her sleep a little better, kept the boogeyman and nightmares away. Just another delusion, I suppose, but one I enjoy.

However, the way the house feels now, it seems as if it might be some time before I'll sit down with a glass of wine and a book. I decide Zeus needs a distraction, a little redirection. Hyped as he is from dropping poo, the walk, and playing at the park, the only diversion is siccing him on the poor, innocent cat.

"Go get Tyler." Zeus perks his ears up. His eyes get bright. He cocks his head as if I've asked him to solve a difficult algebra equation, one he feels he should know the answer to. "Go get Tyler, Zeus. Where's Tyler? Where's Tyler? Go get him, Zeusy. Go get Tyler."

Zeus blinks once, twice, then realizes it isn't cosines and tangents he's after, but a stupid, orange fur ball of a cat. "Tyler!" Zeus gives a short, animated bark, spins on his haunches and launches all hundred and thirty pounds of himself upstairs like a lightning bolt. "Run Tyler! Run!"

Somewhere upstairs a tired kitty wakes and gives a weak moan of a "meow" in response to my warning and Zeus's rapidly closing scamper.

This not only serves as a distraction for Zeus, but if Francesca is in the house this would indeed ferret her out. And Mirabella would be close behind, crying, "Zeus is going to eat Tyler! Zeus is going to eat Tyler!"

Zeus clatters into a room, and Tyler hisses a warning. If there's one thing Francesca hated, besides French manicures, Marilyn Manson, and flavored iced tea, it was Zeus chasing Tyler around the house. They'd already destroyed approximately $1,750 worth of lamps, glassware, pictures, and other miscellaneous household items.

If I didn't work for an insurance company, my insurance policy would have been discontinued long ago. As it is, I have friends in high places; all has been replaced, and then some.

My hand is still holding the leash and the bag of poo. Okay, first things first. I toss the poo into the garbage, throw the leash on the counter, and get a beer—Pilsner Urquell, a favorite of mine—then go in search of the phone. Between the two ladies, the Wandering Nomads of Chat, the phone could be anywhere between the front door and the attic. I refuse to do as my parents. They have a phone in almost every room, all connected to the same line. If the phone rings it sounds like someone has parked a fire engine in the living room. The house shakes and the teacups rattle. And invariably the phones aren't in the cradles but in a cupboard, under a chair, on the television, or in the car. No one ever seems to know how the phone gets in the car; it just appears there.

I begin my search with the most likely places and work backward. Upstairs, Zeus and Tyler are discussing in no uncertain terms existentialism, nihilism, and absurdism, and their roles in the modern belief system. Minutes later, the two continue to contrast Camus and Christ, and I still have not found the damned phone. Disgusted, as much with their fervor as my ineptitude, I return to the refrigerator for another beer.

"Zeus! Zeus, come!" I shout, before they truly tangle and break something else. "Zeus!" I can hear the big boy padding across the floor, down the stairs and around the corner.

"There he is. Did you enlighten Tyler?" I catch my breath and take a quick draw on the Pilsner. The phone is in its cradle. The phone is in its cradle? But I looked there, didn't I? I must have. It would make no sense not to look there first, but I have no recollection of doing so. And yet it makes no sense not to have. I stare at the phone and sip the beer, hoping something comes to mind. Nothing does, so I call Francesca's mother. Perhaps Francesca and Mirabella have run away to her potted-plant and lace infested haven again?

"Margarita?"

"Sí. Buenas noches," warbles Margarita. *Cops, America's Most Wanted*, or *Judge Judy* plays sporadically in the background.

"Buenas noches, Margarita. This is George." Zeus looks at me oddly, as if maybe I'm not. It's a little disconcerting.

"Ah, Jorge, buenas noches." Since I'd stolen her Francesca from her, I'd been Jorge, never George. Like sorbet and gelato, similar but different. The first year or two I'd attempted to correct her, now it's simply one of many crosses I bear when it comes to her.

"Uh, buenas noches, Margarita." Margarita is a woman of few, but often repeated, words. It will be best if I get to the point, and quick, particularly with the quizzical glare Zeus is giving me. "Is Francesca there?"

"Francesca?" I don't think she's forgotten her daughter. I think Margarita thinks it's simply a stupid question.

Regardless of how stupid it may be I ask again, "Sí. Is Francesca there?"

"No, Jorge. No Francesca here. She is there, no?"

"No, she is not," I answer, snapping my fingers and pointing for Zeus to take his odd glare somewhere else. He ignores me and continues. I turn my back on him.

"No?" Margarita mutes the television. I can picture the confused look on her face.

"No." I reply, not really helping.

"¿Por qué?"

"No sé, Margarita. Gracias."

"De nada, Jorge. De nada." Margarita hangs up, confused as much by the conversation as the action on her television screen.

I hang up and stare at Zeus, who seems as perplexed as me. Tyler has wandered down to join us. He gives me a pissy, disgruntled glare and saunters past us and over to his empty dish. He sniffs it and looks back, first at Zeus, then at me. It seems Tyler, too, knows how things work around here.

Sipping the Pilsner Urquell, I stare back. He meows insistently. Zeus looks at Tyler.

Would Francesca's father, Carlo, know anything? Sure, he may know a lot about fashion photography, but not this. Besides, there's no way Francesca could've gotten to Milan in such a short time. And what's the time there? I can hear his gray gravel voice as he picks up the phone in the early morning and says—

"Meow!"

"Okay, Tyler, kitty, okay. Keep your fur on." Zeus looks at me.

"Meow!" Zeus looks at Tyler.

"Hey, I said, okay." Zeus looks at me, realizes he isn't getting anything, and pads into the living room. He promptly climbs onto the couch and makes himself all too comfortable. Usually I'd tell him to get off, but tonight is gaining a certain irrepressible momentum, and normalcy isn't part of its mass.

I open a can of Seafood Medley and practically crush Tyler a thousand times as he, purring at light speed, zigzags between my shins, rubbing frantically. By the time I smack the can in his dish it feels as if my shins are about to explode into flames from the friction. As he buries his head into the pink concoction I hop up on the counter and attempt to get my hands around the dilemma of where the hell the ladies have gone.

I consider calling a few of Francesca's friends—but why? If they were coming back, they'd come back. If not... well, that's something else, entirely.

I'll give them an hour. An hour? A few hours? And then what? Okay, a day. One day to come back, or contact me, or whatever. No, one hour, then readjust based on what has, or hasn't, transpired in that hour. I think this makes sense.

I take a long, satisfying, blinding swallow of the Pilsner and push a tingling sensation (impending doom?) back down my throat.

I look at the photos covering the refrigerator. Mirabella playing soccer and basketball; the balls are almost as big as she is. Mirabella and her friends making their Halloween haunts. Francesca has the photos running down the side of the refrigerator in consecutive order. Mirabella was first a sunflower, then a ladybug, a bunny rabbit, an angel, then as Zeus (the photos of her and Zeus together are amazingly cute, almost to the point of making one want to cry), as Tyler (not nearly as cute as Zeus and her; sorry, Tyler), and, finally, Princess Fiona (green version).

Maybe they went to the store for chocolate or ice cream or gummy bears or Oreos or anything sweet enough to alleviate the sourness of our marriage. Maybe to Home Depot for weed killer? Francesca despises the tufts of grass growing between the sidewalk's slabs. Maybe Mirabella needed something for school? Glue? Erasers? Shoes? Socks? Probably not. She has practically everything. Oh, God, not tampons. It's way too early for Mirabella, right? Sure, she probably eats too much hormone-infested meat and such, but eight is way too early for a period, isn't it? God, I hope so. Last thing I want to deal with right now are TWO women and their monthly cycles. Not to mention the possibility of Mirabella getting pregnant. No. No. No. No. I do not want to think about that. About being a *grandfather*. That right there simply seems another way to say Old, say Dead, say Good-bye.

Regardless of the errand, it should realistically only take twenty minutes, right? So, if that's the case they should be home by.... Oh, yeah, there was that damn note.

I drain my beer, and stare, bewildered, at my reflection in the darkened windows. My reflection stares back. Both of us are unsure of what to do next.

Tyler, finished with his Seafood Medley, slinks off around the corner, unconcerned. After a brief moment he's scratching in his litter box. From the living room Zeus snores.

Gradually my annoyance of Zeus and Tyler's cavalier attitudes toward Francesca and Mirabella's disappearance begins to infuriate me. Bubbles of frustration form, rise, and explode inside me. And if I wasn't going to explode, cover the walls with a glossy, red sheen, I needed a distraction.

All that seemingly remains are the leftover dishes from the uneventful dinner, Marquez's biography, the glass of wine, then the ritual lock down of the palace.

Reluctantly, I attend to the items on the list.

Hot water and white bubbles begin swallowing the stained plates. I pick up the blue scrub pad and begin loading the dishwasher. As a macabre distraction to the unpleasantness of scrubbing I ponder the possibilities. Could they have been kidnapped? Perhaps Francesca was forced to write that cryptic note? Has some strange catastrophe befallen them? No, the place was too pristine, too "as I'd left it." Alien abduction? Maybe. I'll ask June next time I'm at the park. She's sure to have plenty of insight about abductions, particularly alien abductions.

Not ten minutes later the sink is empty, the dishwasher loaded and running, and the kitchen is cleared, clean, and ready for the next mess.

Hey, maybe there was a school function tonight? A play?

A game? A teacher-parent-student consultation? No. No. No. Besides, there's that damn note. God, I hate that fucking note!

Stomping into the foyer, I grab Francesca's note and march upstairs to my den, or, more correctly—as I'd been corrected by Francesca more than a million times—*our library.*

Okay, who is this Murakami? Some Japanese magician? Some master of...of Japanese paper-folding? Why can't I think of the term for Japanese paper-folding? Why? I write,

> What is
> Japanese
> paper-folding
> called?

on another yellow sticky.

I sit at my—*our*—desk, connect to the Internet, and search for information on Murakami.

Quickly I discover he's some avant-garde writer, very cutting-edge, at least where the Japanese are concerned. He's written some books. That's all. Nothing spectacular. I might get a copy, or two, in hopes of trying to figure out what Francesca means by "*like smoke.*"

As I begin typing, What is Japanese paper-folding? a thought sidetracks me: I'll have to take Zeus to doggy day care tomorrow. Shit, that will cost me at least half an hour, if not more. To be prudent, I should plan on forty-five minutes, if not an hour, for the side trip. Then another thirty minutes at the end of the day to pick him up.

I log off and begin mentally putting tomorrow together. Okay, remember to set the alarm for an hour earlier. Up at six, shower, shave, eat...no, feed Zeus and Tyler first, let Zeus out, then shower, shave, eat. Get Zeus to doggy day care by a quarter after seven, fill out paperwork, then head to work. Simple, sweet, and efficient. Work I'm not going to think about. Work is going to be hell and high water, and I'll wait to discover if I can swim when I walk through the gates.

I read Francesca's note once more and slam it inside my briefcase, disgusted, infuriated, angry, confused, pissed off, exasperated, perplexed, baffled, bewildered, and befuddled, but, mostly, just simply worried.

Francesca couldn't have picked a worse time to pull this stupid little stunt. Next week will be exceedingly busy and I'm not going to have any extra time or energy to invest in placating her and her mysterious tantrum.

Suddenly I notice someone staring at me. And just as suddenly, I recognize it's my reflection in the darkened window. I rub my forehead as I shake my head slowly in despair. I give my reflection the finger; he dutifully responds in kind as I lean back and switch the light off. Thankfully, I/he disappears and the world outside is magically revealed.

I wander downstairs, get Zeus up off the couch and let him out back to pee, while I lock up and turn the lights off.

It takes ten minutes to get him back inside. Zeus acts like he knows something about the odd silence infusing the house. Something he'd rather not be part of, or tell me about.

As Zeus resettles on the couch, I wander into Mirabella's room. I find myself staring, lost, at Mirabella's empty bed. Tonight I was supposed to relate how the intrepid crew of our fable, *The Improbable Adventures of Sir Dog Fart-A-Lot and Squire Laugh-Cat*, traversed the Dingle Dangle Desert. How they outsmarted the Hell Scorpion Zar to drink from the Chalice of Perfect Giggles. But to the surprise of Sir Dog Fart-A-Lot, Squire Laugh-Cat, and Mirabella, the chalice would have been empty. And then, my plan had been to tickle Mirabella until her pure, sweet laughter would fill the chalice. All would gather round to drink of the joy.

But the Dingle Dangle Desert chapter will have to wait for another night.

Like most nights I reluctantly turn off the light and shuffle down the hall, an unnerving silence follows me. Once, twice, I turn around to confirm no one, no thing, is behind me.

When I crawl into bed, Francesca doesn't ask why I tell Mirabella such "make believes," nor does she lecture me about raising a child on fantasies. And I don't nestle beside her, spoon her and explain life is short, and, besides, plenty of adults are living and dying on fantasies.

Francesca doesn't ask, and I don't explain, because she isn't here. I stare at the ceiling, listening not to the midnight symphony of scrubbing, but to my heart beat-beat-beating in an attempt to fill the empty space.

Needless to say, I don't sleep. Needless to say, I keep expecting Francesca and Mirabella to walk through the front door. Needless to say, they don't.

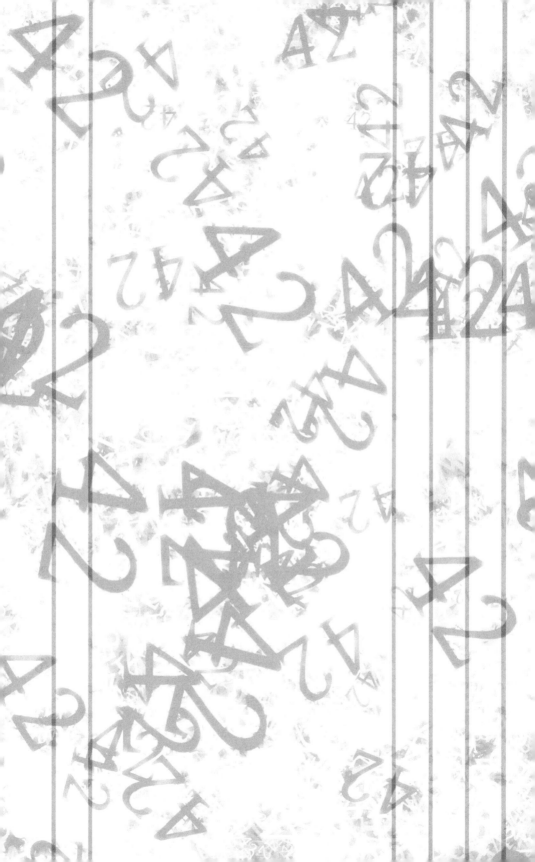

Thursday:

March 25, 2004

Tomorrow doesn't work out as planned.

Throughout the long, sleepless night, I keep thinking I hear the phone ringing. Each time I turn over, it stares back, innocent and silent—its cyclopean green eye glowing accusatorily.

Frustrated at staring at the ceiling, at thinking the phone is ringing, I get up and attempt to do some work. One of the smaller projects is putting together a pamphlet for our clients in Florida. Telling them how we appreciate their business and how we admire their fortitude for sticking it out through one of the worst hurricane seasons ever. It's basically a plea to keep them insuring with us, to keep them in Florida. After any large catastrophe, particularly after so many hurricanes, a certain percentage will move out of state, to someplace "safer." Subsequently we lose a certain percentage of that business. My mission with this brochure is to seduce policyholders into believing they're being brave, upholding the pioneer spirit, and not simply being stupid.

I try not to think about how my life, and all it contains, is derived from other people's fear of loss, from attempting to *insure* their lives would continue on without too much loss or change, regardless of the catastrophe. "God won't, but we will."

The first few paragraphs of the Florida pamphlet made me queasy with disgust. Probably because the words were so heartfelt and genuine, but mostly, because I knew Slater, the copywriter, and his penchant for cocaine and college girls.

To repress my unease I fetch a glass of wine and surf the Internet for European vacation spots. It's been over ten years since Francesca and I have been over. Not once since Mirabella's birth. Maybe now? Mirabella is old enough to appreciate it and not be too much of a pain in the ass. I looked into Greek islands, little hotels on the Adriatic, and small, mountain villages in the Pyrenees.

After forty minutes of surfing, a thin blanket of fatigue falls across my eyes. It seems that the wine and this hopeful diversion have worked.

I stop looking for vacation spots, trundle off to bed, and attempt sleep again. Immediately I fall into a restless unconsciousness. Though it can't rightly be classified as sleep. It is as if I am simultaneously conscious and asleep. My dream-self watches my conscious-self. My conscious-self watches my dream-self. Each waits to see what the other will do. Each waits for the other to make a mistake. Invariably neither does, and nothing happens. Except my not getting any sleep.

$$\infty$$

The alarm doesn't ring. Or maybe I simply slept through it? Either way I don't wake until nearly seven. I turn the clock over. The alarm is set, it just didn't ring. Odd.

$$\infty$$

Somehow I'm out of shampoo, which also seems odd. Okay, these things do sneak up on one. Not that odd (I guess). I use Francesca's shampoo instead. I'll smell like her the rest of the day. I'll catch brief glimpses of her scent rolling over my shoulder, around me. I'll turn, expecting to see her, but will discover nothing, not even myself.

Perfectly distracted, I cut myself shaving. I actually watch the razor scratch the glistening, white foam from my face. A red spot, blood, raises its head, blooms. I stare, confused, perplexed, and unsure how I knew it would happen, yet unable to do anything about it. I place a patch of toilet paper over the cut. It helps. Momentarily. On the third piece the blood is quelled and I continue on into my hurried morning.

By the time I feed Zeus and Tyler, and give Zeus some time to take care of his morning "business," I'm thirty minutes behind schedule.

∞

The woman at the doggy day care says she's completely full and can't take any more dogs. "Particularly Rotties." She says it like some alien venereal disease, "Rotties." Like, "Oh, my God, I'm going to just die. Zoeteck gave me the Rotties."

I say very calmly, ignoring the poodle clock behind her, its tail wagging incessantly, telling me I'm thirty-five minutes behind schedule and very, very late, "Zeus is exceedingly well behaved. Aren't you, Zeusy?" He looks up at me, unsure what he's doing here in the first place, let alone why he's supposed to be placating the bottle-blonde dog sitter.

"I really can't," she says, ignoring Zeus's imploring brown eyes.

"Please. Look, my wife left me last night. Just up and took off with my daughter and everything. I've really got no choice here. I have to be at work in—" I look up at the poodle clock, "—three minutes. I'm willing to pay extra. Clean up after the dogs when I get back. Anything, just name your price. And if anything should happen, I'll pay for it. I'm in the insurance business. I'm covered for practically everything." My wallet's out and I'm opening it up, prepared to pay the bribe. However, it's empty.

"Goddamn," I say to no one in particular, not even Zeus, or the poodle clock, "she even took my money." I had something like sixty bucks or so, didn't I? I rub my eyes, attempting to fight back both fatigue and tears. How could this be happening? How?

I'm three seconds away from taking Zeus and myself down to the nearest bar and tossing back a few dozen when the bottle-blonde dog sitter says, taking Zeus's leash, "Don't worry about it. Let's say it's my gift to someone else left holding the bag."

"Seriously? What about a credit card?" I offer, attempting to pluck a card from my wallet.

"Don't worry about it. It sounds, though, like you got off easy. I got saddled with two kids and a mortgage."

"Oh. Sorry." Zeus looks back forlornly, and then notices the other pooches behind the chain-link fence. That's it, I'm history and he's in doggy heaven.

"Thank you! Seriously!" I yell above the barking as I exit hurriedly.

She smiles, waves, and suggests, "Get that toilet paper off your chin!"

∞

One of Portland's problems, besides dreary, wet winters, is being bisected by a river with an inordinate number of drawbridges spanning it. Presently the Hawthorne Bridge is up. I and the miscellaneous conglomeration of commuters wait five minutes for a tug to push a barge full of sand down the river. Cars, buses, and cyclists back up. When the bridge finally goes back down, the subsequent chaos and hurry only make things worse.

I pull into the building's underground parking lot only to discover someone is parked in my spot. Some blue Vega piece of crap. I drive around to the valet kiosk by the elevators. No one is there. I wait a minute. I wait two. Then three. Four. Five. Ah, fuck this. I go and quickly park in the first available spot around the corner.

∞

The first thing my secretary Anne says to me is, "You're late," with a playful smile.

"You're observant," I shoot back. Sans smile. Sans playful.

"Sorry, boss," she says honestly, because she means it, because she's a truly a nice person. "What do you need? What can I do?"

I'm halfway past the desk, almost to my door, when my momentum slows. It seems for the first time in forever I notice the gold nameplate on the faux-wood door. It strikes me as terribly odd that it doesn't seem to be the right name.

She asks again, "What can I do?"

"That's the same nameplate, isn't it? I mean, no one's changed it, right?"

"No, boss. Same one."

"Good." However, it still doesn't look right. It still seems either misspelled, or...or simply the wrong person's name. I glance left to the filing cabinets and bookcases behind Anne's desk, then to the right to the production room and the copywriters and layout people, and then back to the gold nameplate. It still looks wrong.

I say the name slowly, barely audible to myself. It even feels odd in my mouth, even leaves a strange, empty sourness in the back of my throat once it's escaped.

"Boss? Uh, Mr. Olson?" Then the disconcerting moment is gone, and I move immediately on.

"Anne, I'd love a huge cup of coffee, and some kind of pastry. Or three. And we're still on for lunch with Andrews, right?"

"Yes. Noon at Murata."

"Okay. Then tell James I need to see the printer's proofs by eleven, at the latest." Reluctantly I take the last few steps to the office door. I turn the knob, slowly. As I open the door, expecting to find someone behind the desk working diligently away, Anne says offhandedly, "Your wife called. She said she'd call back later."

I spin quickly and nearly shout, scaring her, "What?!" I notice Anne's bewildered face, and immediately apologize. "Anne, I'm sorry. Look... what about my wife?"

"She called," Anne says, annoyed. "And she'll call back."

"Anne, thank you." I don't sound as sincere as I should.

"Sure." She turns and stomps off. The coffee shall taste like mud, the pastries like spackle. I can't blame her.

∞

Every ten, twenty minutes I check for messages left at home. There's nothing until late afternoon. It's Margarita asking about going to a movie with Mirabella. For some reason, out of a desperate kind of hope, I save the message.

The day, as far as work is concerned, passes along like any other: slowly.

Finally it's done and I gladly close my door and leave. I can feel the eyes of the nameplate glaring into my back. I want to turn around and verify the name. See if it hasn't changed since the morning. Instead I walk on and into the night.

∞

The blue Vega piece of crap is still in my spot. Disgruntled I walk on, around the corner to where my car should be. It, of course, is missing. I look up and down the row. At nearly 6:15, there are few cars for mine to hide behind. Besides, this is the spot I parked in this morning. My car is missing. Probably towed, I think. Maybe stolen.

I stomp over to the valet kiosk, prepared to vent, prepared to take all my frustrations and grievances about the world out on the unsuspecting and innocent valet. Again, though, much to my disappointment, there's no one there. I wait. I listen to tires squeal as a car rounds a corner. I wait. People's voices echo as they walk to their cars. I wait.

Finally I leave. I walk to the front of the building and the little turnaround driveway for the unloading and loading of passengers. I call for a taxi on my cell phone. I wait five minutes. The taxi arrives and I tumble in; the Black Box looms above me.

∞

Zeus isn't too sure about the taxi, nor is the driver about Zeus, but in the end we make it home safe and sound.

The house is the same, empty. After checking for nonexistent messages, I let Zeus into the backyard. He lopes around and looks back, not sure what he should be doing. Tyler comes and sits next to my ankles and stares at Zeus. Tyler is also not sure what Zeus should be doing. Zeus, finally discovering his raison d'être, saunters to the azalea, and begins peeing.

Tyler and I return to the kitchen in hopes of discovering Francesca and Mirabella unpacking ingredients for a magnificent dinner. Like the house, though, there is only emptiness.

Tyler's feast tonight is something titled Vegetable Chicken Liver. The contents are as incongruous as the title and Tyler stares, dubious, at the clump. However, by the time I dump Zeus's Savory Country Beef into a bowl, Tyler has discovered a frightening voracity that borders on madness. He's emitting little kitty growls each time his bared, bright teeth dig into the gray, tapioca-like clump. Zeus, having returned from the azalea, hesitates before his meal and joins me in a perplexed stare. He gives me a glance and I shrug, each of us realizing the impossibility of discovering such enthusiasm in the contents of our dinners, let alone our lives.

As Zeus grudgingly begins eating his clump, I prepare myself a luxurious, sixteen-ounce banquet of ninety-nine percent fat-free turkey chili. I watch the green, microwave-safe ceramic bowl turn and turn and turn. The brown, can-shaped brick slowly melts into a sludge of edible ooze. Ding!

Behind me Zeus and, particularly, Tyler chew and chomp noisily. I sit down at the table and sadly stare at my bubbling, brown ooze. I'm sure, based on their relative enthusiasm, theirs tastes better. I attempt to create the pathetic enthusiasm I use for taking out the garbage or mowing the lawn. It doesn't work—the spoon only plays idly with the skinned surface and accomplishes nothing. Accepting this as an omen, I stand and place the bowl, and its pathetic contents, in the sink.

"Okay, Zeus," I sigh, "let's roll."

He looks up, gives a few licks to his bowl, and follows me toward the door. However, before we get there, I notice the answering machine inexplicably blinking demonically. There are suddenly three messages! How? I checked and there were none. And now? Three.

Tentatively, hoping, I press the button, and the messages play.

First, Margarita's lethargic, Spanish lilt: "Mirabella, I take you to movie this weekend. Sí? I think good time is…."

Delete.

Next is another woman's, smoky, blue jazz—Jessica, one of Francesca's friends: "Francesca, don't forget, six o'clock wine tasting tomorrow night at Vino. Spanish reds. Yummy. Oh, hey, do you happen to have a recipe for bread pudding? I'll tell you why tomorrow. See you. Ciao."

Delete.

Another woman, less smoke, less jazz, but very blue—Leslie, another of Francesca's friends: "I tried Jess, but her line was busy. How, with all of today's technology, can a phone be busy? Can you say call-waiting? Hello. Anyway, I just need to know where and when the wine tasting is tomorrow night. Give me a call. Thanks. Bye."

Delete.

Once the messages are deleted, a surge of disappointment rushes across the shore, undermines the weak castle of my hope. I guess I was expecting Francesca's sultry, honey-infused voice, "Sweetheart, I'm sorry. I was rash, I was wrong, I was misguided. Mirabella and I, we wait for you at a secluded little inn on the coast. We'll be waiting for you." She would then, of course, leave an address and give directions.

Alas, that's not the case, and the only thing I have to look forward to is picking up Zeus's warm, steamy poo. However, by the time we reach the park, the swaying bag, like a hypnotist's unsuccessful watch, begins to annoy and I throw the bag into an overfilled trash can bordering the park.

Zeus and I don't stay long at the park. Tuesday isn't here, nor is June. And if they were, I think I would've left before we could chat. Or I like to think so. Probably because I'm afraid June could explain a dimensional vortex, which manifests itself when people are neglected. This vortex transports the neglected to another world, another dimension. It sounds all too likely. I'm sure she has a theory about it. We leave before I begin pondering the trials and tribulations awaiting those left behind.

On our return, I again find myself staring at our illumined house, waiting. Waiting for me, the one more real than the me watching for me, to walk by a window. Waiting, hoping Francesca and Mirabella have returned.

Zeus and I stare, but don't see anyone, just bookshelves haphazardly stuffed with books, a stairway, a few lamps, bourgeois paintings—simply the standard accoutrements contained in a well-appointed, two-story Victorian. We're both disappointed.

Suddenly, somewhere, a phone begins to ring. It echoes back and forth, up and down, the deserted street. It's from my house! I sprint across the street. I know it's Francesca. She's calling to tell me there was a landslide. I have to take a left onto a back road before I get to the bridge that crosses the river if I'm ever going to find the inn.

With Zeus right behind, I bolt up the steps and through the front door. Just as my hand grips the phone it falls silent, dead.

"Hello? Hello? Francesca?! Hello?!" The connection flatlines like a cardiac victim. I dial *69 in hopes of getting the number. However, a recording states the number is not available. I try again. The number is not available. The recording's voice, a woman's, is as cold as a knife. The number is not available. She sounds tired, forlorn. Is not available.

Because there is nothing else to do, Zeus, Tyler and I, reluctantly, begrudgingly, go about our routine.

Eventually I place a selection of Vivaldi cello concertos on the stereo and settle down with a glass of wine and a book. Zeus pads over and looks questioningly at me.

"Okay, what the hell." I pat the sofa next to me. He bounds up and settles in, happy and thankful. I give his big head a shake. One good sip and three paragraphs later, Tyler is snuggling up on the other side of me. I prop my sock-shrouded feet on the coffee table. Within half an hour we're all asleep, Vivaldi having slowly rocked us unconscious.

∞

Sometime during the night I must wake and carry myself upstairs. I must also undress, put on pajamas, and crawl into bed, because that's how I find myself the next morning, in bed, wearing pajamas.

41

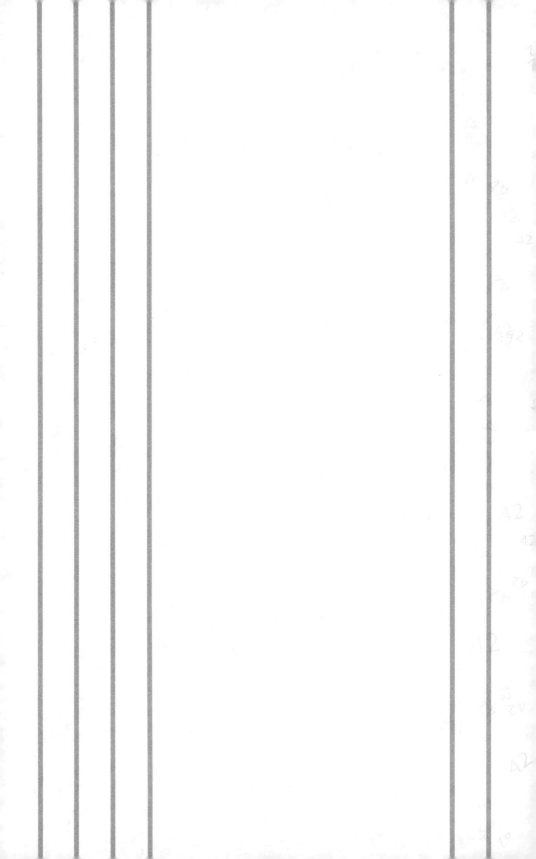

Friday:

March 26, 2004

Today—Thank God it's Friday, T.G.I.F.—begins more smoothly than yesterday. Probably because I again don't sleep, so waking at the crack of dawn is much easier. It also helps that I follow my plan.

I feed Zeus and Tyler first. Have a glass of orange juice. I am prepared to smell like Francesca. Don't cut myself shaving. However, I have to take Francesca's car, the VW Eurovan which I haven't driven since the testdrive. I have to adjust the seat, the steering wheel, mirrors, everything. It takes me five minutes to find the switch for the window wipers. It's an odd sensation driving this instead of my old Mustang. It's the altered perspective, being above everything and able to see a little farther ahead. Not to mention the lingering scent of Francesca and Mirabella. Or is that my hair, her shampoo?

∞

I have no problems getting Zeus to doggy day care. And this time, because he was so good yesterday, and I'm ahead of the masses, there isn't any pleading, though I do give the woman a twenty-dollar bill for yesterday's generosity.

She says, "It's not necessary."

"I know," I reply. "Please. Call it payment for yesterday's 'personal hygiene consultation.'"

She laughs and reluctantly takes the proffered bill.

∞

This time the blue Vega piece-of-crap is gone and I park in my spot.

∞

Anne isn't at her desk. I write her a note about checking with the building's valets, or whoever, to see what may possibly have happened to my car. I then walk into my office without glancing at the nameplate. Unconcerned if it's correct or not.

I spend the morning ignoring work and attempting to take care of some personal business. Namely, attempting to figure out where Francesca and Mirabella may have gone.

First, I call Francesca's therapist, a Mrs. Sandquist, an LMFT. Supposedly, and according to Francesca's limited experience with therapists, she's a "very insightful woman." I hope she is, based on what she charges. I leave some vague message, ultimately asking her to call me back, which she doesn't.

Next on the illegible list scrawled on the yellow sticky note are the credit card companies.

"I'm sorry, sir, but it can take up to three or four days for some companies to process—"

"Okay. Okay. But, what about airlines or car rental agencies or...or coastal inns?" There's still hope, isn't there?

"No, no, sir. Nothing like that. If you have Internet access, this information is available on our website at—"

"Yeah. I heard you the first time. Thanks. Bye."

It's the same for each card. Some young, crystal-voiced idiot reading from a script telling me the same thing: "No, nothing like that. If you visit our website you can access your account via—" Yeah, whatever. Bye.

Of course I get online and check, and, of course, there's nothing out of the ordinary. No one-way ticket to Zihuatanejo, or Mallorca, or Fiji, or Katmandu. No guns, scuba gear or C4 purchased. No nothing. Just Costco. Just normal, standard, daily, boring purchases—gas and groceries. Nothing out of the ordinary. It's a little upsetting, if not suspicious.

I call home. There are, of course, no messages.

∞

A bike messenger, cadaverously thin and dressed in various shades of black, stops by moments before I exit to pick up Zeus. I sign for a manila envelope from our mortgage company, which I toss into my briefcase. It's probably the preliminary figures for a second mortgage. About a year ago, Francesca and I started looking into getting a vacation home, and only recently have we started crunching the numbers. However, right now, a second mortgage, and a vacation home, are as probable as Tyler learning to juggle.

As the messenger exits, I turn to Anne and ask, "Have you heard anything about my car?"

"I'm afraid not. But they did say they towed one parked in your spot today."

I look blankly at her, confused, attempting to make sense of what she's just told me, and the possible ramifications.

"Did they happen to mention the make of the car?" I ask, knowing all too well the answer.

"Yes," she says tentatively. "Why?"

They have records of the license plates and make of the car (or cars) for the corresponding parking spot. I never added Francesca's car after we purchased it a year ago. It's a little late to do so now.

"Red Eurovan?"

"Shall I call a taxi?" she asks, attempting to restrain a smile.

"Please."

And before I can ask, she answers, "And have them deliver the van to your house?"

"Would you mind?"

"Not at all," she replies through her gradually growing grin.

After I retrieve Zeus, I discover the cabdriver has a problem, a *big*, BIG problem, with dogs.

"Hey, he stays out." The man points a long, accusatory forefinger at Zeus. The tip is missing and brutally scarred, as if lost in a carpentry accident, or bitten off by a baby shark.

Zeus looks at me, confused.

"Oh, come on," I reply, trying to make us look über-pathetic in the thickening mist swirling and falling around us, "He's just a dog."

The cabbie isn't buying. "No, he's not *just* a dog—he's a *Rottie*." Out of his mouth it isn't a disease, but some ancient demon come to pillage, rape, and kill every last innocent villager. "And he stays out."

"He's trained," I plead, as if I'm being accused of the atrocities, "And a good, old boy. Come on."

"He stays out." The man's glare is a gleaming butcher knife.

Pointing to the driver I command, mockingly, "Zeus, kill." Zeus blinks and stares as if I had told him the air speed velocity of a laden swallow.

"Mister, that might be funny," his voice goes cold with anger and emotion, "*if* my sister hadn't been killed by one."

"I'm...I'm sorry...." But nothing I could ever say could make up for that. Sometimes life does kind of sit back and kick one between the legs, doesn't it?

"It's eleven fifty." His tone relaxes, but the butcher knife remains in his eyes.

Recognizing these bills are worthless to a loss like his, I give him fifteen. He slowly, quietly, as if proving a point, drives away. No way was I getting my change back, even if I'd asked for it.

From my cell phone, as the mist begins to gradually thicken to rain, I call for another taxi.

I specify that I have a dog with me. He's—I pause as I attempt to make Zeus sound like a walnut covered in caramel, dipped in Swiss milk chocolate, and sprinkled with powdered sugar, "—a Rottie." I add a dollop of whip cream and a cherry. "He's friendly and trained, though. Perhaps there's a driver that's okay with dogs?"

"Uh, sure. No problem," the dispatcher says. Then she adds, "Though it could be a while. Twenty, thirty minutes maybe."

"No problem. Tell the driver to give a good honk. I'll be in the park across the street." And add, uselessly, "Waiting."

First Zeus and I walk around the corner through the growing drizzle and get two slices of pizza from It's A Beautiful Pizza. The Hippie Boy at the counter looks at Zeus.

I say, "Don't worry. It's to go," in a smooth jazz voice that obviously implies, "like, cool your jets, man, he's just a dog. Dig?"

Hippie Boy makes change from my twenty, wraps the slices up, and rambles, "Dogs are interesting because they'll love anyone. Except for Cerberus, right? Guard dog to Hades. Supposedly he had a snake for a tail and snakes all along his back. Three heads and stuff. Must've been one mean 'n' ugly hombre, eh? Not like your guy." We look at Zeus. He's fighting back gallons and gallons of drool. I put a dollar in the tip jar and return the rest of the change to my wallet. "Your guy," continues Hippie Boy, staring intently into Zeus's eyes while Zeus stares right back, "has the eyes of...of a monk." For a long moment they stare into one another. Hippie Boy must be high. Then the connection is severed and the world rushes back in and continues wherever it's headed. There's no explanation, only the definitive severing of the connection. He must be high on blue mickies, or yellow nuns, or crack, or crank, or whatever. On a yellow sticky I scribble,

> What's the
> difference
> between crack
> and crank?

"I'll...I'll keep that in mind," I mumble as I attempt to juggle my briefcase, the slices, and Zeus's leash. Once everything is stabilized, I leave. "Thanks," I say on my way out.

"No pro-blay-mo. Chowder," Hippie Boy says, playing the counter as if it were a bongo, accompanying the music on the pizzeria's sound system.

∞

Zeus and I take our pizza to the small park across the street from the doggie day care center. We hunker under a large tin canopy, which covers four graffiti-riddled picnic tables bolted to a cracked and weathered slab of concrete. On the table we choose, someone has scrawled in crazy, black marker script, don't let them know! Someone has added, They already do!

Before I ponder too much and too long, Zeus nudges my thigh. I look down at him. Long strands of drool ooze from his jowls.

Once again he's right. I hand him his slice of plain cheese and unexpectedly withdraw with all my fingers.

The way he gobbles his slice I'm not sure he even tastes it. Toppings, any and all, give him gas, particularly pepperoni and green peppers. After one of Francesca's frantic departures, Mirabella and I made the mistake of giving Zeus a slice covered thick with toppings. Watching *Finding Nemo* was more like finding a breath of fresh air.

Anyway, my slice, a Veggie-Carnivore combination, tastes like perfection, like a five-course meal elegantly downsized to pizza pie dimensions. I'm disappointed I didn't get another slice, or a whole pie. Next week. I'll call ahead and pick it up before Zeus. Yes, a good plan.

The increasing rain pounds the tin roof. Somehow, though, the maddening cacophony becomes soothing, mesmerizing. Cold, bright drops fall around us; puddles gradually grow where the edge of the cement floor meets the tired grass.

Wait a minute—next week? Could they be gone that long? A few days, maybe. Definitely not a week. If it's a week, something's definitely wrong. And then what?

One of the puddles begins to slowly inch its way toward us.

"Zeus?" He looks up at me, nervous at the tone of my voice. "What the hell's going on? I mean, where the hell are Francesca and Mirabella? Where are they?" Zeus begins to climb up with me. I assume for comfort, probably his and not mine. "No. Sit, Zeus. Sit."

He does, reluctantly.

Sitting on the metal picnic table in the middle of an empty city park, as the day gradually grows colder, darker, wetter, I wish for a pint of scotch. Something to sip on through the night until an innate understanding seeps into me. Understanding about where, but mostly why, Francesca and Mirabella have gone. Because, realistically, I don't know anything, particularly without that scotch. As it is, my ass slowly freezes. The puddle gets closer and closer.

So, as Zeus and I wait for the taxi, we watch the wet world move along. A few cyclists cower into the rain and wind. A handful of pedestrians walk through the park on their way to Belmont and the restaurants there. We sit and wait and watch—a man and his dog, and his misunderstanding, which hovers over his right shoulder, growing larger and larger by the minute.

∞

By the time the taxi drops us off, I'm tired and, for lack of a better term, thin. The island of uncomfortable silence that is the house doesn't help. Not even the reassuring rhythm of Zeus lapping at his dish consoles me. I call out for Tyler. Silence, a guilty criminal, replies. I sort through the mail. Zeus comes and dutifully drools on my feet. Thankfully I have my shoes on; my socks and feet stay dry.

"Nice try, big guy. Nice try." He looks up with understanding—the understanding there's always tomorrow. "Hey, kitty, kitty. Tyler?"

I give the few envelopes a cursory glance. Junk, bills, and this month's *Simple Living*—one of many magazines Francesca subscribes to.

I begin to notice there's something slightly deeper to the silence. Accompanying it is a growing edge of annoyance.

I throw the mail across the bureau and yell for the cat. "Tyler! Hey, kitty, kitty, kitty, kitty." Nothing. "Hey!" I scream too loudly for myself, too loudly for Zeus, who pops his head up at me. "Hey, cat! Hey, Tyler! Get your furry, fat, orange ass down here!!" Nothing. No tired "meow." No slow, sad, sultry saunter from a hidden corner. Nothing. Only silence. I chew my lip. I don't like it. The house was locked up as tight as a bank. It rained all day. Tyler hates rain. If available in his size, he'd use an umbrella and galoshes just to drink water. Anger, pure and simple, wells inside me. "Tyler!! Get! The Fuck! Down Here! Now!!" Zeus looks at me, confused, perplexed. I pat his head and make my way upstairs like a convict to the gallows.

"Hey, kitty, kitty. Hey." I attempt to sound less manic and more inviting. Like fresh ahi in a solid gold bowl. Nothing. "Hey, kitty, kitty. Hey. Hey, kitty, kitty. Hey. Hey, kitty, kitty. Hey. Hey, kitty, kitt

At some juncture I recognize he isn't here. The cat has flown the coop. Hopefully he's found Francesca and Mirabella. Hopefully. Hopefully that damn dimensional vortex will either spit Francesca, Mirabella, and Tyler back out—or else swallow Zeus and me, too.

Suddenly, somehow, I find myself at the top of the stairs wallowing in a specific sadness, a specific fear, a specific silence. I can't hear him. I can't hear Zeus.

"Zeus! Zeus! Come here, boy! Come here!" There's a brief moment where it feels as if my heart will collapse, implode from the silence, the expectation. Then, "Woof!" and the answering scramble of big limbs off of the deep, comfortable couch. The silly lunk was asleep on the couch. That's all, just asleep. Nothing to be worried about. No big deal. Really? Really.

I'm back to an acceptable form of calm as he turns the corner. His rear slips under him. His speed and adrenaline are proportional to the fear and anxiety that filled my voice. Immediately he's on the steps beneath me, slobbering my knees as I attempt to shake him off.

"That's my boy. Easy. Easy." We tussle and tangle for a moment. I think how, if given full reign, he'd be a lethal pile of flesh. Thankfully he loves me as much as I love him. "That's my boy. That's my boy." The initial enthusiasm wears off and we both kind of wonder what we're doing at the top of the stairs.

As a final hope and plea I say, "Tyler?" Zeus pricks his ears up, expectantly. "Tyler?" He cocks his head. "Tyler? Go get Tyler, Zeus. Where's Tyler? Where's Tyler? Go get him, Zeusy. Go get Tyler!" Zeus just sits there, his head at a forty-five degree angle, staring at me as if I were a piece of driftwood. "Tyler," I say slow and flat, "Tyler." Zeus stares and stares.

Stupid, stupid dog.

I head downstairs. At the bottom I turn back to where Zeus remains at the top. He looks at me, I at him.

"Tyler, dummy. Tyler. Go. Find. Tyler." Zeus straightens his head as if asking for a definition. I comply, "The orange, four-legged feline. He likes licking his ass and shedding in your water bowl. Ring a bell? Hello?" Nothing. Zeus is a rock of incomprehension. I turn the corner and head for the kitchen to find wine and dinner, though wine alone would suffice.

After my second glass I found myself in the attic, tearing the place apart, searching for that damn cat. He wasn't in the basement stuck behind cobwebbed pieces of leftover sheetrock, or eaten by the washer or dryer. He wasn't stuck in any closets or cupboards on the first floor. Nor was he up the chimney, hiding behind the flue. His window box, on the second floor in the spare bedroom overlooking the backyard, was empty and cold. It was like an open grave. I honestly almost started crying. That's when I got my third glass of wine and returned swiftly to the hunt. He wasn't taking a bath, or playing in Mirabella's Little Princess castle. Nor was he trying on my suits, or Francesca's skirts and lingerie. He wasn't anywhere. Not even in the attic, which looks as if a tornado and a hurricane have had a lover's spat.

Far, below, a dog barks. It's Zeus. I look outside. The sun has set and the stars are well out. I've forgotten to walk him! Crap—and that's exactly what he has to do.

Despondent, I trudge downstairs and let Zeus out into the backyard. As he squats and looks embarrassed, as all dogs seem to, the phone begins ringing. I rush to it, leaving Zeus alone to finish what he's in the middle of.

"Hello?" It seems my desperate enthusiasm startles the caller. Only silence answers. I strain to listen. I can hear breathing. "Hello? Francesca?"

Finally, "George?" The voice sounds familiar, but seems unsure who it's speaking to.

"Yes. Francesca?"

"George?"

"Yes!"

"Are... are you alright?" Then it dawns on me it's Francesca's friend, Jessica.

The enthusiasm drains from my voice. "Yeah, fine. Thank you."

"Uh, okay." She doesn't sound particularly convinced. But I don't particularly care. "Is Francesca there?" She's on her cell phone; I can hear people in the background enjoying themselves—it's a little annoying. Then I remember, Francesca was meeting friends for the aforementioned wine tasting session.

"Jessica, hello. Hi. And how are you?" Did I sound weird? Hopefully I didn't sound weird. Maybe it was the wine and not the paranoia? Did it sound like I was covering something up?

She tries to ignore the fact we already did the pleasantries once. "Uh, just... just fine, thanks. Hey, we're all at Vino's and we're wondering where Francesca is."

"Oh. Uh, I think she's...." I do sound weird. I've never been a good liar. As the saying goes, I couldn't lie my way out of bed. But that doesn't stop me from trying. "I... I think she took Mirabella to some school thing. Or something. Yeah, some school project." Lately, the past three years, I've become notorious for being a little less involved in Mirabella's upbringing than I should. I think now might be a good time to play that up. It's not like I don't want to be truthful. I simply don't want to seem any more inept as a husband and father than I think they already assume I am. Telling her Francesca and Mirabella have possibly left me would only be direct and absolute confirmation of that hypothesis.

I add a little smoke. "Did you try her cell?"

And I'm hit with red, hot coals. "Yes. The message said service had been discontinued."

"What? Are...are you sure?" Oops, I sounded surprised and confused.

"Yes. I tried the number three times."

"Oh, she...she must not have been able to find it. She...she lost it the other day. At...at a soccer game, I think." Was it soccer season? I continue headlong into the abyss of false testimony. "And...and canceled the service. I'll have to talk to her about that. Look, Jess, I gotta go, I think Zeus is eating the cat. Sorry. Take care and say 'hi' to everyone for me. Okay? Bye."

"Okay. Bye, George."

I hang up like a shipwreck survivor making dry land, unsure if the island was habitable or not. Jessica is sure to know I was lying, at least about Zeus and Tyler. Tyler could hold his own, particularly against Zeus.

It suddenly dawns on me the big lug isn't here. A cold flush of panic sweeps through me again. "Zeus! Zeus!" I yell, running to the open kitchen door to discover the backyard is empty. "Zeus! Zeus!" I hear something behind me, entering the kitchen. Is it the ghost, the alien, the evil force that's abducted Francesca, Mirabella, Tyler, and Zeus, now come to yank me into the cold, dark depths?

I take a deep breath and turn to face my fate. Instead it's Zeus, unsure what the hell my problem is, but he's here anyway.

"Hey, there's the big boy!" And I shake his head playfully, and we wrestle, and tussle. He, I think, out of joy. I, definitely, for relief. Even that slight elation seems insipid and foul in this world, though, in this empty house. The poison will escort us out of the house, into the drizzle, and down the street.

Zeus doesn't know why we're going on a walk so late, particularly in the cold, in the rain, but I try and explain it to him as I leash him up. To him? More like myself.

"Well, Zeusy, it's like this.... First of all, the house is too silent, too quiet, too big and foreboding without Francesca, Mirabella, and Tyler." He pads along beside me, seemingly agreeing. Then I explain how sometimes people fall in love and then over the years things change. The thrill and elation of seeing them dissipates, particularly after seeing them over and over during the long days, the long years. Sure, you can try and practice staying in touch, keeping the intimacy, but it's hard enough when there's only the two of you. Then when you start tending to a child, a house, pets—Zeus gives an offended sideways glance which I ignore—a career, and, finally, one's self, the other person can kind of get lost in the background. Eventually, maybe even invariably, you're liable to have more in common with a blind, one-legged, Sri Lankan beggar than the person you wake up with.

Eventually we arrive at the park. The rain has stopped, but I'm talked out and Zeus still isn't completely convinced. I can't really blame him. A lot of what I said sounded like I was trying to convince myself of something. Of what, exactly, I'm not sure, but something.

The park, not surprisingly, is empty. I let Zeus off his leash and he looks at me, confounded.

"Go play," I say.

His interpretation of play is wandering aimlessly, smelling the grass, and occasionally lifting his leg. I try to recall something I thought I was going to ask June. My mind is a blank slate, and I gaze fixedly beyond the baseball fields, off into the dark distance.

Zeus, having fulfilled his obligation to play, joins me in the mindless contemplation of nothing. Before truth can find us, we leave.

∞

Again I find myself drawn to search for myself in my house. My? Isn't it still *our* house? Francesca's and Mirabella's and Tyler's, as well as Zeus's and mine?

"Where are they, Zeusy? Where are they?" He doesn't even look at me. The rain has him completely discouraged.

We don't cross the street. Instead we stay on the opposite side. From this perspective the house almost seems as if it could be someone else's.

I stand on the curb in front of the Wilson's house. They live directly across the street from us. He's a dentist; she works in the personnel department of a bank downtown. I lean on the maple sapling they planted a few years ago, and accept the pseudo-protection of its budding limbs.

It begins to rain a little more steadily, as if it were going to continue for a long, long time.

The house, our house, my house, the house is lit up like a candle. Apparently I forgot to turn the lights out before we left. Every room is a bright, white eye in the house's skull. I look long and hard, attempting to see myself walking past a white window.

After a few minutes, the realization of the futility sinking in, I step off the curb and into the street. That's when I think I do see a shape, or a shadow, something, move across the den's window. I blink and squint. I wait to see if it happens again.

Maybe it was a bat darting past? Or? I don't know what else it could've been. I wait and watch, but nothing else happens. Rooted in the middle of the street, I'm fascinated at the possibility of seeing myself, or maybe Mirabella, or Francesca, or even Tyler. Instead there's nothing, only a house with all its lights on, and a man standing in the middle of the road, rain seeping into his clothes. I look down the street. It's exceedingly quiet. Everyone is inside watching television, eating dinner, knitting, reading, doing what people do on wet Friday nights in late March. The street, cars, trees, and houses glisten and sparkle.

I think I could stay in the middle of the street and wait and watch time slowly move by, forever. Be an H.G. Wellsian time-traveler in a protective bubble and watch the quick progression of the sun across the sky. Watch the street, the house, the city quickly decay and disappear.

As the sun rises and sinks, rises and sinks, rises and sinks, a heavy sadness weighs me down. I'm not in the mood to fight it. I give in. I collapse. I slowly sit and then lie in the street. The rain pelts me, soaks up off the street, through my clothes and into me.

I let go of Zeus's leash. Smarter than me, he trudges across the street and up the steps to the front door of the house.

The rain falls and falls. I stare into the sky. How do alien abductions work? What is Japanese paper-folding called? How can the dead communicate from beyond the grave? What is the sound of a mummy laughing? And what is the gap between orange slices called?

Pondering everything, I hear a car's engine above the patter of the rain. It sounds like the car has turned the corner a few blocks away. I wonder if it will stop, or simply roll across me. Will it hurt? My limbs are numb from the cold, the rain. If they drive as fast as some of the kids who race around here, it'll be over in a second. I won't feel a thing. Like a bullet to the brain. Besides, I'm not sure my limbs can move quickly enough should I wish to get out of the way.

I wait.

It rains.

The car turns into a driveway a block away.

It rains.

Zeus gives a distraught and confused bark.

I turn my head to him and smile, forlorn. He barks again. Yeah, I know—what the hell am I doing? It's cold and wet and I'm lying in the street. Simple proof, as if Francesca and Mirabella and Tyler's abandoning the ship weren't proof enough, the captain is a lunatic. And it doesn't help that there seems to be a storm on the horizon.

Gradually I raise myself to my feet. Joints and limbs are practically fused together from the cold. Eventually I lumber up the stairs to where Zeus waits apprehensively. For a change I'm dripping on him.

∞

It takes a half hour to get the house, myself, and Zeus settled into place for the rest of the night. The lights are all turned out except for the reading light above my corner of the couch. I've started a fire that crackles perfectly, as if it were in a movie. I've fed Zeus and wiped him off, and thrown a blanket across the couch. I've shed my wet clothes and am in big wool socks, Levi's, T-shirt, and a tattered black cardigan. The CD player is loaded with a collection of string quartets, Baroque classics, and Gregorian chants with Peter Gabriel's soundtrack from *The Last Temptation of Christ* added in for good measure. A bottle of wine, a Sokol Blosser pinot noir, is open and waiting nearby on the coffee table.

The plan is to see which happens first, my finishing Marquez's biography (I have a hundred and sixteen pages left) or the bottle of wine. If I were a betting man I'd wager on the bottle, by twenty or thirty pages.

I pour a glass of the pinot, open the book, and let the world disappear. Ignorance and delusion is what this is about. Looking at the bottle, the book, the fire, Zeus curled up on the couch, the rain falling outside, I realize I'm moments away from being as blind as Oedipus. And it couldn't arrive any sooner.

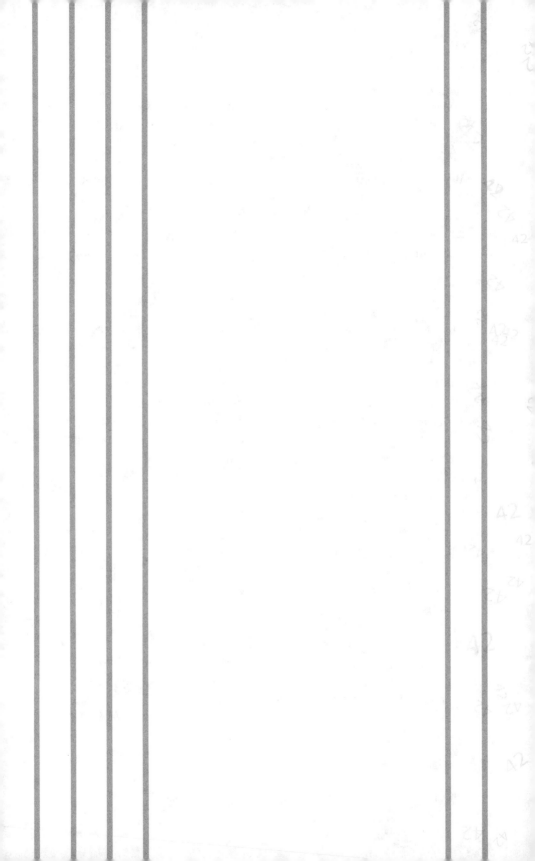

Saturday:

March 27, 2004

Waking, I have no idea where I am. I remember the wine, the book, the fire, Zeus, everything. But I'm not there, slumped on the couch fighting Zeus for space. I assume, based on the thin light, this is morning. I seem to be in bed, but it doesn't feel like my bed, and not because Francesca hasn't been in it for...for only two nights? No, surely it's been more than that? More like a couple of hundred, right? I do the calculations slowly. Okay, it's three nights, which makes me feel slightly better. But still, that's not that many, and yet it feels like a lifetime, like forever.

However, is this my bed? I'm lying on my stomach, with pillow and sheets piled up over my head, which pounds like a two-year-old Mirabella on a drum. I can't see anything, but I know I'm in a bed. Somewhere I hear a lawn mower and a leaf blower. Music plays softly, reverently, somewhere. I inhale, but nothing smells familiar. Not even Francesca's shampoo in my hair.

Weakly, I call out for Zeus. There's no answer. I'm too hungover, too tired, but the fear of being left alone urges me to wake and rise. As I sit up, the child with the drum in my head is joined by two friends, each with her own drum.

"Zeus?" There's no way he hears my mouse-in-a-coffee-can voice. I'm going to have to crawl out of bed and trudge downstairs and check the couch. Assuming this is the right house.

I rub my eyes. Eventually I create fissures and cracks to see out of. It looks like the right bedroom, but...I fall back. What's the use? Zeus is gone. There's no way he's there, still on the couch, sound asleep. No way. What's next after him? My job? The house? The city? Myself?

Outside, the mower falls silent. The blower, however, continues.

Okay, fine, let's witness the aftermath.

I struggle to my feet. Totter for a moment, then stagger and lurch my way forward. First, to the bathroom—nature, occasionally, does take precedence. Once finished, I stumble an escape from the bedroom. The stairs waver and weave as if viewed through a glass of ouzo, but somehow I make it to the living room. Where the little shit lies sound asleep on the couch.

Taking a seat by his big head, I idly play with his soft, soft ear. I don't know how long I do this, stare at the dead embers of the fire, the empty bottle of wine, the closed book, the family photos crowding the mantle, when a panicked thought drops down the well of my mind—Zeus is dead. He's not moved since I sat beside him. Hasn't sighed so heavily his jowls flap. Hasn't snored. Hasn't done anything. He's dead.

"Zeus?" My voice is still weak and rasping, still caught in the coffee can. I slide my hand to his chest. His heart pounds solidly in his chest. It, disconcertingly, feels almost as if something, someone, is attempting to escape. "Zeus!"

He doesn't stir, though his heart, the thing, the someone, does begin to increase tempo. "Zeus! Zeus!"

Suddenly he jumps up. His swiftness scares me. I leap back, afraid. He barks and growls as if being attacked. A hot wave of fear washes over me. Bright, jagged teeth are bared, fire enflames his eyes. For some reason two words flash over and over in my mind, demon possessed, demon possessed, demon possessed. I hope it's some odd, startled memory from my adolescence and not the truth.

"Zeus!"

Thankfully he recognizes me, and instantly calms down. Realizing his faux pas he bows his head. "Zeusy, it's okay. It's okay. That was my fault. You're okay. You're okay." Tentatively I pat his head. He sniffs my hand, begins to lick it.

I tug him gently over onto my lap. I rub his head, scratch his belly. He rolls onto his back. Friends once again.

The phone rings as I attempt to simultaneously rub Zeus's belly and write a list of errands on a sticky note. There's a brief moment when I think about getting up and answering it. Instead, I scratch Zeus and wait for the machine to pick it up.

"Francesca?" It's Leslie. "Jess and I are going for a walk up at Tryon Creek. Gorgeous day." I glance outside. And sure enough, it is. "Join us? We'll be leaving around noon. Hope you're well. Bye. Oh, call my cell, I'm at the grocery store. Bye."

Ugh! I'm going to have to tell Jessica and Leslie about Francesca's leaving. I'm going to have to tell Margarita. Then there's Mirabella's school. And, well, my mother can simply figure it out on her own. It's just going to get uglier and uglier and uglier.

Okay, what to do today? I look at the list; nothing sounds relevant. Not even showering, shaving, or eating. I ponder staying on the couch scratching Zeus all day, when there's a knock at the door. Zeus bolts up, waits. Did he hear something? Did he? There's another knock. He did. He jumps off the couch, barking, and dashes to the front door.

I think, I believe, I hope, that from the front door you can't see me on the couch. I slowly slide down and elongate myself, attempting to hide.

A woman's voice, Margarita's, is barely audible above Zeus's barking. "Francesca? Francesca? It's momma. ¿Aló? ¿Aló? Francesca? Jorge? ¿Aló?"

I simply cower on the couch and wait. It seems I'm not ready. Not ready to tell anyone about myself as failed husband, failed father. Not yet prepared to confess I was unable to support a wife and daughter emotionally. Sure I could keep them in Disney DVDs, Eurovans, and such. But that's not happy. That's a Band-Aid on a bullet wound.

Margarita eventually gives up and drives off. Her old Volvo sputters off down the street. Well, that's one reason right there I'm glad we never gave her a house key. When we first moved in Francesca and I had a contentious discussion about exactly that.

I said, "No."

She said, "Yes."

We went around the ring a bit. Finally, I made a good point, "If you want her to be able to walk in on us as we're fucking, fine. But in that case, give her a photo. It'd save the near-sighted old woman a dangerous drive over."

The thought of Margarita walking in on us truly scared Francesca. She conceded. No key for Margarita. And a small victory for me.

Lying on the couch, the leaf blower having fallen silent, I somehow fall back asleep.

∞

This time upon waking I know where I am, but not exactly when. The shade and shadows of the room are slightly askew. I sit up, scratch my head, rub my eyes. I go get a glass of orange juice and try to wash the sticky morning cotton from my mouth. Looking at the time on the coffeemaker, I scratch my stubbled chin in disbelief. It's nearly two in the afternoon. Holy cow! How the hell did I sleep that long? Not even in college after a bender with the boys did I sleep this late into the day. Is it a sign of age? Or wisdom? Maybe stress?

I have another glass of orange juice. Then..."Zeus!" Nothing. It was only a matter of time before I was completely abandoned. It's only expected. It's well deserved. "Zeus?" Then I hear him padding down the hall. "Zeus, are you really so stupid? The ship's sinking, buddy. Best to get while the getting's good."

I reward his loyalty, reinforce his stupidity, with a can of food. I'm about to go upstairs and shower and finally get this day underway, when the phone again rings.

It's Leslie again. "Francesca, where are you?" That's exactly what I'd like to know. She continues: "We had a fabulous walk, but missed you—just like at wine tasting. We're going to the spa tomorrow. You have no choice. You're going with us. Pick you up at three. We'll do dinner and wine after. Bye. Oh, and tell your husband he better not be erasing these messages. His life depends on it. Love you, George. See you tomorrow, Francesca. Bye."

Slowly, slowly, I walk down the hallway to the phone on the bureau—my own green mile. Without hesitation my forefinger reaches out and pushes the erase button.

Two steps up the stairs, heading toward a shower and a shave, I stop and return to the kitchen. I watch Zeus finish his meal. He seems as if he's truly enjoying it. As if there's something magical about the ground-up meal, the miscellaneous, leftover beef, sheep, and pig parts compacted into a mucous loaf. I stare, bewildered and mesmerized—strangely reminded of Tyler. Eventually he finds the bottom of the silver bowl. However, that isn't enough. He licks and licks it clean. The bowl scoots across the kitchen floor. He follows with his tongue. Not stopping until it shines, pristine and new, until he can clearly see himself reflected in the surface. Satisfied, he saunters to the back door and sits. Time to poop. I let him out and follow him into the backyard, playing prison guard.

On that second step to the shower I decide I'm not going to lose him. I'll take him everywhere, never let him out of my sight. I'll be vigilant. He will not disappear. Not on my watch. No, sir.

After he's done with his business, I take him upstairs with me and leash him to the bed where I can see him from the bathroom. I take my shower, occasionally peeking out at the confused dog just to make sure he's still there.

Shaving I take slow and diligent. I don't need any more razor inflicted contusions, so I attempt a new, right-to-left pattern. Halfway through my shave, at the equator of my face, the doorbell rings. Zeus immediately jumps to attention, immediately starts barking.

I peek out the bathroom window. No old rusted Volvo. However, thankfully, there is a Speed's Towing tow truck with my Mustang on the back.

"Hold on!" I yell above Zeus. "Hold on!"

A reply comes: "Okay!" as I quickly wipe my face free of the shaving cream. I throw my clothes from the night before back on, grab Zeus, and go downstairs to claim the car.

The driver doesn't know anything about a red Eurovan. Honestly, I don't particularly care. I have my Mustang back.

I sign the paperwork and he leaves. Ten minutes later Zeus and I are on the road. Driving aimlessly around, I put together a mental list of things to get: yellow sticky notes, Murakami novel(s), shampoo, and...and.... Could I send out cards to notify people that Francesca and Mirabella have left me? Maybe ask for help, if they know where they are? Even any help with Tyler, the little orange kitty, would be greatly appreciated. Okay, the cards are probably not the best idea for announcing my inadequacies and losses. I'll think of something else then. Perhaps a brochure?

∞

I stop at a corner convenience store and get sticky notes and shampoo. I'm unconcerned about price, or brand, but I can see Zeus the whole time.

The Murakami novels pose more of a problem. However, desperate times require desperate measures. Zeus and I simply march into the Powell's bookstore on Hawthorne like the vanguard to an angry and accursed army. It takes only a few moments to find the aisle with Murakami. And instead of going through the selection and reading the back covers I grab his entire collection. Before anyone can say anything, I've paid and left. The cashier even gives me a nice nonchalant smile on my way out.

While running my errands everyone seems to be a little nicer, a little more pleasant than usual. This causes me to smile and give friendly little nods in return.

Maybe the smiles are a sign things are looking up? Maybe the sun is going to break through and shine on Francesca and Mirabella and Tyler. As they're illuminated in heavenly light I'll go to them and we'll live happily ever after.

∞

For a late afternoon lunch and beer, I visit the Lucky Lab Pub. Zeus and I, after ordering inside, settle in at the outside table I've reserved with the heap of Murakami novels.

On a very cursory quest, I go through them. I don't find Francesca's "*like smoke*" reference.

As I'm reading about a goat man and a beach hotel, my sandwich arrives. It looks as appetizing as a whale corpse washed ashore. I order another pint and give a few of the accompanying potato chips to Zeus.

Technically I'm not reading Murakami's curious prose, just scanning it. Just looking for common elements from one novel to the next. Attempting to distinguish patterns in his prose, patterns in the impossible.

Eventually, done with another pint, the sandwich having been shared and scavenged, much to Zeus's chagrin, by the other canines, I come to a conclusion about Murakami. He's alright, though he seems to suffer from a fixation on prostitutes, young women disappearing, scotch, and sheep. I'm sure there are more fixations. And in time I'll find them. If necessary (which it seems it is), I'll know him better than myself, especially if it helps return Francesca, Mirabella, and, I suppose, Tyler to me. I'll crawl, through his books, into him. Gain access, discover where the "*like smoke*" originates, and douse the fire—glimpse the constellations of my family on the perfect arc of his skull. And, with one swift blow, unite us in bright, glorious light.

Inevitably, basking in the glow of beer and fantasized success, a dark needle insinuates itself into the fabric—what if they don't come back? What if reuniting is delusion, not reality? What then? What then?

Initially I'd assumed, after reading that stupid, fucking note, they'd be gone a day, maybe two. However, Margarita's apartment isn't that comfortable, nor would she be asking about them, or stopping by.

I'm not one to worry, but this is ridiculous. Usually Francesca vented one way or another, a raving phone call in the middle of the night, a furious e-mail from the Internet café near her mother's. Something, but not complete silence. That was saved for when she was home.

I wonder, can you file a missing persons report if they left of their own free will? I assume Francesca didn't abduct Mirabella. What would be the sense in that? If you're going to abscond, you leave the kid behind, take the money, max out all the credit cards, scrawl *Shit happens, but assholes like you are born* in lipstick on the mirror, and flee to Vegas with the hunky, twenty-four-year-old carpenter, right? You don't take the kid, leave the car, and not purchase anything, I assume without a romantic partner-in-crime. At least from my perspective you don't.

∞

As I round the corner toward home, I notice an old, rusted Volvo parked in front of the house. I drive by as casually and inconspicuously as possible. Margarita is on the front stoop knitting. Immersed with the white needles transforming the red yarn, she doesn't look up. I wonder if somewhere in space and time the me that lay in the street in the rain didn't just get run over. I give a cursory apology to that dimensional me, and drive on.

Now what? I drive a few blocks, take a left, and park.

How long can Margarita sit there? I'll attempt to stonewall her. Hold out until she gives up. But how long will that be? If she's feeling self-righteous, it would be like attempting to get a suntan on the dark side of the moon. Particularly if she's proving a point to Jorge—like mother like daughter. In the rearview mirror, I see Zeus staring at me. I know. I know. Lately, he's become far more judgmental.

Glancing at the Murakami novels cluttering the passenger seat, I make a quick decision—the park. I'll read, Zeus can play, and perhaps June will be there to answer a few esoteric questions about ghosts, dimensional vortices, and alien abductions. Perfect.

∞

I take an oil-splotched, plaid blanket from the trunk and spread it out in the weak light of the early spring sun. I lie down and attempt to get comfortable. Zeus stares at me, perplexed. I snap and point. Reluctantly, he settles himself at my feet. I explain, in no uncertain terms, that I've had second thoughts about letting him play. About my losing sight of him. Therefore he stays on leash and at my feet. Initially he whimpers an argument, but quickly becomes sullen and pouts as he too lies down.

The pile of Murakami novels awaiting dissection, rest at my shoulder. I thumb to the copyright dates and place them in sequential order. However, before I can begin dissecting, my cell phone rings.

The name displayed sends me into a mild annoyance: Margarita. I don't answer. It rings and rings. Eventually voice mail takes over. What am I doing? I'm afraid of talking to a sixty-seven-year-old woman. Sure she's a spitfire for her age, but it's a little sad.

After a moment the message alarm rings. Immediately the phone rings again, and is instantly followed by the message alarm. This time the name displayed sends a cold, expectant chill through me: Francesca.

Quickly I dial voice mail.

"Jorge, you call me. You tell me—" Margarita is quickly deleted.

And then Francesca's sweet voice fills my ear, "George, where are you? Mirabella and I have taken the groceries home. For some reason we're returning. Call me. Soon." In the background, before Francesca hangs up, I hear Mirabella, but can't discern what she says.

A fissure of melancholy, of loss and longing, opens inside me. I play the message in a futile attempt to fill it. And again. And again. And again. And again. I even play it for Zeus, though he doesn't appreciate it as he should—having been woken from his nap.

Reluctantly, as if sentenced to hard labor, I begin reading Murakami. I read until it's too dark to make out the print. June and Tuesday never show up. I write on a yellow sticky note,

Why is June's dog named Tuesday?

∞

This time, thankfully, the old, rusted Volvo is gone. I turn into the driveway and park. Zeus and I lumber out.

As I open the front door, my cell phone rings again. This time, though, it's ▬▬▬▬I don't want to answer, but, call it conditioning, I do.

"Hello?"

"Hi." There's a short pause, as we gauge the other, each measuring the need with the fee.

She asks, "You can talk?"

I answer, "Since I was a child."

She laughs lightly, then throws a rock through a plate glass window. "Meet me for a drink." Not a question, but an open-ended statement. She's famous, or infamous, for them. I think that's how this whole she and me business began.

I look at my watch. It's nearly 6:30. And it's a Saturday. She knows the rules. No weekend nights. Afternoons, maybe. Then I remember the vacant house.

"Why are you calling?" I ask, as I pick up and sift through the mail. Zeus goes to his water dish and drinks and drinks and drinks. It seems he's a little dehydrated.

In some strange parallel way, ▬▬▬ replies, "Because I'm thirsty." I can't tell if that was an honest statement—she could drink lemon drops like lemonade. Or an innuendo? Thirsty for blood, revenge, justice, or, perhaps, something more X-rated? Could she be watching Zeus and me right now? Stalking us? And the "thirsty" is simply a reference to Zeus and his water dish?

Anxious, I walk around the house, peering outside the windows, into the back yard, looking for a stalker, or a killer, specifically a short, attractive woman of Korean descent. I don't see anyone.

"No. I mean, why now?"

"I'm *thirsty*." Okay, she happens to already be a few drinks into the evening. So it was an innuendo.

"Can't do it. Not now. Sorry." The mail is again composed of bills, junk, and another magazine for Francesca, *Modern Woman*.

"Why? Too busy with 'Disney and popcorn'?" I want to take offense at that, but I once lamented spending too many nights watching animated movies (specifically Disney, and not Pixar) and eating popcorn. However, right now, *Beauty and the Beast* and artificial butter flavor sound like heaven.

"No. It's not that."

"Then?" Zeus is still drinking. The light on the answering machine is blinking. There are two new messages. She repeats a little more seductively, "Then?" I think I hear splashing water somewhere in the background, behind ████

I weakly throw out an excuse, not explaining the sad reality. "I've been saddled with the dog."

"Bring him. He can guard us." Zeus is done with the water. He now sits patiently and expectantly by his food bowl.

"What do you mean?"

"I mean, I'm in the bath. Bubbles. Candles. Wine." It sounds like she's losing patience.

"So?" Then she adds something I'm not expecting. Though, I will admit, I've longed for it.

"And shaved."

"'Scuse me?" She laughs and splashes, but says nothing. I look at Zeus. He gazes back, sad-eyed and hungry. I try to ignore the weight in my crotch, growing. Then, inexplicably, she hangs up.

"Zeus?" He tilts his head like he knows I'm about to say something that could affect the entire course of humankind. "What the hell is going on?" He tilts it a little more, realizing this is really monumental. "And—" I'm playing with him, manipulating my voice so it sounds important, intriguing, "—what the hell am I going to do?" He keeps his head tilted and waits for an answer and his food. He probably doesn't care one way or the other what I do, as long as he gets food in his bowl.

Stalling on making a decision about ████, I hit the play button on the answering machine.

It's Margarita. "Mirabella, gran-mamma is to take you to movie.

Be there soon. Ciao." Well, that explains what Margarita was doing on the steps this afternoon, knitting. Delete.

Next is a woman's voice I don't recognize; it's melodic, with an affected cheerfulness that immediately annoys me. "Hello Olsons, this is Nancy Coles from A.A.E.I. It seems we forgot to include some paperwork the other day. You have, of course, my sincerest apologies. George, it should be at your office on Monday. And if you have any questions—nothing too complicated though, nothing like 'what's the meaning of life—'pa-lease give me a call."

Of course I want to give Nancy a call back. I want to tell her to retract the stupid sunshine enema up her ass. I want to tell her the term "we" has become obsolete and is quickly becoming offensive. I also want to ask her, "What paperwork?" However, as I delete Nancy's message it hits me—the manila envelope, the second mortgage, the vacation home. The envelope I put in my briefcase. And my briefcase was where? I had it last when....

My cell phone begins ringing, again. It's ▬▬▬▬. "Yes?"

"Did I mention I shaved? Did I mention I'm horny? Did I mention I want you to come over and fuck me silly, straight, and serious?"

For some reason I look at Zeus. He's still staring at me, patiently waiting for his dinner.

"No, but I think it was implied. Shall we say, implicit in your tone and innuendo?"

"Okay. Let's say that—'implicit in my tone, implicit in my innuendo.'" She is really, really pushing the point. Never had she pushed this hard for me to spend time with her. Initially it'd been, "meet-here-at-such-and-such-a-time, fuck, bang, lick, suck and see-you-later." The only recent change was her turning thirty a month ago. And, unofficially of course, our one-year anniversary is two weeks away. I wonder if there's some correlation? Her birthday? Our meeting? Perhaps. On a yellow sticky note I write,

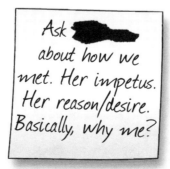

Ask ▬▬▬ about how we met. Her impetus. Her reason/desire. Basically, why me?

Of course I don't write the same questions for me.

"Did I mention I have the dog?" Zeus stares at me. I'm pretty sure he's offended by the phrase "the dog." I can't say I blame him.

"Did I mention he could guard us?"

"Yes. Yes, you did." I wonder if she thinks it's necessary. Do I?

"Good."

"Indeed." We've arrived at that fateful juncture—a decision must be made. Zeus sniffs his empty bowl. The house sighs with the increasing winds outside. It seems a storm is rushing headlong over the hills and into the city, and tomorrow.

"And so?"

"And so...."

∞

As I back out of the driveway, I try to ignore Zeus's sullen stare from the backseat.

"I've already explained, she's got a couch, too." He sits down and stares into the shadows of the footwell.

In the middle of the street, I hesitate before shifting into first. I look up at the darkened house. Perhaps it was the light that kept the me I was looking for away from the windows? Perhaps now I can discern Francesca and Mirabella, both creatures of light, in the darkness. The car idles and I wait and watch. But, like when the house was lit, there's nothing, only an empty house.

Disappointed, I drive off into the night, expecting the same thing around each corner: disappointment.

∞

████ greets me at the door in a green and red silk kimono that gives her skin a deep, luxuriant glow. Then I remember the bath, the wine.

"Hello," she smiles.

"Hi."

"You need a drink." Again a statement, not a question.

"Probably three," I admit.

"So, this is the infamous Zeus?" Zeus looks up at her, unsure, unsure about everything. Guardedly he sniffs around.

"Yes. Yes, it is." We watch him sniff the doorjamb.

"Look," she says. I look into ████'s dark, brooding eyes. "If you're not going to enjoy yourself...go home. I'm sure Zeus and I can find something to talk about."

"What?" She obviously means my tone is missing a certain enthusiasm. However, her smile seems to speak of something else. I ask again, "What?"

The smile remains as she answers, "Your face."

"What's wrong with my face? I thought you liked it."

"Go look in the mirror," she says, closing the door and taking Zeus's leash. Before I protest, she gives a gentle shove, and commands, "just do it," unconcerned about copyright infringement.

Her apartment has gone through a transformation since I'd last visited, which was about five months ago. A Thursday, the week before Halloween, I think. At the time there'd been mostly boxes because she'd just moved in. Now it's elegantly decorated in sleek wood end tables, comfortable, well-appointed chairs, and a large couch which Zeus is sure to love. The lights are turned low, and a handful of tea candles burn here and there. In the background Norah Jones plays. There isn't a cardboard box to be seen.

A residual humidity, scented with lavender, vanilla, and eucalyptus, lingers in the bathroom. Again, a few tea candles sparkle in the dark. I switch the light on and destroy the ambience.

Quizzically, I gaze at myself in the mirror. I notice half my face is covered in thick stubble, the other smooth as a baby's butt. Apparently, after my car was dropped off I'd forgotten to finish the rest of my shave. Now *that* explains people's reaction to me while in Powell's, while shopping for sticky notes and shampoo, while drinking my lunch. I was obviously some freakish eccentric with his "Rottie" and a half-shaved face.

I want to laugh, but can't.

I lean forward and squint into my eyes, attempting to discern an image flickering in candlelight. Instead of a towel, or the shower's ornate etched door, I see myself leaning and looking in the mirror, where, reflected in my eyes, is me, leaning forward and looking in a mirror. I imagine, if I had a magnifying glass or telescope, I could discern hundreds of me's gazing and staring back and forth at me.

Before I ponder more than I should, ███████ enters with two robust glasses of red wine. She places one on the dark marble countertop near my hand.

My explanation about being interrupted by the tow truck operator sounds pathetic, like something made-up. Even I don't actually believe it, which is odd because I'm pretty sure it happened.

██████ comments, "It almost makes you look as if you're two people. Or, I guess," she takes a long, seductive sip of wine as Zeus sidles up beside us, "one person split in two."

I look back at myself, seeing exactly what she means. She makes it more apparent by running her hand through my hair, but only on the side that corresponds to my unshaven face.

Zeus, disgruntled, lies down in the hallway just outside the bathroom door. It's as if he's accepted some implicit covenant of staying longer than he'd hoped for, of reluctantly guarding her and me. I don't think about what that might mean.

██████ laughs at the bipolar, split image of me and takes another sip of wine. I look from my reflection to her. She smiles mischievously; I stare, perplexed.

"So, whom do I get tonight?" she asks. I look from me to her, her to me. "Good George, or Bad George?" I want to wipe that assumptively self-satisfied smile off her face. "Good George, or Bad George?" she repeats. I want to wipe that blank, confused stare off of my face. I want to replace it with... with what? "Good George, or *Naughty* George?"

██████ turns the light out and walks to the edge of the bath. I follow her reflection the entire way. She hesitates. I turn to mine. Now I don't even know if it is me. The candles illuminate my shaved face, my smooth hair, my "good" side, while the "bad" side is cast in shadow, like the dark side of the moon.

Zeus is already asleep in the hall, snoring and chasing dream rabbits.

██████ lets her kimono drop from her shoulders and steps into the empty bath.

I continue to stare into my reflected eyes, one bright with flame, the other dark with shadow.

She turns the water on, adds bath salts and a few scented oils. Gradually, the room fills with steam. The mirror slowly fogs over. She leans back, closes her eyes, relishing the hot water rising up her legs, her thighs, and asks idly, "George? Are you joining me?"

I stare until I disappear in the thick, thick steam.

Sunday:

March 28, 2004

This time when I wake I really don't know where I am. The sheets are pine colored and smell of incense. Raising my head, I nervously take in the room. The mute walls are decorated in bright tapestries with medieval motifs. There is an ornate scene of a joust. There is a dinner party full of revelry and merrymaking. There is a knight offering a nondescript object to a princess on bended knee, while on an overlooking hill, a unicorn watches. The fourth wall is nothing but windows, from floor to ceiling, overlooking the city.

The implications and interpretations of the whole scene make me a little dizzy and I bury my face back beneath the pillow, where I'm shrouded by the scent of incense. The scent reminds me of something. Of something I should know, but I can't, for the life of me, remember.

Maybe this is the actual me I was expecting to see in the house? Maybe I've finally switched and this is the real me, but I don't know it yet. It's too early. Eventually the uncomfortable sensation of displacement will disappear, will be forgotten. Days of drudgery and nights of lethargy will be replaced. But replaced with what?

Instantly I'm answered by a tongue in my ear, the weight of a naked woman pressing herself against my back.

"Morning," she whispers, again licking my ear and gently tugging the lobe with her teeth.

"Morning," I echo, turning over to glimpse myself reflected in the beautifully dark, dark eyes of ▇▇▇▇.

Instead of recalling last night—the wine, the bath, her mounting me, the waves, chasing Zeus to the couch—and dealing with the guilt, I ask as a diversion, "What's for breakfast?"

"It was going to be crêpes," she replies, "but someone got up and ate them." Not me, right? I would remember eating crêpes, wouldn't I?

"Someone? W-who?" I ask, nervous, afraid of the impending implication.

"Your dog."

"Zeus? Is he okay? Is he still here?" I attempt to get up, but ▇▇▇▇'s weight holds me.

"Yes, he's fine. Relax." All the characters in the tapestries are resolutely staring at me. "Are you alright?" Each time I return someone's gaze they turn away, pretending they weren't staring. "George?"

"Yeah, yeah. Absolutely great." Again I lie. This is becoming a habit, and a bad one at that. "So," again I go for diversion, "what about crêpes and breakfast?"

"He ate them."

"Oh. Sorry." I think I sound sincere. "Did he break anything?"

"Just my nose," she says smiling.

"I'm sorry, what?" Her nose looks as cute as ever.

"He had a little—check that, change that—a *big* poop problem."

"Yeah, he's kind of conditioned that way. Food in—poop out. Sorry. Anything I can do?" ▇▇▇▇ smiles, and coils herself around me.

"Yes. You can screw me. Then take a shower and shave. That beard of yours is beginning to look ridiculous. And then take me to breakfast." I echo her smile, and dutifully comply.

While in the shower, steam rising around and blurring the shower door, I wonder, could ▇▇▇▇ have somehow disposed of Francesca and Mirabella? Tyler too? Hoping to supplant them? Hoping to be the next Mrs. Olson?

First ▇▇▇▇ would "accidentally" run into them at the grocery store, or a coffee shop. She would do this many times, though it would always seem to be coincidental. Eventually a friendship would be established. Mirabella would come to trust ▇▇▇▇. One day after school, or at a soccer game, ▇▇▇▇ would explain to Mirabella that Francesca has asked ▇▇▇▇ to take her home. ▇▇▇▇ would then tie Mirabella up and take her to a warehouse. ████ would call Francesca. Francesca would show up at the warehouse, be forced to write the note. Then everything falls into place exactly as it has.

Suddenly there's a loud knock on the shower door. I drop the soap and it skips and hops around my feet, hitting my ankle sharply.

"Ouch! Uh, yeah?!" I yell, a little too frantically.

"You get lost in there?"

"Yes!" There's a brief pause as we ponder the possibility, impossibility, of that. "What's up?" I ask, preparing to dodge the thrusting knife, the chainsaw, the Molotov cocktail, the hot lead from the .38.

"My hunger. If you don't hurry up I'm liable to eat your dog." Of course! She'd dispose of them by eating them! Of course!

"Rotties are good eatin', sure. But I prefer donuts, or pastries. Can you wait?"

"Not long. Hurry your ass up!"

"Okay!" Again my hair is going to smell like a woman, the "other woman." This, my life, is simply getting better and better.

∞

As a third choice to crêpes and Zeus for breakfast, we get pastries and coffee at the Pearl Bakery. We then take ourselves, and Zeus of course, for a long walk down the park blocks running through downtown. For some reason I'm attempting to ignore how nice it is to be walking with ████ Chatting about inconsequential items, trivia, while the city, in its weekend way, wakes. I also notice how nice it is to be walking Zeus without holding a poop bag.

Eventually, we make it all the way to Portland State where the farmer's market is in full swing. We decide to forgo the mingling masses searching for some personal nirvana in organic produce, whole grain breads, and free-range chickens.

████ is relating an adventure she recently had while visiting Japan on business. It has something to do with karaoke, sushi, lipstick, and the misunderstanding that she was a famous Broadway actress.

"The last thing I remember, a drunk businessman was French-kissing a tuna they'd pulled from the kitchen, while three of his friends were attempting to sing Steve Miller's 'Jungle Love.' After that everything blurred and eventually went black. Sake and jet lag, you know?"

"Who'd you wake up with?" I ask, honestly curious and a little afraid.

She answers sincerely, flatly, telling the truth, the whole truth and nothing but the truth: "The fish. Naturally."

Laughing, we turn around and take a few steps from whence we came. Immediately, almost as if we were being followed, we run into Leslie and her husband, Nate.

Keeping eye contact to a minimum, I haphazardly mumble some weak, pathetic, "Hello-Hi-Good-to-see-you-Beautiful-day-Take-care-Bye," gibberish-bullshit tainted with embarrassment, insincerity, and guilt.

A few steps past Leslie and Nate, I glance back as if they're Nazi S.S. agents following us on a secret assassination mission. ▬▬▬ asks, "So, who are they?"

I try to play it down, play it cool and smooth. "Enemy agents on a secret assassination mission." I'm a complete failure. It sounds pathetic and forced.

▬▬▬ sips her coffee meditatively then asks, having swallowed a kernel of insight, "Aren't all assassination missions secret?"

I want to argue with her simply for the sake of venting my guilt and anxiety. However, she, unfortunately, has a point. I remain quiet and chew my anger like a racehorse chews its bit at the starting gate.

We pass a block in silence; the tension grows and grows. I want to glance back, see if Leslie and Nate are watching, taking notes or a video. I can hear the people on the park benches, at the café tables, talking about the odds, placing bets. Another block passes. I want to assault Leslie and Nate. I'd like to beat a convincing explanation into them, pound an intricate lie about what I'm doing on a Sunday morning with this beautiful Asian woman. Instead, I finish my apricot scone.

Finally, at the end of the third block, the bell sounds, the gate opens: "I'm sorry. Truly. But I have to go. I'll call you later. Honestly."

I'm practically across the street when she yells, "Hey!"

This is where and when I'm expecting to be clubbed with "don't I matter..." "why is it..." "we should..." "you should..." "couldn't we...?"

Instead ▬▬▬ asks, "Aren't you forgetting someone?"

I knew it. Here we go. It was only a matter of time before the accusations, the demands, the expectations, the public spectacle. I turn into the expected storm, only to be confused by her smile and her offer—Zeus's leash.

"Th-thanks," I mumble inadequately, trotting back to take his leash.

"Sure. Anytime." I turn to go. Again, she calls, "Hey!" I turn around and look at her beautiful smile, into her beautiful dark, dark eyes. "I want you to know I had a really good time last night." She means it. Every letter, every word, is gilded in sincerity. "And," a hand that holds me from turning and running, "and a better one this morning."

"I did too." I'm sincere, but it sounds, at least to me, as if I've just sacrificed my daughter so I could go to war. Weakly I smile and turn away, once again expecting disappointment.

∞

Turning onto my street, Margarita's old, rusted Volvo is once again in front of the house. The plan, again, is to drive by as inconspicuously as possible. This time, though, instead of the park and Murakami, it's going to be beer and bourbon.

I need to resolve my fear of telling people Francesca and Mirabella have left me. I'm unsure what the correlation between beer and bourbon is, but surely there must be one—call it instinct.

I slow to keep the engine down, attempting to give her no reason to look up from her knitting. This time, however, I don't see her on the stoop. I look closer. Try to find her in the shadows. Maybe she's found the key under the flowerpot? Shimmied a window open and snuck in? Maybe.... Suddenly a shape leaps in front of the car. Some kid after a ball? A raccoon? A— Immediately, I apply the brakes. Maybe a...a...Margarita? Margarita! My reaction is good, but...she's hit solid—*thunk*—by the front bumper and grill. In slow motion, she's sent flying. The tires and brakes squeal, sending a cloud of blue-gray smoke into the air. Instantly following the *thunk* is Margarita's piercing scream. Zeus begins barking. Two knobby stick-legs clad in old, hole-y pantyhose and two dark shoes are tossed up into view, and immediately disappear. One shoe, thrown at the apex of the arc of the legs, shoots off and clatters down the street. There's a dull thud as Margarita collides with the pavement. Zeus continues barking. A long, low, agonizing wail—Margarita's—wakes the neighborhood.

Like I was telling myself earlier, life just gets better and better.

∞

I have crappy hospital food while Margarita is in surgery. It seems, thankfully, she'll survive. I knew she was a little spitfire.

It's difficult, though a few embellishments assist, to explain to the police and hospital staff exactly how I ran into her. I can't imagine attempting to tell the same story to Francesca, particularly if I'd killed her. Things are bad enough between Francesca and me without my having killed her mother.

Francesca and me? It's as if she's still around. As if Mirabella might tug my sleeve and ask to be escorted to the video store. Or explain some word I know, but can't define.

While Margarita is in surgery, I attempt to keep Zeus by my side. However, my pleas—"Honestly, this is her dog. No, really, he is a 'seeing eye' dog. Yes, that's right, we're with security,"— fall on deaf ears. It seems there are strict regulations prohibiting dogs roaming hospital hallways. Much to my dismay, I'm forced to leave him in the car. However I park on the top floor of the parking structure, where I can constantly peek from a hospital window and see him staring confused from the back seat.

Eventually Margarita is safely out of surgery and tucked into a private room. She's suffered a compound fracture of the femur (that's what the surgery was for), a broken hip, a dislocated shoulder and, for a garnish, a concussion. Interestingly enough, in an *X-Files* type of way, all her injuries are on her left side. The EMT at the scene said he sees it all the time. I didn't mention the curious coincidence of forgetting to shave that side of my face the day before.

The young surgeon (who looks like my paperboy) asks, "What is that? Assinno? Asasno?"

We turn to Margarita, unconscious and wheezing a word over and over, a word he can't understand.

"Well, she is Spanish," I reply. "That could have something to do with it."

"Yeah, maybe. It could also have to do with the gallons of sedatives we've given her." As he scratches a small scar over an eyebrow he adds, "I mean, she's been mumbling that since they brought her in."

He's young, still a bit rough around the edges with the bedside manner.

"Well, I gotta go shove some intestines back inside a guy. You take care. And don't worry about her. She's a fighter. She'll be fine."

By the time Zeus and I return from the hospital, it's late afternoon. When we pull into the driveway, I notice the lawn is getting a little long. Perhaps I'll mow it sometime soon. Perhaps I won't. But right now it's time for a quick beer and a long nap. Hopefully long enough to forget the word Margarita is mumbling over and over, "asesino." Assassin. Directed, I assume, at me.

∞

The Pilsner hasn't had the opportunity to get comfortable in my belly when the doorbell rings. Thankfully, Zeus, after the snack I've just given him, is out in the backyard consecrating the azalea again. Stealthily I creep around the corner and into the kitchen. More than likely, glancing at the clock on the coffeemaker, it's Jessica and Leslie come to collect Francesca for their afternoon at the spa.

Beginning to close the back door, I hear the front door open and inquisitive voices. I must remember to lock the door. "Francesca? George?" Jessica is always too snoopy for her own good. Leslie is the more practical. "Zeus? Hello, Zeusy?"

"I don't think they're home."

"Someone has to be here."

"Why?"

Zeus is done with the azalea; hearing voices, he saunters over.

"Because George's car is here." Great, Leslie thinks she's fucking Colombo. And to prove the point she continues, "Did I tell you? I saw George downtown this morning."

Zeus, recognizing their voices, attempts to squeeze past me. I hold him back, one hand on his collar, the other on his muzzle.

"So?" Jessica says, sounding like she's snooping through the mail.

"He was with some woman."

"What do you mean—some woman?"

"I mean *another* woman."

"Not Francesca?"

"No."

"Did he say anything?"

Zeus pushes hard enough for me to recognize we're moments away from an awkward scene. One I'd just as soon avoid.

I want to hear what they've got to say about me, about "some woman," though I probably already know. However, their footsteps echoing down the hall are gradually getting closer and closer. Quietly I close the door, tug Zeus by his collar, and hurry us into the garden shed. There's barely enough room for Zeus, let alone me. Both of us have a number of lawn and garden implements poking and jabbing us. I've left a crack in the shed's doors for gazing into the house, and also to allow a modicum of fresh air into the grass clippings and wet leaves— one of the few areas to escape Francesca's cleaning regimen.

After a long moment, during which I have to readjust to get a pair of hedge clippers out of my ribs, Jessica and Leslie make their way into the kitchen.

Zeus gives a slight start and a yelp as he backs into a rake.

"Easy Zeusy. Easy. It's okay. It's okay."

I watch them look around. They nod their heads, agreeing on something, which of course annoys me.

As they snoop, I hear me ask myself and answer myself, What the hell am I doing? I don't know. You're hiding. I know. From what? Jessica and Leslie. Why? Because....Why? Shut up, it's too late now; our fate is sealed to this action, deal with it. I hope a spider bites your ass. Shut up! And I do.

Watching the ladies is interesting in a voyeuristic kind of way. I wonder if this is how stalkers and serial killers feel. Jessica has gotten a piece of paper and a pen. She sits at the kitchen table and begins to write a note. Leslie, I think, is still worried about Zeus turning a corner and ripping them to shreds. She paces slowly back and forth. Calling around the corners, "Zeusy? Zeusy?" And down-stairs, "Zeusy? Zeusy?"

While Jessica writes, they talk. Obviously I can't hear them, though I know exactly what they're saying.

"This really isn't like Francesca."

"I know. Dishes in the sink and the recycling hasn't been taken out."

"Mail piled up. And did you see the lawn?"

"Something's wrong."

"When was the last time you talked to her?"

"Tuesday sometime. Let's leave a note. And if we haven't heard back by Tuesday—"

"Monday night."

"—From either Francesca or George we call the police."

"Agreed. Now let's spaaaa!"

"Were you getting waxed? Because I hear they have that new Australian bee pollen gel." On cue, they exit the kitchen.

I give them a few minutes, then flee the suffocating shed.

I pat Zeus and tell him what a good boy he is for being so quiet, for putting up with all the discomfort of the shed.

Glancing up, I notice James Dudley, my next-door neighbor, on a ladder cleaning his gutters. He's staring at us with a very perplexed look on his face. James tends to wear a sorrowful, hangdog face anyway, but this is different. It's almost as if he's witnessed something suspicious, like the neighborhood's dubious mystery—the carnivorous, three-headed squirrel.

"Hey, James. Find anything interesting?"

He shakes his head. Says nothing. Just stares; the perplexed look on his face seems to have taken up permanent residence.

Upon entering the house, I verify Jessica and Leslie have left. Their absence confirmed, I immediately lock all the doors and windows, get another beer, and read the note they left.

Jessica's handwriting is nothing like Francesca's. It reminds me of an elderly woman writing to her even more elderly sister about the proper way to can pears or bake a pecan pie.

Francesca and George (and Mirabella!),

Hello! Stopped by to take you to the spa. Just Francesca. Sorry George. ☺ The door was open so we let ourselves in. Will either of you please call either of us? (Oh, Leslie is here with me.) We're beginning to worry. Hope you all are well.

Love and hugs,

Jessica and Leslie

P.S. Mirabella, Brittany wants to know if you'd like to spend the night for her birthday, Saturday, April 10. Hope so! Bye.

After reading the note, the beer tastes flat, sour. I put the bottle down, but immediately pick it up again and drain it in one long, carbonated, stinging swallow.

I'm angry. I'm confused. I'm regretful. I'm confused. I'm perplexed. I'm pissed off! Fuck!

What am I doing? What am I not doing? Why haven't I called the police? Why haven't I been racing around the city, the state, the nation, the world, looking, questing, hunting, searching, delving, and diving for my wife and daughter? What made me think she would only be gone for a day, or two? Am I that sure even now that Francesca is calling it quits? Couldn't it just as well be some test? A test like when we first met, just a few days after the hurried thrusting in the shadows of St. Michel, in Paris?

When I woke to Francesca's absence from the bed, I stumbled into the bathroom. Taped to the bathroom mirror—we'd splurged and gotten a room with both a shower and a toilet—was a note.

Sweetheart— If you can find me, you can have me…

Hungover as I was, I put in a cursory search to find her. Sure, I was head-over-heels, but the wine at the bistro, the bourbon at the blues bar, the tequila shots at the disco, the Spanish coffees at the late-night lounge all added up to a catastrophically massive hangover.

I honestly was impressed she'd had the energy and gumption to crawl out of bed and pack, let alone be able to write a note, and a legible one at that.

I thought, while necking and dry humping on the Metro's final train from Versailles: A) No way we were making our eleven o'clock check out. B) No way was I ever letting this woman out of my sight or arms. And C) Forget flying to Greece for some sun, let's stay in Paris! Yeah!

Initially, on a very cursory search, I pulled the shower curtain back, opened the armoire, checked behind the curtains and on the small fourth-floor balcony (I write,

> What room were
> we in, in Paris?
> What was the
> hotel's name and
> address?

on a yellow sticky note) and, finally, under the bed. At that juncture, I stood a little too quickly and was washed under by a tidal wave of blood rushing to my head. The room spun and spun, around and around. I had barely enough time to notice the handful of coins on the bedside table, the used condom sticking to the side of the garbage can, and someone in the hotel across the street stretching on their little fourth-floor balcony, before I ran into the bathroom and threw up.

After cramming my stomach back down my throat and jabbing my eyes back into their sockets, I took a long, hot shower.

Still, I wasn't worried. I figured she'd be downstairs—slightly annoyed, but there in the little café doubling as the hotel's reception area—hunched over the daily Le Monde and a cold espresso.

Eventually, I made it downstairs only to find the café-reception area empty.

I fumbled idly with the room key while I contemplated. I could walk out. I could walk away. I could claim, "c'est la vie." I could return home and have a great story to tell. I could proclaim her as one of those things. A woman I traveled with for a few weeks, we did this, we did that, in the north of France, in Paris. Then she left. That's what happens on a summer vacation in Europe. Friends, gathered together on my return as if for a Last Supper would all nod sagely—everyone except me. I would be both savior and traitor. I would be the one on bended knee. I would be the one holding the sword. I would create a myth she could never live up to.

I pondered the key. I looked at the empty reception desk, at the empty slots for mail with keys hanging above. I gazed at the little, white marble tables and golden chairs of the café, also empty. Outside, cars and pedestrians, mostly tourists, trudged by.

La propriétaire, in her dusty, gray-haired, gray-eyed, gray-skirted way, was cleaning something behind the bar. Eventually, before the thing was clean, she noticed me and my indecision. Reluctantly she walked over and took up guard behind the desk.

After a moment, bored with my bourgeois American-ness, she'd asked, "Oui?"

The key gradually gained a weight I was distinctly uncomfortable with.

Suddenly, I blurted out, "Si possible, je voudrais rester ici pour un nuit plus. S'il vous plaît. D'accord?" She, as well as I, had been surprised. Not only did the sentence make sense, and was, I think, grammatically correct, but my accent was impeccable.

She'd stared, only able to nod a reply, as I'd dashed upstairs to throw my backpack on the bed.

Five minutes later, after another bout with the toilet and the dislocation of my eyes and stomach, I began aimlessly wandering Paris. I was hunting a woman I'd only met two weeks before, but knew I'd known for eternity.

I retraced and traced and backtracked, and did it over again, every street, museum, antique shop, bookstore, shoe shop, jewelry store, bistro, cemetery, canal, back alley, bar, club, disco, record store, café, park, and Metro station we'd ever slipped into, thought about, or looked at. In the end, there was nothing but futility.

Like Napoleon at Waterloo, thoroughly defeated, I staggered back toward the hotel. A few blocks away I spotted some down-and-out café. I thought it appropriate, after such a defeat, to drink myself into oblivion. And once exquisitely intoxicated into oblivion, I'd be kicked out into the cold, forlorn night of my loneliness.

Tired, frustrated, angry, and ready to chew glass (again much like Napoleon at Waterloo), I stomped beneath the gilded name La Fin Du Temps and into the café. Once my eyes grew accustomed to the darkness, I flopped into a graffiti-chiseled booth and yelled, demanding the largest beer available.

After a long moment—my throbbing head flat on the cold, scarred table, my cheek and forehead learning to love the gouges—the beer, the largest available, a frothy full liter mug, was brought.

"What do I owe you?" I asked resolutely, in English.

Instead of a slip of receipt thrown flippantly at me, a voice answered, sincerely, "Votre vie."

I expected it to be expensive, but that seemed excessive.

"Fuck off," I replied, again in English.

A hot breath fell on my ear, my eyes flew open, and a voice whispered, also in English, "We have." A slight giggle followed this answer.

Slowly I raised my head, accepting the power of fate, of destiny. Francesca, dark-eyed and solemn, stood before me—as I'd expected all along, from the moment I woke, from the moments I'd traipsed back and forth, up and down, over and around and through this infernal city of light, Paris.

"Buenas noches," I said coolly, ignoring the welling tears in my eyes.

"Buenas noches," she said, cooler, also ignoring the welling tears in hers.

I stood without taking a sip of the magnificent, golden, glowing ale. Time stood still, waited. The city stopped and held its breath. The world, the universe, did the same.

She and I, we took a step forward. We tentatively touched fingers, gripped hands. Then, because this was something dictated by physics, like the sun and moon, we threw our entire weight, our beings and souls, into the arms of the other.

We began as coal, and separated, diamonds.

Nothing has ever felt that good, that satisfying. Nothing—ever.

Through the backhanding glare of tears, I paid for the beer, though it was abandoned untouched.

Silently, she led me to the hotel. If the streets were crowded, or empty, I don't know, I don't remember, I can't recall. We also attempted to climb the rickety stairs in silence, but to no avail—they groaned and complained with each step. I'd like to think we forgave them. The door to our room I unlocked and held aside. She, ignoring the shadows, the shapes outlined and lingering, stepped in—our fate sealed.

We made love passionately, desperately, perfectly, knowing this was all we could do to keep the inevitable tide of death at bay, for the moment. Inexplicably, we understood everything about time, distance, and eternity, about the tenuousness of life, of love. And this understanding, this wisdom, was translated to our fingers, our tongues, our entire bodies, and our souls.

All night, until the waning moon collapsed beyond the horizon, we twisted and entwined. Entwined and twisted. Gripped and groped. Licked and nibbled. Twisted and entwined. Wrote and deciphered the fables on our skins.

Finally, during the low tide of our bodies, she asked, "Why so long to find me?"

I couldn't help but inject a certain contemptuousness into my voice. "What do you mean 'long'? I think it was, and please excuse my French, a fucking miracle."

In the thin, milky light of the arriving dawn, I could see her forehead curl on itself, salt on escargot. I'm sure it hurt.

"You... you did not look on *the back*?"

"What do you mean *the back*? The back of what?" Clearly our lovemaking was so profound it'd knocked something loose, like her common sense.

"The back...of the note." Obviously she sensed my inaudible gasp, because she added, "Did you not look on the back of the note?"

This, I thought, must be how the pigeon feels immediately before it's introduced to the talons of the peregrine falcon.

"No," I replied, offended. Her forehead shifted, a master yogi. "Why?" I asked, realizing the snow exploding around me was my feathers.

She was silent. Silent in a way I'd never known before. And, honestly, it frightened me.

We waited in the uncomfortable grave of our silence. Outside, traffic and pedestrians moved by. Tires and engines hummed, laughter, voices, shouts. Somewhere a radio played a sad Edith Piaf tune. Finally, Francesca rose and walked naked into the bathroom.

She returned quickly and held out the note—a thin, wavering shield.

I could make out her breasts, her smooth, supple stomach, the dark patch between her legs, but I wasn't able to read a damn word.

"Honey, it's a little dark. What's your point?"

She turned and flipped the lights on. Naked before me, unconcerned in the harsh white light, she held the note, and herself, perfectly still.

...until...La Fin Du Temps.

I squinted, confused. The paper looked familiar, the handwriting also, but the words were nothing I'd seen before.

She turned the paper around, attempted to nudge some understanding, with a slight thrust of the head.

Sweetheart— If you can find me...you can have me...

Still I didn't get it. Wine, bourbon, tequila, Spanish coffees, turbulent sleep, vomiting, a day spent aimlessly wandering Paris, only to be topped off with sex so grandiose and spectacular civilizations could've been founded and destroyed on the passion—I figured I was lucky to know my name.

She turned the paper back and forth, back and forth, back and forth. Outside, from across the street, a group of drunken Australian sailors started shouting up at our illuminated hotel room. Quickly, I turned the lights out, much to the chagrin of the Australian sailors.

In the dark, suddenly, I was struck—a sledgehammer of understanding, accompanied by a pickaxe of insight. My dense skull had been breached. Light leaked in. On the back of the note was the clue to where to find her at Café La Fin Du Temps.

"Honey, I understand—now—but isn't that impossible?"

For a reply, she tore the note. I heard it, crisp bat wings slapping the air. She leaned in and kissed me. Then, with her tongue, she began pressing something moist, lumpy, into my mouth. I tried to resist. She parted, and gently pressed her fingers to my lips. The note tasted of paste and cheap ink.

Insistently she placed her mouth back on mine. Slowly I began to chew and, eventually, swallow.

Once finished with our curious snack, she slipped beneath the covers and snuggled into bed, where we slept for a long, long, long time.

I yawn. Zeus, frighteningly, mimics me. We are quickly losing the afternoon.

Okay, but this sure as shit ain't Paris. And I truly believe this isn't a test. One leaves clues behind, doesn't one? One accidentally drops the gun, the knife, the rope, the syringe. Forgets, in the chaos of the crime, to wipe the fingerprints off the wine glass, wash the lipstick off the shirt, pick the bra up off the bed. One doesn't leave a short note with a vague and obscure reference from some two-bit Japanese writer about *"like smoke."* I mean, come on. You leave clues. You...My skin goes cold. My heart stops. Could she have put something on the back of the note? Something like before? Something like Paris?

Oh, my God! Oh, my God! Oh, my God! Oh, my God! Oh, my God! Oh, m

Where's the note? Where's the note?!

I stop, and Zeus, who has been following my frantic search, slides into the back of my legs.

"Zeus?" He looks up at me, quizzically. "Where's the note?" His head does the all too tried-and-true head-cock to one side. I'm beginning to truly hate that look from him. Surely he can affect some other gesture, can't he? Can't he? Sure he's only a dog, but come on! Shit!

"Where's the note, Zeus? Where's...the..note?" Same, same, same. Dumb-dog stare. Concentrate. **Concentrate!** "You didn't eat it, did you?" Nothing. He's giving me nothing. Shit!

Out of frustration, I return to the refrigerator for a beer. Looking into the cold, bright light, I pull the last Pilsner out. Promptly, I open it and drink half.

Then insight hit me like crows against a cloudy sky. The note I took into my den, our library, and read and reread as

I searched the Internet. Then, frustrated from lack of under-standing and insight, I'd placed it in a sleeve of my briefcase. That was Wednesday, therefore.... My briefcase I...I...I had had with me in Francesca's Eurovan. I had had it with me and Zeus at It's A Beautiful Pizza. Hippie Boy had said, "Your dog has the eyes of a monk." Zeus had had a slice of cheese, while I had had a combo underneath a tin awning. Then? Then a taxi ride. Then? Then...nothing. I left my fucking briefcase in the god-damn taxi. I left my briefcase with the note, the note that's liable to have the clue to finding Francesca and Mirabella and Tyler, in the goddamn taxi! Fuck!

My heartbeat and breathing are sporadic. I don't know the taxi company. There's no way I can remember the driver, the car, anything. The note, my last and only chance, to find my love and my child, is gone. Gone. Gone. Gone. My eyesight blurs. Things begin to slowly spin.

Unsteadily I collapse on the couch. I can't breathe. My heart shudders. Zeus, worried, comes over and licks my face. She left a hint on the back of the note, and I? I've lost it, thrown it away, like our love, like my life, like everything. "Zeus, stop, please. Zeus, go lie down. Go on." Reluctantly, he goes to the far end of the couch, hops up, and settles in.

Eventually, my breathing and heartbeat return to a semi-normal state. Thankfully my mind isn't too far behind my body, and I realize the number should be in the call list of my cell phone. Before calling it, however, I listen two or twenty times to Francesca's message. "George, where are you? Mirabella and I have taken the groceries home. For some reason we're returning. Call me. Soon."

Her voice, an elixir, intoxicates me with hope and joy. I drink. And drink. And drink.

And, yes, eventually, I make the call.

"Don't know who yer talkin' 'bout," states the taxicab company man.

I describe the driver in much more definitive terms.

"Like I said, don't know who yer talkin' 'bout." It sounds like he takes a drink of something, like beer from a can.

"Do you think you could ask someone else there?"

"Only me here." In the background, from a radio, there's the guttural clawing of hard rock 'n' roll.

"Well, did anyone turn in a briefcase? It's black."

"Wow. Black. What else?" He slurps his beer.

I describe the briefcase down to the chewed corner from Zeus, the scratches from Tyler, and the general hinted scent of peanut butter from one of Mirabella's sandwiches unknowingly left a little too long in one of the sleeves.

"Can't say it sounds familiar." This guy is starting to piss me off.

"Can I come down there? Check around? Ask someone... some things... or something?"

"Office is closed. Opens up on Monday."

"Can I come down there Monday then?"

"Fine by me. Free country and all, you know?" Okay, he's an asshole.

"Can I ask your name?"

"Sure." He sips his stupid low-carb, low-cal beer.

"What's your name?"

"Steve."

"Steve?"

"Yeah?"

"Thanks for nothing." I hang up before he replies, before he says, "You're welcome," in his flat, fucking, stupid voice. Asshole.

Could I call for a taxi, and, if it's not the driver I'm looking for simply wave him on? Keep doing so until eventually the right one shows up? How many drivers could they have? What about days off? What about him having a twin? Could I get hypnotized and recall something pertinent, like his name off his taxi license? Maybe I could...I could....

Suddenly it hits me like a bird into a plate glass window: I'm done.

I'm done thinking, done pondering, done speculating the possibilities, done contemplating how to get the note, done worrying about finding the woman who left me. Done. Done. Done. Done attempting to change things I can't alter or affect. I'm just done, with most everything. Done and tired. Tired. Tired. Tired.

Cherishing this small but forlorn nugget of insight, I finish the beer. Done and tired. Tired and done.

I decide the time to take a nap is wasting. Wasting quickly, all too quickly.

Before I settle on the couch, I check the locks on all the doors and pull all the blinds and drapes shut. Zeus, while I hold his leash (he's not getting away from me), settles down on the floor in front of the couch. He's not particularly happy with this arrangement.

Nor is he content. And based on his forlorn look you'd think I was preparing him for the Spanish Inquisition. However, that's the way it's going to be. "Sorry, big boy." He just stares at me.

It takes a few minutes before I'm completely comfortable beneath the blanket. But once there, it's the most satisfying thing to close my eyes and fall into the dark, forgetting folds of sleep.

∞

When I wake, I find Zeus has snuck up on the couch and taken up residence with me. Through the blanket I can feel his heartbeat with my feet. I lie like this for a long time, listening to the world, which is very quiet, and feeling Zeus's heartbeat with my foot.

After a while I get up, use the bathroom, and fix Zeus his dinner. He trots in and eats while I stick something in the microwave and wait.

Looking at the clock, I find I have at least five, if not six, hours before I'll feel like going to sleep again for the night. I look around the kitchen, but there's nothing to do here for that long. It's too late to mow the lawn. I could go upstairs and work on the renter's pamphlet, or the shareholders' brochure. But why? Most of the shareholders I've met are bags of self-important assholes. And renters? God love them, but there are millions and millions of them.

I could finish painting the utility room in the basement. I've put it off for two months and another day, or thirty, won't matter.

"Okay." I make an executive decision, "The usual then? Eh, Zeusy? How's the park sound?" Zeus appears to agree. We leave immediately after I brush my teeth and confirm I've no oddities attached to my face.

With our first few steps down the sidewalk, I feel a strange sense of otherworldliness. As if the world isn't as it should be. Or, maybe it's me, distinctly in the wrong place, the wrong time.

Whatever it may be, there's something specifically wrong, though I can't put my mind on it. I realize this has been the case since I awoke on the couch. Colors aren't quite right—on anything. Sounds are slightly skewed. Birds sound like dogs. Dogs like birds. Even the aroma of cut grass from James's lawnmower, which sounds like a television, is misaligned and smells distinctly like coffee. I notice an airplane flying backward across a sky that moves like the surface of the sea. Zeus tugs on his leash, anxious to get to the park. My arm stretches and stretches down the block.

"Zeus," I ask, "where are you going in such a hurry?" My arm stretches and stretches.

He turns, and even though he's a little dot in the distance, I can hear him when he answers, "To *The House at Pooh Corner* where Francesca and Mirabella and Tyler sip tea and eat honey cakes."

Why didn't I think of it? Of course that's where they'd be! They'd be discussing butterflies and sunsets over tea and honey cakes. They'd be watching sticks float under the bridge. They'd be waiting for me!

I begin running after Zeus. I get perhaps a block farther when a shadow falls across me. A giant me looms over me. He's twenty, thirty, forty, a hundred feet tall. I shudder to a stop as another me, and another, and another come into view. Then I realize...the world is covered with hundreds, thousands, millions of hundred-foot-tall me's. Each wields a huge axe. And they all want to eat me. But there is only one real me to be devoured; a bloody, severed-limb-fight erupts among the giants. Limbs and internal organs and blood rain down. Houses, the entire city—and probably the world—are falling beneath the blood and bodies. For hours, days, and years, the battle rages on. Eventually there is a winner. Deep wounds cover his body; it looks as if he won't live long either. However, he has the strength to pick me up in his giant, blood-smeared hand and eat me, whole.

I tumble down the dark hole of his throat to the darker well of his stomach. His stomach is pitch black, cold, and empty. My hands grope, searching for a way out. Instead they discover what feels like...an axe. And as I begin to chop blindly on the walls of his stomach, I begin to recognize myself thinking, "This is a dream, this is a dream." However, not until I've hacked my way out of his belly, to the blue light from the watery sky streaming down on me, do I wake.

∞

I wake again, this time with a distinct sense of fear, and linger beneath the cover of the blanket, attempting to discern if this is the real world or not. I attempt to discern and decide what exactly that might even mean—the real world. This one seems approximately the same as the one I just left, which makes me all the more fearful. Everything is as it was before: Zeus is on the couch, James's lawnmower whirrs, birds sing—everything is the same. There is, thankfully, no lingering sense of not-quite-rightness.

Again I feel Zeus's heartbeat through the blanket, and I think about doing something differently than I had in my dream, but I can't think of a reason to do anything differently. My choices made sense then, they still do now.

So I get up and use the bathroom and fix Zeus's dinner. My dinner, made in the microwave, is a leftover piece of lasagna Francesca made two weeks ago. It tastes like boiled chicken, or freezer-burned salmon, but not lasagna.

I brush my teeth slowly, purposefully, hoping to dislodge answers and truth, but only minute, red flecks of tomato speckle the mint slime being swallowed by the drain. Disappointed, I look up and find myself in the mirror, staring, bewildered, at myself in the flesh.

Zeus, sitting behind me, checks my reflection, too. I don't notice anything, though that doesn't mean there isn't something there. After a moment, I agree, "Okay, Zeus, let's go to the park."

∞

Among the clutter of other dogs and owners are June and Tuesday. Zeus and I walk over.

"Hey, Zeusy, how are you?" June asks as she rubs his noggin.

Zeus looks at June, looks at me, looks at June, and then notices an ant ascending a blade of grass. He sniffs and then dutifully eats the ant.

"He's perplexed," I reply as interpreter.

"Oh, is he?"

"Yes, indeed. Indeed he is."

We watch the other dogs play and romp. We watch the other owners, chatting in little groups of three and four. Tuesday rushes over. She and Zeus do a quick nose, tail, sniff, wag, lick, bark, fake charge, bark. Then Tuesday takes off, expecting Zeus to chase her. However, I keep him on a short, firm lead. He looks up, disappointed.

June asks, "Is that why? He can't play."

"You mean, him being perplexed?"

She nods. Her sad Icelandic eyes reaffirm it's sad Zeus can't play with the other dogs. I agree, but.... But I can't tell her my wife and child and cat and red Eurovan and briefcase and a large portion of my sanity have left me, can I? Can I tell her Zeus is the only thing keeping me above water? Sure, June and I have had some good conversations about Yetis, vampires, the Bermuda Triangle, UFOs, Atlantis, and the like. However, I don't think that makes us intimate, friends able to share every little tidbit of our personal lives. Hell, I don't even do that with Charles, a graphic designer in the production department, whom I've known for nearly five years. Occasionally we'll go out for lunch or a drink after work. He's told me some things, like having a fantasy about seducing my secretary and doing it on my desk. But that's only been divulged after a beer and on a Friday night, with the weekend as a buffer for everything to grow hazy, hopefully, if not forgotten.

June, on the other hand...I don't even know her last name, where she's from, or anything about her private life. I do know she believes in ESP, government (both local and global) conspiracies, graylings—

What exactly are graylings?

—and every other strange and crazy entity and theory. I know she's a bartender at The Crow Bar up on North Mississippi Avenue. I know not to ask about her love life. Made that mistake only once. She had commented curtly, as we stood in the inadequate protection of a tree in late January, "I believe that subject should be permanently off-limits." The way it sounded, she included all of humankind, for all of time, and not simply the two of us.

I had agreed, then asked (after a few minutes mourning), "What do you know about the Chupacabra?"

"The Flying Goat Sucker?" she'd asked with enthusiasm.

I had nodded, made nervous at how the blue of her eyes crystallized with a strange clarity.

She'd explained more, much more, than I ever wanted to know about the flying, hairy lizard that roams from Puerto Rico to the American Southwest preying on farm animals and occasionally, so some claim, small children.

We've established a relationship based on crazy, twisted surface topics—nothing more. We're not going to, like the others, become a surrogate support group, lamenting our lives to familiar strangers so everyone has an interesting story to tell at a cocktail party. Not June, not I—we're smarter than that.

Tuesday returns after a short run. She barks and jumps happily around us, trying to get Zeus to play. Zeus and June stare at me.

"Zeus?" He looks up expectantly, and dutifully sits before I say, "sit." While kneeling next to him I whisper in his ear so only he can hear, "Don't do anything stupid. If you see Francesca, or Mirabella, or even Tyler, come and get me." June has told many a tale about spirits enticing the living into Other Worlds. Maybe Zeus can discover what door they've entered? Then, hopefully, he can return and tell me its location.

My thumb plays nervously with the clasp of the leash. The metal tapping sounds like Morse code.

Unfortunately, I've no talisman to give Zeus, only my whispered warning words. "Be careful. Be vigilant. Be brave." He barks in excitement and agreement. "You know where to find me, right?" He barks again. I'm sure he knows exactly what I'm saying.

My thumb begins to ache.

"If you keep that up," June says laughingly, "the poltergeists will find us."

Standing, I reply, perhaps a little too sincerely, "Who says they haven't already?"

June doesn't answer, though she glances around, sizing up the other dog park patrons.

Zeus isn't going to be able to protect me from myself, or my future. That, I finally realize, is something I'm going to have to do alone—regardless of how ill-prepared I am for the task. Therefore, I can do nothing else but let him go. If he returns, that's his choice.

"Bon voyage," I whisper as he bolts off after Tuesday.

The last piece of my life floats off like a piece of confetti.

As I watch, June says, "We all need to be free."

Need is a funny word, one I think most people use too cavalierly. Need was a word my wannabe hippie parents—privileged suburbanites more concerned with "life's mysteries and iniquities" rather than work—felt should only be used for absolute extremes. A drowning man would *need* a life preserver. Someone lost in the woods would *need* a map, a compass. Suffice it to say I was brought up with a specific predilection for Spartan frugality. A frugality I've learned to ignore.

I didn't need an adequate career, a big house, a too-comfortable couch the perfect distance from the fireplace, or racks of wine. Not even a nice and clunky collector car. But that's probably easy to say for someone who has never really wanted for anything—one of the few benefits of being an only child.

What I need (or is that want?) is someone to love me, regardless of my faults, for who I was, for who I am. Someone who makes me feel able to occasionally conquer and rule the world, or at least a good portion of the backyard and the living room. Someone who makes me want to make them feel the same way. And that person was Francesca. And part of my world, her world, our world, was Mirabella, was Tyler, was Zeus...was the precarious entity we had created together, a family.

Sadly, too late, I realize I need to have, and be, a family.

Intently watching Zeus and Tuesday race around, June says, "There is a plant in the Brazilian rainforest called sangue pequeno, little blood. Have you heard of this plant?"

I shake my head, noticing for the first time she has a slight accent, though I don't know if it sounds Icelandic. Zeus chases Tuesday around a mastiff and its owner, and then sprints for the baseball diamond.

June continues, "The plant is a tuber. Like a carrot, it grows with a little tuft of dull green to recognize it from above." Tuesday curls around second base and shoots back toward the mastiff and us. "One tribe says if you can find it—it's very rare—and eat it with your love under a full moon you will forever—and they mean Forever with a capital F—be tied soul to soul." Zeus, however, continues straight past the base.... "Another tribe thinks if you do so, you and your love shall forever be lost to one another. I think the image they use is 'same stream, different banks, opposite direction.'"

Zeus speeds past the dugouts, the stands, the little hill with its scrubby trees overlooking the baseball diamond.

"You realize," I say, "this sangue pequeno is probably a radish?"

Tuesday returns, panting heavily, to June's side. Zeus finally disappears into the shadows of the scrubby trees.

June ruffles Tuesday's head, and says, "Yes," just like the captain of the Titanic to a passenger who's asked if the far object on the horizon is an iceberg.

June mumbles something about having to go to work, and she and Tuesday hastily exit.

∞

Once darkness completely swallows the park, I walk home, alone. It takes longer than ever before; perhaps because I'm not being pulled in the right direction I make three wrong turns.

Eventually, I stand in front of my, our, the house. The stars, staring down on me as I stare into the house, are unsatisfied. I am too. After a long while we realize that's the way things are going to have to remain, and I slowly enter without enthusiasm.

∞

The wood burning in the fireplace crackles like the laughter of the insane. The blood-red wine tastes perfect. I do nothing more than watch the fire, drink wine. I watch and drink, until the fire grows dark and cold, the bottle empty.

Sparks, Flames, and Fire

This is the week the shit hits the fan, over and over and over. Day after day I wake, look in the mirror as I shave—very careful to get both sides—and say, "Good morning, Fan. Who is going to be throwing shit at you today?"

I pull the razor across my skin, peeling back the white cream to expose clean, pink flesh. Unsure (considering my luck lately) how there isn't a cut, a slice, a gaping wound. I make my guesses. Invariably I'm wrong. And typically it's more than I thought possible—the shit being thrown, that is.

I don't remember the week as a day-by-day progression. I remember it by subjects, titles, headings. The progression, the evolution of a subject from savory cuisine, to masticated pulp, to stomach sludge, to intestinal gruel, and, finally, shit. The shit is then gathered by an anonymous entity and flung headlong, with measurable force and intent, against the fan—my life. It clings to the fan and dries there. Eventually some sloughs off into the motor. After a while there is a spark. And another, and another, until a brief ball of flame catches and sets the entire mechanism on fire. It burns and smolders. Acrid smoke billows into the air. Flames leap and jump to the ceiling. Eventually what had been an appliance providing a modicum of comfort has been reduced to a pile of smoldering slag. It's something that wouldn't get a dollar at a garage sale. It is, as most things become, now worthless.

Q:

Buenos Dias, Fan.

¿Quién es el que va a estar

tirando mierda a–ti?

A:

Margarita.

Each time I visit Margarita, even if I bring flowers or Toblerone chocolate (her favorite), she glares and says nothing—gives me the silent stink-eye treatment. Now I know where Francesca got it from, and from where, unfortunately, Mirabella has too.

Mirabella had made a slight attempt about a week before she and her mother... left? Disappeared? What is it they've done? I don't know. But I do know Mirabella tried the silent stink-eye on me at Hollywood Video. I had told her, in no uncertain terms, she wasn't going to get that movie (*Fifty First Dates*), and to put it back where she found it. She'd gotten the cutest little pout and glare. For a second or two she'd stared at me, then spun around and stomped off down the aisle. It'd taken a moment to realize what she'd attempted but once I realized it, I had to laugh—then immediately stopped when the ramifications hit me. The last thing I needed was Mirabella pulling the silent treatment, venturing to be exactly like her mother.

Anyway, the first time I visit Margarita in her hospital room I'm sullen, tired, and full of genuine remorse. The flowers and Toblerone, bribes for amnesty, rest neglected in Margarita's lap. I'm in a chair near the window overlooking the city, mumbling inadequacies about how sorry I am.

"Honestly, Margarita, I didn't see you. It was an accident."
Magisterially, with her good arm, she sweeps the flowers and

chocolate to the floor. She shuts her eyes from the pain—I assume from the effort of moving and not my presence. My assumption though may be a misplaced hope; it's good to know I have a little left.

I attempt a different tack; "The sun was in my eyes. And I got a call on my cell phone." She says nothing. Her eyes remain clenched. She is a wrinkled, brown Buddha of suffering. A wrinkled, brown Buddha that would like to rip my eyeballs out and gleefully dance on my corpse. So, maybe she's Shiva, or Vishnu, or...whomever she is, she'd like to see me dead.

For the next ten minutes we stew in a cauldron of silence.

Before we boil over, I pick up the flowers and Toblerone, place them in her lap, and say as sincerely as possible, "I'm sorry, Margarita. Honestly."

As I'm leaving, gripping the door's cold metal handle, I hear her whisper something, one word. A question I have no answer for. "Francesca?"

"No sé," I inadequately reply. Her eyes open, slowly. "Honestly, Margarita, I don't know where Francesca and Mirabella are."

A fire smolders behind the pale brown walls of her irises. "Francesca?" Her voice, flint and stone, becomes clearer, more forceful. "Francesca?" I turn away.

Looking out the door's slit of a window at a defibrillator cart, I slowly tell her, "I don't know where she is, Margarita. She left." The flowers, an eight dollar and ninety-nine cent bunch of stale daisies from the hospital's florist, smack me in the back of the head. Apparently her pain has subsided, or is an acceptable price for the effort. Petals cascade around me. I explain, "Margarita, please, it was a mistake," and turn around, just in time to catch the Toblerone with my forehead.

We stare at one another and understand everything, particularly every inadequacy of mine. Thank you, Margarita. Thank you very fucking much.

After this it's silence, pure and simple and accepted. After all these years, our relationship has finally been adequately defined; it has taken a turn, distinctly not for the better, but for the simpler. God bless efficiency.

On my next visit, I present Margarita with a small stuffed polar bear. Around the bear's neck is an ID tag in the shape of a red-heart proclaiming *Paul* in Monotype Corsiva script.

"They are going to love this," said the elderly woman behind the cash register as she handed me my receipt.

I stuffed the bear and the receipt into my jacket pocket and replied, "I'll accept forgiveness," then head toward the elevators.

Behind me, a cool wind, the elderly woman said, "We all will, dear. We all will."

I present Margarita with the small, stuffed polar bear.

She accepts him begrudgingly. Immediately she places *Paul* in the pitcher of water on her bedside table and extends a crooked knuckled middle finger.

I trudge to the window chair. The next two hours are a condemned man's seconds as we stare and *Paul* gradually sinks.

I don't think I'll be going back anytime soon.

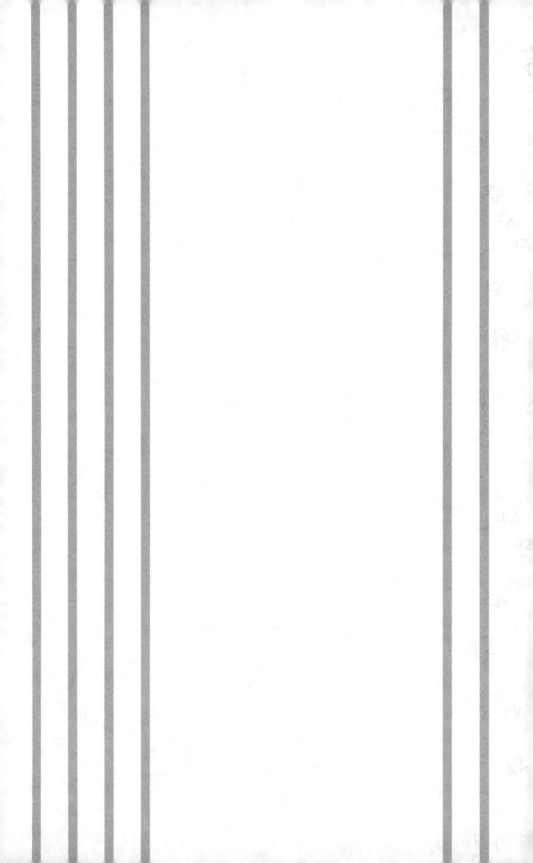

Q:

Yo, what's up, Fan? Who
be throwing shit today?

A:

The Broadway Cab
Company (specifically
Steve).

The taxi company's office, and lost and found, is in a decrepit brick building in the industrial section of the city. The freeway traffic hums along on an overhead bridge, loud and even. After a while I don't even hear it.

The man behind the screen, one of the dispatchers, says, through his rough, unshaven face and past his abused cigar stub, "Check over there. The drivers throw things in there they don't want." His arm points to a large wooden box that once probably housed an engine block. Stenciled across it are a miscellany of numerals and foreign scripts.

I take a few steps toward the box. He adds to my back, "Was there any reward?"

Over my shoulder and the traffic's hum I tell him, "I don't know. I hadn't thought about it. Why?"

"Sometimes," he says, as the cigar slides seemingly out of control around his glistening lips, "it helps."

I turn around, and attempt to gauge if he actually knows something, or if this is just a standard line. I can't tell, so I say, "Well, yeah, I suppose so. It's...it's kind of important I find it. So, yeah, definitely—a reward."

He grunts something in response and asks, "How long's it been missing?"

"Four, maybe five days."

He goes back to the magazine he's reading, *Penthouse,*

Hustler, *Playboy*, something like that, shaking his head, laughing. "Yeah, good luck." He doesn't even ask what the reward is. Somehow I think that doesn't bode well.

There's no way I'm getting the briefcase or the note back. No way. And if the note has something on the back, well, basically, I'm screwed. And Francesca and Mirabella are lost.

"Excuse me?"

"Yeah?" He looks up, bored and apathetic, from the tits and ass on the page.

"Your name Steve?"

"Yeah." He turns the page without looking.

"Thought so."

"Why?" Again he turns the page. It's the same thing—new tits, new ass.

"The driver I mentioned? Well, he said something. Something about.... No, no, forget it." I raise my hand and wave everything off like a signal to the runner at second to wait for a line drive into the gap, or, better, a home run. I figure if I can't get my briefcase, the note, the woman and child I love, the dog I cherish, and the cat I tolerate, I can at least get even. Particularly with someone innocent. "Sorry, forget it, it's nothing." My hand sign quickly changes as I ask, "It's okay if I search through the box?"

Steve squints at me and my flailing hands, curious, suspicious of me. The tits and ass on the page stare at the underside of his flat, unshaved chin and his hairy nostrils.

"It's really none of my business. I just stopped by looking for my briefcase, you know?" Above us the traffic hums and whizzes along.

"What'd he say?" Steve closes the magazine—the tits and ass heave a sigh of relief.

By this time I'm at the wood box—it's larger and deeper than expected—and I'm practically screaming so Steve can hear me. "Hey, like I said, none of my business!" I turn and begin searching, digging through the dark, dank shapes cluttering the box.

"That coffee-and-cream motherfucker mentioned my girlfriend, didn't he?"

I don't say anything. I struggle, searching for my briefcase. Rummaging through the sweaters, hats, glasses, empty purses, books, folders, dolls, and other shit, I don't hear Steve until he's at my side. He grips my elbow and forcefully pulls me away from my search.

"Hey, I asked you a question." Steve's breath is a toxic slurry of dank cigar smoke, beef jerky, and halitosis.

Steve, and his supervillain breath, tire me. His bloodshot eyes, the thin scar over his left eye, the flakes of tobacco sticking to his yellow teeth and glistening lips drain my intention. I no longer have the strength for the farce of some rationalized revenge. I'm prepared to accept the Minotaur's horn.

"Look, I'm sorry. I was hoping to get you pissed off. I hoped you'd tell me the driver's name. Maybe you'd call him in and I'd be able to talk to him. Search his cab. Honestly, he didn't say anything about your girlfriend." Steve looks at me hard, searching for the truth in my face. "Honestly."

I don't know what he finds, but he says, "Bullshit."

"Steve, I'm going to go. If you talk to the driver, tell him I'm offering a reward." I start walking backward. Before I can turn around and make a proper, less wary retreat, Steve starts walking toward me. I continue backing up slowly.

Steve launches the dead cigar into the lost-and-found bin. "You know what I think?" I shake my head dejectedly. "I think *you're* the motherfucker that's been seeing my girl behind my back."

"Steve," I continue, shaking my head, "that's ridiculous."

"Yeah, yeah, that's right. Come down here to see what the competition is like. Right?" He gives a hard, two-handed shove to my chest—some misguided precardial thump. "I knew it had to be some clean-shaved puke in a fucking suit and tie. Some puny-ass, no-good prick."

Before I can comment on his accuracy he shoves me again. It doesn't bother me as much as I think it should. It somehow feels deserved. Deserved and due.

"Steve, honest, I don't know who your girlfriend is. Besides, I'm sure we don't have the same taste in women." I hope my tone implies his "taste" is more highly evolved than mine. Where Steve is Penelope Cruz, I'm Pippi Longstocking. Unfortunately, I don't think that's the case.

I ball my right hand into an approximation of a fist. I haven't been in a fight since the sixth grade, during lunch in the cafeteria. It was literally over spilled milk. Brandon McGovern had thrown an apple core at Pete Peterson. The core collided with my milk carton and I, as young boys will, took offense. Perhaps because I'd been embarrassed (or felt I had) in front of Jenny Thurston. I had a crush on Jenny. And, as young kids will rationalize, it was now requisite that I go to Brandon and punch him. He, as young kids will rationalize, had to punch me back. Quickly the situation escalated—a fight, my one and only, ensued.

Brandon and I spent two weeks in detention together and became best friends. Somehow, for a change, it seemed the school administration knew what they were doing.

However, this isn't a grade school cafeteria, nor is the cabbie-dispatching-junkyard-dog Steve, Brandon McGovern. Steve is, plain and simple, an asshole.

Steve's continuing with his diatribe, while I slowly back away.

"Just some tight-lipped, scrawny motherfucker who thinks he's better than everyone else." He shoves me again. It begins to feel less and less deserved.

"Steve, listen, okay?"

Steve sarcastically holds his knobby hand to his cauliflower ear and feigns listening to my pleas.

"I got a fucking news flash for you, Shakespeare. You're going to be—"

I throw my fist blindly at his face. Unexpectedly, I hit him full force, in the nose and cheek. A bright explosion of pain erupts in my hand as Steve collapses to the oily concrete floor.

I run before Steve can get up and kick my ass. I run out the door, around the corner to my Mustang, which miraculously starts up immediately. Thank you Mr. McQueen, thank you. The tires squeal beautifully in a cappella as I accelerate my escape.

I see Steve is screaming, swearing, and bleeding, in the rearview mirror as I drive hurriedly into the night.

By the time I'm home, my right hand is swollen. I can't even grip the steering wheel. I think I may have broken a finger or two, or perhaps dislodged a knuckle or something. No matter the diagnosis, my hand looks like one of those big green Incredible Hulk novelty fists the kids have around these days. It's really rather funny, except for the pain. I take four or five Excedrin, put a bag of ice on my swollen hand, and manhandle a bottle of wine open. It's done so poorly the first glass is filled with cork. I then struggle to put a fire together.

Once the flames take hold, I sit and think about what to do next. Nothing comes to mind, so I watch the fire and drink. The ice melts and becomes lukewarm water. The combination of the pills, wine, and flames make me feel the same way, lukewarm. Eventually I transcend to steam and fall into a deep, undisturbed, and completely unmemorable sleep.

∞

At work the next day, I'm poring over the papers cluttering my desk when the phone rings. I can tell by the tone of the ring it's a direct call. "Hello?"

"Is this the motherfucker who coldcocked me last night?"

"S-S-S-Steve?" I stutter out, incredulous.

"Ye-ye-yeah, y-y-you dick!" he replies. The fucking smart-ass. "Thought you could hide, eh?" I hang up. How the hell did he get my work number? How the hell did he get my number? How? My phone begins to ring, over and over. Finally my voice mail answers. After a moment the phone begins to ring again and again. I go around the desk, follow the gray cord to the wall socket, and unplug the phone. Looking back at the phone on my desk, I wonder why I didn't simply unplug it there. Honestly, I don't know.

A few hours later I plug the phone back in. There are twenty-six messages. Twenty are from Steve. I erase what are sure to be very angry, very vindictive messages every time Steve's number pops up on the display.

One morning there are literally two hundred messages from him. The next day one hundred and seventy. The next afternoon one hundred and thirty-four. It seems he has an obsessive-compulsive behavior pattern and me on his speed dial. I'm really rather impressed and, if the circumstances were different, I'd call and compliment him. As it is I don't, though I do harbor a dark desire for sweet, sweet revenge.

I ask Anne to see if she can arrange a different phone number for me. I don't explain why. She informs me a few hours later the new number should be in effect sometime at the beginning of next week.

I thank her and wonder if the beginning of next week will be soon enough.

Q:

Good morning, Sir Fan. Who, pray tell, will be hurling excrement at you this day?

A:

Mrs. Sandquist, LMFT.

Finally, I receive a return call from Francesca's therapist, Mrs. Sandquist—during lunch. Charles from production, Anne, and I are going over the specs for the shareholders' brochure at Murata when she chooses to call...thus having to leave a message.

"Ah, Mr. Olson," she begins in her thick, cake-frosting English accent. "So, glad to hear from you. Unfortunately, though, due to client-therapist confidentiality, I can disclose none of Francesca's treatment, or issues. You of course understand, don't you? So glad. Should there be anything else I can assist with, please don't hesitate to contact me."

I call her back immediately. It's maybe fifteen minutes after she'd left her message. She doesn't answer. I leave a message, "Mrs. Sandquist, this is George Olson. As I said before, I'm not interested in Francesca's treatment, or her theoretical emotional problems. I *am* interested in knowing if there were any issues which might affect her and my daughter's safety. If you could perhaps find the time to get back to me in regards to these issues," (I said it like her...*iss-yous*), "I'd be forever in your debt. Thank you." I add my cell number, my work number, and my home phone number, including the hours I can be reached at each.

Mrs. Sandquist calls the next day, again during the lunch break. "Mr. Olson, your wife and I discussed no issues which, I should think, in my professional opinion, directly affect her or your daughter's safety." Brief and succinct. I'm tempted to call her back and thank her, then decide it would be superfluous.

Instead, a day later, I call in regards to her capacity to know exactly what may, or may not, pertain to issues regarding my wife and daughter's safety.

"Mrs. Sandquist, please don't misconstrue my intent. I do believe you to be a very competent therapist. However, if you don't mind, I'd like to be the judge of what might or might not be issues regarding my family's well-being and safety. Therefore, I'd like to request a meeting with you to actually discuss these matters in person. Please return my call at your earliest convenience. Thank you. Good-bye."

Strategically, she calls while I'm out. I'm beginning to think that not only is she a marriage and family therapist, but either lucky or psychic as well. Either way, it's starting to annoy me.

"Mr. Olson, again I must reiterate,"

(Re) iterate, what is to "iterate"?

"I cannot discuss your wife's treatment with you. I hold my clients' confidence in me as sacred. Any violation of that promise would undermine their trust in me and make my position as a therapist tenuous. I'm terribly sorry, but I cannot see or speak to you about this matter. Good-bye."

I convince Anne to make an appointment with Mrs. Sandquist.

"Why?" Anne asks.

I, staring out the window onto a city caught in a perfect spring day many floors below, reply, "Because I'm crazy and alone," in such a joking and convivial manner that Anne complies. Surprisingly enough, so does Mrs. Sandquist, LMFT. But that's probably because Anne, after firm insistence from me, doesn't use my real name.

"Because?" Anne immediately asks after hanging up.

"I need to keep a certain amount of anonymity. Alter ego and all that."

"Sure. Whatever." Anne returns to typing while I continue staring out the window—each somehow disappointed.

∞

A block from the shopping quarter of NW 23rd Avenue stands a squat green house with tired yellow shutters, done in an antiquated English country-manor style. Once a single-family residence, it has now, many decades later, been transformed into offices (three) for therapists.

Whoever the architect was, he was a beginner. Whoever the builder, he was even more of an amateur. There isn't a straight line, a ninety-degree corner, or a smooth surface in the entire house. I find this a fitting place for therapy.

Dutifully I fill out my paperwork and wait in the lobby, the former living room. In the background, to block the voices from the sessions above, is a radio, tuned to a classical station. Presently it seems to be, based on the frenetic drums and the sorrowful wind instruments, something by a Russian composer. Outside a spring rain pounds—something I'm not prepared for, having left my umbrella at home, having left this morning in perfect sunshine.

Eventually, I hear voices at the top of the stairs, convivial, but forced and false. A young couple, afraid of each other, their circumstances, and the future, walks single file down the narrow stairs. The dark-haired husband is in front, his head down, averting his eyes from mine. The wife, a blonde thing with roving blue eyes, follows. Behind them is a woman dressed in flowing browns and blacks and black-rimmed glasses. I assume their therapist. I assume Mrs. Sandquist.

The woman follows them to the front door and gives them a smattering of good lucks and goodbyes. Over her shoulder I notice that neither the young man nor the young woman turns to return the wave, or reply, or agree. She sighs. She gives herself a slight moment to transition, and then turns to me as if it were morning, the start of a brand new day.

"Hello. You must be Mr. Nielson?"

"Yes. Thomas Nielson," I reply, attempting to change my voice slightly in case she recognizes it from the messages I've left her. Thomas, middle name; Nielson, mother's maiden name. Anne had grudgingly agreed when I asked her to use it. I'm sure she's writing all this down. Someday there's sure to be a heavy blackmail tab to pay.

Mrs. Sandquist and I shake hands. I hand her my completed paperwork. She gives it a cursory look. "This way, Mr. Nielson," and she begins climbing the stairs. Resigned, as if to the gallows, I follow her to her office.

The room is simply a large bedroom, which has been outfitted as an office. In one corner is a small desk cluttered with paper. There's a couch, though more correctly it's probably a settee, as it's rather small. On a sticky note I write,

124

> What is the difference between couch and settee? Perhaps divan?

There are also two low-slung chairs with a small, barren coffee table between them.

"So, what brings you in today, Mr. Nielson?" she asks, taking a seat in one of the chairs. Obviously I take the couch—or the divan, as the case may be.

"Family crisis," I say matter-of-factly, looking around at the still life prints covering the walls.

"Would you care to elaborate?"

I don't want to, but the prints of oranges and apples, the hanging pheasant, duck, and the fish, seem to require something to be said. And it might as well be the truth. "My wife has left me. Taking our daughter with her." Having kept everything bottled up, it's oddly liberating to confess this, regardless of how I may be implicated in the matter. Something deep inside me shudders, then breaks free. It's as if a large piece of my soul has broken away from the rest of me. I picture a chunk of ice falling away from a glacier and into the cold blue sea.

"I'm terribly sorry to hear that. It was unexpected?"

I nod my head. Suddenly I can't talk. The spray, the waves, from the collapsed piece of ice are rushing up inside me. Freezing my will to speak, to move, to breath.

"How long has it been?" Mrs. Sandquist's quizzical look is tainted with a touch of recognition. "Since you've heard from them?"

My heart begins to freeze. A blue, icy sheen begins to envelop it. I can't breathe. The enormity of my loss, of my ineptitude as a husband, as a father, falls upon me. I can't breathe. They didn't leave me, I lost them. I can't breathe. My lungs begin to shrink and freeze from the cold. I can't breathe.

"Mr. Nielson?" There's a moment when the fallen piece of ice seems as if it might stay afloat, perhaps make the shore, or float out to sea. For some reason, no one, distinctly not I, felt this was possible, even *hopeful* it would happen...a chunk of blue-white ice floating slowly, either to the shore, or out to sea. However, inexplicably, perhaps from the rocks and boulders that have become enmeshed in its icy self on the long journey down the hillside to the sea, it does not float. It simply sinks. Sinks swiftly through the cold, dark water, to the colder, darker bottom of the sea, lost forever.

Once the ice settles reluctantly on the bottom of the sea, it begins to gradually dissolve. Begins to melt, fresh tears in a tired, cold, and salty sea.

The tears slowly surface. I wipe them away. Try to take control. So what if I've lost a wife, a child, a cat, a dog...my life? It doesn't matter. I've still got...I've still got...nothing. Nothing without them.

"It's okay. Just let it go," Mrs. Sandquist says, familiar with ice melting at the bottom of dark, tired, cold seas.

I look at her, tears knocking on the backs of my eyes, my heart frozen and fearful.

"Just let it go."

And I do. My tears flow and mingle with the cold, dark water. My heart shakes with remorse and pain. My sobs rack my thin, tired body. For five or ten minutes, I blubber and cry my heart, my lungs, my soul out. My shirt and sleeves are drenched with my tears. I've used up her box of tissues, the contents of which now clutter the cushion next to me on the little divan, the small couch.

Wiping the lingering remnants of the tears away, I say, "I...I don't think I've ever cried like that. Ever."

She smiles understandingly. "Sometimes a good cry is the best therapy." She gives me another moment or two to compose myself. "Now, Mr. Olson?" I glance up from my attempt to corral all the loose and used tissues. "It's Mr. Olson, isn't it? Francesca and Mirabella?"

"Yes. Yes, it is," I answer, all the more discomfited.

"You realize," she says through a sad smile, "nothing has changed. I *cannot* discuss your wife's treatment with you."

I'm about to protest, but am swiftly cut off. "If at some juncture it's discovered that something nefarious has happened, then, and only via a judge's court order, can I disclose and discuss my records with regards to Francesca's therapy. And only then."

Crestfallen, I throw the handful of tissues and the box into a nearby mesh trashcan. "Is that understood?" she adds for emphasis.

"Yes," I reply. Standing, preparing to leave after my scolding, I notice the rocks and debris left on the sea floor. They look exactly like my disappointment.

"Have you been to the doctor for that hand?" she asks, slowly walking me to the door of her office.

"No, I've been a little busy."

"I believe in holistic treatment. The body, the mind, and the spirit-soul of self are all simply different aspects of a person's entity. You must cultivate all to be whole."

"Fine. I'll go see a doctor for my hand." The rocks and debris are quickly being covered by sediment.

She adds, officially shooing me from her office, "If I can help in any other way, Mr. Olson, please don't hesitate to ask. Good day."

"Thank you," I say halfheartedly to the closing door, as I head downstairs a step at a time.

A few days later I'm sitting on the front steps of the crooked house waiting for Mrs. Sandquist. Eventually she pulls up in a late model BMW sedan. She doesn't notice me until I stand up and she's halfway to the house.

"Mr. Olson, what are you doing here?" she asks, surprised and noticeably annoyed.

"I need to ask you something." The desperation, at least to me, is palpable in my voice.

"I'm sorry, I thought I was clear about not discussing this with you. Besides, I'm expecting clients." She begins searching for the keys to the house in her voluminous black purse.

"Well, actually, they've left."

"Excuse me?" Her eyes narrow to small, black, accusatory holes. "What do you mean 'left'?"

"The young couple—Kid Hot Rod and his girl, Sexy Blue Susan." She gives a slight, reluctant smile at my description. "They've left."

"Please, Mr. Olson, answer my question, what do you mean by 'left'?"

"They drove away, as in left. But they'll be back next week." She doesn't seem any less annoyed by my succinct and descriptive explanation.

"Exactly what did you do?"

"I bought them off, so to speak." The black holes of her eyes are beginning to pull the outlying light of the day in. I'm sure to be next. Quickly, I explain. "Friends of Francesca stopped by and made some accusations. And I spoke with someone who says it's possible.. I need to know.. is it possible to do something and not know you did it? Cover everything up and pretend not to know—or actually not know—what you've done?"

"Mr. Olson, I'm sorry, but I really can't talk about this."

"Look, Mrs. Sandquist, I'm not really in the mood for verbal fencing and subtlety. Okay?" I take a deep, calming breath as her left hand descends into her purse. It's sure to be wrapping itself around a cold can of mace. "Can someone do something, say commit a crime, a murder, what have you, and not know, or remember, anything about it?" June was pretty sure it was possible. And while she was telling me, it was as if she were telling me something I already knew. Honestly, it was a little perplexing. And absolutely disconcerting to imagine I may be harboring a killer, a madman, within myself.

I notice Mrs. Sandquist relenting, beginning to give way. The desperation must be working. For the final little push I add, "Please," very, very genuinely.

She sighs, "Very well. Let's go into my office."

Once we're settled, she begins as if we were still on the porch: "It's called a fugue state, or more technically correct a psychogenic fugue state." I shrug my shoulders as if she's described a lunar moth while speaking Swahili. "Basically due to either stress, or perhaps something organic, say a tumor, the individual loses all sense of normal consciousness, though the individual is still capable of cognition and motor skills. After a while the individual returns to their normal state of consciousness. Usually, these states are relatively short, though some documented states have lasted years. And it's theorized that it's possible to last a lifetime."

Again I find myself staring at the still life prints. I clarify to them, as much to myself, "You mean...living a life out as someone else than who they initially were?"

"Yes. Exactly. Our sense of identity and self is basically a relatively tenuous entity. For some, exceedingly so. A certain amount of stress or a specific incident may trigger some internal reaction that undermines all the pillars of that individual's identity, effectively causing that 'person' to cease to exist."

"How...how do they...return to their original self, to who they were before?"

"That, like the trigger that sends them into the fugue state, could be anything. Most likely it's getting away from, or taking care of, the stress trigger which caused the fugue state in the first place."

"And," I had to ask, "and murder is a possible way of 'taking care of the trigger'?"

She sighs. "Mr. Olson, this is not my area of expertise. If you want, I can give you the name and number of someone who is far more qualified than I to discuss these matters."

"Not necessary." For a moment we simply stare at our knees and listen to the traffic and birds outside. From the prints, the fish, duck, and pheasant stare dull-eyed and dead, almost accusingly. For clarity's sake, and not mine, I ask again, "But murder, something as you said, 'nefarious,' is a possibility?"

Reluctantly she nods. "Yes."

"And, I assume, they could be cognizant enough to dispose of the body, or bodies, hide any evidence? Do any and everything along those lines to cover the heinous act up?"

Again she nods, reluctantly. "Yes."

"Thank you, Mrs. Sandquist, you've been a great help. If a very disturbing one."

She doesn't answer, but simply watches me leave.

I walk out into a day ending, typically, in sunset.

Slowly I walk down 23rd Avenue to a pub, The New Old Lompoc, where I get a sandwich and a pint. As I chew and drink I ponder the possibility of harboring a dark, sinister second me inside of me. I don't finish the sandwich, or the pint, afraid I may be somehow nurturing *it*, too.

Intermission

Ignoring the fan, my life, disintegrating around me, I lumber to the park.

Like an infiltrator, a dirty spy, I glide into the general pack of dog owners and mill about. Casually, I smile and say hello to a few of the other regulars. Each time a sharp spur of guilt strikes me.

Then a voice startles me. "Where's the Zeuser?"

I turn to June and lie. "You know dogs. Wandered off. He's probably smelling or eating something he shouldn't as we speak." She laughs lightly. Then I ruin everything, by adding, "Best case scenario, abducted by aliens." She doesn't ask about the worst case scenario. Actually, June doesn't say anything for a long time. She takes alien abductions very seriously. Supposedly, that's how she lost her last two cats. Cats, rumor has it, are far more intelligent than dogs, hence why they're abducted far more often. And which may also explain why I prefer dogs.

Finally she says, "I don't think so."

Peering intently into the shadows beneath the scrub trees, searching for movement, for anything that looks familiar, I've lost track of where I am, where we were in conversation. "Uh, 'think so.' What?"

"Abducted by aliens," June says. Naturally.

"Because why?"

"Zeus was smart, too smart."

"Smarter than a cat?" I smile. She frowns. Like I said, she takes abductions seriously.

"Perhaps. But smarter than the average alien." Coming from June, that's high praise. Honestly, I don't think she'd say the same about me. "I think," she adds, playing with one of the studs in her ear, "he found a portal to another dimension."

She then goes on to explain how it's easier for animals to discover the windows between worlds. How dogs and cats, both domesticated and wild, have an innate ability for inter-dimensional travel. This ability was derived many millennia ago from witch doctors who captured cubs and used them in various experiments. "And it's pretty common to confuse the use of dimensional doors with abductions."

"Of course it is."

She pays no heed to my sarcasm. "Hence, the misinterpretation of the disappearances of the Mayans, the Aztecs, and the Anasazi." June now launches off on a brief defense of her thesis. After a few minutes, her momentum wanes.

Because I have my own abandoned temple to return to, I prod her for more information—a weak attempt at postponing the return to the dusty, stained altars of coffeemaker and couch. June, unfortunately, is simply an intermission in my disintegration. So I ask, "Is that also your explanation for the Martians?"

Unfortunately she isn't having any of it, and replies, "Long story. But I have a hint: Amelia Earhart."

Quickly, as I attempt to assess the correlation between Earhart's disappearance and the theoretical disappearance of the theoretical Martian civilization, June calls Tuesday. Tuesday saunters over and they immediately leave, leave me wanting more and afraid to return home.

Q:

Hello, Fan. Who will be hurling poop at you today?

A:

████████

I'm somewhere in the cadaverous valley of a good wine buzz when my cell phone rings. Who'd call at this hour? Francesca! She's calling to explain the circuitous route to the dimensional door she and Mirabella accidentally walked through. She's calling to invite me to open it and join them.

Hastily I stagger off the couch, wave good-bye to the fire, and make it to the bureau in time to answer. Unfortunately, it's not Francesca, it's ██████████

"Hey, what's up?" she asks, a bit too enthusiastically for me.

"Nothing," I reply, rubbing my eyes red, "What about you?"

"Can I come over?" I look around as if she's mentioned a chainsaw-juggling penguin riding a plaid unicorn in my living room.

"What? What are you talking about?" She's never asked, never mentioned once, not once in the long, angular year of our cavorting, to stop by, to come over. And not once have I mentioned, offered, suggested, hinted, or intimated at her stopping by, coming over. But there is no penguin, no unicorn in the living room.

"I'd like to come over. To spend the night. Spend it with you. There."

"Okay, I'm sorry, but, and don't get me wrong, I don't mean to be rude, or...anything. But, ██████honey, what the hell are you talking about? First, do you know what time it is? I mean it's pretty damn late. Secondly, what makes you think it'd be

okay to come over? To spend the night? Particularly *here*."
I'm attempting to use a very firm, very understanding voice,
though one that's also compassionate. I don't know if it works
or not. She hangs up. I conclude not.

Outside, I hear a car door slam and an engine start up. I go
to the front window and pull the curtain aside. Across the
street, down a few houses, is what looks like the late-night
sparkle of a new Mini Cooper pulling away from the curb and
driving away.

██████does own a Mini Cooper, racing green, sports package.

Confused, I return to the couch and my glass of wine. I attempt not to think too much about the implications of ███████
and her...stalking me? I probably would have been more at
ease if I had found that chainsaw-juggling penguin and the
plaid unicorn. Maybe next time.

∞

The next morning she's sent an e-mail. It reads: G—Please don't
feel as if I were placing pressure on you to respond. I had such a great
time with you and Zeus the other day I was hoping to relive it, though at
your place. I realize the surprise of me stopping by, particularly so late,
might've been too much. I'm sorry. As you can imagine, my judgment
might've been impaired by alcohol. It, I should have you know, is also
impaired by my deep feelings for you. I recognize we've never talked
about or expressed our emotions for one another. We've kept everything
very physical, very businesslike. I wonder if now isn't the time to discuss
our feelings? What do you think? I'm curious. Please tell me what I, and
we, should do. Thinking of you...██████████

I don't write back. I send it directly into the trash can. For a
long time I ponder how she knew Francesca and Mirabella weren't
home. It only takes me a moment to realize I don't know.

I get a phone call from her at work, while my line is unplugged. Her message happens to be snarled among the long
series of angry and vindictive messages from psycho-Steve.
I'm so conditioned by punching the erase button twenty-four
consecutive times I erase ██████'s message before I'm able to
listen to it.

This is sure to have consequences, but I'm so busy delet-
ing Steve's messages I have no time to think about them,
or ██████.

I get a letter from her. It's delivered to my house. However,
I notice there isn't a stamp on the envelope. She dropped it by.

I pour a large glass of a Sokol Blosser pinot noir and open the envelope. It's a greeting card of two dogs, both mutts, sitting on a small couch (or maybe it's a divan), one on top of the other. There's no caption, it's a blank card, except for what she's written.

Dear George—

These days of silence have become exceedingly long. I miss you. I will also admit, I want you. Until you can admit the same I shall also abide in silence. Perhaps as your days without me become longer and longer you shall recognize it's me you want and need.

Always Yours,

Is it simply coincidence she's pushing things now? Spring fever affecting her and her judgment? Or, is she somehow tied to this? Tied to the disappearances of Francesca and Mirabella and Tyler and Zeus? And, if so...how?

∞

The next morning, as I step off the elevator, late again for work, I immediately notice Anne's face. It's covered in bemused curiosity.

Slowly, as her smile grows, I walk to her desk and ask, "What?"

First she hands me a few messages, the mail, then falls into a petulant silence. I'm forced to repeat myself. "Come clean, Doll Face. What is it?"

Anne pretends to be chewing gum, takes a pencil, and begins to twirl her hair with it, and says in her best Jersey accent, "Well, boss, you got a visitor." Steve! He's found me! He's ransacking my office before he kicks my ass and throws me out the window to the sidewalk below. However—thankfully—Anne adds, "And she's a real looker." I'm simultaneously relieved and slightly disappointed. The avenging shadow of Steve is haunting me mercilessly. I simply want the deserved retribution, as painful as it may be, to be over with. I have a normal life to get back to squandering.

Before I walk the plank into the cold sea of my office, I ask Anne, "Can you make lunch reservations for Murata...for when they open?"

"That's eleven-thirty, boss."

"Yes, yes, it is. What's your point?"

She drops the Jersey accent, along with the pencil, and flatly adds, "None. Consider it done."

"Anne?" She looks up, a little startled, partly because I used her name but mostly because I sounded sincere, genuine. "Thank you."

"Sure. Anytime." She looks at me as if I'm someone else. As if she's not sure who I am. There's a certain sorrow in her eyes. Before I can ask who it might be she sees, I step into my office.

███ is at the window, looking out across the city. She doesn't turn to me. She's wearing black high heels and a black knee-length coat. Really rather formal, I think. Something one wears to a funeral, not—Is this when and where the jilted lover kills the man who wronged her and commits suicide? The classic love suicide? My skin goes cold. That form of tragic drama is right up ███'s alley.

Well, so be it. It would be well deserved. Besides, it'd save me having to deal with Steve, and Jessica, and Leslie, and....

Silently I close the door, take off my coat, and walk to the windows. I almost want to keep going and step off into nothing. Though, instead of falling, I want to be able to keep walking. Keep walking on air, until...until...when?

Until I'm back where I began? Until Steve hunts me down? Until time stops? Until I find Francesca and Mirabella? Until I'm comfortable with my death, my mortality?

Something moves to my left. And I'm surprised to discover ███ still here. Didn't she leave? Or, did she leave and return? Could she have been here all this time? All this time—what does that mean? All this time. I don't know what that means. Just letters, squeezed together to form words, placed next to one another to create a sentence, which means, what? I don't know.

███ insinuates herself between me and the window.

Slowly she unbuttons her coat. Of course she's naked underneath. Though it's a cliché, it's a very unexpected and enticing one. Unfortunately, I'm all too cliché—myself—a neglectful, middle-aged, overweight, receding hairline, abandoned husband and father. I'm a punch line to a joke. Or maybe I'm just the joke.

Remorseful, I look into ███'s eyes. I want to say something, anything that will explain, but words at this juncture are inadequate. I close my mouth. Once again I undermine the probability of proving myself a fool.

A wan, understanding smile graces her lips as she buttons her coat.

She slips past me like water around a smooth rock, and leaves.

I don't move until Anne knocks on my door. "Lunchtime, boss."

Intermission

"What about a psychic?" June asks, throwing a tennis ball into the outfield for Tuesday.

"For me?"

"For finding Zeus." I haven't told her about Francesca, Mirabella, or Tyler. But then I haven't really told anyone. For some reason I don't think Mrs. Sandquist counts. Therefore June, in her ignorance, shouldn't feel special. I did, however, mention Zeus's "running away." How else could I explain his absence paired with my presence at the park?

"I guess I keep coming back to the park in the hope he remembers.. here.. and having a good time, and Tuesday, and.. and you, you know?"

"Yes." For a while we watch the dogs play.

"So, you mentioned a psychic?"

"I did." She takes the returned ball from Tuesday's mouth and throws it again.

"And?"

"Nothing." Tuesday runs the ball down and begins loping back toward us.

"Okay." June throws the ball again. Again Tuesday returns with it. And again June throws it.

This happens a few more times until I dredge up something to ask June. "What do you know about the bombardier beetle?" I've become nervous, some would say fearful, of returning prematurely home to discover my double enjoying dinner and a movie with my missing family. To extend the trips to the park, I've started looking up curious topics on the Internet for June to discuss. I'd like to ask her about doppelgangers, but sometimes the truth is the last thing one wants to hear.

June gives me a calculated and quizzical stare. She throws the ball one more time, then answers, "You mean the beetle that shoots boiling hot, caustic chemicals out of its posterior by combining hydrogen peroxide and hydroquinone, and igniting them? Generating temperatures in the range of 212 degrees Fahrenheit?" I nod, already very impressed. However, she has more. "Rumor has it one species of the beetle is even capable of three hundred pulses per second, and is being used as a prototype for some highly-secret military propulsion engine."

"Uh, yeah, that's...that's the beetle."

"And why do you ask?" Tuesday's too tired to bring the ball all the way back and lies down a few feet away from us.

"I was thinking, in regards to spontaneous human combustion, what if the beetle were the trigger? The match, I mean. Is there perhaps a higher incidence of spontaneous human combustion where the beetle is indigenous?"

"Curious hypothesis." June stares at Tuesday. Tuesday stares at June. "However," June continues, "the last known SHC was in Northern England, I think in 1992."

"And the beetle," I ask attempting to keep an eye on both of them, "is indigenous where?"

"Pretty much most every continent. Savannahs, temperate zones, woodlands and grasslands." Tuesday doesn't move, simply lies there panting in a seemingly vain attempt at catching her breath. Something, however, in her canine eyes tells me it's a ploy to keep the ball out of June's evil, diabolical, throwing hands.

"So there's a North American species then?" I ask.

"Yep. Not sure which one or anything, but yeah. Why?"

"Well, I remember you mentioning a while ago the 'wick effect' and smoking in regards to SHC and I thought, what about those incidences where the victims didn't smoke? Then I heard about this beetle. It's just a hypothesis."

June remains silent and thinks about this little beetle crawling near a sleeping, overweight person, and the beetle being startled by something and setting the person on fire with its posterior discharge. Gradually a smile grows on her lips. "It's an intriguing hypothesis. I'll ask a friend."

That's enough for me. I don't say anything else.

We stare at Tuesday until she caves under the pressure and finally brings the ball back. June happily pats Tuesday's panting sides in exchange. Once Tuesday has caught her breath, they say good-bye and walk slowly out of the park. I wait a solemn minute, maybe two, and do the same.

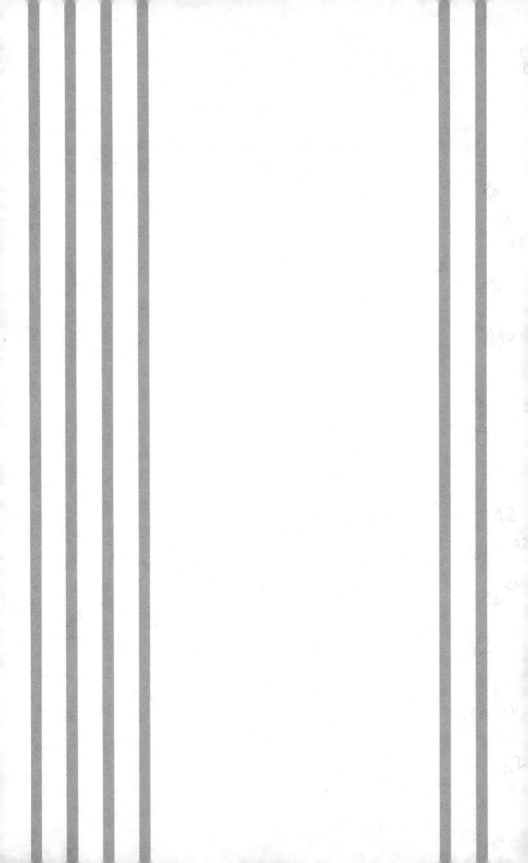

Q:

Good morning, Fan. How
may I direct the shit hurled
at you today?

A:

The Searching Quest for
Francesca, Mirabella, Tyler,
and Zeus.

In a vain and futile attempt at circumventing my fate, I begin a blind attempt to find my family.

I've gone around the neighborhood and plastered every—and I do mean every—telephone pole with photos of and information about Zeus and Tyler. I even try to increase people's incentive to keep an eye out for the furry beasts by offering a reward. Fifty dollars for Tyler, and a hundred for Zeus.

I've traipsed to every grocery store, deli, supermarket, pizzeria, burrito joint, convenience store, coffee shop, and gas station and placed posters in all of them. Using the stapler and the duct tape I've attached nearly a hundred posters to one thing or another.

However, no one calls with specific information, or says they've actually got Tyler or Zeus. There are a lot of messages like, "You know, I think I saw a dog that looked like him over at that park, or school, or whatever on Fremont Street, or is it an avenue, or maybe it was Fifteenth and Tillamook, or maybe.... No, no, I'm pretty sure it was at a park." I delete these.

There are messages like, "My cat (or dog) (or both) just gave birth to the cutest litter. You should see these little guys. They are just sooooo adorable. I know how losing a pet can be very tragic, but sometimes the best thing is to get a little kitten (or puppy) (or both). Oh, this little guy wants to say hi... say hello. Hello. Helloooo." I delete these.

Occasionally the messages are incongruous and insane: "How much was that washer and dryer? Because I can't go over a hundred and fifty dollars." "There's a dog fight comin' up. And your Zeus looks as if he could handle himself in a ring. What d'ya say? I'll give three to one. What d'ya say?" "Sugar, if you need a shoulder, or anything, *anything at all*, to cry on, give Darlene a call. Okay?" I, of course, dutifully delete them all. And then I get something to drink.

∞

One night I, and two bottles of wine, call every known airline in the civilized world. We ask if they can tell us anything about a beautiful Spanish woman and a beautiful eight-year-old girl who may or may not have flown on one of their flights about a week or two ago.

At first everyone is very respectful, very helpful and considerate with their, "I'm sorry, sir. But without any flight information it's impossible." Or, "Sir, I do understand, however, I'm not authorized to give out that information." In which case I attempt to get a name and a number, of who is authorized to perhaps give that information. They, of course, have no information pertaining to Francesca and Mirabella. However, for certain FAA and security considerations, they do take my information.

As the night wears on, with the bottles losing their enthusiasm and my patience thinning, the airlines' staff become less and less understanding, more and more terse. "I'm terribly sorry, goodnight." "No. Try another airline." "Your inquiry, sir, may best be directed to a psychiatrist. Have a great night! And thank you for flying International Air America."

"Fuck off, you fucking cracked-up, crack-whore! My wife and child are probably tied and gagged in the fetid basement of a serial killer!" And the line goes dead. "Fuck!" I slam the phone down and wait. And wait. And wait. And realize I don't know what I'm waiting for. That's when I go to bed and try to sleep.

That's when I wake and listen to Francesca's message, and scrub the coffeemaker into a pristine, sparkling, silver sun.

That's when I wake and forlornly stare at Mirabella's empty bed, whispering the next chapter over and over.

That's when I wake and open a can of Seafood Medley and place it on the back porch for Tyler. That's when I microwave a frozen, Deluxe Combination pizza and place it on the front steps.

That's when I go back to sleep, when the alarm rings.

Q:

Good morning, Fan. Who is going to be throwing shit at you today?

A:

The Lake Oswego Police Department.

"Anne, I'm sorry, I can't take the call." I don't look up. I keep my head down and nose to the grindstone. I wave a hand as if flailing at invisible insects. For once this week, I'm actually trying to get some work done.

"It's the police," she says. I don't have to look up to know she's smiling, satisfied, "Calling about the Eurovan."

"Can I ask you something? Why do all the graphic designers think they're creating layouts for MTV or *Vogue*? We're a stupid insurance company. Plain graphics, plain text, and straightforward presentation are what the shareholders expect. No frills. No sprinkles. No whipped cream or cherries. Just give them the numbers sunny-side up and inject a little 'it's all going to be okay' warmth up their hemorrhoidal asses. That's how they stay with the tried-and-true, our company, red, white, and blue. The designers can save their 'creativity' for the twenty-to thirty-year-old demographics of the renters' insurance blitz this fall. Therefore, I ask you—" I hold up one of the proof sheets; it's covered with layered graphics, insert boxes and bubbles. It even calls for an echoed watermark. "—what the hell is this?"

"I do not know, boss." Anne's sarcasm causes me to glance up. I find her shaking her head in mock repugnance. She then sticks a finger down her throat in support of my aesthetic position.

"Neither do I. Neither do I." Disgusted, I throw the proof sheet on my desk and spin around to gaze on the buzzing city below. Offhandedly I comment, "If you were a coyote caught in a trap, do you think you could chew your paw off?" Anne has learned not to answer these questions, because the answer invariably leads to another question, another personal predicament and then, of course, to another question.

After we each ponder the question in our own way, she asks, "So, what should I tell the police?"

"Police?" I ask, puzzled as to what their connection with chewing one's paw off might be.

"About the Eurovan." She is making no sense at all. And that self-satisfied smirk is really beginning to annoy me.

"Eurovan? What Eurovan?"

"Your wife's." I swear she's speaking in a foreign tongue. Something familiar, yet unrecognizable, like Portuguese instead of Spanish.

"My wife's what?"

"Eurovan." For some reason I cock my head as if I were Zeus. "Boss, you okay?" Something finally begins to surface, slowly.

Turning around to face her, I say methodically, reinforcing my own memory and a small portion of my sanity, "My wife's red Eurovan. It has a smiley face bumper sticker? Smells like soccer fields, grape juice, dogs, and aloe vera? A pulp novel rests, dog-eared, under the driver's seat? Right rear bumper is dented because she miscalculates the turn out of our driveway and constantly scrapes the retaining wall? Is full of soundtracks from kid's movies? And is affectionately known as Red Robin?"

Anne nods. "Yes, *that* Eurovan." Somewhere a switch is thrown inside me and it suddenly makes sense—the police are calling about my wife's *missing* Eurovan! Of course! That's it! Eureka! They've found the Eurovan camped out in the Redwood forest where Francesca, and Mirabella, and Tyler, and Zeus were camping and relaxing, roasting marshmallows and telling camp stories.

"Okay, Doll Face, patch 'em through. And," I add before she exits, "take yourself and your beau out to lunch. Put it on my expense account, okay?" The prospect that the discovered Eurovan equates to reuniting with my family makes me magnanimous and slightly giddy.

"Sure thing, boss," she replies, smiling and pertly flipping an ankle up as she leaves.

Before Anne forwards the call, and Francesca explains everything, I decide the practical thing will be for me to fly down to Eureka, or Shasta, or one of those other Northern California outposts. Where Francesca, having taken Mirabella to Ashland to watch a few plays, can then pick me up. Afterward we can make a leisurely return up the coast.

Unfortunately, the City of Lake Oswego police detective, Detective Nugent, is direct and to the point, like a bullet being slammed into the chamber. Immediately, expertly, he shoots my hope from the sky.

"We pulled your Eurovan out of Oswego Lake this morning. You got any idea how it got there?"

My magnanimity is quickly set aside, particularly for stupid questions and without mention of Francesca, or Mirabella, or Tyler, or Zeus. "Someone drove it in there?"

"Look, Olson, I'm trying to carry out an investigation here, okay? If I want grief I'll call my ex-wife."

"Sorry, detective. It's been a long week."

"Aren't they all?" He has a good point; the weeks must be particularly long in his line of work. I might as well play nice. He may actually know something about my family.

"What can I do for you, detective?"

"Well, you're right. Someone did drive the van into the lake. Only one problem."

"Oh?" I sound distant, like I'm waiting for bad news, like watching bombs being released from far above with nowhere to run. Did Francesca carry out some crazed-mother–murder–suicide pact and drive the car into the lake? Are the bodies of Mirabella, Tyler, and Zeus, slowly floating to the surface, one after the other after the other? "What's the problem, detective?"

"The guy that drove your van into the lake?"

"Yes?" This is perfect Perry Mason. This is a perfect cocktail party story. If I wasn't mesmerized by the bombs' whistling descent I might attempt to write this down.

"He was still behind the wheel when we pulled it out this morning."

"He? He, as in a man, and not a dog?" Zeus knew where I kept the keys, but his paws surely couldn't have steered, could they?

"Uh, yeah," the detective answers curiously, "It was a man. What do you mean by 'dog'?"

Before we get too far down that path I ask, "And you think I can tell you who this guy is?" There's a short pause as I quickly go through all the possibilities of who it could be. No one comes to mind. You'd think there'd be a few suspects. Maybe he's a quiet computer geek from work, or the pale, blond man with the Great Pyrenees from the dog park? Or the postman? Or, as a last resort, a pimpled valet. Honestly though, I have no idea who could be sitting dead and wet in the front seat of my wife's Eurovan. Though some quiet, silent portion of my mind thinks it could be me they found resting, waiting there in the Eurovan, in the lake. That same portion of my mind hopes it isn't—otherwise who am I if I am there?

The detective waits for me to tell him. He waits patiently. Very patiently. Unfortunately, though, I've nothing. There's only the silence, the unknowing within me, which seems to be something I'm incapable of conveying. So, the expectant silence grows and grows.

The detective, seemingly out of necessity, chews his pencil. I ponder the comic scene of Zeus driving the Eurovan, with Tyler pressing the gas pedal, into Oswego Lake. Of course, I have to ask the obvious. "Why is it you think I should know who's behind the wheel?"

"Maybe because it's your car?"

Again I have to laugh—he has a point. I probably should know, but I don't. I don't know a lot. And he was about to find that out.

"Detective, I'm sorry, I really don't know. The car was towed out of the building's parking facility nearly a week ago. Since then it's been missing. MIA. The towing company was supposed to get it back to me. They never did. That's kind of the end of the story—at least on this end." It sounds like the pencil is nearing the eraser. "Sorry."

"Okay. Fine." He adds, "For the moment." It seems he doesn't like dead ends. Can't say I blame him. "What's the name of the towing company?" I give him the information one of the incompetent, pink-pimpled valets gave Anne, who then gave to me. I also convey what I remember from the man who dropped off my car.

"Anything else?" the detective asks.

"No, that's pretty much it." This is the moment I should ask about reporting Francesca and Mirabella as perhaps missing persons. He could also probably clarify for me if they're classified as missing if they left of their own volition. But I suspect that would be more suspicious than a body found in the Eurovan in the lake.

Before I hang up and have a chance to contemplate my inadequacies over sashimi and sake, he hits me with a shovel, full in the face. "One more thing: I'd like to talk to your wife about all this."

"My...my wife?" My stomach lurches into a tight fist of apprehension; there's now only room for sake.

"Yes, her name's...I have it somewhere." I hear him turning papers, searching his records.

"I know my wife's name, detective. It's Francesca."

"Right. Francesca." It still sounds like he's chewing a pencil. Maybe I should ask him to stop? "You know, of course, the van is registered in her name, so I just want to ask Francesca, your wife, a few questions." I don't say anything. Basically because I don't know what to say. The detective continues chewing his pencil and hitting me in the face with the shovel. "I called and left a message at your home. I even tried your wife's, Francesca's, cell number. Though it seems service has been canceled. I assume you know about that?" I don't say anything. I still don't know what to say. I seem to be sinking to a very dark and cold place, not unlike the bottom of the sea. "Mr. Olson? Do you know how I could reach her?"

"Who, detective?" What little light leaks in from above begins to dissipate.

"Your wife."

"Francesca?" Wasn't there a switch here a moment ago? Something to flick and illuminate this curious, cold, and dark world? But now there's nothing.

"Yes, Francesca, your wife. Is she out of town? Visiting relatives? Perhaps on vacation?"

"Detective, and you can believe me or not, but she left me. Just up and left." It's curious how not even the truth does anything against the thick, black wall of deep darkness. It's curious because confession feels so good. Why had I postponed it so long?

"Is that so?" He sounds dubious.

"Yes."

"Mmmmm. Really?" Okay, he's exceedingly dubious, but that's his job. I can't say that I care, or blame him. "Okay. Let's say that's the case—for the moment." Again, for the moment? All these considerations of time. Time to do, or not do. He interrupts my thoughts with another smack of the shovel: "I'm going to need you to take a look at the body."

"The... the body? The one you found in the van?"

"Yes." Again, that damn sound of him chewing the pencil! "What other body did you think I meant?" He sounds suspicious. Perhaps that's an occupational predilection?

"Detective, I'm very busy at the moment. Is there any way we could expedite this experience?" Words flounder out as a seagull flies by. For a moment our eyes meet; instantly he's gone, a block away. I place my hand on the window, envious.

"I can fax a picture. Or send you a digital photo via e-mail."

"E-mail. I don't have a personal fax number." I give him my private e-mail address. I don't need morgue photos roaming my business account.

"Okay. It'll probably take an hour or so before I can send it. Oh, one last question." This must be the prestige question, the one he whips out which causes me to confess my dastardly and heinous crimes. "Do you own a gun?"

Thankfully I know the answer, and it's one of innocence. "No. So, that's how he died?"

"Yeah. Two shots to the chest and another, for good measure, to the temple. How'd you know?"

"You asked about a gun. I made an assumption."

"Yeah, well, we also pulled him from a lake. Thanks for your time, Mr. Olson. I'll be in touch."

I look at the phone as if it's a strange, exotic marsupial from Australia, or New Zealand. Before it bites me, poisons me, pulls some glistening entity from its pouch, I hang up.

∞

I receive an e-mail from the detective. The message reads: Mr. Olson, Please take a look and see if you recognize this man. Let me know as soon as you can, either way. Be forewarned, it's not the prettiest picture. I also still need to speak with your wife in regards to this matter. Thank you for your time and cooperation.

With the e-mail is an attachment, the picture of the dead man found in the Eurovan.

Hesitantly I open the attachment, unconcerned about being on company time, company equipment. Gradually, I'm beginning to care less and less about a lot of things.

It's a color photo with a remarkable amount of clarity. I'd forgotten how precise, stark, and bleak digital photos are. It seems those sad characteristics are only enhanced when the photos are of the dead. I guess, like most of the world,

I've become inoculated by the shading and spraying, erasing, and enhancing capabilities of Photoshop. It seems the Lake Oswego Police Department doesn't employ graphic designers for their photographs. If they did, would the dead be recognized more often?

As it is, the face is of a man who seems remarkably familiar, but one I do not know. However, I've not seen many dead men's faces, so perhaps all dead men would seem familiar to me? Dark hair, wet and glistening from the waters of the lake, is set atop a thin, unspectacular forehead. His eyes, which I assume were once much brighter, appear to be green, or hazel. Perhaps their dullness is from the water having seeped and soaked its way in. An uncomplicated and slightly larger-than-average aquiline nose rests above a mild mouth and a sloping, square chin. He has a bit of stubble, otherwise nothing of remark, except for the gunshot wound to the right temple, where a red, watery mucous oozes.

I decide to print a copy and keep it in case I want to reference it later. Maybe as an attempt to shake a memory loose.

I reply to the detective's e-mail: Detective—Agreed, pretty he is not. But then, he is dead. He seems familiar. He reminds me of the man on the nickel. Unfortunately, I do not recognize him. Sorry. Let me know if I can be of any more assistance, though I don't believe I've been much at all. Perhaps next time, though (and forgive me for this sentiment) I hope there isn't one. Good luck with the investigation. George Thomas Olson.

I send my reply, and delete his e-mail.

A little later he replies: Thanks for the look and the time. Right now we don't even have a name on the guy. A John Doe, as we call them. I'll let you know if something comes up. By the way, I still need to talk to your wife about this. Please let her know and have her call me at her earliest convenience. I assume you can contact her, right? I think we'd both like to know this man's death and your wife's leaving weren't related, wouldn't we? Anyway, thanks again.

I don't reply. Instead I delete the message. "Asshole."

The idea the unknown man's death and Francesca's leaving are somehow connected grates on me. The detective obviously knows what he's doing. If I wasn't earlier, I am now well over my head. "Asshole!"

Later that afternoon I receive another message: Mr. Olson, I cannot stress enough the necessity to talk to your wife. Have her call me as soon as she can. In regards to the Eurovan, it's presently State's evidence and will be held until the investigation is closed, which could take some time. Bureaucracy and all, you know? Again, thanks. P.S. I'd like not to be forced to bring either of you in to get a statement. Please have her call me.

I think about replying. About mentioning the strange circumstances of Francesca's disappearance, about not knowing where she is, or Mirabella, or Zeus, or Tyler. I contemplate disclosing the afternoons when I'd claimed fatigue rather than attend a soccer game. The nights I drank more than was prudent instead of mingling and melding with Francesca. The past week I've longed to be given the opportunity to amend my many mistakes, but the nature of time conspires against such desire and I'm forced to accept my past.

Alas, no amount of mourning or confessing will amend such sins; therefore, I delete the detective's message. I mean, isn't it easier this way, really?

∞

There's a tentative knock on my office door, and Anne slips her head in. I look up.

"Yeah, Doll Face? What's the...?" Something in her eyes causes me to stop and fall silent. I imagine Steve standing behind her, dark gun in her ribs. He plugs her twice. She falls to her knees, and dies. Steve steps casually over her body, aims at the window. It takes three shots to completely break it to the point where a body can be flung out. He directs me to stand in front of the jagged wound. I do. Wind sweeps around me. Somewhere I hear a seagull cry. Before he pulls the trigger, I jump. Finally I throw the words off my tongue and finish my sentence, "...the deviled egged problema?"

She mouths one word, causing me to quickly alter my feigned granite glint to something nearing true concern. "Police."

"Ah, is it Detective Nugget?" I ask, standing and adopting a pleasantly casual demeanor. "Please, Anne, show him in." She gives a hard, quizzical squint at my faux-secure self. "Anne, please, show the detective in." I proffer a magnanimous, welcoming hand.

She nods curtly, throws the door wide, and announces, "Detective *Nuge-N-t*." I give a painful smile at her emphasis on the forgotten and neglected N (her Christmas bonus shall be coal, one piece, very small), "This is Mr. George Olson."

Detective Nugent and his wrinkled suit walk in. He extends

his hand, as Anne gives a bow and flourish he doesn't see. She humbly backs out, bowing as she goes, over and over. Finally she closes the door behind her. (Okay, not even coal. Maybe a rock or a petrified toadstool.)

"Detective," I say, jovially shaking his calloused hand, "so pleased to finally meet you. But I must admit, I have a certain amount of confusion in regard to your visit. Please, have a seat." I offer one of the dark leather chairs semicircled around the front of my desk.

"You know, if you don't mind," he counters, walking to the windows, "I think I'll stand."

"Of...of course. Absolutely. It's a fabulous view." For a long time, longer than necessary, he stares out the window. Unsure of what I should be doing, besides acting naturally, I stare out the window with him. Cars cruise down Market Street. Seagulls, crows, and a few pigeons, fly around and disappear back into the city. Clouds, nondescript and sporadic, slip along the sky like hazy puzzle pieces.

Before my guilty, telltale heart, buried beneath the soft wood floor of my chest, begins to beat and beat and beat, the detective turns to me.

"Wow," he sighs, "a seductive view, isn't it?" A few moments pass. Is he expecting an answer to the obvious? I open my mouth to answer, to utter another lie, but he supersedes me. "So, why...why am I here?"

I don't think he's *that* dumb. I remember Columbo and his mild-mannered confused-cop gimmicks.

"Honestly, detective, I don't know. You tell me." He smiles, broad and genuine. It seems he too has seen many a Columbo episode.

A few more awkward minutes of silence slip by.

Finally, having glimpsed the appropriate omen, he says decisively, "Okay," turns from the window, and throws himself into a chair. It takes me a moment to catch up and collect myself in mine. Once he's begun, Detective Nugent is all business. "A red Volkswagen Eurovan, registered to a Francesca Olson, your wife, was found in Oswego Lake. You know it's Oswego Lake, and not Lake Oswego, like the city?" I shake my head, shuffle my shoulders. I didn't know. I don't care. My phone begins to ring. I ignore it. "Do you need to get that?"

"No." It sounds like a forlorn bird.

"You're sure?" A hungry, starving, dying chick.

"Yes." Is that suspicious, not answering? Besides, it's probably Steve leaving angry, psychotic message number eighty-four. Or Jessica or Leslie crying crocodile tears of worry. Or perhaps Margarita calling to whisper a dire curse on my soul. Regardless of who, there's a high probability it's no one I want to talk to. And wouldn't answering and immediately hanging up be more suspicious?

Thankfully, the small, starving bird immediately dies.

"Okay," the detective says into the renewed silence, taking a small notepad out and flipping a few pages. He reads, "A Mrs. Alright, love that name, I mean that's like right out of a British…." He catches my eye, my annoyance. "Okay. She, while she's walking her two Pomeranians, notices a van, which ends up being your wife's Eurovan, slipping into Oswego Lake."

"Detective, I do honestly understand how this pertains to me. But I'm hard-pressed to know *exactly* how the specificity of the event alters what you've already basically told me."

He ponders his notes. He nods and nods. He nods as if I've made a very succinct observation he, somehow, neglected to take into account. Then, as I glance at the proofs and other miscellaneous disorganized chaos covering my desk, he again hits me. This time, though, instead of the shovel, it's a heavy club and I'm a baby seal.

"First, it's your wife's van. Second, your prints are the freshest found. Oh, yeah, the tech-boys have got tools and techniques that would make the best twenty-dollar hooker blush. And, get this, your fresh prints happen to be all over the place—literally, everywhere. Third, your wife hasn't called me. Fourth, you didn't reply to my e-mail. Fifth, e-mail and phone etiquette aside, I don't trust you. Something about constantly looking from this height gives someone a misconception, a misconceived perception of things. Then there's the oddity of you perhaps not being home the night of the murder." Before I can comment, or argue, he adds, "Your next door neighbor. Seems he's got a remarkable memory for the mundane, and the mysterious. I suppose you've also heard the tale about the three-headed squirrel?" (I guess he's not bluffing. Therefore, remind me to never, ever, so long as I live, or am trapped in hell, or heaven, or disappear into complete and absolute darkness, play poker with this man.) He begins relating the tale of the infamous three-headed squirrel.

However, I've heard it numerous times over many a dull and lethargic neighborhood barbecue, or a likewise dull and lethargic dinner party. I know all about the squirrel's predilection for stealing dirty socks, hiding car keys, and becoming drunk on bird's blood and singing Sinatra while tap dancing on roofs beneath the full moon.

"Detective?" I interrupt him. I don't pretend there's something I wish to add after that disgusting nine-letter moniker. I simply pound a pencil's eraser into my desk, once, twice, thrice, turn it over, pound the pencil's lead into my desk once, twice, thrice, turn it over. Do it again. Then again. I can wait for eternity here. I can wait until forever.

"What is it?"

"Forgive me and my metaphor, but you seem to be a cat scratching for a place to crap."

Detective Nugent shuts his little book. He gazes at his calloused hands and raises his sharp gray eyes to meet mine.

"There's something wrong here." His forefinger touches his chest, points to my desk, out the window, circles here, there, everywhere. "I know it. You know it. In time," he threatens, "everyone else will, too."

He stands, tired but firm, and says, "Have a nice day," exactly as if he were driving a stake through a vampire's heart.

I reply, "You too," exactly as if I were doing the same.

Q:

Howdy, Fan. Who

is gonna be tossin' dung

yer way today?

A:

The Lynch Mob

(aka Jessica and Leslie).

Jessica calls my home phone: "Francesca, if you don't call me in a day, I'm calling the police. This is not a joke. George, if you don't call me in a day, I'll call the police." She hangs up. She sounded forceful and sincere.

I don't call her.

Leslie calls my cell phone: "George, listen, I don't know what's going on with you and Francesca, but could you please call either Jessica, or myself—we're worried? Thanks. Oh, and George, Jessica's serious about calling the police. Okay? Call us. Please."

Leslie, also, sounded forceful and sincere, but also scared. Not of me, necessarily, but of something else. Of something else? What might that be? Could she have some second sight, see Mr. Hyde lurking behind my irises, smiling malevolently, waiting patiently to lurk from the shadows and strike? Maybe she was cold, the shivering affecting her voice, making it sound like fear rather than frigidity? Yes, that's it. It's her temperature and not my temperament.

∞

Returning from Murata, I'm pleased to have had the perfect amount of perfect sushi, sashimi, and *sake*. However, I'm exceedingly displeased to discover Jessica and Leslie milling about inside the glass doors in front of Anne's desk. Particularly since I'd declined a second order of sake.

Before I can call for another elevator, or slip down the hall to hide in the men's room, they notice me.

Instantly I adopt a carefree, no-problem, hello-how-ya-doing, nice-to-see-you, demeanor. Anne's dour smile tells me the reviews will be harsh, critical, and all too poignant. Basically, I'll be content if I can survive to the curtain call.

"Ladies, hello. I'm so pleased you're both here. Been meaning to call...just far too busy. Isn't that right, Anne?" She opens her mouth, but I continue headstrong and headlong into oblivion. "Sure is. Sure is. Anne, do me a favor, please? Hold my calls—and I mean all my calls. Okay? Thank you, Anne." I march on through my door, leaving it wide open, the ladies far behind and bewildered. Having already shed my jacket and made myself comfortable behind my desk, I wait for them. Idly pondering the growing chaos of the printer's proofs, I call out, "Ladies? Hello? This way, please." Like ducklings they finally enter. "Sorry, but this is probably a private matter, I assume?"

"Yes, actually, it is," Jessica replies, as confused as I am by my robust façade. I have no idea how long this can last.

"Then would you mind closing the door? Please. Thank you. And, please, take a seat—if so inclined, of course." I indicate the two chairs in front of my desk to them with an open and benevolent hand. I need to hurry. I feel the sweet poison of the moment dissolving quickly in my veins. Dr. Jekyll, Mr. Hyde am I, I am.

Before they can speak, I jump in, hoping to find something to save me, near the bottom, shrouded in seaweed, hidden by a shadow, under the sand, at the very last moment. "Ladies, I must apologize first. I didn't mean to offend you, at all, by not returning your calls. It's simply been a very trying week for everyone. Both Zeus and Tyler have disappeared. And I needn't tell you what they meant to Mirabella, Francesca, and me."

Jessica and Leslie exchange dubious glances. Headlong, I surge on through the cold water. Surely someone has hidden that little golden Oscar statue somewhere close by. "And, to make matters worse, Margarita has, well, had an accident." I don't particularly see any reason to explain the circumstances. That'll only muddy the water more, right? "So, while Margarita has been in the hospital, Francesca and Mirabella have been at Margarita's place. Tending the hacienda, so to speak." Now how perfect is that? Wrapped tight *and* with a bow on top. Ladies and Gentlemen, accepting the award for Best Male Lead in a Major Motion Life...the envelope please.

Jessica decides to jump in and attempt to play detective. "Can you explain why her cell phone service is canceled?"

"Because," quick-quick, don't think, react, "we've decided to go with a different provider. One that includes an entire comprehensive family package and overseas functionality. It supposedly won't roll over for another week or so." They aren't buying it, but neither are they throwing my blather back in my face. I offer a distraction. "Either of you care for coffee, or tea, or something?"

In unison they shake their heads, and Leslie sits in one of the leather chairs, though she seems none too comfortable. Adjusting herself to the mature leather, Leslie asks, "Why hasn't Mirabella been in school?" Jesus, they've done their homework, haven't they? Or is it Brittany, Jessica's daughter, who ratted me out? From the corner of my eye I see Jessica hesitate, then give a slight nod of approval.

Beautiful. Appreciate this, bitches.

"Well, we heard there was," I offer a dramatic pause, a kiss to Oscar's cute, shimmering gold head—there is the supernova of flashbulbs— "...I assume this is just between us? Correct? I mean, we know how rumors get around, don't we? How they can twist and taint reality from a kitten into a man-eating tiger. Right?" Both nod, both irritated at the innuendo I'm throwing back in their silly, pinched, spoiled, suburban housewife faces. "Good."

I take a calculated moment to look at a bell graph representing provider premiums and millions of dollars in claims, which is supposed to appear on page twelve of the shareholders' brochure. I make a note and toss it aside, then finish the rest of my point. "There was the rumor the father of one of Mirabella's classmates was...I guess the term is unstable. He'd threatened, supposedly through anonymous phone calls, and in very vague terms, to stalk through the school, shooting, killing, maiming, and raping everyone. Francesca and I decided, for safety's sake, to take this seriously. Besides, from what I've seen, the school still has a few unresolved security issues." I don't mention the issue is parents smuggling noisily wrapped snacks into school plays. I finish convincingly, "Prudence alone dictated our course of action."

A long, unsatisfactory silence pervades my office and their hearts. The pressure seems to cause the objects in the room to shrink, the windows to swell and billow. My breathing becomes shallow and rapid, while my heart slows and slows and slows.

Jessica, breaking the spell, erupts. "This isn't like Francesca, George. We all know that. This isn't like her. Why hasn't she called?! Or stopped by?"

"Jessica, I'm sorry, but that I don't know. I'm not privy to all of Francesca's emotional nuances." Nor am I privy to all of mine. I have no idea why I'm lying to them. Is it really so difficult to say Francesca and Mirabella left me? Possibly. Maybe because it's none of their business. I'll tell them what I want to when I feel like it. Until then they can fuck off.

"Can we have Margarita's address?"

"Why would you want to visit Margarita?" She only knows one word, and one gesture. And don't bring flowers, chocolate, or a stupid stuffed bear. But do attempt to ignore the word asesino, and her weak attempts at clawing your eyes out with her scabbed fingers.

"We want to see Francesca, not Margarita. You said Francesca was visiting her."

"She...she is." Reluctantly, I give them Margarita's address. Neglecting, of course, to tell them she's actually in the hospital, and would be for a few more weeks. I also neglect to mention Francesca and Mirabella aren't there either. There's only dust and dying plants I'm supposedly watering every other day.

"George," Jessica asks, "what'd you do to your hand?"

Looking at it as if it were attached to a stranger's wrist, swollen and in the first stages of bruising, I answer straightforwardly, though I still sound confused and unsure. "I hit something."

Neither replies. You can tell by the squint in their eyes a few suspicious thoughts are roaming rapidly through their minds. We stare awkwardly at my swollen, bruised hand. I decide to close this long and uncomfortable moment. "Ladies," their squints narrow at my weak attempt at a compliment, "is there anything else?" I pick up a few miscellaneous papers and throw them haphazardly back on the desk for emphasis. "Because, unfortunately, I've work to do."

They shake their heads, disappointed and unsatisfied. As they leave, I feign returning to the grindstone, realizing I am exactly as they are—disappointed and unsatisfied.

The door closes behind them, tight and secure as a coffin lid. For five minutes I don't do anything. I'm not sure I'm breathing. The papers on my desk blur into an amorphous, monochromatic spill. The dull white blur drips and runs off the desk, stains the carpet. The carpet contracts the pale virus, which begins to collect at the base of the walls. It tries to climb, in thin wavering arms, toward the ceiling. When it reaches the windows, it simply flows out and over like water. Falling, falling, to the street far, far below. The bookshelves, too, are succumbing to the creeping blur.

A book, *El amor en los tiempos del cólera*, lodged center stage on one of the shelves, seems to be making a gallant attempt to resist the devouring blur. The runny arms have reached the ceiling, and with nowhere else to go, begin dripping back to the floor. The book happens to be the only non-work-related book crammed onto the cramped shelves. Strings of pale mucous fall in clots from the ceiling. It's a hardbound, first edition, and is actually signed by Marquez. Stalactites and stalagmites begin to form, begin to fill the office. Francesca, much to any collector's chagrin (not my own; I'm not a collector) has also written inside the jacket:

Mi Amor, Mi Vida, Mi Sangre, Mi Respiro, Mi Hueso,
Mi Alma, Mi Absolutamente Todo. In other words you, George
Thomas Olson (GTO). I know not time, nor ever have I liked it.
However, I know, if nothing else, I want to spend this life of mine with
you. Please allow this fine and magnificent author to speak for me.
Eternally Yours (regardless how far fate—ultimately—may
keep us apart),
~Francesca

It's curious, but the only words I understand, as the book is of course in español, are those written to me by Francesca. And though I had an inkling of their intent, she actually had to translate the first series for me: "My Love, My Life, My Blood, My Breath, My Bone, My Soul, My Absolute Everything."

The room is nearly filled with strips of wavering, foggy cotton. Somehow I'm able to get up from my desk and walk, ever so slowly, to the bookshelf. Streamers trail from me like ethereal wings. My hand reaches through the thickening veil of fog for the book, and what's hidden behind it—a bottle of scotch.

The bottle had been purchased and sequestered there a few days before ████ and I illicitly consummated our affair, many months ago. Unsure exactly why I bought it—for strength or solace—it has remained untouched.

I've had two good, satisfying pulls on the bottle before Anne walks in, unannounced.

I look up, guilty.

"Sort of a second lunch?"

"Kind of. What's up, Doll Face?"

Slowly she saunters over and makes herself comfortable on the corner of my desk, while I...I stare out on a city I no longer know, or care to know.

"Those friends of your wife's...." she let the sentence hang and dangle, like a body.

"Yeah?"

"They don't like you," and this is the part that aggravates, though is completely expected, "or trust you."

"You know, Doll Face...." I begin. For some reason it's easier to keep the established charade than let Anne glimpse exactly how disturbed I am. "I don't blame them."

Minutes gradually tick pass as we consider this statement. Once we're aware of its significance, she hops off the desk.

Smoothing her skirt, she asks, completely out of character, "Would you trust the whale, or what the whale swallowed?"

I have a general idea of what she means, a rather specific idea at what the question hints at, but nothing remotely close to an answer.

"Doll Face, that's the most poignant question anyone has ever asked me." Goddamn if I didn't mean it. "Give me some time to think about it? Please?"

She replies cryptically, shutting the door behind her, "Sure. I mean, it's your funeral, isn't it?"

Later that afternoon, or the next day, I honestly don't know when it is, I get a phone call. I answer it simply to keep from putting a match to the papers on my desk.

"George, um, it's Leslie," she sounds confused. "We went to Margarita's. Francesca and Mirabella weren't there."

"Leslie, I'm sorry, but I don't know what to tell you. Maybe they're out running errands. I mean Margarita is pretty spry for her age." Oh, good, the charade continues.

"Didn't you say she was sick, or something?"

"I...I did. Yes."

"And isn't that why Francesca was supposedly over there?"

"Maybe she got better. Maybe she got worse and went to the hospital. I don't know. I'm not her mother. Okay?"

"Well, actually, we'd like to—"

"Les, I'm sorry, but as I said before, I've got work to do. If I hear anything from Francesca I'll let you know. Otherwise... go live your own life and stay out of mine." I hang up.

I get another call immediately. I don't answer. The message is from Jessica, explaining Leslie's irritation at both calling me and having to call for Jessica, who indeed would've lacked a certain amount of tact. Needless to say, Jessica was a little angry. I don't need that kind of negativity, I have my own. I erase the message.

∞

That night, or the next, while ruminating over what pathetic piece of shrapnel to prepare for dinner, Jessica calls again and leaves messages, on both, no, sorry, all three phone lines, home, cell, and office. Her voice is like a meteor striking a flat, virgin plain on a lonely planet somewhere. The dust and debris are kicked high into the atmosphere. Darkens the sky. Causes the world to gradually grow colder and darker. The strange animals populating this small, insignificant planet no longer look at one another. They simply wander into quiet corners to die, hoping someday, the dust will settle and life, new and better, will be reborn.

"George, just for your FYI, your fucking information, we've talked with Detective Nugent. And have discussed everything. Even chatted with Margarita. Who doesn't know what the hell's going on either." (Shit, I could tell you that.) "I hope you're prepared for—" Suddenly she's crying. What the hell's going on? I hear her crying for a long moment, then she composes herself and proclaims through a myriad of sniffles, "Expect absolute hell, you murdering fucking bastard!"

This exact message is on each answering machine and voice mail I have. With each listen I grow more and more intrigued by how she could've duplicated the message, duplicated her voice full of fear, hatred, and sniffles. I'm less intrigued by her words, her message. Regardless of the technology and personal fortitude used, I delete one message after the other, after the other, religiously.

Once the ordeal of listening to Jessica's sobbing is finished, I sit with a bottle of wine and drink, hoping to discover in the red, glistening surface what the hell she's talking about. But the settling dust is too thick; it obscures the sun. And I can't really see anything. Even the fire is a small, hazy pinpoint of light on the horizon. Sleep, like the thickening ash, weighs my limbs down. I'll wait until morning to see if I wake.

Intermission

"I asked a friend of mine about you."

I stare at June, mildly confused. "Me?" For some reason I'm bothered and annoyed by her confiding in a stranger about me. I feel an odd comingling of threat and betrayal. "What about? The butt-flaming beetle and spontaneous human combustion?" I ask, attempting humor to deflect my annoyance.

Her Icelandic eyes stay averted from mine for a long time. I assume, from the way they move here and there, she's following Tuesday around the park.

She ignores my question. "My friend does past life regression."

Something tells me this is going to get worse before it gets better. I make another sad, diversionary attempt. "Why past? Why not future?"

"Oh, she does that too. But she only gets past lives where you're concerned." Like I said—worse before better.

"Well, that's comforting," I say sarcastically, hoping Tuesday would get bit by the little pit bull puppy she's playing with.

"It is," June clarifies, "if birth is simply the incapacity for wisdom and knowledge. And that the cessation of birth, of a 'next life,' implies gaining advanced spiritual insight into Nirvana in this one. So, that's very good." The little pit bull still hasn't bitten Tuesday. It looks as if they are getting along, wrestling and romping.

"That is good. Though, at this juncture in my spiritual development, highly improbable."

"Perhaps. But then...." She falls into a petulant silence, and kicks a knot of grass with her tennis shoe. I wait. She continues when Tuesday wanders over and takes a rest at her feet. "There is also something called erasing, or recycling. It's where the spirit, for whatever reason, doesn't gain another birth cycle. It simply falls away and gets erased, or recycled."

June kicks another few knuckles of grass free, before I finally ask, "You mean, disappear? No falling back to a beetle, or great glory of working for an insurance company? Nothing? No chance for nirvana either?" She shakes her head and seems all too depressed. "It could be worse, right?" She looks at me exactly as if there was nothing worse. Nothing. I attempt to keep it light. "I could be a beetle working for an insurance company."

She gives a wan smile and kneels to pet Tuesday. Tuesday rolls over on her back. June scratches Tuesday's pale belly, but doesn't say anything. After a moment it seems odd to simply watch, and I say good-bye and wander off. Theoretically back home.

Q:

Good morning, Fan.

Who is going to be throwing

shit at you today?

A:

The Job. The Career.

The Grindstone.

The first thing I hear from Anne isn't "You're late," but, "You won't like this, boss."

She follows me into my office with papers and memos. Dramatically donning my comic book role, I toss my coat off and stand, back turned to the room, defiant before an antagonistic city.

"Hit me with the news, Doll Face." To be really convincing I'd need a cigar and a burly, dust broom mustache. Something like that guy in *Spiderman*.

I admit I'll miss these brash moments of mimicry and mockery. This young, go-get-'em reporter reports to the dour, pessimistic section manager rapport we've come to create. Earlier there was no rapport. There was verbatim dictation. There was a new secretary, hired by some gray-haired–bun-head, and a new section manager, promoted from some obscure post from some obscure section inhabiting a floor below.

"Hi."

"Hello." It took us a week before we knew one anothers' first names. After that it was all downhill.

Finally, on a Friday after work, having survived two interminable months of working with Miss Stilted-Stick-Up-Her-Ass, and she working with Mr. I-Don't-Need-Your-Help-I-Know-And-Can-Do-Everything-Myself, we went and had a celebration, of having mailed our first mass mailing, a brochure directed to senior citizens who fall down and can't get up.

We got drunk on sake and ate too much sushi and sashimi.

"Look, Anne, I don't think you plan on doing this your entire life; nor do I. I don't even like the job. I'm actually surprised I even got it. Anyway, what I'm saying is...." I took another long sip of sake, because I really wasn't sure what I was saying.

She, however, did know. "You're saying we can either get along, have a good time, and try to make the best of a very boring, very mundane, very soul-sucking experience, or we can...we can..." She faltered, and I accepted the challenge.

"Or, we cannot." She nodded. Then I made a toast, "Here's to getting along, having a good time, and—"

She chimed in: "Making the best of a boring, mundane, soul-sucking experience."

We drank a toast and nothing was the same after.

So, I've flung my jacket across the room to an idle chair, which catches it expertly. I stand defiant before an antagonistic city. She's said, "You won't like this, boss."

I've answered, "Hit me with the news, Doll Face," as she's followed me into my office.

There's a slight hesitation as she closes the office door behind her, a precursor to truly bad, bad news. I steady myself, opting for the pose of the persecuted—leaning against the window, hands pressed firmly above my head against the glass, back slightly bent, legs slightly apart. *Atlas at Window* is how an artist, good or bad, might title it. Or maybe, *World Contemplating, Man, Above.*

"Mr. Dietrich has," Anne clears her throat—the man looks down and watches a few pedestrians jaywalk across the street—then continues, "a few additions he'd like to include."

I whirl, angrily breaking my pose. "What?!"

Hurriedly she explains, "I know, and he does, too, or so he said, that the deadline is this week."

"What are they?" Dietrich is the PR manager, technically above me and with ten years seniority, so he could pull this last-minute bullshit, which he tended to do all the time, as a point of remembrance—like a dog repeatedly peeing on the same pole, even after no other dog has pissed there for months, or even years.

She hands me a few sheets of paper. I look them over, in a very cursory manner. Granted, the changes are complicated, and are probably for the better, but it meant ten to fifteen added hours, *if* we were lucky. It also affects the entire scope of the layout and the brochure, which only means having to redo everything.

Reluctantly, I initial where it's needed and hand the papers back to Anne. She, also reluctantly, being the messenger and bearer of bad news, takes them down to the design boys in production. The shit is flowing, falling, sliding downhill.

It seems as if I can get no work done at work. Between the phone calls from Steve, the cops, Jessica, Leslie, and███████, my occasional attempts at calling airlines, or Amtrak, or Greyhound to vainly ask if they've seen Francesca and Mirabella, I'm really rather surprised the brochure is progressing at all.

And what work I do take home tends to get left behind in the morning. Mostly due to the fact I don't work on it at all. Instead, I wander to the park and chat with June. Instead I call airlines and drink wine. Instead I stare at Mirabella's empty bed. Instead I listen to Francesca's phone message. Instead I stare at Zeus's empty food dish, Tyler's empty window seat. Instead I hold out Francesca's dresses, attempting to remember, if not her face, at least her shape. Instead I drink wine and watch the fire slowly grow cold.

∞

The Big Boss, Mr. Naismith, swings down, and gives his customary, *dum-dum-de-dum* rap on my door, and enters all smiles, all jowls.

"How's it progressing there, Chief?" Regardless of the fact he's the division manager, and regardless of whom in the company he is speaking to, he calls everyone "Chief." Something about being from the Midwest, I guess.

"Well enough." I shuffle a few sheets around to cover up the color print of the dead man found in the Eurovan and to make it look as though I'm actually doing something. "Though you could tell Dick to—" Mr. Naismith gives me a quick, sharp look. He doesn't like his boys not getting along. "Okay. You could tell Richard to—" Who am I kidding? Naismith doesn't care about Dietrich. And I don't care about either one. As long as the shareholders' brochure is halfway presentable, everyone's happy. We keep our jobs and get a bonus. The tried-and-true continues. "Actually, Mr. Naismith, everything's going smoothly. A train on greased rails."

"Now that's what I like to hear. That can-do attitude." He doesn't look at me or the mess on my desk, or ask about the train on greased rails—going nowhere—as he walks to the window and gazes out on a city he thinks he owns, on a world he believes he understands.

"Yes, sir, that's what we strive for up here—can-do." If the windows opened, would I push him?

"When can I take a look at your love's labor?" I assume he's referring to the brochure. I wouldn't push him. I'd stick a foot out. If he tripped and stumbled and fell out the window, I suppose it could be construed as his own fault.

"I should be able to get the finalized proofs on your desk no later than, say..." I lie; we'd be lucky to have them done by the end of the month, "...Thursday afternoon. Though, depending on the graphics for the cover, it could be Friday morning."

"Make it Thursday. Golfing Friday out at Pumpkin Ridge." He pauses and pretends to hit a ball through the window and out over the city. "Stay left, stay left. Stay left. Right on the green, three feet shy of the cup. Let's hope I shoot that well Friday, eh, Chief?"

"Yes, sir. Let's hope so."

"And George," he says, eyeing his putt, "I don't need to necessarily see the cover. Something about a book and its cover, you know?"

"Yes, sir, don't judge it by it."

"That's it," he says, practicing his stroke, before stepping to the ball. "You're a smart one, aren't you? That's why we hired you, isn't it?"

"I'd like to think so, sir."

Finally, he putts. It must go in.

"An eagle—now that's what I like." Throwing the invisible putter to me he says, "Finish the back nine for me, George, I gotta take the kids to the pool."

I catch the putter. "Yes, sir."

Leaving, not closing the door behind him, he says, "Nose to the grindstone, Chief. Nose to the grindstone."

Wielding the putter like a club, I whisper behind his back, "You fat-jowled bastard," and take a good swing.

∞

One of the few benefits of being a section manager is there aren't many people I have to answer to. However....

"Morning, Anne, what's the news?"

Anne looks up and has a very...I don't know what kind of look on her face. It's one I've not seen before. I guess the closest I can come is pensive.

"Doll Face, why so—" I notice my office door is wide open, "—pensive?"

"You have a *visitor*." The way she says "visitor" makes me think of an alien with an anal probe device. I look at my watch; sure I'm late, but it's far too early for aliens, isn't it?

"Who?"

She whispers, "Naismith."

That bastard again? I give a faux smile and nod. Okay, let's go play nicey-nice with Mister Jovial Jowls.

"Mr. Naismith, once again a pleasure to...see you." However, I don't see Mr. Naismith. "Uh, Anne?"

Then I notice a pair of glistening black shoes sticking out from behind my desk. I take a few tentative steps.

Mr. Naismith is flat on his back. Shades of blue and red undulate over his strained face. A heavy, gurgling wheeze rasps, bubbles, out of his mouth. Scattered around him, outlining him, are miscellaneous layout pages. A few inches from his left hand rests the photo of the dead man found in the Eurovan.

I rush to Mr. Naismith's wheezing side, loosen his tie and shirt around his fat neck. I yell, "Anne! Anne, dial nine-one-one!"

"What?" she asks, confused by the command and the desperation in my voice. There's a chaotic clatter as she scrambles from behind her desk.

"Call nine-one-one!!"

Anne hurries in, far enough to see me at Mr. Naismith's side. Immediately she pirouettes and exits.

After a short second spent appreciating Anne's artistic departure, I return my attention to Naismith.

His breathing is weak and shallow. His pulse is, too. However, as I place my hand on his chest, his heart jumps and kicks in a frightening manner. It shakes and quakes like a burlap bag of kittens thrown into a muddy river.

"Hold on, Mr. Naismith. Hold on. I...I'll...." I don't know what, but I'll do something.

I take the photo of the dead man and place it in the desk drawer. Hopefully, there is no correlation between the photo and his condition. Hopefully. Though the way my life is going, that is highly unlikely.

Next I...I stare aimlessly around the room. I search for something to do besides feel this man dying beneath my palm. But I'm unsure as to what that may be.

Anne, thankfully, returns to report: "They should be here in five minutes or so." We look at one another, then at the prone, heavyset, elderly man sprawled on the floor, wheezing. "They say we should continue monitoring his breathing and heartbeat."

"Okay." We stare, back and forth, me to her, me to him, her to me, her to him.

Suddenly, extremely tired, I can feel myself shrinking. Shrinking to a pinpoint. I take my hand from his chest. By now the bag is on the bottom of the river. By now there's a sad, theoretical stillness descending. I lean back against the window. I heave a sigh and pat a spot next to me, which Anne dutifully takes.

"He's going to be okay?" she asks, settling in beside me, averting her eyes from the blues and reds undulating beneath Mr. Naismith's skin.

"Probably." Oddly, I'm relieved and disappointed by such an unsatisfying answer.

Anne and I, unable to do much else, simply stare at the old man. The ensuing silence is extremely awkward. In some vain attempt to cover up Mr. Naismith's wheezing inhalations, I begin telling a story I created for Mirabella when she was six.

Suddenly, during that uneventfully mild summer, Mirabella had become afraid of sleeping alone. Neither Francesca nor I could discern why. She and I had convened about Mirabella's diet, movies, friends, school, exercise, toys, allergies, toothpaste, soap, and shampoo—literally everything. However, nothing stood out. One night everything was fine, we're sleeping relatively content in our bed, then the next night...Mirabella, wide-eyed and frightened, so out of breath she can't explain her fear, has to, unequivocally and desperately, sleep with us for protection.

We never figured out why. We humored her for a week. Then we forced her into her room, but the poor girl cried and whimpered long into the sleepless night. We asked, but she would only shake her head and hug us, burying her tearful face deep into our shoulders. We, of course, inevitably, acquiesced.

After another week of being incessantly kicked by Mirabella's thin legs, something had to change. That's when I began telling her the story. That was when she was able to return to her bed, alone. Eventually the fear and the anxiety wore off. Eventually I no longer had to tell the story. And everything returned to normal. Until that occurred, this is what I told Mirabella, and this is what I tell Anne, and, I guess, Mr. Naismith, too.

"Floating on the bluest waves of the bluest ocean is the greenest island. Above the greenest island, floating on the bluest ocean, are the whitest clouds floating on the bluest sky. Living on the greenest island floating on the bluest ocean beneath the whitest clouds that float on the bluest sky is the most beautiful Unicorn." (The first time I had to explain what a unicorn was to Mirabella. I don't do so with Anne and Mr. Naismith.) "The Unicorn, though, is sad. Regardless of how beautiful, how magical it is, it wants to fly. It can weave gold into stars. It can make trees dance and fish sing, but it cannot fly. One day the Unicorn hears from Howard, the town's friendly ogre—he's just like Shrek, but blue—that there is an enchanted cliff at the far end of the island. All who travel there, once they leap off the cliff, are able to fly. However, to get to the Flying Cliff is a long and dangerous journey. And none, regardless how brave and ninja-like, have ever been able to adventure their way through the trials and dangers to stand at the edge of the Flying Cliff.

"The Unicorn nods sagely at what Howard has said. However, the sky is filled with stars, the trees are tired of dancing, and the fish are tired of singing. The Unicorn decides it will adventure to the Flying Cliff."

∞

Four minutes and twenty-four seconds late, the EMTs, flanked by a few rugged and ready firefighters, arrive and stop on the threshold to my office.

They find Mr. Naismith still heaving, gurgling, and Anne, still intently listening. I, however, find myself on the last stretch of the bottle of scotch hidden behind *El amor en los tiempos del cólera*. It seems at some juncture, probably when the Unicorn had been captured by the despicable Crab Pirates, a drink had been in order. And so I'd woven the story as the scotch slowly slid along its designated path.

The EMTs expertly stabilize Mr. Naismith and bundle him off. Both Anne and I give our account of the tragedy. Mine, of course, is more accurate, more convincing, more entertaining.

Once left alone, I give Anne an abbreviated ending to the story.

Afterward she smiles awkwardly, and says, "I'll just go finish my work." She closes the door, leaves me floundering and feeling foolish—something I'm getting distinctly used to.

Instead of taking a nap on the nonfunctional, neo-retro, overpriced designer couch in the corner, as I'm wont to do perhaps a bit too often, I stagger back to my original position against the window. There I slide like a glacier down a mountainside. Millions of years from now I'll wake at the water's edge, thinking, as I plunge in, "Finally."

After my brief, unsatisfactory nap, I go downstairs to purchase a large burrito from the cart across the street. I eat at the foot of the tumbling fountains across the street from Keller Auditorium. After the beans and rice and salsa, I lazily return to the drudgery awaiting me.

Instead of working, I stare out the window. I decide to take the rest of the day off. Hell, I just saved a man's life; don't I deserve a slight respite?

However, respite is not immediately in sight because Anne knocks and enters. "Mr. Naismith is stabilized and should be fine. But...." Again it seems she leaves a body dangling and swaying.

"But?" I echo, nervous. Then immediately request, "Please define that nervous qualifier." I feign an attempt to make sense of the disorganized mess on my desk.

"But Mr. Naismith would like to speak to you," she says as if announcing the sentence for a guilty man—life without the possibility of parole.

"Did...did he mention about what?" Unfortunately, I sound guilty, but I'm satisfied the sentence isn't lethal injection or the electric chair.

"No. Though he was adamant about speaking to you directly."

"So, he's...he's conscious enough to...to speak?"

"Yes, it seems so."

"I mean, that's great, isn't it?"

"You tell me." There's a hint of a challenge to her voice, in her eyes.

"Wish I could, Doll Face. Wish I could." I'm doing nothing with the papers, except making them more disorganized, if that's possible. She and I know it. I stop, and smile pathetically.

"When you can," she says, "let me know. Otherwise," she shrugs, "I'll be at my desk." Slowly, sadly, she turns and leaves, closing the door firmly behind her.

James, one of the graphic designers working on pages ten through sixteen, is attempting to blow smoke up my ass about why his pages aren't finished. At the far end of the room, I see Anne waving to me. She holds her hand up like a phone to her ear. I nod.

"James?" I shake my head, tired of playing babysitter to a thirty-year-old computer geek more interested in gaming than living, or doing his work.

He stops his litany of excuses.

"Please, just get the pages done," I tell him. He's about to exhale more smoke. I stop him. "Please. Otherwise I will erase every EverQuest character you've ever created. I will find porn photos of you and your girlfriend, assuming you have one, and put them on the Internet. I will attach a message virus to every e-mail you send, that reads, 'I am nothing more than a lifeless hunk of dead flesh consuming gallons of Red Bull, Rockstar, and Cheetos for no reason other than to waste air and energy because I'm too stupid to do anything of consequence.' Now, do I make myself clear?" He nods. "Good. You have two days to finish those pages."

I walk, spurs echoing in my ears, down the dusty, ghost town aisle, past the other cubicle clones, who duck their heads and clatter shutters closed, to where Anne waits.

"What've you got?" I ask, a slight sense of Clint Eastwood lingering.

"It's Naismith." Her eyes show she is frightened at the possibility of being an innocent bystander to a showdown, a gunfight.

"Great, Doll Face. Patch him through." I give a slight nod, a tap of the dust-covered, sweat-stained Stetson and saunter into my office. The door, of its own accord, closes behind me. The phone quickly calls out, like the old, muskrat-faced derelict on the saloon's stairs, "high noon, high noon." I adjust my stance, making sure the sun is to my back. In one quick, clean, lighting-smooth move I snatch it up and immediately slam it down.

Occasionally that's the difference between life and death, knowing when to do the wrong thing.

∞

Returning early from lunch, I discover Dietrich in my chair, leafing through the chaos of proofs on my desk.

"Can I help you?" I ask, attempting to hide my annoyance behind my annoyance.

"Seems I should be asking you that." He stands slowly as I walk over.

"I'll ask again, can I help you?" I yank page seven from between his fat, sausage fingers.

"No," he says, wiping his hands mockingly while making a slight amount of room for me at my chair.

I throw the sheet down. "Then what foul wind blows you in here?"

"Naismith."

"So, you think he's a foul wind?"

Dietrich continues as if I've said nothing, as if I were a ghost. "He asked me to check on things. Asked me to be the rearguard, so to speak."

"It is your forte."

He walks through me, and says, "He wants me to double-check the proofs before the shareholders' brochure goes to press." Dietrich, too stupid even to think about it, continues, "When does it go to press?"

"Friday. Early. As soon as we get the proofs to them."

"Good. I'd like to see everything on my desk no later than Friday morning, first thing—I think you might even call that Thursday night."

It's the same thing Naismith wanted, but Dietrich presents it like it's his idea, like he's the one pulling the strings and calling the proverbial shots. I look at him as if he's a condemned man living on borrowed time.

"Consider it done," I say, almost believing it can actually be accomplished.

"I will." He leaves, and Anne comes in, after an appropriate amount of time passes and my cursing has ceased.

"What'd he want?"

"Permission to pull his head out of his ass." She doesn't reply, just smiles and leaves. I wish I could've done the same. Instead I admit to the faux-wood door, "I, of course, gave it."

∞

Thursday morning I'm not as late as usual, and I read through the proofs religiously. I make a few changes and send them back down to the cubicles. They're returned, corrected, by noon. I reread them, confirming the changes have been made and all is in good order. I initial them and place them in a manila folder. James even gets his pages in by three. I proof them. Surprisingly, they're perfect.

For Dietrich I write,

on a yellow sticky note, which I attach to the front cover of the brochure. I place the proofs of the entire brochure into the folder and ask Anne to take them up to Dietrich.

Very shortly, Anne returns with the manila folder still in her quivering hands.

"So," I say, satisfied, "after four years we finally get it right, eh? I mean, that was quick." Something is tight and pinched in her eyes, around her mouth. "Almost a little too quick, for Herr Dietrich." Are those tears? "What is it, Doll Face?"

"This... this morning...."

"Yes?"

She drops the folder on my desk and says, "Dietrich's dead," as if I already knew, as if it were my fault.

∞

Friday and finally, after nearly two weeks, I'm on time. Anne, to my surprise, says nothing. She seems to be harboring something distinctly against me in regards to Dietrich's death. Rumor is his wife found him hunched over the breakfast table. His cup of coffee is Rorschached across the *New York Times'* crossword puzzle, a gob of cold, leftover filet mignon snarled in his esophagus.

Anne, I think, fears I somehow assisted in Dietrich's demise, despite my stealthy, ninja-like removal of the "Choke On This" sticky note from the proofs. I'd like to mention fate or destiny to her, but it would be hard not to smile slightly and, therefore, I remain silent.

So, it's Friday, and in celebration—of finishing the shareholders' brochure and not of Dietrich's demise—I ask Anne to organize a Halo tournament.

"No," she says, sternly, flatly.

"Anne," I reply, perhaps a bit too defensively, "it's for morale. This isn't about Dietrich."

"It's in poor taste."

"They don't even know." She throws me a quick scowl. I dodge it and continue, "Besides, there's so much tension and frustration pent up in those gray prison cells; if they don't release it one way, it'll be another." We both turn and imagine one of the usually mild-mannered cube clones standing, a pair of black Uzis in his hands, and rattling the office into confetti.

"No."

And it's definitive, because as I'm about to suggest this is a way of remembrance, Anne angrily begins slamming on the keyboard. I don't know what memo or letter she's writing, but I do know I don't want to receive it.

Okay, I need to find another accomplice. Reluctantly I glance toward the dull continent of the cubicles.

"What's the winner get?" James asks.

Staring back down the row, I see Anne leveling her judgmental gaze—still flat, still stern.

I expound an answer, knowing more than likely Anne is probably right: "A bottle of single malt and a gift certificate to Murata or Carafe."

It's not a new Pentium processor, or Hyperlight's Mylar gaming glove, or a case of cheese flavored soda, but he'll do it.

As James begins accepting names and organizing brackets, I shuffle meekly past Anne. I go down and around the corner to purchase a bottle of scotch—no, two—from the liquor store.

On my return, and much to my chagrin, I find myself assigned to do battle against a little blonde pit bull of a second-year copywriter named Carin.

Carin, with a bit more glee than I think necessary, quickly hands me my hat. I, therefore, take an early lunch.

Upon my return, I give Anne and her glare the rest of the day off. We don't need her negative energy spoiling the atmosphere of camaraderie derived from killing one another electronically.

She doesn't say anything, simply stops typing, gets up, and leaves—the perfect petulant exit.

The rest of the afternoon I spend sipping single malt and ignoring the incessant ringing of the phone. I also diligently ignore the urge to open the folder containing the shareholders' brochure. There are bound to be gross and negligent errors we've inexplicably missed, and finding them now won't help. It's a miracle it even looks like a brochure, let alone a brochure in the English language. And, honestly, I'm content with that.

While I wait for the messenger to pick up the proofs, the office empty and sullen, I order a cord of cherry wood. The wood man mentions they're having a spring sale. He doesn't give the specifics of the sale, and I don't ask. They'll deliver my cord on Sunday.

As if on cue, the phone rings as I hang up, and the messenger, with a buzz cut and wearing orange riding glasses, walks through the door.

Once again I ignore the phone, and I hand him the folder.

Professionally, with one bike-gloved hand, he assesses its weight. He squints, curious, at the address, and asks, "Is this right?"

The only lights in the place are from my office, and James's desk light. The little bastard is sure to be playing on the Internet, practicing for the next time he gets to steal a bottle of scotch and a gift certificate.

"Yeah," I say, a sense of melancholy suddenly stalking me. What a long, fucked-up week.

"This is just downstairs, isn't it?" the messenger asks.

I look at the address as if I don't know exactly where it's going. As if I don't know the owner, the manager, the press person of AlphaGraphics on the ground floor.

"Yep, sure is." He looks at me, still confused. "Don't ask me," I say. "It's company policy. Something about personal liability. Never know what's liable to happen between here and there."

"You're telling me." He smiles and tucks the package into his bag. There's a brief moment of expectation, which is followed by nothing. He asks, "That's it?"

"Yep, sure is. Probably want to ask for Marcus."

"Consider it done. I'll catch ya later."

"Okay." And that's it. There's nothing more to do. Nothing but turn the lights out and flee before that melancholy pulls the trigger. "James? James, make sure you lock up after yourself. Okay?" He doesn't reply. He's sure to have his headphones on. Sure to be pulverizing demonic aliens and saving the world.

Envious, I close the doors and trudge to the elevator. I have to push the button three times before the down arrow is illuminated. This innocuous sign triggers the realization the week is finally—thank the heavens and hells—fucking over. And, surprisingly, after this week I'm actually looking forward to the next. I mean, it can only get better, right?

I notice my reflection in the elevator doors staring at me quizzically. I think I smile in reply, though I can't see it in my reflection. I want to mention to myself, as an explanation for my reflection not reflecting the smile, how long and tiring the week has been. I need to explain it to myself, not out of choice, but out of necessity, as a weak attempt to learn something about mistakes, lest I make them again and again and again.

To my reflection, in sincere tones, I whisper about arriving late every day, except today, Friday, April 2. How Margarita finally learned fluent English, though it was with the middle finger of her right hand. Then there was Mrs. Sandquist, reluctantly seduced by my sincere tears to admit nothing that helped in the quest to find Francesca and Mirabella. And also the altercation with Steve, the cab company dispatcher. Not to mention his incessant calling. I don't remember exactly what that was about, though I think it had something to do with his girlfriend, his insecurity, and my anxiety. Jessica and Leslie, for some twisted reason, think I killed someone. Mr. Naismith's little episode in the middle of my office. And me, or you, or us, hoping it wasn't due to the photo of the dead man found in the Eurovan. Then there's Dietrich's choking and dying on a piece of cold, leftover steak he was having for breakfast. Not to mention Detective Nugent believes I may have been responsible for something nefarious. What exactly, he won't say. And to top it off, there's Francesca and Mirabella and Zeus running away. Oh, yeah, and Tyler-kitty has also disappeared.

I don't know what else to say. My reflection, though, seems unconvinced. Should I mention ████? Maybe the price of gasoline? June's friend's curious observation about me and my soon to be recycled soul? Or? Or maybe I shouldn't say anything at all. Just stare at it until one of us begins to understand the other?

Finally the elevator arrives and opens. My reflection parts in two, quickly disappears. Without ceremony, I step inside the mouth of the beast and descend toward tomorrow.

∞

The weekend is like nothing I've ever known. Like nothing I've ever read, or seen, or dreamed. It was something completely unique. Completely.

It was quiet. It was peaceful. It was perfect.

I drank bottles of wine reserved for years to come. It was almost like living the future.

I ate. I slept. I listened to the rain. I made a fire and kept a log always on. The phone rang. I didn't answer. The phone rang. I unplugged the phone. Someone knocked on the door. I didn't answer. They left. I pulled all the blinds in the house shut. Someone knocked, rang the doorbell. I didn't answer. Someone left. I disconnected the doorbell.

I slept. I ate. I listened to the rain. I drank bottles of wine reserved for years to come. It was almost like living the future over again.

It was quiet. It was peaceful. It was perfect.

I watched the fire burn and burn and burn.

Unfortunately, though, it couldn't stop time. Monday, as expected, eventually arrived.

Monday:

April 5, 2004

Waking from a long, dreamless slumber that's been more like hibernation than sleep, I find myself in remarkably good spirits, with an abundance of unexplained energy and optimism. Therefore, the morning's chores (rising, showering, shaving, eating, commuting) are less painful drudgery and more pleasurable monotony, which unexpectedly causes me to find myself early to work and I have over half-an-hour to spare. It also helped that traffic was much lighter than usual, and I simply cruised along.

After I park, I pull the yellow sticky notes off the steering wheel and review the list of items I created over my energized and optimistic breakfast of instant apple-and-cinnamon-flavored oatmeal.

On today's agenda: Call people (this includes ▬▬▬, Jessica, Leslie, Detective Nugent, Margarita, Mr. Naismith, Mrs. Sandquist, and whomever else I've neglected while in my fugue-like funk). Not only do I plan to call them, I plan to be completely and absolutely honest, straightforward, and forthright. I will apologize and explain. I will explain and apologize. Return e-mails (my God, how they pile up!). Confirm monthly schedule with Anne. Order flowers for Naismith and Dietrich (if Anne hasn't already). Clean and organize office. Shred photo of dead guy. Check printed brochure. Mow lawn. Call a house cleaning service. Grocery shop. Work out during lunch. Go to park and talk with June. And finally, I will go to sleep.

Sure, the list sounds daunting, but I feel as if today is the day to get things done. I'm feeling exceedingly good about everything. Perhaps it's getting a good night's sleep and having breakfast?

I can't explain why I'm infused with all this optimism, but I'm going to attempt to use it while I can. And it's this spring optimism which explains why I believe Zeus will show up. As will Tyler. This optimism caused me, this morning, to leave the doors and windows wide open and food on the porch. Thieves can take what they want, but as long as Zeus and Tyler return, I don't care.

I also—another delusion of the optimism—have a suspicion I'll receive news about Francesca and Mirabella. It's a strange hunch, an unreachable itch in the middle of my brain. I suspect things will return to me in the reverse order they left—Zeus, Tyler, then Mirabella and Francesca.

Heading toward the elevators, I recognize I'm too wound up for the office. I decide there's time to saunter to Starbucks, get a latte, and linger in the spring morning air.

∞

Having survived the line behind the other addicts, I order and pay for my grande skinny latte. Waiting for the latte's delivery from Pert Barista Jamie, I idly play with two packets of raw sugar and a stir stick.

Near one of the front windows, two students, I assume from Portland State, have avalanched a slew of textbooks across their table. From the diagrams and schematics I hazard a guess they're physics or mechanical engineering texts, and the students, of course, are nerds.

One, wearing dark glasses and a black sweater, is vacantly doodling with a mechanical pencil in some spilled NutraSweet and saying, "You're not talking about Douglas Adams's *The Hitchhiker's Guide to the Galaxy*, are you?"

The other student, wearing black-rimmed glasses and a gray sweater, meekly replies, "Yes, actually, I am."

"That the meaning of life is forty-two?" Black Sweater asks, decidedly skeptical.

I've never read the book—heard about it, but never read it. Quickly, juggling the stir stick and sugar, I scribble,

Adams,
Hitchhiker's
Guide

on a yellow sticky note.

"No," says Gray Sweater, "that's actually the answer." The answer to life? The answer is forty-two?

Black Sweater counters with a classic rebuttal. "Whatever."

Gray Sweater presses on. "There is the *probability* that Adams is right." Probability is said as if Gray Sweater had placed her hand on a sword's hilt.

Black Sweater stops playing with the NutraSweet. Some hint of curiosity and insight sparkles in his eyes. Apprehension, however, begins to surge into mine.

A few more jittery addicts escape with their fix, and I move a few steps closer to eavesdrop more easily.

"Exactly," replies Gray Sweater, excited. "If there's the probability the universe started from nothing, or there's enough dark matter for it to collapse back upon itself, there's the probability—"

"Three monkeys at a typewriter," Black Sweater chimes in.

"Or a coin tossed eighty-six times."

"Or...." Black Sweater's voice drops a few hundred degrees, freezes, stops.

Gray Sweater plows on. "Or an English author flippantly states that forty-two is," Black Sweater joins in, and they finish together, "the answer."

In the following reverential silence my skin blooms goosebumps. It takes a moment, but finally my brain begins to recognize what my skin instantly knew—I'm forty-two.

"And what about that book, *Eight*?"

"What book?"

"*The Eight*. It's by, oh, I don't remember...Katherine Neville."

"Hey," Black Sweater says, "isn't Hebrew a numeric language?"

"That's kind of my point."

Mischievously, Black Sweater smiles. "How many permutations could there be?" Quickly they duck their heads and begin scribbling furiously in their notebooks.

I take another sticky note and write,

Hebrew (?)
numeric (?)
word (s)
for / equate
forty-two?

Barista Jamie's voice calls out pertly, "Grande skinny latte. Grande skinny latte."

It's possible a man's parents were born in 1942, isn't it? And his grandparents, both sets, were born in 1924? And it's also possible both his grandfathers were killed in the Ardennes during the summer of 1944. And both his grandmothers died at the venerable age of seventy-six. Though perhaps not necessarily probable, it's definitely not fate, right?

It must also be possible the man could be born in 1962, stand six feet two inches, and weigh two hundred and four pounds.

Barista Jamie's tone quickly ascends to annoyance. "Grande skinny latte. Grande skinny latte."

But what's the probability the man's address is 4242 NE Sycamore? Slim? None?

Barista Jamie kamikaze dives into derisive disgust: "Grande skinny latte! Grande skinny latte!" Banzai! Banzai!

What's the probability his birthday is February eleventh? I do a slow, but precise count on my fingers. February eleventh is the forty-second day of the year! What's the probability he turned forty-two on the forty-second day of the year?! My forty-second birthday was February 11, 2004. Again my fingers find themselves counting themselves, calculating Francesca and Mirabella's disappearance. A cold fear causes my fingers to stop. Of course it's possible, but how probable is it the family of the man who turned forty-two on the forty-second day of the year, February eleventh, disappears forty-two days later?

That's impossible, isn't it?

No, not if forty-two is the answer.

The two students remain locked in furious calculations; I can almost see the thin trails of smoke rising from the pencils' lead.

Not if forty-two is the answer.

And it must be, because that man is receiving Barista Jamie's mega-manic-stare-of-decapitation, which penetrates his preoccupation like a laser.

"Sorry," I say, waving an apologetic and defensively inadequate hand, "that's me. That's me."

Her smile is a scalpel as she sternly places the cup on the counter, whips her back to me, and stomps off. Talk about humiliation. I pretend to ignore the cuts and blood as I step to the counter.

Picking up the latte, I glance at the clock above the steaming espresso machine. It reads 8:42. Eight? And forty-two? Curious.

Again my fingers begin compulsively dancing, calculating and computing: four times two is eight. My wife is thirty-five. My daughter is eight. Forty-two: four times two is eight. Thirty-five: three plus five is eight. Eight is eight. I was born in 1962. Nine minus one is eight. Six plus two is eight. One plus nine plus six plus two is eighteen. In high school I played football, wide-receiver, ran back punts and kickoffs. My number? Yeah, that's right—eight. I graduated high school in '81. I graduated with a BA in English in '84. I received my Master's in Business Administration in '88.

My name—George Thomas Olson. George (six letters) Thomas (six letters) Olson (five letters). Thus, six plus six plus five equals seventeen. So, one plus seven equals eight.

If I leave now I should be able to make it to Powell's and back in time to circumvent Anne's derisive glare. And, if not, is it really that important to be on time? Do I care what my secretary thinks? Besides, Naismith is probably still out. And, if not, I'll claim I was at AlphaGraphics discussing fonts, paper brightness and weight—everything that makes life meaningful and worthwhile.

However, Powell's doesn't open until nine. Maybe I'll hoof it down during lunch.

Wait. Something's wrong. Slowly I look down at my watch. It inexplicably reads 7:42. I look back at the clock on the wall.

Back to my watch. I do this a couple of times, watch, clock, watch, clock, hoping somehow my confusion will dissipate. It doesn't.

Barista Jamie calls out gleefully, "Triple Americano. Triple Americano."

"Excuse me," I begin to ask, but she's finished with me. I'm scalded milk. She turns and feigns cleaning the steamer nozzle.

I turn to Triple Americano, a dark, arty, guy with a goatee, and ask, "Is that clock right?"

"Ah, time," he sighs, pulling an old pocket watch on a shiny silver chain from his leather coat. "Yes. It's nearly nine."

He notices my sad confusion and says, apologetically, "Daylight savings," shrugs, and exits with his triple Americano.

Hurriedly my latte and I follow, leaving the nerds to their calculations.

The quick march back toward work is fraught with distraction and dismay. I can't believe I didn't set my watch forward. Hence my previous (delusional) optimism founded on the misguided belief I was early and not late.

Quickening my pace, I jaywalk wherever and whenever possible.

All the chaos with Francesca and Mirabella and Zeus and Tyler and the car and the accusations and punching Steve and my swollen hand and the dead body and ███ is stalking me and Mr. Naismith's heart attack and Deitrich's death and everything had me too preoccupied to even notice the simplest thing—altering time.

A car horn and subsequent blur brings me to a swift halt. As I wait for a gap in the traffic, I notice, a few blocks away, the building I work in—the Black Box—looming above.

I speedwalk across the street, mesmerized by the building's glossy contours. I'm reminded of the last scene in *Fight Club*, when the buildings explode into bright shards. However, instead of glass the Black Box breaks, shatters, disintegrates into a great flock of ravens, a murder of crows. I want to write on a yellow sticky note, "Difference between crow/raven—a murder of crows, a *what* of ravens?" But I don't have the time as the crows, the ravens, descend upon me and begin beating about my ears and mind. Black Box. **Black Box.** Eight letters. **Eight letters.** Black Box. **Black Box.** Eight letters. **Eight letters.** Black Box. **Black Box.**

Now two blocks from the soaring, dark building, my pace slows to a crawl. The dark wings beat my mind again toward the answer: forty-two. I'm forty-two. Four times two is eight. Black Box, eight letters. The wings attempt to beat more incidents, numbers, and facts from my memory, from my past. However, I fight back and flail at the shiny beaks.

Desperate, I stop and wait for the traffic light to change. In the interim I attempt to remain calm and appear normal. One. Two. Three. Breathe in. Breathe out. One. Two. Three.

Focusing on keeping my hands at my sides and ignoring the cawing and screeching of the birds, I miss the light twice before my futility is complete and absolute. The crows peck and pull the numbers, the incidents, from me, begin devouring them like bodies on a battlefield. One. Two. Three. Breathe in. Breathe out. One. Two. Three.

My mind swirls and spins. Smoke. Musket fire. Carnage. The injured scream and moan. There are so many dead and scattered. Overwhelmed, I cast my eyes to the next dark wave, which is sure to overrun me. Musket balls rip and shred the air and I notice an omen, a blinking, warning sign—"**don't walk**, don't walk, **don't walk**." (Don't walk, eight letters.) Do I need to gaze deeper into the mystery, beyond the churned-up, body-strewn trenches? Do I?

If this is significant, if I can trust the omens, I can close my eyes. I can step off the curb. I can heed the sign and run—not walk—across the scattered bodies. I can run through traffic, through misunderstanding, through dark claws and beaks, through the shrill cries of the dying to the other side.

My toe stubs on the curb, and I inelegantly stumble to my knees. My eyes slam open to a sign that states the obvious, but unheeded: "**Walk**. Walk. **Walk**." I stand and brush my knees off, discovering, not cannons on the hill, but my black Cole Haan shoes. (Cole Haan, eight letters.) Four sets of eyelets on each shoe. Two shoes. (Four, two. Forty-two. Four times two equals eight.)

In the silence, the marauding birds having suddenly disappeared, and someone is shouting something. They're shouting something about escaping, about luck, about being an "ignorant fuck-stick!"

Yes, I agree, ignorant is no way to exist, but, it has been said, ignorance is also bliss. And that's exactly what I need—bliss. I don't need to delve into the inexplicable. I don't need to ponder why Francesca left forty-two and not forty-one or forty-three days after my birthday. Nor do I need to speculate about my birth date or address or anything. I simply need to wrap the comforting fog of ignorance around me, exactly as I've been so successfully doing.

A half-block away, where the Black Box looms, a small gray mouth yawns, welcoming. The esophagus leads to parking, where the incompetent valets occasionally reside. It also leads to salvation, to the elevators, which will whisk me to my office and the awaiting bottle of single malted bliss.

Seconds later I'm padding into the cement bowels of the building. And there are the golden, glistening doors of the elevators. A quick glance confirms my escape vehicle remains, awaiting me.

And suddenly, as my mind stumbles on a crumb of thought, my pace slows. Instead of a beeline for the elevators I find myself, curious, deviating toward my car. My mind, small child that it is, inexplicably follows the trail. My feet, my body, invariably do too.

Soon I'm standing in front of the Mustang's dull black body and the infamous parking spot.

I attempt to whisper my mantra—**ignorance**-ignorance, **bliss**-bliss-**bliss**—loud enough that my eyes will heed my head's warning. However, my eyes are not my ears and they see what I feared.

A cold shiver runs up and down, up and down my spine. I jab my fingers in my eyes and rub, vigorously attempting to alter them enough that they won't see what they see—the Mustang's license plate: ATE 042.

The cold shiver increases its pace, begins sprinting.

Was that why the old man I purchased it from had that devilish grin? Why this car, and not the three others I looked at? Why-why-why?

Bliss, oh, bliss, where art thou?

As the cold shiver continues doing laps on my spine, I notice the faded black numbers of the parking space. The car casts a milky shadow and it takes a moment to recognize them. But, eventually, I—**ignorance**-ignorance, **bliss**-bliss-**bliss**—see them, see them all too clearly—sixty-seven. ($6 \times 7 = 42$. $4 \times 2 = 8$.)

The shiver suddenly stops, shudders, and dies, leaving me in a cold state of unacceptable dichotomy: calm agitation.

Slowly, very slowly, I inch my way to the bank of elevators. I do not turn my back to the car, or the open maw of the parking garage.

The blind beggar of my hand searches for the button, finds it, and gladly, diligently, presses it over and over and over.

∞

Stepping into the elevator, I press the floor number—seventeen, (one plus seven equals eight). My index finger freezes to the smoky plastic. It takes four floors before I can pull it off the illuminated number.

∞

In the gap between the elevator and the office's shimmering glass door, I attempt to gather and arrange myself.

Wiping cold sweat from my brow, taking a few slow, level breaths, I decide to pick something inconsequential and nip the impending breakdown in the bud.

"Anne?"

She looks up, smiling, not mentioning my tardiness, but simply implying it with an impish grin. "Morning, boss."

But, what should I ask her? What's your favorite book? John Dos Passos's *The 42nd Parallel*. No. What's your favorite band? Level 42. No. What's your favorite color?

"Boss?"

"Your last name? What's your last name?" I have to remind myself not to look at my shoes, not to count the pens in her penholder, not to count the buttons on my shirt.

"Uh, why?" She's sure there's some strange subterfuge brewing.

"Please, for my sake," I insist, eyes askew, down toward the cubicles, "answer the question."

"You don't know it?"

"Look, Anne, maybe I did, at one point, but it's since slipped my mind. It, like most everything, has been buried beneath the flotsam and jetsam of life." I sigh, wipe my forehead dry. Anne just stares at me, as if I were someone else. "Please, what's your last name?"

"Mo," she answers.

"Mow? Like to mow the lawn?"

"No, like mo' better, mo' money."

"Mo? M-o? Two letters?"

"Yeah." She discerns a specific fear and panic behind my eyes, in my voice, and explains, "My grandfather shortened it. Or, as the story goes, had it shortened for him, on his way over from the 'Old Country,' Italy. It was Monachésimo, or something like that. He never actually told us. It was at the height of the Three Stooges' film career. Which is neither here nor there, but my grandfather happened to have curly hair and looked like Larry. So the deck hands, mostly Americans, said he was all three cannolied into one." I smile and nod appreciatively, though I wonder why no one seems to be occupying the gray cubicle catacombs, and why James's light is still the only one on.

Anne, heedless, continues on. "When the Ellis Island authorities asked my grandfather what his last name was, someone shouted 'Mo!' Everyone laughed. He thought it was a good way to begin a new life in a new country—everyone laughing. So, here I am—Little Miss Mo." I try to ignore what Anne Mo is telling me, and the improbable significance.

I think of my own name—my initials really—GTO. My father, so it's related, had a thing for muscle cars. And at some juncture, he and my mother ended up in the backseat of one. Hence me—George Thomas Olson, GTO. I'd hate to think, particularly at this juncture in time, what he would've done if he had a different last name, or a Vega, Gremlin, or Pinto.

"Why?" Anne asks, still unsure and unconvinced of my motivation. I suppose it shouldn't matter that there are four Bic pens and two pencils in the penholder, right?

"No...no reason." She's still not convinced, nor am I. There's still another itching question. "You've a middle name, don't you?" Please, please, please.

She, unfortunately, shakes her head. "My parents had a hard enough time agreeing on my first name. They decided for their collective sanity, and the sake of the marriage, to skip an attempt at a middle name." Great, just fucking great. Because that means: Anne, four letters, Mo, two letters—forty-two.

I again ponder my name, George Thomas Olson. I always thought it was like eating dry wheat toast with unseasoned oatmeal. Sure my initials were a car, and sounded kind of cool, but there was something else. GTO—in the alphabet, G is the seventh letter of the alphabet, T is the twentieth, and O is the fifteenth. Seven plus twenty plus fifteen equals forty-two!

George—six letters, Thomas—six letters, Olson—five letters. Six plus six plus five equals seventeen. One plus seven equals eight!

"Why, boss, what's up?" Anne's questioning gaze sends shivers down my spine to my feet, where they remain, frozen.

On the night of my conception, there's no way my parents were remotely thinking about the significance of forty-two, or eight, or anything for that matter. What I've heard is Dad got Mom, not to mention himself, drunk on whiskey and coke while at a drive-in.

Dad declares, "It was *The Guns of Navarone*, or at least it sure seemed like it!" Chuckle, chuckle. Ha-ha. That's Dad for ya.

However, Mom claims, "It was *The Parent Trap* with Hayley Mills. That's why you don't like blondes, or twins, dear." I'd like to laugh like I did at Dad's comment, but I can't, because sadly, it's true.

So, they weren't thinking, per se, while in the backseat of the GTO. I write,

> What does GTO stand for anyway? Sure, it's a car...

on a sticky note. Anne watches bemused. How is it GTO, George Thomas Olson, fits so, so nice and snug into the forty-two/eight scenario? It can't be chance, or luck, can it? And yet it almost has to be. Perhaps something more sinister? Something disguised as fate or destiny?

"Boss?" I drag my gaze out of the roiling storm clouds of the ceiling. Mirrored in Anne's dark eyes, I see the first few flakes begin to fall.

"Uh, it's nothing, Anne." I lie. "Dorothy, from personnel," I say—it's not a few flakes, but a few thousand—"she called and wanted to verify something." Mechanically, I rub my arms through my suit jacket, curl my hands, and blow into them. "Thanks," I finish, tugging my collar up around my chin.

"Sure. Anytime," she replies, returning to typing up some memo, not noticing how the temperature, and the barometer, steadily falls.

Snow drifts and swirls from the ceiling. Immediately, a blizzard blows in. Deep drifts collect in the corners. I lumber, knee-deep, into my office.

Outside there's a perfect spring day. Clear blue sky. Birds flying. Trees budding. However, my office is frozen, cold. Antarctic.

I'm shivering. I continue rubbing my arms through my jacket in an attempt to dispel the goose bumps, but to no avail. I'd have more luck starting a fire with a flounder.

Slowly turning in the center of the room, I notice...the nonfunctional, neo-retro designer couch has four seat cushions and two back cushions (forty-two). Against one wall there are four bookshelves and two filing cabinets (forty-two). Each filing cabinet has four drawers: two times four equals eight.

Okay, I have to stop this. This will make me crazy. Crazy, crazy, I tell you.

I think maybe I need what I knew I needed earlier—a drink. I gaze expectantly at *Amor en los tiempos de cólera*. Its author, of course, is Gabriel Garcia Marquez. Gabriel (seven letters) Garcia (six letters) Marquez (seven letters). Seven times six equals forty-two. Six times seven equals forty-two. Forty-two, the answer to life, either way.

Okay, I have to stop this. This will make me crazy. Crazy, crazy I tell you—I tell me—I tell the budding spring world outside from the midst of a three-foot-high, swirling snowdrift—crazy.

Again I blow on my hands. Steam, like incense smoke, curls up through my fingers. They remain numb, and I thrust them into my pockets. I find strange, sticky shapes. Thin forms bend and crunch beneath my grip. Nervous at my discovery, I pull my fists out. Each is filled with bright, yellow sticky notes—little, laughing mouths testifying to my ignorance.

Clutching the collected sticky notes, I wade to my desk and methodically answer them, one by one. The Internet is such a glorious thing.

Claimer? No, but claim is derived from the Middle English/Middle French word, clamer. Happy as a clam? The complete phrase "happy as a clam at high tide" is strictly an American phrase, and was first referenced in print in the early 1800s.

Japanese paper-folding? Origami. Difference between crack and crank? Crack is cocaine. Crank is methamphetamine. I'll have to wait to ask June why she named her dog Tuesday. How did ████ and I get together? That, too, will have to wait. As will what hotel and room in Paris Francesca and I stayed in. The difference between crows and ravens? Ravens happen to be one-third larger than crows. And yes, a flock of crows is called a murder, supposedly for holding judgment on an accused and then killing him if found guilty. Incredibly, and this is disturbingly suspicious, there are forty-two different species worldwide.

This seems to be the perfect omen to begin my quest for the larger answers. These little ones are pretty much answered.

Therefore, I begin compiling a series of lists. There are basically three. One is a list of everything that is predetermined. Factors out of my control: i.e., both parents being born in 1942, my birthday (2/11/62), my height (six-feet-two, six plus two equals eight), things like that. The second list is of everything incidental that is predetermined. These are like my parking spot (sixty-seven), or the address on the house (4242), or the license plates on our cars (ATE 042 and Francesca's ODB 1205). The third and last list is subconscious inclinations/dispositions and curious coincidences: there's my football number in high school (eight), there's both Francesca and Mirabella's names having nine letters, there's Zeus, Tyler, George (four, five, six).

It takes a few hours, but I believe I've squeezed a good majority of the information out of the twisted crevices of my mind. Tonight I'll go through the boxes of photos and watch all the home videos to glean more numbers, more hints and clues.

From the lists I'll extract numbers from dates, addresses, and telephone numbers. These numbers I'll begin to attempt to place into meaningful sequences. Hopefully, some pattern will be discernable.

I group the information I have in a sequential manner, which seems the most logical. Therefore I begin with grandparents' birthdays, my addresses growing up, and continue all the way through working here on the seventeenth floor with parking space sixty-seven. Nothing seems to float up and out of the numbers. I try it based on groups and headings. Birth dates. Addresses. Names. License plates. Height. Weight. Shoe size. Anything I can think of. Because anything, even the smallest clue, is liable to affect the outcome. It is monotonous work, but I know something will eventually emerge. Something will lead to a certain clue, which then can be followed to a path that will wend its gradual way to understanding, insight, and my missing family. Why? Because forty-two is the answer.

∞

Eventually I'm overwhelmed with numbers and calculations. I realize I've worked through lunch and go downstairs to get a bite at Carafe, a little French bistro on the ground floor.

I'm finishing my croque-monsieur et pommes frites when two elderly gentlemen and a woman enter. One gentleman elegantly explains to the server his name is Cecil Chamberlain and the other gentleman is, curiously enough, also named Cecil Chamberlain. I stop mid-bite and stare. The woman, the first Cecil explains, is the other Cecil's wife, Kay. I put the sandwich down. With numbers spinning through my mind I recognize Kay—K—happens to be the eleventh letter in the alphabet. Kay sits between the two Cecil Chamberlains. As they ponder the menu, I recall C is a Roman numeral. Quickly I take out a sticky note and write,

What is C
in Roman
numerals?

On another I write,

On another,

Vitamin C—
significance?

"Too much. Too fast. It's got to slow down. I'll miss something. I'll—" I glance up. The Cecils and the single Kay are staring at me. Okay, I should be using my internal voice.

I say, "Long day. Sorry."

The first Cecil replies, "That's because you're young." Kay and the other Cecil chuckle and they return to the menus. I, on the other hand, slap a twenty on the table and exit before I lose.. something.

∞

Once back at my office, my first priority, after Anne reinforces her ignorance of everything pre-dating Billy Joel, is to answer the yellow sticky notes. Quickly, via the Internet, of course, I discover C is the number one hundred in Roman numerals. And K, besides being the eleventh letter in the alphabet, is the physics abbreviation and designation for the temperature scale established by Lord Kelvin. Zero degrees Kelvin, the temperature and not the Lord (though who's to say as he's deceased) is equal to -273.15° Celsius or -459.67° Fahrenheit.

I write the numbers down, try to place them in some coherent order, and instantly the mathematics overwhelms me. Fucking numbers! **Fuck!**

Frustrated, I sweep everything off my desk. The miscellaneous shrapnel cascades from the desk all the way to the far corner where Marcus from AlphaGraphics placed the two boxes of shareholders' brochures.

Immediately I'm on my knees picking everything up and returning the office to a more dignified state. If I'm going to extract the clues from this mess, I have to be calm, organized, and disciplined.

I tell Anne to hold all my calls. If I can be left alone, if I can concentrate long enough, hard enough, I know the underlying meaning—answer—will make itself known. I will find it, I will.

Slowly, methodically, I begin again.

Somewhere in the interminable calculations I find myself simplifying things down to ones and zeros. The permutations of six ones and eight zeros fills a page before I realize it's binary code! Binary code! I pound the nub of the pen, attempting to figure it out. Black ink begins to drip onto the paper. I throw out the pen and get a pencil. Finally, two broken pencils later, I settle on two to the sixth power. Which, I think, if my math is correct, which I'm sure it isn't, would be sixty-four different sequences.

I begin writing out each sequence on a separate piece of paper, but quickly decide to visit a programmer tomorrow. Aren't they paid to do the leg work? I wonder what it translates to? I can't wait to see what the calculations reveal. See? C? What if I alter C's translation to "see"? Or "sea"? Or even "sí"?

I snatch another sheet of paper and begin.

Quickly the pages fill. Every few minutes I have to rub and shake the blood back into my hand in an attempt to keep it from cramping. The fact it's still slightly stiff and swollen from the collision with Steve's face doesn't help either. My work, though, gradually progresses. It seems to be growing, maturing toward something truly significant and insightful.

The multitude of papers aligned in strict, organized rows over my desk, on the floor, and along the windows, are the nightmarish roadmap to some crazed mathematician's mind. However, regardless of how chaotic it may seem, I know them to be stones and breadcrumbs left along a path that ultimately will lead to a sweet and singular destination—my family.

Excitement wells inside me. Finally, it seems as if the clues and answers are being uncovered, revealed. This, I know, is the beginning to finding Francesca, and Mirabella, and Zeus, and Tyler, and...and, the most elusive one of all, myself.

I gaze and stare, mesmerized by the possibility of the implied discovery. Somewhere in this curious scripture is the first clue to beginning the journey to the next clue, which will lead to the next step, on and on until I'm lead to my family. I know it's only a matter of time before all is back as it was. Us, in our little home, happy.

Somewhere hidden in the numbers and phrases, the secret, forty-two, hides. I look. I ponder. I stare and gaze. Occasionally

I hold a single page up for ten, fifteen minutes, attempting to discover the truth, the hint. I then set it down and move on. First comes familiarity and recognition of a new language, then understanding and insight. It is only a matter of time before I am fluent in this new tongue.

I do this (it could be hours or days) until my phone rings. It's the inner office ring from Anne. Obviously, when I told her to hold my calls, I lacked conviction; I wasn't emphatic enough.

"Anne, I told you, no calls. This is serious. Really. If you want," I tell her, as inspiration hits me, "leave early, leave now. Put up a 'No Vacancy' sign and go enjoy yourself. Really. I mean it. I can't be bothered."

She peeps up, "Boss?"

"What?" Something in her tone says stop selling and listen.

"It's the fire department. They—"

I don't have time for her long-winded explanations, My grandfather blah-blah-blah-blah-blah. I interrupt her.

"Anne, I don't hear any alarms." Nonetheless, I find myself frantically scrambling about, picking up the strewn papers, while simultaneously looking for something to put them in. Anything to keep them away from the flames and secure in my hands. I'll not lose this work, these hints and clues.

"No. No," she says. "It's not the building. They're on the phone."

"Fine. Fine. Fine." I don't have time to bicker with her over minutiae. "Well, put them on. And, Anne, seriously, 'No Vacancy.' Leave early. Leave now." Hopefully that sounded less like a warning and more like a friendly command.

She says, "Okay." But it's not "okay." It's "you'll be sorry, because you're going to be eating your own shit soon enough." I'm unsure how she might know, but that's the subtext to her "okay." She, grudgingly, dutifully puts the caller through.

"Is this Mr. George Olson?" He sounds middle-aged and fatherly, sincere yet guarded, like he's having a conversation with his daughter's new boyfriend.

"It is. And I'd be happy to purchase tickets for the ball. Say two pair? But just call back tomorrow and talk with my secretary. Okay? She'll be happy to take care of all the details."

"Uh, that's very generous, but it's actually about—"

"Okay, okay, for the silent auction, the vaudeville show, the cakewalk, the fun run, or whatever. Christ, I'm signed up and onboard, but call back tomorrow. Please."

Before I can hang up, he says, "No, Mr. Olson, it's about your home." Of course! This is about Francesca, Mirabella, Zeus, and Tyler. Tyler was probably in the neighbor's tree. Zeus, having followed the thick, succulent scent of cooking chili, wandered in and fell asleep on the station's soiled couch. While Francesca and Mirabella? Well, they'd just stopped by to make paella and tiramisu as a midnight snack.

"You found them?!" I shout before he finishes his sentence, which ends in, "it's on fire." Once again, I feel as if I'm being hit in the face with a shovel. Though it's still unpleasant, I'm getting use to it.

"Fire? What fire?"

"Sorry, Mr. Olson, but them? Who?"

"Francesca, Mirabella, Zeus, and Tyler!" Why am I surrounded by idiots?!

Anne knocks, and peeks around my door.

"I'm sorry," the fireman is stuttering, "but...who...who are they?"

Holding a hand over the phone's mouthpiece, I say, "Anne, I told you—day off. 'No Vacancy.' Leave early. Leave now. Really." And I too shoo her out with an insistent waving of my hand.

She has her own agenda, however, and declares loudly, "Visitors." The way her face is scrunched up she might as well have said vampire-flesh-eating stormtroopers.

"They're my family," I quickly reply into the phone, as I continue to attempt to wave Anne out the door.

"Actually," the fireman says, "I don't know anything about them." Idiots. I'm going to have to do everything myself.

Two men, each wearing glasses ("four-eyes," four eyes, two men, forty-two!), step around Anne with bright, shiny police badges proffered casually in front of them.

"Sorry to interrupt, Mr. Olson," the first detective says, giving an unenthusiastic, uncaring shrug. I stare at him as if he were driftwood. He, heedless, adds, "My name's Bliss and this is Detective Smith." Detective Smith gives a bored toss of the head, which I assume to be a greeting.

The fireman on the phone is saying, "The initial assessment is that it seems to have started near the fireplace. Perhaps a spark ignited something. We should be able to discern exactly where, why, and what in a week or so."

He hesitates. "Also, we're almost positive the house was empty at the time. We really doubt anyone was trapped inside."

Detective Bliss says, "If possible, we'd like a word with you. It's in regards to the Lake Oswego—"

"Detective, I'm on the phone."

Bliss and Smith exchange a conspiratorial look, nod, and begin to look around my office as if they're *not* looking around. While attempting to listen to the fatherly fireman, I methodically, but, I hope, casually, begin picking up the papers with my calculations.

Bliss replies, appraising the books on the shelves, tapping knowingly—for which I hate him all the more—*Amor en los tiempos de cólera*, "I understand that, *sir*. However, we'd like a word with you."

"However, detective," I extend the receiver, shake it for emphasis, "I'm on the phone."

"I can see that." For a brief moment our eyes catch. Suddenly my office is transformed into a mixed martial arts octagon.

"Good." We stare, we wait for the bell.

Inexplicably, Detective Smith is testing the couch's cushions. He seems satisfied and moves to the chairs as Bliss idly toys with a filing cabinet's handle.

I place the phone back to my ear as Fireman Bill says, "It seems most of the windows and doors were open, which, unfortunately, helped with ventilation, but would've facilitated escape. So, there should be no concern that anyone was trapped."

"However, we have questions," Bliss says, deadpan, insinuating.

"Who doesn't, detective? Life is one question after another. Anne?" The spotlight suddenly cast upon her, she shudders herself out of her voyeuristic reverie. "Can you have these gentlemen wait outside?" They seem to be confused by this reasonable request. "For a moment. Please. And, you...you go home." She, for some reason, looks as if she's about to cry. Almost as if she's watching something very sad transpiring.

"Actually, Olson, I'm afraid—" Detective Bliss doesn't want to shut his piehole.

"Will you shut the fuck up! I am on the goddamn phone! Fuck!" Everyone, even Fireman Bill, falls quiet. I ask, my blood so thick with ice you could walk across it, "Trapped? What do you mean, trapped? Who's trapped?"

Anne hesitates; she wants to stay. She wants to watch the plane crash, the sinking of the ship. I point a finger and scream, "OUT!"

She pouts, but exits, closing the door behind her—a professional to the end. Her Christmas bonus is reinstated. Good for her. Unfortunately, she's neglected to take the detectives with her. They, at least, lower their badges.

"No, sir. No, sir. No one was trapped. We're pretty positive about that. However—"

Smith sits in one chair, appraises it, and moves to the other. Bliss, on the other hand, has followed a circuitous route to my desk. He attempts to pick up the sheet with the CC Kelvin CC computations. I, however, beat his slimy, smoke-stained fingers to it.

We smile at one another, knowingly. Fucker.

"However, what?" I ask Fireman Bill.

"Well—" He has a distinct problem with getting to the point.

"Goddamn, man, corpses are more direct than you. Get to the point, will you?" I give the detectives another fake smile and flap my hand like a flailing mouth.

Curiously, my office door begins to open again.

Before "Anne, I said leave!" can escape my mouth, there's a large officer in blue, then another, crowding the doorway. Both are stern-faced and serious.

Fireman Bill, tragically, continues pontificating. "The house is a complete loss, I'm afraid. Burned to the ground. I'm sorry. Though barring any discrepancies, your insurance should cover it. You do have insurance, yes?"

"Like the sea has salt water," I reply, gathering up a few more pages.

"Perfect." He then rattles off a miscellany of information about whom to contact, and who the investigating officer is, what and where and with whom to do what and when, exactly.

I don't hear anything he says. Not because I don't care, but because Detective Bliss is saying, "We'd like you to come downtown with us."

I and Smith and the two uniformed officers smirk, because, well, we're already downtown. Bliss continues, unperturbed, shrugging his shoulders. "Fuck you guys. I just like saying it." We stare, and wait for the next inevitable and automatic lines. "George Thomas Olson, I have a warrant for your arrest for the murder in the first degree of your wife, Francesca Áureo Octavo Olson, and—"

"I'm sorry," I interrupt, "but what the fuck are you talking about?" The officers bring their hands quickly to their dark guns. Ah, this is how I finally get launched out the windows—full of bullet holes. All of those many nightmares falling, tumbling into the dark oblivion, one way or another, explained—gunshots.

Bliss attempts to clarify. "Your wife, Francesca; we're arresting you for—"

"Yeah, yeah, I fucking know. For her murder. No shit, Sherlock. Which, by the way, I *didn't* commit. Nor do I believe she's dead. But, and this is where, 'what the fuck are you talking about?' becomes pertinent—" They grip their guns tighter; obviously, the police force doesn't appreciate verbally astute suspects. "But, what the fuck are you talking about, her middle names are Áureo Octavo? I mean what the fuck does that mean? Áureo Octavo? Her middle name is Verdad! Áureo Octavo? That sounds like some fucking heroin-addicted porn star from Ciudad Juarez for Christ's sake! Is that who you think my wife is? Is it? Is it, you stupid, fucking, flatfoot detective?"

After that there was pepper spray, hog-tying, and a few swift kicks to the back, ribs, and face, but only as window dressing, only as seasoning on steak, frosting on cake.

Sure the police report would imply: "Resisted arrest."

Of course it would infer: "Yelled profanities. Resisted arrest."

Obviously it would claim: "Grabbed miscellaneous papers. Yelled profanities. Resisted arrest."

It even would go as far as to state: "Subject was irritable due to a simultaneous phone call from the fire department about the burning of his house. We informed him of our purpose. At this juncture he shouted, 'My wife is not some fucking hooker from Ciudad Juarez! She is a goddamn angel! As is my daughter! Not to mention my goddamn dog! And, yeah, the fucking cat, too! Hey, leave those papers the fuck alone! Do you have a warrant?! Do you?! Well those are the key, the secret to finding my angel, my wife and daughter, my dog and... and the fucking cat, too! Fuck, for all I know, I'll even find myself! Now give me my goddamn papers! And get the fuck out of my office! I *am* being reasonable! It's my goddamn wife and child and dog! And cat, too! And, AND it's my fucking office! OUT!' Subject then grabbed miscellaneous papers from arresting officers in a threatening and exceedingly aggressive manner. At which point subject was subdued using pepper spray, hog-tying technique, and administrative blows."

∞

That night, in one of the urine-scented interrogation rooms, the Bad Cop (Bliss) is asking, "Could there've been someone else?" He means like some young football buck, or the dead guy in the Eurovan (obviously, before he was dead), ramming Francesca on the side while I was at work. Hence motive. Motive to kill the beloved wife, as well as kill the theoretical guy fucking the beloved wife. The guy in the Eurovan, by the way, happens to remain a John Doe.

"No. Absolutely not," I say through my swollen lip. We glare. I glare through my swollen, bloodshot eyes, both darkening to black and blue. He, the four-eyed bastard, glares through his glasses.

"Why?" he asks.

"Because you kicked me, asshole."

"Because? What?"

"Because she's not like that."

"No? But you are?" We glare.

"What do you mean by that?"

"Suppose you tell me?"

Okay, how could they've found out about ▇▇▇? She and I had our own private thing. No one knew. I told no one. Not even Charles over lunch and martinis. And I believed ▇▇▇ when she said, "No. You are mine. My little private secret I'll carry to my grave." Or do I believe her? Maybe this is part of her plan?

Could Anne have spilled the beans? No. ▇▇▇ and I met discreetly at Higgins Bar only occasionally, if we felt like having a glass before stripping one another clean and bare, attempting to discover solace in the skin of the other.

Could ▇▇▇ have ratted me out? It's the only thing that makes sense. But why? What kind of vindication is there in that? Sure, hell has no fury like a woman scorned, but I didn't really scorn her, did I? It was an affair. Nothing more. No, that's actually incorrect. It was an affair in the beginning, but somewhere it became something else. Something much more. I suppose I couldn't blame her if she did rat me out.

Or maybe this is simply one of those detective lines listed in the manual to throw out at the confused suspect to see what he can be tricked into volunteering. Much like fishing with dynamite.

I tell the detective, "I can't say I know what you're talking about," as if I believed it and we were in a small boat fishing.

"Fine, play hardball. We'll see how far that gets you." He

turns some pages of the report over. Turns them back. Then again forward. Frowns. Then looks at me.

Then asks, like slowly inserting a cold knife in my chest, pulling it out, inserting it over and over, searching for my heart, "When did you find out your daughter wasn't yours?"

Initially I don't say anything. Or maybe I just can't. I'm trying to figure out why he would say something like that. Why would the manual suggest using that line? That's just mean. What's the trick? Where's the catch? I don't get it. Why would he say that?

"Goddamn," the detective says. "I'm sorry. Really." And he means it, sincerely. "I thought you knew. It could be the hair samples from the van weren't hers, or maybe the lab boys.... Look, I'm...I'm sorry."

Goddamn, he's serious. I...I don't know what to say. Nor does he. We linger in an awkward silence. I notice my hands, my fingers, seemingly for the first time ever. I begin to gradually compare and contrast the moons on each finger with the corresponding finger of the other hand. There seems to be no correlation. Confused, I ask, "Mirabella wasn't...isn't...isn't my daughter?"

He doesn't say anything. And I haven't looked up from my hands, my fingers, my moons.

"Would you mind?" he asks, motioning to the dented, gray door. I shake my head, not caring what he means. My pinkies don't even have moons. I hope he means, "Slam your cranium against it until the truth leaks out of you." I believe I *have* the truth, but I believe I don't *know* it, can't *confess* it. Hence, the necessity of beating it from me. Please. Please. Let's see what bright words flow like blood from my mouth and mind as he kicks and hits and strikes me over and over.

Instead, Detective Bliss exits.

Disappointed, I continue looking long and hard at my hands.

What's that mean, pinkies without moons? I want to write on a yellow sticky, "Significance of moons on fingers? What?" But of course I don't have a pen, or a sticky note, and it'd be difficult to write, handcuffed to a table as I am.

Bliss is gone for at least ten minutes. Finally, when I'm beginning to recognize my hands as my own, he returns with the Good Cop (Smith).

"Mr. Olson," Detective Smith asks, "is it true you didn't know your daughter wasn't yours?"

I'm listening. Honestly. But I'm more focused on attempting

to sift through the information, the numbers, the incidents, the clues that have drifted down over the past few hours. If I lose them now I'm liable to lose them forever. Everything would be lost. Everything. Somehow I can't make myself clear enough to get the detectives to leave me the fuck alone.

If I could be left alone, just be given a little silence, a little time and peace, I'm sure I could figure out what exactly is going on. What the equations mean, and where they'd lead to. I'd figure out exactly where Francesca and Mirabella are. Where Zeus and Tyler are. How the house caught fire. Who the dead guy in the Eurovan was. If EVP—electronic voice phenomena—is real or a hoax. Where am I headed and what should I do?

As it is, all I can hear are these stupid detectives and their stupid, stupid questions. "So, you didn't know the John Doe in your wife's Eurovan? What were you doing with your dog in the shed? What was in your briefcase you so conveniently lost? Why'd you try to run over your mother-in-law? What'd you do with the bodies? Why'd you see Francesca's therapist? Ask her about psychogenic fugues? Were there any other women besides █████? What do those equations mean? Are they some kind of demonology? Are you some kind of closet Satanist?"

No matter how much they talk, regardless of how poignant and insightful their questions, all I see are my fingers. My fingers with, and without, moons. My fingers, weak and shriveled on pathetic hands attached to thin arms, a sad torso, a bumbling, stumbling heart and soul. In other words, little ol' me.

The small, airless interrogation room is filled to capacity with the stench of sweat and fear of the other sad souls who've been here before. There is also the acidic scent of myself—and I, too, am covered in sweat and fear.

I drop my head and scrub my scalp. The handcuffs laugh at the hope of scratching Francesca's scent free. I sniff the air, but there is only sweat and fear. I scratch harder, longer. The handcuffs laugh and laugh. Sweat and fear. Eventually, my hands cramping, my hair tossed and crazed, my scalp bleeding, my hope dead, I become nauseous and throw up over and over. I continue until there's nothing left inside me, until I'm completely empty.

Somewhere, thankfully, I black out.

When I wake I don't know where, or who, I am—typical. Fucking typical.

Summer in a Snow Globe

"Do you understand the charges being brought against you, Mr. Olson?"

Looking around, I notice a small courtroom. It's one of the older ones. It's all wood. Not Formica and plastic and carpet. It's wood and marble. It smells of dust and hate, lots of hate.

"Mr. Olson, I'm speaking to you."

Behind the bench is a judge with gray, popcorn hair and bright eyes of an indeterminate color. His name, embossed on a gold nameplate, is the Honorable Judge Asher.

"I will ask this once again," the pink mouth beneath the gray popcorn and indeterminate eyes mumbles, "and only once more. And I expect an answer. If you do not reply I shall hold you in contempt of court. Is that understood, Mr. Olson?"

"Your Honor," interrupts a man looking a little too slick, smooth, and styled for his own good, "my client is obviously in a state of catastrophic traumatization. If you'd please—"

"Mr. O'Conner!" Judge Asher booms out, "This is an informal arraignment, not a trial. You say anything more and I shall hold *you* in contempt. Is that understood?"

I look at Mr. O'Conner, realizing this is my lawyer. Joseph O'Conner, an associate of my family lawyer Duncan McGee, will handle my criminal case.

We've not spoken, Mr. O'Conner and I. My one call was to Duncan.

Duncan had said, "I think I know someone."

I had said, "Good," and hung up.

"Now, Mr. Olson?" I turn back to Judge Asher. He's now fondling his gavel. It seems to be something he enjoys. "I will ask you one more time—do you understand the charges being brought against you?"

I nod. Judge Asher squints a dubious stare.

"Are you mocking this court, Mr. Olson?"

I shake my head.

"You're sure?"

I nod, as genuinely as possible, afraid any more shaking or nodding will cause my swollen lip and eyes to pull me irrevocably to the floor.

"Very well," Judge Asher declares. "Make a note. The accused has nonverbally agreed that he understands the charges filed against him." As I smile my appreciation, I notice a vast miscellany of initials carved into the surface of the small desk I sit behind. "Now, Mr. Olson, I have a few questions for you." This, I think, is how a guillotine sounds.

"Your Honor?" Mr. O'Conner interrupts demurely.

"Yes, I know, Mr. O'Conner, this isn't a trial. I simply want to know how your client is going to conduct himself *if* I allow bail to be set."

Mr. O'Conner says, "Oh. Excellent. Thank you. Thank you, Your Honor," and sits back down.

"You seem like a reasonable man, Mr. Olson, regardless of what the police report claims. The charges brought against you, however, are exceedingly serious. I need you to promise you'll carry yourself as you have in the past...should you be released. With the utmost dignity, and as a productive and law-abiding member of society." I nod. "You will show up for trial." I nod. "You will be a model citizen." I nod. "You will not run away." I shake my head. "Very well, then, I will grant you bail. However, due to the nature of the crime, bail is set at," Judge Asher hesitates, glances around the courtroom for insight and then is finally hit by inspiration as he pronounces, "$420,000." He strikes his gavel and says, "Next?" like I was in line at Burgerville.

∞

Joseph, my intense-eyed attorney, tells me not to worry, "It's only temporary." I think he's talking about the lingering effects of the pepper spray and the administrative blows, and not the sensation of being a stranger in my body.

"Right now," he says, as we sign release forms, "is the hardest part of the fight. Right now you've got to relax and settle back. Rope-a-dope, ya know?" He steps back and gives a brief example as if he were Muhammad Ali. "Take it easy. Recover. Let me and my team be your shield and sword. Okay?"

I smile. I nod. I like his enthusiasm. I like his optimism. I like his brash demeanor. Hell, I even like his suit. He even seems as if he knows what he's talking about. Somehow, though, I don't think it'll matter. One way or the other, I think I'm guilty. It seems on that alone this is a lost cause.

"Good," he replies to my nod. He gives me a gentle, reassuring pat on the shoulder as he accepts the plastic bag containing the items I had when I was arrested. They also give him my jacket and belt. My shoelaces and tie are in the bag.

We don't say anything until we're outside and I appear back together. Shoes laced and tied. Belt on. Jacket on. Tie in a pocket. Wallet in the same pocket. My watch is missing, though I don't say anything. The last thing in the plastic bag is a circle of worn gold, my wedding ring. It stares at me, a forlorn, lost animal searching for a home.

"Go on, champ, put it on. You gotta start somewhere, right? And it might as well be at the beginning."

Returning his sad, understanding smile, I slip the ring on. Though it feels a little tighter, a little colder, than I remember, nothing changes. Not even the sensation of floating in my body. Or, maybe, it's my body trapping me? Or, maybe, it's having more than one me in my body? How many could possibly fit? I wonder.

Joseph continues, "We'll hit them so hard it'll take a pro-wrestler and a pry bar to get their heads out of their asses. We're going to stay aggressive and proactive on this. Okay?"

I nod.

"What?" he asks.

"Is it cold, or just me?" He looks around. It's midday. Spring in full swing. For a moment he gets a worried look on his face. He smiles broadly.

"That's temporary too, my friend. It'll wear off." He gives my shoulders and arms a quick and friendly, invigorating rub. It doesn't help. I remain covered with goose bumps like stalagmites.

As I attempt to rub my skin smooth, Joseph hails a cab. We

get in, but not before he glances around, as if looking for something, or someone.

Once inside and a few blocks from the courthouse, he says, "Now, here's the plan...."

∞

The plan is this: I will stay at Joseph's law firm's apartment.

"We use it only sporadically for clients and such that need to keep a low profile. And you're lucky enough to fit the criteria." He gives another broad smile. "Anyway, it's relatively quiet. A nice enough place to collect your thoughts, you know?" I nod. "That's also where we'll pretty much do all our interviews and such. We're going to keep you out of the public eye as much as possible. Particularly until that shiner clears up. You really caught one, didn't you?" I nod. "Thankfully we've got over a week before the preliminary hearing. By then you'll be back to your normal self." He sounds sure, though I can't necessarily agree. I hope; I just can't agree.

∞

The cab drives through a neighborhood that's an odd mixture of stately Victorians, old duplexes and little, dumpy apartment complexes.

The plan is to get me (and I quote) "made over and made up" including a haircut, a new suit, everything. "Maybe even a dietary consultant. Try and clear your complexion up. You've been drinking a lot?" I shrug. "Yeah, well, who wouldn't, right?" He gives me another friendly pat on the shoulder. I'm quickly learning to hate Mr. Joseph O'Conner. And if my hand didn't have the residual effects from Steve, I'd think of punching him.

Eventually we stop in front of a white, two-story, stucco thing. Above the front door, gilt letters proclaim it as The Alamo.

Joseph pays the driver, and again glances around as if looking for something. I don't ask. I'm a little afraid of what he'd answer.

"We'll take the back stairs. The neighbors are, well, interesting. Best if we keep to ourselves." We walk around the corner and down the tired driveway. In back there are parking spaces and an overused trash dumpster.

The apartment is on the second floor.

Entering the kitchen, we're met by a thin vanguard scent of old newspaper and vinegar followed by an assault of hot, stagnant, stale air.

"Yow!" Joseph yelps, heading immediately for the front of the apartment, "It's as warm as Poseidon's balls in here!" Next time I see June I'll offer that as a possibility for the Boiling Sea phenomenon off the north coast of New Guinea. Joseph calls out over his shoulder, "I'll turn the air on. And look around. This den will be your home for awhile."

The plan is to have one of his assistants visit and take my statement. That's all I'll be doing for the next few days—confessing my story.

The plan is to talk and verify the facts. The plan is to talk with witnesses. The plan is to find Francesca, and Mirabella, and Zeus, and Tyler. The plan is to ignore the possibility that there are no witnesses, and Francesca, and Mirabella, and Zeus, and Tyler can't be found.

"But," I say, pointing out the obvious, "you don't have my papers."

"Papers? What papers? For what?"

Briefly, succinctly, I tell him about forty-two and eight. I explain the subtle nuance of four times two equating to eight. I expound eloquently on the curious synchronicity of my car's license plate and the parking space, sixty-seven. I explain the subtle nuance of six times seven being forty-two. I present definitive truth in the form of my secretary Anne Mo, four and two.

"Mo? M-o?" Joseph asks, puzzled. I'm tempted to tell him how she garnered her last name, though don't believe he's interested, nor do I believe it would help. "M-o, that's short for something, isn't it?" he asks.

"Modus operandi, right?" I answer reluctantly, not liking the implication.

He shakes his head. "No, no. Well, yeah, but I was thinking of something else."

Extracting a yellow sticky note from my jacket pocket I write,

Look up
abbreviation
M-o

Joseph looks at me quizzically, mildly concerned, mildly annoyed, like being forced to use a fifty to pay for a candy bar.

In order to deflect any inquiry, I mention the two Cecil Chamberlains and the one Kay. I explain the binary code and the subsequent equation with Kelvin.

The plan is to have me talk with a psychiatrist. "This process can be pretty taxing. Best to get you as healthy inside as out, you know? Just to make sure. Right?" I nod, walk to the thermostat, and turn it up a little. Nothing seems to be helping my chill. I feel as if we're in a meat locker.

Joseph hands me two crisp twenties. "For dinner and breakfast," he explains. "Keep the receipts, okay?" I nod, and pull my jacket up around my chin. "My assistant, Naomi, will be over tomorrow before lunch with groceries and things. Also, I believe I heard the fire department was able to salvage a few items from your house. I'll have her bring over anything pertinent." I nod. "You going to be okay?" I nod. "Feel free to use the phone. Call long distance. Friends, family, whomever. Hell, if you want, surf porn all night on the computer. Whatever you need. Relax. And recover. Rope-a-dope, ya know? The place is yours. Okay?" I nod. He gives me a nervous, curious stare. "You're sure?"

My body, not the floating me inside, answers, "Yes. Absolutely," as if I mean it.

Once Joseph leaves, I quickly turn the heat back up.

As the hot air sighs through the vents I aimlessly wander the apartment. It's a long and large one-bedroom, and is split into thirds. The front room, done simply, elegantly, reminds me of some English professor's bachelor pad. The middle is the dining room, which even has enough room for a nice sideboard for plates and such. The last third is bedroom, kitchen, bathroom. The entire place, except for kitchen and bath, has gleaming hardwood floors.

I check the place out. Pick up the books in the shelves. Flip them open to see if there are any inscriptions. No. I check the stereo out. It's a little Pioneer number with a nice collection of CDs. I select a collection of Miles Davis's blues numbers. I open the cupboards and look at the board games, the tableware, the Tupperware, the Ziploc bags, the toilet paper and towels.

On the sink in the bathroom is a collection of new toiletries for me.

Closets, for the most part, are empty, except for a few dresses in the bedroom. There is a black overcoat and umbrella in the closet near the hallway.

The apartment, based on the hot, thickening air, must be relatively comfortable but I'm still freezing. I turn the heat up higher and notice the slight aroma of incense, of burned candles, lingering in the background. It reminds me of ████'s condo. But, regardless of how nice it is, it still feels like a prison. In comparison with last night's actual cell, this prison is the Waikiki Hilton. For the moment it will have to do.

Still cold, I turn the thermostat up again. My bones have been replaced with ice. I return to the bathroom cupboard and find an old afghan that smells of mothballs. It and I go curl up on the brown leather couch in the front room.

I fall instantly asleep, and dream of nothing.

∞

I'm woken by my shivering, by the rattling of my teeth, which sound like castanets in an epileptic's hands. My entire body is quaking. I clutch myself tightly, fearing my ice-blue bones shall be thrust up and shatter through the surface of my skin, splitting it like fault lines. My hands aren't big enough. My grip isn't tight enough. My skin shall explode like dry earth. My bones shall shatter like glass.

Nothing warms me. Not rubbing my skin red. Not covering my head with the afghan. Not turning the thermostat up to full. Not throwing the overcoat over the afghan. Nothing. I'm shaking the teeth from my skull. As a last resort, I run into the bathroom and turn the shower on. Steam rises in deep billowing clouds. Quickly I strip and jump in. The scalding water is just enough to send the chill shivering back from whence it came.

I stay beneath the hot spray until it begins to wane.

Drying my red, red skin, I catch a glimpse of my shadow-self moving, lurking behind the curtain of steam draped across the mirror. With my hand I clear a swath and stare at a man I do not know, and who, honestly, frightens me.

∞

Dressed in my two-day-old clothes, with the overcoat from the front closet draped over me, I'm once again shivering in the living room. Maybe I need food? Something in the belly to fuel the body's furnace? There's nothing in the cupboards, so I walk to a sandwich shop down the street and grab a turkey-avocado on wheat. Somehow, while chewing, I become colder. Maybe what's sucking my energy from me is the quick, crazed transition from married man with a wife, a child, a dog, and a cat, to a lonely, confused man—to a man charged with murder. Forcing myself to finish the sad sandwich, nearly gagging on the last bite, I notice a Goodwill a block down the street.

At the Goodwill, shivering, I collect a wool cap, gloves, a thick plaid lumber shirt, a scarf, and a down jacket.

Outside, I pull the clothes from the plastic bag and put them on. I stand awkwardly on the sidewalk, attempting to adjust to the added bulk. I feel like that kid in *A Christmas Story* who is so bundled up he can't lower his arms. Thankfully, my shivering slows and finally stops, though something deep inside feels as if it's still shaking, quivering.

∞

I return to the apartment and spend the early evening frantically rewriting the equations on paper I find beneath the computer desk. Due to my shaking glove-clad hands, the script is barely legible.

I stare at the sheets for hours, attempting to make sense of the figures. Occasionally, I make a notation between lines, off to the side, or circle a number with a comment nearby.

Eventually, the silence of the late night grows heavy, so I put on a CD, a collection of Mozart concertos, and go to the computer.

I am tempted to surf porn, but the idea of gazing at young bodies (which Mirabella would eventually be), who are obviously someone's daughters—strikes me. Strikes me as revolting and slightly disgusting.

However, Joseph's comment about Anne's last name reverberates. Not modus operandi? Then what?

I google M-o; something, thankfully, besides modus operandi, comes up, an abbreviation for molybdenum. I click on the link. Even with the gloves, my fingers are so cold I can barely move them, barely click the mouse.

The web page contains the periodic table for atomic weights and measures and is provided by the Los Alamos National Laboratory. I find Mo, molybdenum, and I again begin shaking all over. Molybdenum's atomic number is, of course, forty-two!

I look at the number, forty-two, the answer, the meaning of life. Why? Douglas Adams. What's the probability of all of this? I should find those PSU nerds and shake the truth out of them. Instead, I google Douglas Adams. I select a site, www.42.com. I get on the site's forum and ask, "Why did Mr. Adams believe the answer was forty-two?"

I get all kinds of stupid answers: "Because your grandmother said so :-)." "Because it's funny." "Because forty-two rhymes with poo." "Because your mother said so :-)." "Because it was easier than writing *Being and Nothingness*, or the Bible." "Because in Hebrew, which happens to be an alpha-numeric language, forty-two can be translated into the syllables/letters Bet-Samesh, or BS—bullshit. Get it? Life, and the meaning, and the search for meaning is BS, bullshit. Get it, idiot?" The last comment was signed by The Dark Overlord of Nihilism, aka DON.

I don't reply back to any of them, particularly DON. I do, however, search Hebrew language sites. I want to investigate the Bet-Samesh possibility. Though I honestly don't wish to verify life is hopeless, meaningless, bullshit.

An hour into my quest, I run across the Kaballah Center. On their site are curious statements about the forty-two-letter word for God and the seventy-two names of God.

Quickly, excitedly, I pull out a second ream of paper and notice, like the proverbial pot of gold, a case of sticky notes gleaming in the shadows. Forsaking the paper, I gleefully grip the sharp edges of the sticky notes.

The entire night is spent writing, copying and transferring, the information gleaned about the number forty-two, about eight, about Anne Mo's grandfather, about the hand in the soup on the ferry from Ireland to France, about everything, from the pages to the sticky notes.

Well past the hour of the wolf, I begin making an extended family chart. It's curious, but exceedingly comforting, to write names on little yellow sticky notes. The chart includes me and my immediate family, as well as friends and business associates. I make charts, as best I can, for my friends and business associates. I spend the night placing, arranging, and rearranging the yellow notes on the walls. It's necessary to remove a series of large, black-and-white photos of Venice, as well as to relocate all the bookshelves into the dining room.

By the time I turn the lights out, the walls are scaled in yellow. Air from the heater makes them dance and rustle, mesmerizing me. I decide to sleep on the couch and listen to their compelling whispers, hoping they'll disclose where truth lies.

∞

I wake to the sound of a key rattling in the back door. Then I hear the precise movements of someone unpacking and placing groceries in kitchen cupboards. It sounds like something I've known before, for many years.

Groggy, tired from lack of sleep, from staring into a computer screen for hours, from writing significations on sticky notes, from administrative blows, and from dozing on the lumpy couch, I stumble down the hall to the kitchen.

"Francesca? What *are* you doing? Come back to bed, please." I rub my eyes. The gloves chafe. Sleep has collected in the grooves and fissures of my eyes. It's painful to press my fingers in the creases, attempting to squeeze wakefulness out like paste from a tube. Heedless, I continue. Francesca remains silent, observant, beautiful, a can of chunk light tuna cupped perfectly in her hand.

I lean against the doorjamb, adding, "Sweetie, let the Zeuser out. Throw some cereal at Mirabella and come back to bed. Please. I want to fuck you, so long, so hard, we become blind and can only recognize one another through our hands."

My gloved fingers free themselves from my newly cleared eyes which discover, not Francesca, but a young, African-American woman.

Not knowing what to say, what more I could do to offend her, I close my gaping mouth, turn, and walk back into the front room, crawl back beneath the afghan, and descend back into sleep. I hope when I wake (unsure if I want to), Francesca will have returned, or enough time will have elapsed that Joseph's assistant, Naomi, will have seen it in her heart to have either forgotten or forgiven me.

∞

When I wake, Naomi is gone. I can't say I blame her. I wonder if I blame Francesca? Blame Francesca for leaving, blame her for growing silent, for cleaning instead of cultivating; blame her for accepting the seduction of suburbia, of allowing me to descend into who I am? Do I? Do I blame her? Or should I blame myself? Can I blame *us*? And if so, what's that mean? Blaming us?

I don't know what it means. I do know I've given myself time to think about it. But that was the idea. Think about it and it would depress, it would affect, it would make me go insane. Instead I walked Zeus, chatted with June, slept with ████████, drank, did everything, everything *except* think about it.

Ignorance, as I've said, is bliss. And I? I'm an impeccable samurai.

Before I slip too deeply into introspection, I pull myself from beneath the comfortable confines of the afghan. Tucked into one of my shoes, Naomi has left me an itinerary she's compiled for the next few days. It's typed, not handwritten, and very legible. I look at my wrist to see when I am. There is only a pale band where my watch should be. To discover the time, I have to walk into the kitchen and find a clock on the stove. I'm mildly disappointed and slightly annoyed there isn't a clock on the coffeemaker.

If the stove's clock is right, I have under an hour before Naomi returns with a stenographer to begin taking down my statement and story. According to the schedule, that is all I'll do for the rest of the day—make my statement, tell my story. Like I care—I already know it, and have been diligently attempting to forget it.

Paper-clipped to the itinerary is a note, Naomi, in her own handwriting, has also suggested a few things:

> I might advise, Mr. Olson, that your
> "project" be cleaned off the walls. We must
> maintain an amount of "secrecy" where your
> defense is concerned. Also, we should attempt to
> project an attitude of security and surety, both
> within one's "self" as well as one that will affect the
> perception the world has of us. These are only
> suggestions. Heed them, or not.
>
> ~Naomi

Basically she's telling me to shower, shampoo, and shave. No one believes someone that looks like a killer isn't a killer. Jesus, tell me something I don't know.

I take a shower and shave. I find a whole set of casual clothes—Levi's, T-shirt, a sweater, socks, underwear, and shoes—lined up in the bedroom. I make a pot of coffee.

If I am acquitted it's going to cost me an arm and a leg. These people are professionals. I'm just thankful I work for an insurance company, otherwise I'd be in more trouble than I am, (which doesn't sound possible, but somehow I'm sure it is).

∞

To keep from thinking about how lost and precarious my freedom, my life, my love is I go back to searching for clues in the numbers.

While piecing together the significance of Paul Warfield's (wide receiver for the Miami Dolphins and Cleveland Browns during the '70s) number forty-two, the lyrics of the band Level 42, and Enrico Fermi achieving the nuclear reaction in the year 1942, there's a mouselike knock at the back door.

It's probably the stenographer. I don't answer. I make a note that the signing of the United Nations declaration, in Washington, D.C., coincided with Fermi's discovery. I postulate a few possibilities on another sheet of paper. Also curious: the UN World Headquarters is located on Forty-second Street in New York City. I make another note.

Quickly I calculate Washington (ten letters—more binary code, which I make a note of. I also note George as the first U.S. president), D.C. (D is the fourth letter in the alphabet, C the third. Also I note DC as an electrical current.) Therefore, if we...ten (zero doesn't count, it's nothing)...subtract one from forty-three, we get...forty-two. Slowly the wavering images coalesce. Slowly. I must be patient.

There's another knock on the door. Once again, I ignore it. I have to. I have no choice. The answer is right here. Right in front of me. I simply need to be methodical, organized, and, most importantly, left alone for the answer to appear. I must also be patient.

Not much later, annoyingly, the phone rings. Not surprisingly, I don't answer. I'm presently noting the Electronic Industries Association, founded in 1924, has its headquarters in Washington, D.C.

A little later the phone rings again. Stops. Rings again. Stops. I'm reading a poem by Stephen Crane (author of *The Red Badge of Courage*). It doesn't have a title, but is instead numbered forty-two.

After reading it, I recall Emily Dickinson also numbered

her poems. It takes me a moment to find Emily's forty-second poem. While I do so, I can't help but marvel at all this information tucked snugly away on the Internet.

I print copies of the two poems, spend an hour attempting to memorize them, then, before falling asleep on the couch, diligently transcribe them onto yellow sticky notes and place them appropriately on the fluttering walls.

∞

The morning is spent rereading, rechecking, and verifying numbers and dates. It's spent adjusting and reconfiguring the walls. Moving a note here or there clarifies the hieroglyphs and causes me to smile, broad and genuine. This is good. Very good.

∞

Based on my hunger, my thirst, it must be late afternoon when the back door opens and Naomi enters. She's closely followed by a young woman carrying a large, square satchel.

"Mr. Olson?" Naomi says, steaming in as I, hands full of yellow notes, add one to the wall's configuration. "Why didn't you—" She stops and looks around the room, at the yellow-gold, glistening walls. It takes a moment for Naomi to quell her fear. But, once it is quelled, she is again imperial, an empress. "Why didn't you let Ms. Vilasovic in?" Ms. Vilasovic gives a thin, wan smile. "Or answer my phone calls?" I place a note here, another there. "Mr. Olson, what *are* you doing? Didn't I suggest something," she flicks a note, and then another, "less odd?" Ms. Vilasovic continues smiling.

"Well, yes. Yes, you did. But I...I was thinking." I take a deep breath and begin explaining, "See, presently I'm reading Masumi Kato. He happens to be the founding father of a Japanese style of ballad called Kato-bushi. I'm reading his death poem. See, he died when he was forty-two."

"Of course he did," Naomi cuts in. I ignore her. Ms. Vilasovic's smile is slowly sinking.

I continue, "Stephen Crane and Emily Dickinson both seem to have also numbered their poems instead of giving titles. Though there is some contention if that was actually done by them or their editors. Anyway, Crane's poem forty-two deals with God and existence. Which is interesting because supposedly, according to Douglas Adams, forty-two is," and I put quotes around it with my fingers, "'the answer.' Now, have you seen *The Last Samurai* with Tom Cruise?" Naomi nods her head, slowly, carefully. Ms. Vilasovic does the same, her smile now a flat line of concern. Both know you don't step on the grass, feed the bears, or disagree with lunatics. "Do you remember when he has his existential crisis in the hotel room?"

"About returning to either the bottle or the samurai?" Naomi judicially offers.

"Yes. That's it. Well, the number on his room's door is forty-two. Which I believe is how old he is, isn't it?" I quickly scribble down the remaining notes and go to the computer to search Tom Cruise and verify his age.

"Mr. Olson," Naomi asks, "*what are you doing?*"

"I'm online," I reply. They have a separate DSL connection, so I've been online for most of the past day or two. I look at the pale band of skin where my watch once resided. It confirms many, many hours. "I'm looking to see if Tom Cruise is forty-two."

"Yes, but *why?*"

"*Why?*"

"Yes, *why?*"

I'm going to have to be patient. Very patient.

I begin explaining. I too, like (perhaps) Mr. Cruise, am forty-two. I turned forty-two on February eleventh, which is forty-two days after the New Year in the Year of 2004, the year of the Goat. Francesca, my wife, is thirty-five. Mirabella is eight. My football number in high school was eight. Four times two is eight. Three plus five is eight. And eight is eight. I was born in 1962. One minus nine is eight. Six plus two is eight. One plus nine plus six plus two is eighteen. My parking space is sixty-seven.

Naomi stops me before I get to Anne's last name, M-o, my home address, my car's license plate, my parents' birth years, fucking everything.

"Eight? I thought it was forty-two?"

"No. The answer to *life* is forty-two. The answer to *existence* is eight." Both ladies scrunch their brows in confusion. I point out the obvious, "Eight is the vertical representation of infinity." For a visual reference I draw the symbol for infinity on a piece of paper, then turn it—now it's eight. I turn the paper again—infinity. I do that a few times. 8 ∞ 8 ∞

Naomi smiles appreciatively. Ms. Vilasovic, however, remains perplexed. Her vanished smile has incrementally turned to a frown of fear.

"That's very *agile*, Mr. Olson."

"Thank you, Naomi," I reply, tipping an invisible cap in appreciation. "That means a great deal, coming from you." I think I sound sincere. I hope I sound sincere. Unfortunately, the ensuing silence does nothing to confirm my delusions of sincerity.

Then Naomi, the wily huntress she truly is, swings at me with the baseball bat she was hiding behind her back, "But what, Mr. Olson, is the difference between life and existence?"

"Well," I reply, ducking and swinging back, "Life, at least in this context of meaning, is individual, while Existence is holistic, taking into account the entirety of the universe, or multi-verse, or multi-verses. In other words, Infinity, with a capital I." I smile, self-satisfied, and very pleased. To drive the point home, I add, "I also believe if I can discover how everything is interconnected—if you will, discern the universe's handwriting—I can read where my wife, my child, my dog, and even that ridiculous orange cat are hidden."

"And that's what this is all about?" Naomi waves a magisterial hand around the room, attempting to dismiss the implied connotations of so many intent, yellow eyes.

Yes, it's true, Ms. Vilasovic is frightened. She takes a step back, nonchalantly hiding behind Naomi.

I reply, "Yes. These are the clues." I mimic, mock, her hand waving. "This is the first step to reuniting with my family."

"Well, to do *that*, Mr. Olson," Naomi says pointedly, "we'll need to keep you out of jail, won't we?" I nod slowly. "Ms. Vilasovic, can you stay a little late today?" Grudgingly Ms. Vilasovic agrees. "Very good. Seeing how you are," Naomi looks at her watch, "an hour and a half behind, you should begin as soon as possible."

Ms. Vilasovic and I concede.

Ms. Vilasovic sets up her little stenographer machine and its stand. She seems far more comfortable now that she has something concrete to do.

Naomi exits to her car. She returns with a cardboard box and a small, charred, portable home safe. She sets both in a corner of the front room. I immediately move them to the center room—they were blocking a section of wall that defined the relationship between Mars (the god and the planet), tapioca pudding, and Tyler.

"Promise me, you'll wait?" I believe Naomi means wait to open the box and safe—and not wait to go insane. I believe she means wait until Ms. Vilasovic and I have finished transcribing for the day. I nod, forlornly staring at the safe and its charcoaled exterior.

Quickly I go to the kitchen, fighting back tears, to make lunch, to ignore the loss, to pretend everything is going to be just fine. Just fine.

I attempt to lose myself in the complete concentration of the mundane world of slicing a tomato and spreading mayonnaise on whole wheat bread.

Naomi updates me on the life I'm not living anymore, as I make my sandwich, careful to keep my back to her.

I've been given an indefinite leave of absence from work. The house fire is, of course, under a far more thorough and rigorous investigation than initially related to me by the friendly fireman on the phone. They expect to have conclusive results within the week. Mr. Naismith is in stable condition. And Margarita is replanting her forest of decimated houseplants. Naomi has contacted all my creditors and has, using very vague terms, explained the situation. Somehow she was able to get a six-month hiatus during which I don't have to make payments to anyone for anything. However, I am now on a very strict budget. Otherwise everything—where Francesca and Mirabella are, Zeus and Tyler, the man in the van—is under investigation. Yeah, this is going to cost me an arm, a leg, and an ear. Too bad I'm not an artist, or a poet. Maybe, if I'm lucky, in the next life.

Before Naomi leaves she asks, in a concerned tone, referring to my wool cap, gloves, scarf, lumberjack shirt, and jacket, "Are you cold?"

I reply cutting the sandwich in half, "Not any more."

∞

The rest of the day is spent dictating my story to Ms. Vilasovic. Her clackety-clack machine takes everything down. Joseph has given her a set of questions, which she dutifully reads with a thick Baltic accent. I dutifully answer in a monotone.

She'll take the transcription and then give it to Joseph.

He'll have Naomi read it. She'll highlight sentences for questions, for clarification, for discussion. They'll again send Ms. Vilasovic with her clackety-clack machine over so I can answer these new questions. Eventually they'll know as much about my life as I do. Perhaps more. Good for them.

Somewhere around sunset Ms. Vilasovic leaves, and I humorlessly make a tasteless dinner.

Unacceptably, Naomi has neglected to bring any form of alcohol whatsoever. Therefore I'm forced to go to the store and purchase a six-pack of beer and a bottle of wine. Selection is good.

"Aren't you hot?" the cashier asks.

"No."

She squints suspiciously at me, unsure about my cap, scarf, gloves, shirt and jacket, "Is it that cold out?"

"No."

She smiles. My answers seem to define my unresponsive credit card. She tries once more. We watch in silence. Other shoppers pile up behind me. Then it dawns on me: suspended payment equates to suspended credit cards. The people in line behind me shuffle, annoyed. The line grows longer, more annoyed. I look in my wallet. "How much is the wine?"

"Eight ninety-nine," the cashier answers, unconcerned, nonchalantly handing my card back.

"And the beer?"

"Six ninety-nine, plus deposit." She unwraps a stick of gum, places it in her mouth and begins methodically chewing.

Someone down the line comments, "Come on, mister. It's not like you're saving lives here. Make a decision."

The cashier shrugs her shoulders, rubs something off a nail.

"The wine."

She looks at me, curious.

I say, "Socrates: 'wine makes everyone hopeful,'" and hand her my sad ten dollar bill.

"Remind me," she says, "to start drinking more wine."

Taking the bottle and my change, I comment as I leave, "Drink more wine." She laughs and blows a big pink bubble.

∞

It's like being transported back to sixth grade biology class. Instead of a splayed frog, the sickly sour smell of formaldehyde, and weak, unsuccessful attempts at peeking down Sara

Albright's blouse, there's a brand new cardboard box. Besides being closed with yellow police security tape, the box also has my name and address written on top in bold, black print:

George T. Olson, 4242 NE Sycamore, 4/5/04

As I move the box to the middle of the room, where the opened bottle of wine and a glass wait, I discover it to be remarkably light. In fact, its lightness is disturbing and not to my liking. Immediately I don't trust it, or its contents. I look for something else to do—walk the dog, do the dishes, scrub the coffee-maker, mow the lawn—but, in this vile world of introspection, there is only the box and the subtle, wavering walls of yellow. Whispering. Watching. Waiting.

Tentatively, I open the box. Initially I can see nothing in its dark confines. Then, as my eyes adjust, I notice two oddly sharp-angled outlines. I reach into the mouth. My hands disappear down into the dark throat and extract the charred remains of a family photo album and a Murakami novel, *Sputnik Sweetheart*.

Perplexed, I stare back into the shadowy confines, expecting something else, something more. But there is only the photo album, and the Murakami novel.

I set the photo album and the novel off to the side. I turn the box over and wait for something else to fall out. Nothing does. There is only the photo album and the novel. It's difficult for me to believe, and comprehend, how these are the only two items to survive the fire.

Confused, I hesitate to pour the wine. Instead, I simply drink straight from the bottle. I take another drink. Then another. So be it.

Not wishing to delve immediately into the mysteries of the book or photo album—there's bound to be some image to haunt and inflict its will upon me—I grudgingly turn to the safe.

The safe, in comparison to its pristine brother, the cardboard box, is scorched and charred to a deep, ruddy black. The handle is melted into a lump of slag. Remarkably, the tumblers on the lock work and it opens without complaint.

Inside are birth certificates, CD certificates, a list of passwords for all of our accounts, insurance policies, an emergency credit card with the activation sticker attached, ten one hundred dollar bills, and passports. No, just mine. Francesca's is missing. Odd. Very odd. There are also original copies of some poems Francesca wrote me when first we collided. There are copies of both of our wills. Otherwise there's nothing unexpected, just the same old, same old.

The ten one hundred dollar bills, my passport, and the credit card I put in my jacket pocket. Everything else I keep locked in the safe. I put the safe in the box, the photo album on top of the safe, the box's lid on, then Murakami's novel on top of that.

Something bothers me about the book, and it's not the woman on the cover. It's not her red lips and dark eyes. It's the idea that *any* paper could survive such a fire. Not just the novel, but the photo album, too.

There should be noncombustible materials here. Like maybe a bowling ball, though we never owned a bowling ball, so that would be a little out of the ordinary too. Maybe the small stone Francesca and I took off the rock wall surrounding a vineyard near the town of Pommard. Maybe one of Tyler or Zeus's tags. Maybe one of the NASA shuttle cooking pans Francesca bought from a television infomercial. Maybe anything, but definitely not a photo album, and definitely not a book.

I take the book and thumb through its pages. Bits of burnt paper flake off. The charcoal scent of fire, of singed paper, fills the air. Francesca's Dear John letter comes back to haunt me, (à la Murakami) *"like smoke."*

The last thing I want to do is read. The absolutely, positively very last thing I want to do is read Murakami, particularly in search of some obscure reference. I shake the book. I want to shake the pages free from the spine. Impossible, then, to read it. Then I'll indeed have an excuse not to.

I shake it. And shake it.

Bits of black, burnt pages fall like dandruff to the shining wood floor, then a piece of paper. A piece of paper? My hand continues to shake dark dandruff from the book, but my eyes are glued to the piece of paper lying at my feet. Small black flecks pepper its surface. My hand shakes and shakes. Subconsciously, I must want to cover it up, bury it, pretend it isn't there, staring at me, staring at me, staring at me.

I toss the book on the couch and quickly find the bottle of wine. Two long swallows, and I decide.

∞

It's a circuitous route, but eventually I find the gap where our house used to be. The gap is like a missing tooth in an otherwise perfect set of teeth.

It seems as if at some point they must've decided the house was a complete loss and the best thing was to protect the surrounding homes. Only the foundation and the front steps are left. Otherwise there's nothing, only the charred remains, sunk into the basement.

The bottle in my hand, empty for three blocks, is a metronome by my side. The arc gradually grows. Until, finally, I release it and send it into the dark maw of the burned and collapsed house. Or home? House seems impersonal. *Home*, though? Maybe in the beginning, but for the past few years? A house.

The bottle shatters, and somewhere a dog, probably the Dudley's terrier, Buddy, barks in response. Eventually sad, abused and stupid, Buddy falls silent.

The silence is a sign, and I slowly walk up the steps to where the front porch should be, but isn't. Before me lies nothing. There is no longer the bureau with the keys, the phone, with the constantly changing seasonal flower arrangement. The comfortable couch? Gone, destroyed. Francesca's paintings destroyed. Mirabella's stuffed animals and DVDs, all destroyed. Zeus's slobbery water bowl is destroyed. Tyler's scratched cat seat destroyed. And my...my...? My what?

Nothing particular comes to mind. It's not one thing, but everything. The smallest grain is part of the largest beach. And that is what I've lost...every grain of my life. Every little fucking grain. And the funny thing? The funny thing is I read the little slip of paper that fell out of the book. The funny thing is I thought it was a clue. I thought it might help me with the insurmountable gravity of falling.

But I was wrong.

It only added to it.

It was something I'd read before.

It was like adding salt to the wound. It was exactly like that, like adding salt to the wound.

Standing at the edge of the burned-out foundation, atop the stairs that lead nowhere, I can't think of what to do. I don't want to revert to staring at the clear, crystal sky, somehow expecting, though not wanting, an answer. Nor do I want to throw myself headlong into the dark maw, so very close and enticing before me. I wonder if...if a few bottles could've survived? If the book, and a photo album did, why not a bottle, or two, or three?

I think about wading into the debris. About stripping my clothes off and questing into the malignant shadow. Not worrying about glass shards cutting my feet, or splintered timbers jabbing and thrusting through my ribs and thighs. I would wade into the dark tide, naked, searching. Searching for something unexpected, like the truth.

Instead I stare, realizing I'm not that crazy...yet. However, to prove I'm on my way, I unbutton my lumberjack shirt and jacket, and pull up my T-shirt, and attempt to write what Francesca wrote on a note years and years ago. And what, more recently, inexplicably, impossibly, fell from a smoky book.

If you can find me...you can have me...until...La Fin Du Temps.

I attempt to write Francesca's words on my chest with a stick of charcoal.

However, the stick is dull and brittle. It simply crumbles beneath the pressure of my hand and makes an inelegant, jagged swath of darkness across my chest and ribs. My hand, too, is stained. I release the remnants of the stick and walk home, somehow satisfied.

∞

After the next few days of talking, talking, and more talking to Ms. Vilasovic and her machine, to Mr. Mortimer, the psychologist, to Naomi and Joseph, I'm told in no uncertain terms, by Joseph, "Man, you've got to clean yourself up. You're fighting for your life here. Okay? You need to stop with this—" He waves erratically to the sticky notes filling the walls "—this schizophrenic search for truth in the trivial and mundane. You need to focus on the task at hand, and that is presenting yourself as a mild-mannered family man on whom a great tragedy has befallen." Curiously, he sounds sincere, as if he hadn't rehearsed at all.

My voice, though, sounds strained as I answer, "But I *am* a mild-mannered family man on whom a great tragedy has befallen." Unfortunately, I don't sound sincere, or convincing.

We look around the room at the walls filled with my mysterious notes.

After a long, uncomfortable silence Joseph says, "Read, watch a movie, knit, paint, collect baseball cards, exercise, build a popsicle stick house. Hell, bake a fucking cake for all I care. Do anything, anything, but bury your head in the flotsam and jetsam looking for little gold nuggets. Anything except wear a big, stupid wool hat—" (I don't mention it's a cap and not a hat; nor is it wool, but a poly-blend) "—scarf, gloves, and stupid lumber-boy shirt and jacket."

Reluctantly, I take the cap off and stare forlornly back at the walls and all the work and clues represented there.

He doesn't seem to see the pain and turmoil in my eyes, because he continues, "The question you have to ask yourself, George, is do you want to spend the rest of your life free, or in jail or a psych ward?" I look at a wall, thick with bright notes. It explains the correlations and relationships between the earth's rotations, revolutions, and direction through space-time, the poetry of Arthur Rimbaud, the paintings of Thomas Hart Benton, the female orgasm, dark chocolate, and my orange kitty, Tyler. It alone is perhaps worthy of a Nobel Prize. With the other walls and ceiling, not to mention the papers, I perhaps have a decade of prizes locked up.

"It's your choice, George: freedom, or captivity? Which is it going to be?" Another wall: Sri Lanka, Madagascar, World War II, Stan Ridgeway, sake, Zeus, the color mauve, bumblebees, and Milton. "Which is it, George?" I look at all the intertwined and woven facts, each and all subtly pointing toward my family. "Because, right now, you and your delving are simply wasting everyone's time." He again points and waves his hand around at my annotations, equations, and notes. "You might as well confess, because this isn't helping."

The ceiling is where I converge and tie the four walls together. It's where everything focuses on a single significant point, a perfect union of everything forty-two. Regrettably, Joseph and Naomi have a point. I could either prove my point and be locked away, or relinquish my argument.

Reluctantly I answer, "As you wish," condemning myself, I hope, to freedom.

"Good," Joseph says, clapping his hands together and rubbing them vigorously, "I'm very pleased you said so. Now, perhaps you can do one other thing for me?" I've already lost my only child, so I don't know what else he could possibly ask for. "Don't visit your house again. Okay? I don't know why you went back, and frankly I don't care. But someone's liable to think you took evidence, or souvenirs, or...or something. I'll let you know when you can go back—if ever. Okay?"

"How...how'd you know?"

"A private eye. I mean we gotta know what the client does and doesn't do, right?"

I lie and answer, "I.. I guess so."

"Also, George, I have a court order asking for your passport." They must have spy cameras and one-way mirrors. Then Joseph adds, "That is, if it wasn't lost in the fire."

Again I lie. "I assume it was."

"You're sure? It wasn't in that salvaged safe?"

"No. That only contained certificates and such. If you'd like, I can open it for you."

"Won't be necessary, George."

However, our eyes and the long, uncomfortable silence that ensues belie our words. The walls, huge tablets of bright truth, sag with disappointment at my dishonesty and their impending doom.

Joseph, again clapping his hands together, says, "Excellent. Then it's settled—the walls go and you stay," with a finality that's literally painful.

∞

Naomi has been left behind to supervise the slaughter of my work. I don't know which is more difficult, pulling the notes from the walls, or having her watch.

The notes are placed in a dented, green metal trashcan.

Unsure of what to do with such a mature and significant harvest, I turn to Naomi. Handing me a box of matches, she says, "Outside. By the dumpster."

After the pyre has cooled, the wind whipping black wings from the trash can, I wipe my eyes and return upstairs. I find Naomi taking the pages of copious notes and shredding them. She says, as the metal teeth devour my future, "Unless you feel like pleading insanity, these need to be destroyed, too. We don't want them falling into the wrong hands."

I don't ask if there is a pair of correct hands she could give them to. Nor do I inquire about pleading insanity. It might be the correct course of action; unfortunately though, like many things, the correct course often requires too much time, thus making it, ironically, impractical.

∞

Time, in this cocoon, doesn't so much pass as disappear. It disappears in eating whole grains and organic, free range foods.

In dispensing with coffee and incorporating green and barley teas. Minimizing processed sugars and animal fats. Replacing cow with soy—indeed the most difficult of tasks.

Naomi explains, "Basically, Mr. Olson—" I've told her a dozen, thousand times she can call me George, and a dozen, thousand times she's ignored me; at this juncture I've decided to concede defeat in every corner, "—we're creating a product to sell. The product is you, Mr. Olson. We need to make you *look* as desirable, honest, confident, capable, and, most importantly, innocent as possible."

"Do I get a secret-weapon–utility-belt and a sidekick?" Mirabella, for this next Halloween, wanted to be Violet from *The Incredibles*. I, it had been decided, would be lucky enough to be her sidekick. Exactly what that would entail was under discussion. Particularly as it was a role I, apparently, was already fulfilling.

Naomi ignores me—doesn't blink an eye. Naomi, I'm discovering, has the sense of humor of a flea, and the seriousness of a whale.

"Only as a last resort are you going to take the stand. And only as the most desperate of measures are we going to let you speak to the press. Therefore, we are creating a...a package that requires a certain look and demeanor." She hesitates, pondering internally how far she can take her metaphor before she offends me—*if* she hasn't already. "The package—you, Mr. Olson—needs to be someone people instantly empathize and sympathize with. They may not know *why* they like you, just that they do. It could be something as obvious as your smile, or something as subtle as the way you squint with concern when someone on the witness stand says, 'love.' It may even be having an American flag pin on your lapel."

"Is this when I ask, 'Are you creating a man, or a monster?'" She looks as if she's almost ready to smile, but doesn't.

To prove it, she answers, "I'll tell you this: sometimes even monsters are innocent."

"But what if I...I actually—" I don't say killed, or murdered, or anything; it's implied when I add, "am a monster?" She's read my psychological profile, the reports, seen the hieroglyphic walls, researched psychogenic fugues, and shredded the pages and pages of my unified existence dissertation.

"Mr. Olson." Her tone sounds like she's explaining how to

glue leaves on paper to a three-year-old. "That's not really the point, is it?"

I look at her, as if for the first time. I survey the lines of her face, the angles of nose, of eye, of cheek and ear. I'm attempting to discern her past, her history, in the shape and shadow of her skin. And the only thing I can conclude is that she is remarkably beautiful. Nothing else. She is beautiful, period. It cannot be argued. Her beauty, if anything, is a universal constant. I believe the entire world would agree. Every soul, some six billion and counting, down to the last man, the last woman, the last child, would agree—she is beautiful. Somehow, though, I find this to be the saddest thing I've ever known.

∞

And so time doesn't so much pass as disappear. It disappears in exercising. It disappears lifting weights one day, in cardio-vascular work the next. Gradually repetitions are increased. Gradually distance and speed are increased. Muscles, once firm in youth but fallen into midlife atrophy, rediscover their tautness. Because I'm sequestered from the world, I'm stuck with simply lifting five and ten pound dumbbells in the living room, and running on the treadmill in the bedroom.

It's my own lovely little torture chamber, this apartment.

∞

Initially the press only has my mug shot, taken on the day of my arrest. Honestly, based on the photo, even I'm sure I killed someone, if not hundreds. A photo of me at a Christmas party a few years ago is found and circulated. Thankfully, the press adopts it instead.

∞

And so time disappears. It disappears in reading. Reading Murakami. I realize, only after I'm done with *Sputnik Sweetheart*, I was supposed to be looking for a smoke reference in regards to Francesca and Mirabella's disappearance. Somehow, though, it seems less critical, less necessary, than before. Time, I guess, does that, undermines momentum and conviction.

I decide if I'm to simply be a shell, it doesn't mean I can't be filled with something. So, I read the *Bible*, the *Bhagavad Gita*, *Zen and the Art of Motorcycle Maintenance*, *The Tibetan Book of the Dead*, *Foucault's Pendulum*, and *The Da Vinci Code*.

And inevitably, obviously, I read Mr. Adams's *Hitchhiker's Guide to the Galaxy* series. Unfortunately, like the other titles, I glean no great insight. Yes, the *Guide* does state the answer is forty-two—this conundrum is presented by a supercomputer (thus reinforcing my hunch regarding binary code). However, in the book, the question is ethereal and mysterious, unknown. In my world, in my reality, I know the question, and I know the answer. And regardless of how improbable they may be, the truth of them can't be denied.

∞

And so time doesn't so much pass as disappear. It disappears in practicing, by rote and repetition, the correct answers.

"I thought you said I wasn't going to take the stand. Or speak to the press."

"You're not," Naomi insists. "However—"

"However?"

"This is, shall we say, internalizing. Internalizing answers so that they're externalized." Her explanation doesn't help. "We want you to be able to answer for yourself, what others will answer about you. Does that make sense?"

My ego wants desperately to say "Yes," but my head slowly, steadily shakes itself, "No. No. No."

"Okay. It's along the lines of *The Art of War* by Sun Tzu. Or 'know your enemy.' Or something similar to that."

I hesitate, but still ask, "And the enemy is who, exactly?" Already I think I know her answer.

"That's a funny thing," she says, not smiling.

"Is it?" I sound skeptical, because I am.

"Yes."

"Because?" I'm still skeptical.

"Because it's you, Mr. Olson. You. You and your life." Naomi continues, ignoring the void of my stare and incomprehension. "Every witness is going to use your actions and your words against you. They're going to interpret you and your life through themselves. They, these 'impartial' witnesses, are going to filter every experience they've ever had, thought, or heard of you and repeat it back. Repeat it like it was the truth, so help them God." Finally, I begin to understand exactly how much trouble I'm in. "Therefore, we need you to be prepared to hear and accept these views of you and your life.

We need you to know exactly why people believe you are a cold-blooded, calculating killer, capable of butchering and burning his family."

Regardless of how attractive she may be, after what she just said, I hope and pray I never see her again, ever.

But that's not the case.

I see Naomi, every day, for hours upon hours. We practice. We repeat. We rehearse. We eventually come to understand exactly why everyone thinks I'm a cold-blooded, calculating killer, capable of butchering and burning his family. The insight doesn't help. Not at all.

∞

Finally, the arduous torture of anticipation is over and the day of the preliminary hearing arrives.

I am sitting in the park across the street from the courthouse, diligently waiting for Naomi to appear and escort me over. She and Joseph believe this ruse will aid in my defense. If I'm initially seen as alone, as vulnerable, needing assistance simply to cross the street, somehow, so they believe, the general populace will equate this ineptitude with being incapable of butchering my family.

As I attempt to ignore the panic rising inside of me, I search the cluttered horizons for Naomi. Alas, there is only the chaos of six news crews surging around, three local, three national. There are also another half-dozen or so newspaper reporters and photographers scurrying around like intoxicated mice in a maze.

Behind the news crews lurk the most desperate of all, the curious, faceless, nameless masses, the watchers of "news."

However, the most intriguing aspect of my panic, my dilemma, is glimpsing an elderly woman step off a bus and slowly, methodically limp forward. Resolutely, head bowed, occasionally lifting it to confirm she has not drifted off course, she begins her trek toward me. As she gradually nears she looks more and more familiar.

"Mr. Olson, what do you think is your strongest defense? Truth, or insanity?"

"The prosecution proposes to show money as a motive. What do you have to say to that?"

"This ▬▬▬, this mystery woman, do you think she'll testify on your behalf, or the prosecution's?"

The elderly woman is halfway along her journey. And I? I am no closer to knowing who she is than an ant is to building a spaceship.

"Do you have a comment in regards to the DNA evidence, inconclusive as it perhaps may be, proving your daughter isn't yours?"

The cane and the limp of the elderly woman seem familiar. I try to concentrate on those items in hope of discerning who she is. However, the dancing reporters and crew continually get in the way. For all I know, the elderly woman is George Steinbrenner.

"Do you think the Laci Peterson case has any bearing on yours?"

Somehow, without the use of her cane as a cattle prod, the elderly woman makes her way through the crowd and stands in front of me. I look up. Maybe it's the way the sunlight strikes her perfectly through the trees—insight finally dawns on me. Margarita!

I start to stand, take her in my arms. Hug her. Tell her everything will be all right, fine, okay. Tell her I'm sorry. Tell her to pray for the signs to reappear. Pray for the signs I found to be remembered. Pray that I discover them again. Pray that they lead to Francesca and Mirabella and Zeus and Tyler. Tell her I understand. Tell her I love her, simply, if for nothing else, for being the last living link to the woman of my dreams, of my life—her daughter, Francesca.

Before I can tell her anything, Margarita, instead of offering her arms, gathers herself to a remarkable height and power for such a frail and elderly woman. She hovers, an avenging angel, not to accept my apology, my remorse, my confession, but to spit full in my face.

Cameras like angry insects click
-click
-click
-click
-click
-click
-click
-click
-click
-click
-cli

Immediately, her mission accomplished, Margarita turns and limps away. Slowly, like she arrived, she makes her way to where the bus let her off. She crosses the street and enters the courthouse, never once looking back.

Margarita's spittle drips off me. It makes minute Rorschach images on the concrete between my feet.

Staring at those dark, little images, cameras click-click-clicking, I realize time is no friend of mine.

∞

Joseph admits that night, "If you get convicted, that image alone—" he rewinds the image of Margarita crossing the street to where she stands before me and hits pause "—will cost you approximately five to ten years." He hits play. We watch her gather herself, pull spittle and mucous up her throat, then without further ado spit into my face.

It's odd to watch this. It's odd to know what it both looks like *and* feels like. It's perhaps more disconcerting to watch getting spat on by my mother-in-law while drinking B & B and smoking a Cohiba.

I close my eyes. It seems as if the smoke has invaded my lids. Thin trails of dark, wavering rivulets flow like thin water over them. Taking another pull on the cigar, I realize I too am on fire, fading into smoke. The difficulty is not running around, screaming insanely, feeding the flames, but instead sedately, stoically accepting the pain and waiting for the rain.

I take another long swallow of the liqueur and gaze upon a horizon, clean and pristine, completely free of storm clouds.

∞

The testimony plays out slowly, perfectly, as if it were also captured on tape and being played over and over again. It's much like Joseph fast-forwarding past Margarita limping from the bus stop and hitting play as I get spat in the face. Therefore, there are no huge media mob scenes with reporters shoving microphones and cameras in my face. There are no bystanders shouting, "Hang him high!" There are no monotonous lunch breaks methodically masticating dry turkey sandwiches. There is not the ironic swearing in of witnesses, "So help me, God."

There is only time disappearing.

∞

Detective Bliss: "The man in the van was eventually identified as a John Francis Ferdinand. He was the adopted son of a Mr. Franklin Naismith."

Leaning to Joseph, I whisper in his ear, "Francis Ferdinand was the Archduke of Austria. Assassinated by Gavrilo Princip, I think on June 28, 1914." Lightly I thump the table with my fingers, adding numbers and dates. Quickly something comes to light. "Year of the assassination, I believe, was 1914. Gavrilo Princip, fourteen letters. Francis Ferdinand, sixteen letters. June 28, six plus two plus eight equals sixteen. If you'd let me have a pen and paper, I might be able to decipher the correlations."

Joseph writes on a yellow pad of paper with his gold pen, "Be quiet. Please."

He turns back to listen intently to the detective's very boring diatribe of how Mr. Naimsith stumbled upon the photo of his son in my office and subsequently had a mild coronary attack. The district attorney, with his slick hair and inexpensive suit, asks a few questions, but the detective—like every witness—is pretty much on autopilot.

Detective Smith: "Honestly, I don't think he knows. Sure, he may've done it. But I don't think he knows if he did, or didn't. And that would suck. Imagine not knowing. There would always be that gnawing question in the recesses of your mind. Am I innocent? Or am I monster? Personally, I'd almost prefer to be the monster. I mean at least you'd know what you were. Right? Yeah, okay. Sorry. Uh, the body in his wife's Eurovan was.... Yes, Detective Bliss was very accurate. We don't know. No, we don't know. It's not like buying crack at the corner store, okay? He was confused. What'd you expect? Initially, he was angry and pissed off. It's pretty natural. But there's a little problem with the sample. Well, initially there may've been a mix-up in the samples, and then there was a spill. You'd have to ask one of the technicians. My understanding is.... In a nutshell? Okay. We don't know if the child was his or not. It was discovered the lab's samples have been contaminated. And therefore the accuracy of the initial findings are suspect. It seems some rat pissed in a few vials. Sorry, Your Honor, my apologies. I don't know. Because that's the Fire Department's investigation. Yeah, anytime. I said, 'anytime.' You're welcome."

The gallery of spectators laughs. The district attorney doesn't. The judge, a Judge Bailey, Judge Asher's tall, thin, golden-good boy, evil twin, just shrugs.

I watch everything as if I'm in a crowded movie theater where the last seat available is in the front row. I don't like the angle, and the sound is a little too overbearing.

Margarita: "He kill my Francesca! He kill my Mirabella! He try to kill me! He crazy, crazy man! He threaten me in hospital. He stare. He say, he ask, 'Where Francesca?' He know. He kill her. He try to kill me. He never like me. I never like him. He try to kill me. Sí. Sí. Sí. He.. he not at home for long time. I call, but he no call back. I stop and wait. He gone for long time. Then he try kill me. He come to hospital to poison me. But he no care. At hospital? Try kill me. Again try kill me! Bastardo!!"

Margarita gets a strange glare in her elderly eyes—as if she's seeing something that never happened. She screams, and, with remarkable agility, hops from the witness stand and charges me, her cane raised for a death blow.

"Bastardo!! Bastardo!! Bastardo!! Bastardo!! Bastardo!!"

She gets a couple of good attempts in before being restrained by the guards. However, she is old and slow, and somehow my not moving out of the way seems to confuse her. It confuses everyone—including me.

Once the commotion has dissipated, they put another witness on the stand.

Anne: "I don't think it was derogatory or demeaning. I think it was an attempt to make the job interesting and fun. Dealing with words all day, it's kind of easy to lose sight of the human aspect of things. Besides I've read all the Sam Spade mysteries. It was…. No. Well.. once, but we'd been drinking. Nothing happened. Nothing. He was under a lot of pressure. No, never. Yes, that was odd. But I think that was a story he told his daughter. I think he thought it would somehow help. Maybe because he didn't know what else to do. Maybe because there wasn't really anything else to do. I don't know. But I don't think he killed them. No, he did not. I don't know. Because we really never talked about personal matters. That was just our understanding. I'd seen her before, yes. Around the building. You tend to see the same people day after day. You may not know exactly who they are, but you know them. Her stopping by was a little odd, yes. Only the once. A few days before the fire. Yes, a few days after his wife went missing. I did see them. Probably forty or fifty pages. I wasn't sure. I thought they might've been figures and numbers from…from a study, demographics and such. No, that was the first time. I don't know. I really don't know."

Jessica: "He had ample time and opportunity to tell us about her leaving. I think he was covering something up. I think he killed them and burned them."

Joseph interrupts, "Objection, Your Honor, that's complete speculation!" Judge Bailey interrupts Joseph by banging his gavel. Joseph continues, "This is speculation! How can there be a fair trial if speculation rules?"

The gavel bangs and bangs, nearly splinters.

"Mr. O'Conner! Mr. O'Conner!" Bang, bang, bang goes the gavel. "This is a preliminary hearing, not a trial. Save your energies—" bang, bang, bang, bang, "—and interruptions for if we get that far! Please! Or you shall be found in contempt!"

Jessica (continued): "We, Leslie, a mutual friend, and I, called a couple of times to invite her for a run, or something. No. Never. One thing that was odd—well two, actually—her cell phone had been canceled, and one day the house was unlocked; the doors and windows were completely wide open. Uh, we went in. The place was a mess. It looked as if she hadn't been there for months. We, I…I didn't notice anything. It was…was really messy. She would've told us if she was going anywhere. No, he said nothing. Nothing. I think he killed her. I think the asshole killed her. I hope you fry, you bastard! I hope you fucking fry!"

I don't say anything in response to Jessica's outburst. However, I understand her pain and frustration, which she demonstrates admirably. And regardless what hopes she has for my future, I keep an appropriately concerned look secured to my features. Naomi has taught me well I think, as Jessica, fighting back tears, returns to her seat. Naomi has taught me well, very well.

Leslie: "He didn't mention anything. Once we even stopped by his office. Still he didn't say anything. He actually kind of played it off like it was no big deal, like it happened all the time. The Saturday before her 'disappearance.' We went for a run at Tryon Creek. No, she seemed normal. Like all was fine. That...that was the last time. The house was complete chaos. You could tell she hadn't been home for a long time. Yes, she liked to keep things neat. An affair? Her? No. Absolutely not. You'd have to know her. There was no way. No way at all."

Mrs. Sandquist: "No, I don't believe he was attempting any subterfuge. He seemed genuinely concerned about the possibility of a psychogenic fugue. From my impressions of Mr. Olson, I believe he's more a candidate for psychogenic amnesia. That's difficult to say, but some characteristics involve immaturity, egocentricity, and a desire to avoid unpleasant situations and circumstances. Yes, I would think an overtly active fantasy life could be a sign, though it doesn't necessarily implicate an individual. That's dependant on the individual. You must understand this isn't my area of expertise. These are just.... Very well. As short as a couple of hours, a day or two, as long and complete as establishing an entire new life and identity. For Mr. Olson? This is not a diagnosis. You must understand there are tests and.... Very well. I'd say either selective or localized amnesia. Selective is.... I'm sorry, but I'm very uncomfortable giving a.... Yes, but to imply Mr. Olson.... Selective amnesia doesn't refer to a conscious decision on the individual's part to keep certain memories, or forget others. It's simply a byproduct of internalized and/or externalized stress. It's completely out of the individual's control. It either happens or it doesn't. No one can really say, or know. You're welcome."

Nancy Coles: "No, I never spoke to him. I left a message in case they had any questions. But otherwise everything was pretty straightforward. She basically signed everything over. Odd? I suppose. But I try to not.... The papers were signed by her. I reviewed the signatures and initials from when they first purchased the house. Everything was consistent. Everything. Though his did have a slight variation, but we checked that. He'd supposedly hit something."

Steve the taxi dispatcher pipes up, "Yeah, my face," which gets a little laugh from the gallery, and a few raps of the gavel from Judge Bailey.

"Maybe a week. It matched. You'd have to ask her. I know. You're welcome."

James Dudley: "I only really clean my gutters out once, maybe twice a year. The pine needles tend not to clog like maple leaves and such. I'm tempted to buy some of those screens you can drape across the top. I hear those are.... Right. Sorry. Well, it's hard to say. But I know what I saw. He and his dog went into the shed. A couple of times I heard the poor guy—the dog, yeah—yelp. Oh, yeah, there was plenty of...of other noise. Just metal rattling and such. No. We didn't talk much. He always seemed too busy. Had something better to do. Somewhere he'd rather be. I did notice at the end there, he made an awful lot of fires. You could tell by the smoke from the fireplace. I mean it was going practically from dusk to dawn. I wouldn't put it past him. I mean, he's in the insurance business, right? Probably had them and everything insured to the hilt. I imagine he gets a pretty penny if let loose. Get himself some fancy chateau somewhere. Fucker. Right. Sorry. You bet."

Mark Wilson: "Well, let's see. There was him lying in the street in the middle of the night in the rain. There was him standing and staring into his burned house and then writing, or trying to write, something on his chest. There was him driving by his house a couple of times when that old woman...his mother-in-law, yeah...was sitting on the front steps. There was the time he ran over her. There was him just staring into his house. Oh, a few times. Ten, twenty minutes. Maybe. Started, now that I think about it, right around the time when his wife supposedly disappeared. I think, maybe, it would've been the Saturday or Sunday before. No, it wasn't the first. Yeah, he'd occasionally drive by his house. Don't know. Never asked. Odd, yeah, I suppose. But, that's George. No, I don't think he hit her on purpose. I mean, she's kind of short. Okay. Sorry. I will. You're welcome."

Steve: "I didn't know who the fuck he...oh, Jesus, sorry. Oh, sorry, sorry about...Jesus...Sorry. Yeah, I'm...I'm just a...a little nervous. Yeah. Okay. Okay. It was like a Wednesday, maybe. Sure, it could've been a Thursday, too. Okay. I got a call from some guy about a briefcase that was left in one of our cabs. He didn't have any real information about anything. Real vague.

And I thought he was fishing for something. We get that a lot. 'Oh, I lost a wallet.' 'Oh, I lost a watch.' Just in hopes of us maybe having something and being careless enough to give it out. So, I get this real vague phone call about a briefcase. And I just told the guy nothing had been turned in. I mean, he didn't even have the cab number, or the driver's name. So, then about a day or two later this guy shows up. He's dressed pretty nice, suit and all. But that really doesn't mean much, if you get my drift. Anyway, he's asking about a briefcase. I tell him the same thing as I did on the phone—nothing has been turned in. It's like he doesn't really hear me, or maybe he doesn't care. I don't know. But he starts going through our lost and found. I tell him, 'Hey, you can't just go wading through there.' And one thing leads to another and he hits me square in the face and runs off. You mean before he sucker-punched me? Nervous, kind of agitated. No, nothing about her. Yeah."

As Steve walks back to his seat, he gives a quick wink. I think he wants me to fry, too. I know I want to be able to hit him again.

███████: "We met in the elevator at work. Yes, the Black Box. I don't know. It just kind of happened. I have a friend on the twelfth floor and George works...worked on the seventeenth. I'm on the fourth. Occasionally we were on the elevator together. We said hello once or twice. Then we started having a little conversation. One afternoon I was getting takeout from the Japanese restaurant, Murata, and he walked in. We ended up having lunch together. And...one thing led to another. Yes. I don't know. I never met her. I don't know. No, no, he never mentioned anything. I guess I thought she was on vacation, or something. It really wasn't something we talked about. There was my life, there was his, and there was ours. When he and I were together nothing else seemed to matter. We...we were lovers. Over a year. No, no I suppose not. Emotions? That was another thing we didn't talk about. I loved him. I don't know. Maybe. Yes. He seemed comfortable. Fine. Normal, I guess. Though one afternoon we did run into a friend of his wife's. No nothing. He made light of it. As if it wasn't a big deal. No, he didn't mention anything. I already told you, I loved him. No, I'd...I'd do most anything for him, for us, except that. For me? There's a part of me that wishes he could, but there's a greater part that knows he couldn't. Not for anyone. He's pretty selfish."

Confidentially I lean over to Joseph, asking, "Who *is* she talking about?" I turn back to ██████ on the witness stand as Joseph writes something down and gives it to Naomi. Naomi nods, but doesn't look at Joseph or me.

June: "We'd see one another, once or twice a week at the dog park. Yeah, it's just off of Fremont. He was...nice, you know. He'd listen to me talk. About stuff, you know? About *X-Files* stuff. Out-of-body experiences, UFOs, Yetis, other dimensions, that sort of thing. Though I wasn't really sure Zeus had run off. Yeah, that was his dog. Right. I guess because he didn't seem that distraught. I thought it might be some kind of...of come-on, you know? Maybe like if I started feeling sorry for him, well.... Well, I guess because it always sounded like he wasn't happy with his wife and child and stuff. I don't think he was unhappy, maybe a little disillusioned, or maybe he felt he deserved to be happier. Does that make sense? No, I never met her. Let's see...one was about alien abductions in regards to Zeus. I couldn't say. I suppose he may've been. There was also...uh, I think...spontaneous human combustion. People burning up on their own, yeah, exactly. I...I don't remember. Maybe a couple of days or so before. Yeah, it is kind of odd."

Mr. Naismith is unable to make the hearing. He's still in the hospital recovering from triple by-pass surgery. It turns out his discovery of the bloody photo of his son and subsequent heart attack may've been a good thing. Rather than having a massive coronary in a few years, this small attack was an alert of sorts. The doctors discovered the narrowed arteries and have subsequently operated. Though, I don't expect a thank-you card.

Since Mr. Naismith's surgery has him incapacitated, a statement is admitted into the court records on his behalf.

Mr. Naismith: "I always felt George was someplace else. That he would rather be someplace other than wherever he was. I don't believe he knew where he would rather be, simply that he would rather be someplace else.

"Weeks before the deadline for the shareholders' brochure, I noticed a sharp disintegration in his attitude. He no longer cared if you knew he wanted to be someplace else. Previously he attempted, as best he could, to hide this nervous vagabond spirit. However, that changed. Why, I don't know. Maybe it was a midlife crisis. Maybe it was a lack of sex. Maybe it was eating too much dairy. I don't know. Maybe it had something to do with his birthday. Whatever it was, there was a sharp disintegration.

"The inexplicable fact that my son was found dead in his wife's car has shaken me to the core. I don't know what George was doing with that sickening photo. I don't know what any-one would be doing with a photo like that. Regardless, I believe he had it and kept it for no good. For some kind of a trophy. It was luck, maybe fate, that I stumbled upon it. I think it should be just retribution to find someone guilty for my son's death. I believe that person is George Thomas Olson. Sincerely, John Randolph Naismith."

Mr. Naismith's signature is nothing more than a crooked scratch on the page. It looks as if someone has dotted the "i" and crossed the "t" for him. I'm sure there are those saying the same thing about how I look.

Fire Investigator William Anderson: "Unfortunately, the investigation into the cause of the fire is inconclusive. I can tell you that it started somewhere in the vicinity of the fireplace and that there were no accelerants involved. Basically, everything is consistent with an accidental blaze. However, that's not to say.... No, we didn't find any remains. Spontaneous human combustion? Not really. To the best of my knowledge the fire tends to be localized to the body and the immediate vicinity. I believe the fire does consume the bones of the victim, yes. Um, I'm not positive, but I think because of relatively low temperatures combined with a slow burn time. Right. Crematoriums burn hot, but for short periods of time. I think it takes a few hours, or longer. Well, I suppose it could've smoldered for that long, sure. Then it would've had to come in contact with something more flammable, thus igniting the house. No. If that were the scenario we'd pretty much find the same burn pattern. No, we'd still find nothing, particularly if they were in the fireplace. Absolutely. You're welcome."

∞

It's agreed there's enough hypothetical, theoretical, and circumstantial evidence to go to trial, if not convict me.

Therefore, I'll go on trial for the premeditated murders of my wife, Francesca, and my daughter, Mirabella.

Everybody feels there's some twisted mystery lurking in the dark recesses of my mind. Everybody thinks a trial will finally allow the truth, regardless how dark, despicable, and ugly, to come out. I don't know which I want more, to know the truth or continue living in this state of hopeful delusion.

Living in a Coma

Honestly, I don't know what happens with time and, for that matter, myself. One moment Judge Bailey is banging his gavel and stating, "Trial is set for—" and the next, he's been replaced by a three-hundred pound, bald garden gnome named Judge Maundy, who's banging his gavel and asking the district attorney to make his opening argument.

Time and the summer and my life simply slip somewhere and return, a lover rising to use the restroom and returning.

The actual trial is a longer, more excruciating version of the preliminary hearing. People repeat what they'd initially said. Though, interestingly, they're now more secure in what they remember, what happened, what I said, and how I said what I said.

It's amazing, but for everyone except me, time and distance have solidified the past. It's remarkable. And I'm very envious.

Besides the witnesses saying the same things, but better, the prosecution shows a video of some British scientist burning a pig to prove the possibility of spontaneous human combustion—and also to prove I could burn my wife and child the same way. Once burned, the human ash would be effectively lost and destroyed in the house fire. No bones, no nothing, all very clean, all exceedingly methodical and premeditated.

Once the lights are turned back on, as the video's last image lingers and fades, a cold, angry hush descends on the courtroom like a barn owl on a mouse. No one says anything for a long time. Eventually, after the mouse has been devoured, Judge Maundy's gavel breaks the tension, and we recess for an uncomfortable lunch.

$$\infty$$

266 Ultimately, it seems nothing is answered. Everyone, including myself, is disappointed.

How does my signature match the signature on the mortgage paperwork I never signed? A mystery.

How did Mr. Naismith's son end up in the front seat of our red Eurovan with a hole in his head? A mystery.

How did the fire ultimately start? A mystery.

Is Mirabella actually my child, or not? A mystery.

There are plenty of people giving their theories, hypotheses, speculations, and opinions.

Does anyone know anything for sure? No, not really.

Once again, all are disappointed.

Throughout the trial I nod sagely. I nod exactly like that's what I expected. I expected my signature on the papers that signed everything over to me. I nod sagely that Mr. Naismith's son was of course found in the front seat of our red Eurovan. Where else should he be? I nod sagely about the tragic possibility of burning Francesca and Mirabella in the fireplace exactly as if it were a spontaneous human combustion incident. I nod sagely about the interesting idea Mirabella isn't my child but of either a mysterious jogging partner, the man who replaced the kitchen cabinets, Mirabella's kindergarten teacher, or the wine guy at the Wild Oats grocery store. All of whom, interestingly enough, are either dead, out of the country, or simply missing. I again nod sagely; and I begin to wonder if it looks as if I'm agreeing with everything...as if it were some perfectly executed plan.

The Corpse Talks

It's decided the last resort of last resorts is necessary. No one is happy about this, least of all me.

Joseph has cross-examined everyone, which seems only to have solidified the prosecution's case. He called a few of his own expert witnesses in regards to the fire, psychogenic fugues, and amnesia and such. In the end, nothing is conclusive. It will basically come down to whom the jury believes. A group of outside and impartial witnesses relating what they saw and knew about me and the circumstances. Or nothing. I had no one. Somehow everyone I figured for character references ended up being classified as a witness for the prosecution. Thus, desperation calls for desperate measures—it calls for me to take the stand. No one is happy about this, least of all me.

"This is suicide," Naomi states matter-of-factly.

Joseph agrees, "I know, but we have to if he's not going to plead insanity." (Pleading insanity is something the papers, the television commentators, and, to a lesser extent, myself, feel would be the appropriate and safer course of action.) I try explaining, in very simple words and phrases, my "forty-two-week window of opportunity" theory.

"After those weeks pass my family will be lost to eternity. I'm sorry, but presently I don't have the time to invest in insanity." I can tell Joseph and Naomi are disappointed. As slight consolation I add, "Maybe later, just not at this juncture."

Joseph sighs, finally understanding the situation, and says, "Well, if we can't force a mistrial, what do you expect me to do? Pull a miracle out of my ass?"

No one answers. We all wish it were possible, but know it isn't. (Joseph has narrow hips and a pretty small ass.)

∞

The next day, Judge Maundy commands, "Mr. O'Conner, please call your next witness."

"Thank you, Your Honor." Joseph adjusts his tie, looks at Naomi, then me, stands, and says, "The defense calls," a collective breath is taken and held as the courtroom waits and waits and waits for Joseph to finish his sentence, "—George Thomas Olson."

A surprised and excited murmur courses through the courtroom. I stand to a few veiled epithets and hisses directed at my back. I trudge to the witness stand. I can feel every eye boring into my back with the glaring conviction of my guilt. I want to walk forever. Keep them there, to my back. I can't face them. I can barely face myself. However, there's only the witness stand and nowhere else to go.

∞

I tell Joseph and the court truthfully, honestly, exactly what I did and what I remember. I tell them everything with the correct demeanor of self-assured innocence, trustworthiness, forthrightness, and honesty. I do so without looking at Margarita, or Jessica, or Leslie, or...anyone. As I've been instructed and reminded, it is the jury I need to convince.

"The entire world may believe in something, but if you can convince those twelve individuals then screw the world." Surprisingly enough, that's something Naomi said, not Joseph.

Unfortunately for my case, my telling of my story is no better than a compilation of the other witnesses' testimonies. I have no new insights, no contradictions in time and place, nothing. It's the same old story simply told by someone new, myself.

The other problem is, once the cross-examination begins, I say, "I don't know," far too frequently.

"If you didn't kill Francesca and Mirabella, where do you think they are?"

"I don't know."

"How do you think the house fire started?

"I don't know."

"What do you think happened to Zeus and Tyler?"

"I don't know."

"How do you think the body of Mr. Naismith's son got into your Eurovan, and was subsequently pushed into Oswego Lake?"

"I don't know." Even though Joseph and Naomi keep their heads high and backs straight, you can see hope waning in their eyes.

"How do you explain your signature on these documents you supposedly never signed?"

"I don't know."

"Mr. Olson, I'm sorry," the prosecuting attorney pauses for dramatic effect, "but is there anything you do know?" There is a little twitter of laughter from the gallery. Even Naomi and Joseph relinquish a smirk.

Suddenly, and I don't know why it's taken so very long, but everyone thinks I'm guilty. All these faces. All these eyes. And not one thinks I didn't kill Francesca and Mirabella. Each blank face staring expectantly at me, waiting for me to confess to something I didn't know, but they were sure of. I'd never felt more alone.

"Mr. Olson, I asked you a question." The prosecuting attorney is looking for buttons to push, and also hoping I'd confess what I didn't know. Something you see on *Perry Mason*, or *CSI*. My ignorance isn't feigned though. "Mr. Olson, tell us, please... what you do know?"

"I know this—" Anger and humiliation well up inside me. I'm indignant enough and don't need anyone to dig my grave for me. I can do it well enough on my own, thank you very fucking much. "I know I don't know if I harbor a monster inside me. I don't know if there is some junction box where a switch is thrown, because of some trivial frustration, and mild-mannered Mr. Olson quickly transforms into Dr. Ogre. I don't know. I do know I loved my wife, Francesca. I loved Mirabella. I don't mean to put them in the past tense. I love my wife. I love my daughter. Even Zeus, I love. The cat?" I hunch my shoulders. I mean Tyler's a cat. He didn't care, why should I? "However, that's easy to say, on the stand, when my life is in the balance, right? But, honestly, if it comes right down to it—" Everyone leans forward, holding their breath, waiting for the confession. "I don't know. Maybe I did." There are shouts and a rapid rise in the murmurings of the crowd. It's far too loud for anyone to hear my disclaimer, "Maybe I didn't."

Joseph, and then Naomi, begins objecting. They're claiming I don't know what I'm saying. Claiming I don't know anything. I don't know what I'm saying. I don't know anything or what I'm saying.

Judge Maundy bangs his gavel, over and over and over and over.

"Maybe I didn't," I say. Still no one hears me. Again it's like watching a movie, though this time I'm definitely on the wrong side of the screen.

The two large guards step simultaneously forward in front of the Judge Maundy. He bangs and bangs his gavel.

"Maybe I didn't. Maybe I didn't," I repeat, though now I can barely hear myself. Perhaps because I'm whispering. "Maybe I didn't. Maybe I didn't."

Eventually, an agitated calm pervades the courtroom.

"Now, if no one minds," Judge Maundy says, out of breath, glaring at Joseph, "can we get back to this trial?" Everyone is quiet. Even Margarita and her cane are mute as mimes. "Good. Now, I believe Mr. Olson was being cross-examined, wasn't he?"

Joseph is about to say something, but Judge Maundy simply slams his gavel down once, twice, for clarification.

It's true, Judge Maundy is right, I was being cross-examined. Joseph and Naomi want to say something. Want to argue, want to yank and rip me off the stand before I say anything more incriminating, more convicting than I already have. However, they can't.

The prosecuting attorney smiles knowingly and asks, incongruously, "So, Mr. Olson, how old are you?"

"Uh, forty-two." I see Naomi and Joseph begin to sag and slump. I don't know why. This is finally a question I know the answer to.

"And your birthday?"

"February eleventh, 1962."

"Why...why does that seem familiar?"

I offer, "Well, it's the same as Jennifer Aniston's."

"Ah, Jennifer," he replies, going somewhere in his mind and shortly returning. "No, no. I was thinking of something else. Oh, well. It'll come back to me." Naomi and Joseph are attempting to be subtle in the shaking of their heads. "So, you're a Pisces?"

"Aquarius, actually." Four right answers in a row. This is getting better and better.

"And aren't you, yourself forty-two?"

I look around, confused. Didn't I tell him my age a moment ago? If he's not paying attention, who is?

Judge Maundy apathetically requests, "Just answer the question, Mr. Olson."

"Yes, I am. I turned forty-two on the forty-second day of the year."

The prosecuting attorney, rubbing the back of his neck, says, "Wow. That's curious."

Naomi and Joseph are shaking their heads. They've given up the subtlety. I think it's curious, my turning forty-two on the forty-second of the year of the year 2004. I really don't know why Joseph and Naomi don't think it's curious. Not to mention remotely significant.

"You're telling me," I reply, attempting to hide my enthusiasm. I add, as if it were necessary, "Particularly when you consider it being 2004."

"Excuse me?" replies the prosecuting attorney, slightly confused.

"Well, two-zero-zero-four. See, zeros don't count, and then you invert the numbers. So 2004, two-zero-zero-four, twenty-four, invert and it becomes forty-two."

"I'm sorry, Mr. Olson, I can barely play Tetris on my son's Gameboy."

Slowly, succinctly, I explain, "I turned forty-two on the forty-second day of the year 2004, which inverted without the zeros is also forty-two."

"Oh, I see. That's rather amazing. I imagine that's some bizarre coincidence, though, right?"

"Yes and no." Finally we're getting to the heart of the matter.

"That's rather cryptic, Mr. Olson."

Naomi and Joseph are conferring between themselves. Naturally, I continue on, heedless of their trepidation at my fate.

"Interestingly enough," I explain, "forty-two days after I turned forty-two on the forty-second day of the year 2004 was March twenty-fourth."

"The twenty-fourth?" Deftly, accurately, the prosecuting attorney replies, "Let's see, the mirror of forty-two, without the zeros, because those don't count, of 2004?"

I stare, in awe. Finally someone who understands! I attempt to hold my enthusiasm. "Exactly!" But I can't.

Joseph attempts again to interrupt, "Your Honor, I object! I don't see how this has any pertinence to the case." Joseph, at this juncture of the proceedings, lacks enough enthusiasm or credibility to be effective.

"Objection overruled," Judge Maundy states, slamming his gavel for emphasis.

"But, Your Honor, I don't believe my client knows—" Joseph sounds tired and whiny, like a child who's missed his nap.

"Overruled, Mr. O'Conner." The gavel barks and barks. "Besides, I myself am rather curious to discover where this leads." Joseph sits reluctantly back down. Naomi whispers something to him. He shakes his head and broods. "Please, Mr. Olson," Judge Maundy prompts, "do carry on."

Dutifully, I say, "March twenty-fourth was forty-two days after I turned forty-two on the forty-second day of the year 2004."

"And the significance is what?" The prosecuting attorney must be absolutely horrible at Tetris.

"Well, that's the day Francesca and Mirabella left me." A glimmer of understanding falls and ignites his eyes.

"So, you're saying forty-two is the reason they disappeared?"

"Yes, exactly!" And I begin explaining Stephen Crane, Emily Dickinson, and Pablo Neruda. I explain the atomic number of Mo (molybdenum) and its correlation to the number of eyes in a standard deck of playing cards. Which, oddly enough, corresponds to the year Cleopatra became Marc Anthony's mistress (42 BC). Which, incidentally, happens to be the distance in kilometers of a marathon. And also how many people died at Chernobyl. Before mentioning the age Elvis and his father died, or the year the Toronto Maple Leafs came back from a 0–3 deficit to win the Stanley Cup, the prosecuting attorney turns stupid on me.

"Kind of like *The Matrix*?"

"No. Not like *The Matrix*. Jesus, are you stupid? That was an artificial construct. Some machine consciousness, or some such inanity. This? This is a natural process. It's a byproduct of Life and the Universe's existence. For example, both Jerry Garcia and Jimi Hendrix were born in 1942. Both have eleven letters in their names. Both my parents, born also in '42, Bob and Sue, have three letters each. See, there are these patterns in what we call the chaos of life. Slight ripples on the surface, little wrinkles in the fabric.

"So, if we keep these as examples, but expand our scope slightly to incorporate my case, the truth can't help but be discovered. For example, Mr. Naismith's son, John Francis Ferdinand, and the Archduke of Austria, Francis Ferdinand, have certain peculiar similar facts. Gavrilo Princip, the assassin of the archduke, has fourteen letters. Year of the assassination? Nineteen fourteen. Francis Ferdinand, sixteen letters. Month and day of the assassination? June twenty-eighth. Six twenty-eight. So, six plus two plus eight equals sixteen.

"Don't you see? These are the examples of the slight ripples on the surface, the wrinkles in the fabric. The patterns in the chaos. If somehow I, we, can discern their significance, we can know everything. Even know where my wife and child have gone."

For some inexplicable reason, the gallery doesn't give me a standing ovation. Judge Maundy doesn't even approvingly bang his gavel. I believe I hide my surprise, and disappointment, well enough.

"Mr. Olson," the prosecuting attorney says, in a strangely berating tone. "Do you really believe that's possible?"

"Yes. Absolutely." The prosecuting attorney turns to the gallery and takes a slight bow. "Fuck off." He raises an eyebrow, gives another slight bow. The gallery twitters. "What if forty-two *is* the answer, at least for me? What if Mr. Adams was right? Out of six billion people, the odds are relatively good he'd be correct for someone, regardless what he chose. It just coincidentally happens to be me. For you it might be strawberries. For her it might be Jesus. For the Honorable Judge it could be fishing for sturgeon. What I'm saying is forty-two is *my* answer. And the questions—where is my family and how do I find them? They have the same unbelievable answer—forty-two."

Naomi and Joseph, heads plowed together, are conferring in shallow whispers. The prosecuting attorney applauds condescendingly and says, "Bravo, Mr. Olson. Bravo."

All I have for my defense are the facts. And considering where I am in that defense, I launch them like ICBMs. "You don't find it odd there are forty-two women and twenty-four men in this courtroom?" Everyone starts looking and counting. "You don't think it interesting the two large entrance doors each have four panels on them? No one seems to care about the significance of the eight overhead lights, and the four wall sconces on the two sidewalls?" I point out everything I can. Someone has to. It might as well be me.

Eventually, however, my momentum comes to an anti-climactic end, and I stumble to a finish with, "Given enough time, enough worlds, there was bound to be a place, a person, where forty-two *was* the answer. Why not now? Why not me?"

A dull disappointment lingers over the courtroom. They, like me, wanted a bigger, stronger finish. Alas, it's too late. And instead we find ourselves adjusting in our chairs and looking around, wondering if that's all there is?

The prosecuting attorney, having taken up residence on the corner of a table, stands and states, "No more questions, Your Honor." He returns to his long-empty chair as if something significant has finally been decided.

The entire courtroom waits and waits.

That can't be it. I've more to say. I need to explain to them the correlation between Sri Lanka, Madagascar, World War II, Stan Ridgeway, sake, Zeus, the color mauve, bumblebees, and Milton. Yes, it's obvious, but so was the letter in Poe's "The Purloined Letter."

I look at Joseph with pleading eyes.

There are the interwoven relationships between the movie *Planet of the Apes*, tennis, breast implants, Death Valley, the rock group U2, macaroni and cheese, Persephone, diamonds, bagpipes, and Mirabella, to clarify to the gathered masses.

Joseph doodles on his yellow sheet of paper without looking up. Naomi looks as if she's about to cry. She, I believe, could never be more beautiful.

"Joseph?" I ask, hoping. There is the Yangtze River, great white sharks, dominoes, Kevin Bacon, sculling, pigs' knuckles, Mozart, lace curtains, Blue Tick hounds, and Zen Buddhism to explain and correlate.

He looks up, the pen still fidgeting across the paper. He smiles meekly, sadly. I'm unsure what he's afraid of. Perhaps it's me.

"Joseph? Please." There is also Sicily, tattoos, poison oak, peregrine falcons, Prometheus, hockey, and Abbot and Costello. "Please."

Joseph returns to the scribbles on his sheet of paper, his mind attempting to understand the mysteries there.

"Joseph. Please," I implore. He doesn't look up. It's impossible to tell if he even breathes. "Joseph? How can I be held responsible for such an improbable fate?"

Finally he raises his head. A strange sadness fills his eyes as he looks at me and simply says, "Your Honor, the defense rests."

Learning to Fly

It's Monday, November 1, 2004. It's cold. It's wet and woolly. The bar, though quiet, is thick with cigarette smoke. Tomorrow the jury will hear final arguments and then go into deliberation. Joseph has assured me that if I'm acquitted, which seems rather dubious at this point, there'll be a civil lawsuit brought by Margarita. He says, and I quote, "The gimpy little bitch seems hell-bent on vindication."

If I'm found guilty, we'll appeal. Joseph also says, "Sometimes it's time and not truth that wins a case." So, it would seem, one way or the other, this trial is going to drag on and on.

It's this dire prediction of my future that precipitated venturing out of the apartment and aimlessly into this bar. I want to spend a little elbow time with civilians taking their neglected freedom for granted. As a sidelight and bonus, *Monday Night Football* is on.

I sip beer after beer as the game and the night progress. Eventually the game and the night stumble to an inevitable end.

Subsequently, I toss back the last golden ounces of my last beer and notice the final score, Jets, 41, Dolphins, 14. An old-fashioned ass whooping has taken place here. It's also a nice mirror image. And through the smoke and chaos of time I recall two elderly men and a woman named Kay. It takes a moment, but I recall their mirrors. CC K CC. Another mirror, behind the bar and the rows of bottles, reflects a man gazing curiously at himself. It reflects a man with tired, unenthused eyes. Reflects a man and his thinning hair, where gray strands have begun to own and rule far too much property.

I can only gaze at myself for so long before the eyes become clouded with concern. Therefore, I return to the television screen.

The commentators are talking, but the sound is off and I transpose my thoughts and their words. The chubby animated one says, "Jets and dolphins—one is air and sky, the other sea-water. Each are elements, of sorts. Each has tails and fins and—" The other commentator, thin, gaunt, with flushed cheeks like he's been drinking good bourbon, interrupts. "Precisely. One is man-made, the other is nature. Thus the score, 41–14, like the beings' nature, transposed, flip-flopped, mirrored, is the answer." He does something odd with his hand, which I understand as him meaning earth, sea, sky, fire—everything, the Multi-Universe.

Overwhelmed, I stare into my empty glass. Again I have that strange idea something is going on besides what's readily apparent to the eye. It's not a football game with languid men discussing the intricacies of pulling guards and blitzing line-backers. Instead it's the swirls and undulations of the cosmic fabric, which I just can't quite grasp. Or can, but simply can't hold it, keep it.

I want to...4 [1 + 1] 4...make it...4 2 4—either way, the answer for my life. Forward-backward. Backward-forward. But I can't. I'm not supposed to. Naomi has instructed me well, though not sufficiently. I continue. November 1, 2004 (November, the eleventh month, 11 or 1 + 1 = 2. Placing the day makes 21. 21 x 2 = 42. And thus using the last number in the year, 4, creates the mirror of the mirror reflecting into infinity). I think something is written in all that circles and happens around me. I can't help it. Regardless of what the authorities say. And today, now, here, inexplicably, there's a convergence of signs.

"Get ya another?" the bartender asks unenthusiastically.

I'm attempting to sift and sort the congealing thoughts and numbers. I shake my head.

"Ya sure?" he remains unenthusiastic.

"Yes." I sound a lot like him. "What do I owe you?"

"Four pints, right?" I nod. This doesn't help with the settling thoughts and ideas. Curiously, before the bartender answers, my ears begin sweating. "That's eight bucks." I look at him. He adds, attempting to alleviate my expression of agony, "Monday night special, what can I say?" I drop my head and rub my eyes. Sweat now breaks out across my forehead like a flash flood "Mister, you okay?" Again I nod. It seems that's all I can do. Drops of sweat cascade around my empty pint glass as a thick bead begins running down my back. "Ya sure?" the bartender asks, unconvinced.

"Of course." Nervously he smiles. He's seen this before. He's just not sure when, or where. Taking my gloves off, I ask, "What time is it?"

Nonchalantly, playing it Bogart as best he can, he answers, pointing to the dull digital clock by the register. "Uh, it's 8:42."

I close my eyes, attempting to listen—there's a whisper of an answer on a breeze gently blowing over a smooth mountain lake, somewhere. However, I stand in the middle of rush-hour traffic in the middle of a busy, bustling city. I *know* there is this breeze, this whisper, this answer, blowing, but I can't hear it. I can't hear it!

To my left a gray hunchback of an old woman is bent like a gargoyle over a small glass of brown liquid. She's whispering something beneath her breath, an incantation, perhaps.

"Excuse me, ma'am? Ma'am?" Much to my chagrin, I'm going in search of proof.

"Mister," the bartender advises, "leave her be."

Taking my poly-blend cap off, I hold up an annoyed forefinger. "Ma'am?" The gray woman turns to me. Her eyes are bloodshot and set deep in a weathered face. She stares at me steadily. "Might I ask," I adopt a formal, rather British air in hopes of coaxing an answer from her, "your birth date?"

"Ya mean my birthday, don't ya, mister?" She says birthday like it's an old dish towel, finally dry.

I smile. The hag has gumption. "Yes, actually, I do." My feet rest in a pool of molten lava. My calves begin to melt into the glowing red magma. The bubbling runoff cascades down my back, hisses and steams behind my knees.

"Darlin', for a glass," the gray hag says sweetly through her missing teeth, "I'll tell ya anythin'." And she gives a willowy Macbeth witch cackle, which mutates into a wet, hacking cough.

After she's done battling the phlegm, she presses it with pale lips into a bar napkin. When she gathers herself as best she can, I buy her next round.

Her voice is pristine, her eyes gaze far off, as she answers, "A fire-hot day in the great state of Washington, sometime in August of '42."

The wind swirls and sweeps white caps off the lake. Traffic begins to slow. People arrive and enter their homes. Still I can't *hear* it! I can't!

Sweat pours down my chest, collects in the folds of my stomach, stains my shirt.

The bartender takes a dark bottle and pours the gray woman another glass, which he sets in front of her. She smiles thankfully; it's a prize well earned, well deserved.

"That's another—" something in his voice, like my eyes and mind, wavers "—eight bucks. Mister?" His Bogart demeanor seems to be leaving him. Maybe it's the hoisting of the hurricane warning flags?

Holding a cautioning hand up, I rub my eyes, attempt to concentrate. Attempt to block out the idling engines, the slamming doors, the wandering conversations, the obscure radio and television voices, the clutter and clank of dinner preparations.

I take my jacket off and wipe my hands on my jeans. The sweat begins to rise around my barstool. The steam supplants the cigarette smoke. No one knows what's going on, not even I.

"Hey, mister," the bartender asks, "You said you'd buy it for her. Right?"

"It's not that. It's not that," I mumble. He's unsure of my intent and quickly glances around for help and understanding. I, too, do the same. It's so hot I feel as if I'm melting. I swear I'm the Wicked Witch of the West. WWW. The World Wide Web. Charlotte's.... No, no, don't tangent. Stay focused. I'm melting. Melting. I take my dripping scarf off and loosen my damp shirt.

"It's Madeira, ya know?" the bartender says and shows me the bottle verification. The label is a coat of arms drawn in sparse lines. The shield is quartered and depicts the sun, the sky, the sea, and the grapevine. Instead of crossed swords behind the shield, there are two femur bones. Below the muted coat of arms is a saying in Portuguese—thankfully, it's translated into English—"Wine Wakes Even the Dead to Life." Below the line is a word I assume translates to established, then the date: 1842. Placing the bottle back, he says, "Sorry, but it's kind of expensive."

The gray woman, smiling ominously, cackles, "A lot like me."

"Emily, that's unsavory," the bartender says.

"You know I prefer Em."

"Whatever."

I wipe my eyes with the back of my hands. Sweat runs down my wrist like a river.

Out of the shadows at the other end of the bar, a dull, dripping wax man calls out, "Douglas, my diligent squire, perchance another?" I wipe my brow and the nape of my neck with the cap. It's like using a paper napkin to mop up a swimming pool.

"Jake," the bartender flings back, "ya know that's five? Right?"

"Indeed I do. Indeed I do," the dull, melting man replies. "'Tis my limit. I know. I know all too well." Douglas the bartender, pulls a brown bottle from a shelf and pours directly into Jake's glass of melted ice. The bottle is Seagram's 7. Five glasses of seven. (5 x 7 = 35. 3 + 5 = 8.)

I can't help but ask, "Douglas, your... your last name isn't... Adams, is it?"

Tentatively, looking around for help as if it were a trick question, he answers, "No. It's Briggs. Why?" Douglas Briggs. (6 x 7 = 42.)

The trees on the lakeshore begin to sway rhythmically beneath the growing gale. The city is slowly quieting. Lights are being turned out. People are brushing their teeth, going to bed.

"Just... just curious," I say. The numbers, the coincidences of fate and destiny, everything begins to stare and glare. They stare, they glare, expectantly—as if I should know something.

On the television, the remnants of the football fans are filing out. The camera pans around the stadium. A lone fan sleeps in the upper deck. The camera zooms in. Gradually it's discernible he's a Dolphins fan, and the number on the jersey is forty-two, with the name Warfield on it. The chubby announcer comments, "It's strange, don't you think, that the only team to go undefeated in a season had a wide-receiver wearing a running back's number: forty-two?"

Suddenly queasy, I turn away, searching for salvation and quietude in the shadows where the wax man lingers. Unfortunately, above him is a blue screen where Keno games play incessantly every few minutes. A yellow ball begins jumping for a new game. I watch in horror. Each time the ball arcs out, it explodes on a number. Forty-one. Each time it feels like a stake driven deep into my heart. Fourteen. Each time, a green wave of nausea sweeps across me. Eight. Each time, a club smacks the back of my head. Sixty-seven. Each time, a hot poker is thrust into my eye. Thirty-five. They should take me out back and shoot me. Two. Bury me in a shallow grave. Four. Build well-appointed Victorian houses over me. Twenty-one. Allow decent families with decent pets to move in. Forty-four. Let my ghost seep in and steal unsuspecting souls. Eight. Wait, they already have. Forty-two.

The hurricane winds blow me clean off my stool. Stumbling along, I throw two twenties at the bar top and stagger into the bathroom. Once I've rattled into a rusted stall, I'm immediately sick. Over and over I heave my stomach out. I heave until there's nothing left but dust-dry, wheezy gasps. Sweat rolls over me, drips into the filled toilet. A twitching hand flushes once, twice. I sway, I wobble to my feet.

My hands clutch cold metal as I catch my breath. My eyes, finally back inside my skull, slowly focus. With a thick pen someone's scrawled on the wall, **The joke's in your hand.** Someone has replied, in ballpoint pen, *my foot-long ain't no joke!* Another has clarified, in pencil, Twelve inches? In your dreams!

My addled mind inverts twelve to twenty-one; twenty-one is half of forty-two.

I-can-take-no-more! I-can-take-no-more! I-can-take-no-more! I-can-t no-more! I-can-take-no-more! I-can-take-no-more! I-can-take-no-more!

NO MORE!

Hastily nearing a trot, I exit the bathroom, the bar, as Douglas asks, "What about your change?"

I don't reply. I have to get out. I have to get away. Away to someplace quiet, someplace green, someplace blue and quiet. I have to get out! Out!

∞

Suddenly, instantly, in the cool, calm, quiet of night, it's too surreal for comfort. The air is too clear, too crisp. The streets are too vacant. No cruising cars, no wandering pedestrians, no frantic cyclists or stray dogs. Nervously, I look around. There's nothing, only me under a clouded sky with a waning moon, which attempts to gaze through the occasional gap.

Far off I hear something…a leaf is lost from a limb, swept up and whisked out over the water. It lands gently, yet I can distinctly hear the little plop as it glides upon the surface.

I wait. I wait for something I already know. So this is when my bones will burst forth as fiery brands, singeing skin and air. This is when and where I will spontaneously burst into flames. The ashes of myself will gradually be washed away. Nothing shall remain. I know, irrefutably, I'll disappear if I stay here, sweating and burning and melting, for a second longer.

I see, a few blocks down the deserted street, headlights turning onto the street. The car gets closer and closer. As it nears I discern it to be a taxicab. Inexplicably, of its own volition, my arm raises itself. The cab, just as inexplicably, pulls slowly over to the curb. I climb in.

The driver and his sour yellow eyes are vaguely familiar, but I'm as silent as a corpse. I'm going to begin blocking things out and listen. Listening to the thin wind barely whistling across the surface of a high mountain lake.

The driver asks, "Yeah, where to?" and slaps the meter's lever down with a disconcerting pleasure.

Unknown inspiration has inspired a plan from the chaos cluttering my mind. I say cryptically, "Your last fare?"

"Yeah? What about 'em?"

"Take me to where you picked them up."

Curious, his eyes squint in the rearview mirror. "Hey, sir?"

"The last fare you just dropped off?" He nods and I say slowly, making sure it makes sense to me, too, "I want you to take me to where you picked them up." His squint narrows, attempting to measure either my sanity, my capacity to pay the fare, or both.

Convinced of something, he pulls away from the curb. As I take my sweater off, I catch the name of the bar out of the corner of my eye. The sign above the bar's languid entrance reads in blue letters on white, _The 715 Inn_.

Outside, the rain begins to increase, causing the lights to smear and twinkle.

The plan is to follow the river backward to its source. The confluence of the river and the sea was obviously the bar—or, I suppose, the Inn. However, that was as much an inn as Zeus was—is a camel. Regardless, I'll follow this thread, this trickle of coincidence, until it ends, high on the mountains of truth and understanding, or until I die.

That's all that's left to me now: absolute truth and understanding, or death.

∞

The ride is longer, more mundane, than initially expected. As the shimmering city speeds by, I tumble into an uneasy unconsciousness.

"Yo, we're here," says the cabbie as we pull in front of a large, bright terminal.

Through the rain-streaked windows, I squint into the glare of Portland International Airport.

"Is that enough?" I ask, handing him a twenty as I exit the cab.

"Yeah, it sure is." I'm only a few steps nearer the glass and steel edifice before he's yelling at me. "Hey! I ain't no Goodwill! Get this shit out of here!"

I ignore his tirade about my leaving items—gloves, scarf, sweater—in his cab and continue toward a future I know nothing about.

∞

Inside the terminal there's a cacophony of numbers floating around. Instantly, easily, I'm overwhelmed with the vast array of possible meanings and interpretations.

Slowly I turn, mesmerized. If the Inn was the confluence, then this is the delta, crisscrossed and stitched with small streams and side channels.

If I'm not careful, I could spend days, weeks, caught in the labyrinth of dead-end marshes and shallow, silted bogs. Somewhere, though, is the way back to clear spring water. I simply need to be patient, to be careful.

I walk to a television screen displaying the status of airplanes preparing for departure. It gives gate numbers, flight numbers, airlines, and whether the flights are on time or delayed. All the pertinent information. It lists flights in order of departure. Another monitor, directly next to it, lists arrivals. For ten or fifteen minutes, I stare at the screen, watching the flights scroll up and out of view, corresponding to their taking off.

I'm astounded by the number of flights, and thus the number of people, going here, going there. Osaka, Chicago, Seattle, Yakima, Denver, Boise, Eugene, Oakland, Sacramento, Los Angeles. And the flights keep scrolling, keep taking off.

There's simply too much information scrolling past, too many possibilities. It's as if I'm blind. I can't see the interconnections and entwinings of the world any longer. Once on the voyage, the wind and current are discernibly lost. I flounder in stillness, unable to do anything, not even paddle for shore. For there is no land in sight, only the flat, vast, hazy horizon.

A current grips me and I feel myself being washed farther out to sea. If I'm going to drown I know I'll need a drink. I turn to find the bar, take a half step, and collide with an oversized and very heavy suitcase wrapped tightly closed with silver-gray duct tape. My momentum and my buckling knees take me head-over-heels over suitcase. I land heavily on my shoulder. I don't hear, so much as feel, something snap. A sharp, nauseating pain erupts in a bright flash between my neck and shoulder. I roll onto my back and writhe in pain.

An elderly man's panic-tainted voice calls out, "Senhor! Senhor!" I hear his clumping footsteps as he runs to me. He kneels and assists me to a sitting position. The pain is not alleviated, but doubled, by his grip. Colors explode across the sky of my eyes like fireworks as I nearly pass out. Instead, I grind my teeth to a dust that whites out everything.

In the ensuing monochromatic stillness, I appraise my shoulder with a shrug and a light pass of my hand across the growing wound. Something, probably the collarbone, is broken. So much for being careful.

I open my eyes to discover a dark pair of eyes, concerned and friendly, staring back.

"Senhor, you are okay? Yes?" Sweat rolls off my forehead and stains the ancient gray of his suit sleeve. I nod. He's unconvinced. So am I.

A small crowd gathers around us.

I gaze around at the faces as the elderly man says, "I sorry. I think you hear me when I ask for you watch the bag. You hear me? No?" Those watching don't say anything. Not to me, or the elderly man, or their gathered neighbors. They simply stare and watch.

"No," I reply, attempting to stand. He takes me by my arm, but I wave him off. I can only accept so much pain.

As I gain my feet, his wife arrives, slaps him across the shoulder, and begins berating him in... not Spanish, but... something else. Something similar to Spanish, but not.

He begins to berate her back. She raises her voice defensively. He does the same. Their screaming and arguing, over the many years of their lives, has been choreographed to perfection. Regardless of how irate they seem, there is still an undercurrent of love.

A larger crowd begins collecting around us. This only seems to feed the couple's frenzy.

Through the gazing curious, I see a pair of stern-faced security officers striding our way. Is an APB out for me? Do they already know I'm escaping? How suspicious would it be to be picked up at Portland International Airport?

I try not to think about consequences and simply attempt to calm the arguing combatants. "Con permiso. Con permiso." They seem to understand, not my poor Spanish, but my sentiments. They fall into a petulant and brooding silence. "Where...where are you from?"

"We are Portuguese. We fly from Barcelona to here. We visit daughter. She is in school here. She is student."

"Barcelona?" I ask, and ponder the city, as a very probable mountain lake. A very probable place to return to, without ever having been there before.

"Sim. Barcelona. There we have friends. Daughter is here. She is student. We visit her."

"Okay, what's going on? Is everyone okay, or what?" One of the security officers, charging past the picket fence of bystanders, has decided to take charge. The other officer picks up the offending suitcase and brings it closer, in case it attempts to escape.

The elderly Portuguese couple looks forlorn, lost, and exceedingly nervous.

"Everything's fine, officers. Really." I jump, both feet first, from the plane, prepared to put out the smallest fire. "I accidentally tripped over their suitcase...while watching it for them. And we...we got to talking and—" And suddenly, from nowhere, I hit myself in the face with a snowshovel, "And they happen to be from Barcelona and I'm going to Barcelona, so we got to talking."

"You?" the security guard sneers, "you look as if you're *returning* from Barcelona." I'm flushed and sweating profusely—I see what he means.

"No, actually, I'm going." Vigorously I nod, attempting to convince both myself and the officers.

"Which flight?" he asks dubiously.

"Uh, the next one," I say, not blinking. His eyes narrow.

"You have ID?"

"Of course. Passport, driver's license, library and Hollywood Video cards." I begin reaching for them, attempting to ignore the pain in my shoulder as I do so.

"Forget it," he says with a tone of disgust. "Just watch where you step from now on. Okay?"

"Gladly," I say, stepping very carefully through the disappointed crowd without a thank you or good-bye to the Portuguese couple.

∞

"Barcelona?" the ticket agent repeats as she types on her machine.

"Yes. One-way, please."

"One-way?" she asks, unsure.

"Yes," I reply. She types some more. I try to ignore her garish mascara; I ponder the probability of getting some ice and a shot of tequila for my arm. I hope I'll have time before take off.

"Luggage?"

"No." Her eyes narrow to suspicious slits. She looks exactly like the security officer. Perhaps the suspicious squint is part of their training.

In reply, I display Naomi's practiced, gracious, and understanding smile. I wait a calculated moment, and then explain, "I've already shipped everything over to a friend of mine, Miguel Torres. I travel light, but prepared." I place the last three hundred-dollar bills, my driver's license, a very wrinkled piece of paper, and my passport on the counter. And lastly, I set down the emergency credit card, which, moments before, I'd activated from a pay phone.

"I'm sorry, sir, but you need to call from your *home* phone."

"What if my home, along with the phone from which to call from, was destroyed?"

"I'm sorry, what?"

My card had been activated after an extended explanation of how fire, particularly home-consuming conflagrations, does not discriminate in its consumption.

Explaining as nonchalantly as possible, I peel the sticker off the credit card. "There's enough worry in this world without worrying about lost luggage, you know?"

The ticket agent knows all too well about lost luggage and

worry. Many a crazed and berserk maniac has stormed her counter in search of satchel, suitcase, duffle bag, handbag, backpack, purse, and briefcase.

Leaning forward, she replies confidentially, "I wish everyone were as smart as you." We smile conspiratorially. "Now," she adds, "window seat, or aisle?"

$$\infty$$

A soft smile lies languid on my face as the plane taxis onto the runway. Time, thankfully, conspired to allot me a few sparse moments in the airport's bar.

I'd interrupted the bartender watching CNN's coverage of another tragedy in another dry, dusty land, and acquired a shot and a pint. I also acquired a small bag of ice, which I've placed beneath my shirt in a vain attempt at minimizing the swelling and the pain.

Onboard I discover the two seats next to me are empty. It seems the fates are consecrating my escape. In benediction to them, I flip the armrests up, and, once we're in the air, prostrate myself appropriately.

The flight to Barcelona via Frankfurt will take approximately ten hours and ten minutes. I really need to find a computer programmer. Binary! Binary! Binary!

$$\infty$$

Every second of the plane's slow arc to cruising altitude, I keep expecting to hear an announcement from the pilot: "Ladies and gentleman, this is your captain speaking. I'm sorry, but I've been informed by the authorities the asshole in seat K48, George Thomas Olson, 'Big GTO' to his good friends, of which he has none, has been convicted of murder in the first degree for the deaths of his wife, Francesca, and his daughter, Mirabella. Rather than turn the plane around and waste my time and yours, feel free, at your discretion, to rip him limb from limb. You may then toss his corpse out of the plane and into the Atlantic to be devoured by all the pretty, pretty fish."

However, that announcement isn't made. I don't know why. I'm tempted to go to the cabin and explain the situation to the pilot. If necessary, if it helps, they can pass out warm, moist towelettes before my dismembering. It's only a suggestion.

As it is, nothing happens. Not even a cataclysmic crash on

take off. I'm disappointed, but there's always the chance for a mid-flight catastrophe.

∞

Once cruising altitude is reached, I call the flight attendant over.

"Do you have any aspirin?"

She—her nametag reads Eliza—explains that because of certain FCC regulations, she cannot give out aspirin, or any other drug.

I nod. It seems to be a reasonable precaution, particularly in these times where sobriety is unflinchingly expected, but not rewarded.

"What about wine?" I ask.

She smiles. "Red, or white?"

"Is it chicken, or beef?"

"Your choice."

"Red," I say, handing her one of the hundreds.

"I don't have change for this yet, sir."

"Keep it. Let's run me a tab. I mean, it's a long flight, right?" She smiles nervously, unsure about my character and intentions. "What's left over in Barcelona," I add, "is yours." Her nervous smile remains steadfast. "Agreed?" I attempt to comfort her with a placating Naomi-like smile.

It takes Eliza a moment to finally agree; I don't think it's my smile which sways her to do so, but her generous nature.

∞

On my second glass I'm asleep like an overplayed puppy.

∞

Hours later, after a dreamless sleep, I wake to my shoulder screaming and an old, cold plate of boeuf du jour. Eliza has been kind enough to include another glass of wine, which rests expectantly nearby.

Alternating between bites and sips, I finish most of the old, cold dinner. Less than ten minutes later, I'm again pulling the dark corners of sleep tight around me.

This time, though, I don't dream, but go on a "visit." June told me once, as we watched Zeus and Tuesday tugging incessantly on a red, rubber hourglass toy, "Dreams, we like to think, always come to us. However, there are dreams where we do the going, where we...visit."

"What," I asked with apprehension, "do you mean by going?" Zeus and Tuesday's circling was making me dizzy.

"Other dimensions, other worlds, or your Dream World People," she replied blithely, as if it were self-evident.

"Dream World People? What?" I asked, while attempting to see exactly how dilated and unresponsive her drugged out pupils were.

"People who only exist in our dreams and minds. They're born through us. They also die with us. They exist in a special place in our subconscious."

"How much acid have you done?"

She ignored me, and continued. "It's called 'to visit,' or 'visiting.' Dreams concern this world. The individual's troubles, anxieties, hopes, and what have you. 'Visits,' on the other hand, are temporal voyages to different times, different dimensions, different worlds. You can tell the difference, because in dreams everyone, everything, leaves you and your world behind. In 'visits,' you leave."

I'd attempted to recall my dreams. Nothing had come to mind. I'm sure, though, my subconscious was filled to capacity.

Of course I'd asked June to clarify exactly what she meant. She'd refused. I'd asked again, as sincerely as possible. Still she'd refused. Though she had added, as if it caused her great pain, "It's because I'm yet unsure if my life is a dream, or a visit." That's when I noticed exactly how sad, how blue, how Icelandic her eyes were. We said nothing else. We simply watched Zeus and Tuesday play with the toy until they both surrendered to fatigue.

This time, though, asleep at thirty-five thousand feet with a broken collarbone, on the lam from the law, with wine, beer, tequila, and boeuf du jour in my belly, I experience exactly what June means by a visit.

I wake staring into a backyard that's simultaneously familiar and completely foreign. The shed, instead of being a sallow, faded, rust-speckled green, is brightly painted as a giant ladybug. The raised beds are meticulously cultivated and seem to be yielding a splendid harvest of eggplant, peppers, artichokes, tomatoes, and squash of all shapes, sizes, and colors.

Perplexed, I pull myself out of a short camp chair and stagger, bleary-eyed, into the kitchen. It's familiar, too, but also completely foreign. The pristine counters have been invaded by the numerous shipwrecks of long-lost meals. The relics of coffee cups filled with cigarette butts and a tin can half-full of congealed fat are scattered among the bones of the dishes. A dead spider plant, its pot filled with the sticks from burned incense, stagnates in the window as a melancholy witness. The faucet drips and drips.

Above, somewhere on the second floor, music stumbles in waves.

Before I investigate the music, I attempt to adjust the faucet—to no avail; it continues to drip, perhaps with even a bit more purpose.

I walk down the hall. The air is thick, like the faucet's water, and it takes twice as long as it should to get to the base of the stairs. I notice the walls of the living and dining room are covered with curiously familiar paintings. They're like snapshots of a life I've heard and read about, but never lived.

I take a deep breath and begin my trek upstairs toward the thin, wavering music.

Eventually, years later, I reach the landing, only to discover the music is emanating from farther down the second floor's corridor. I make my way toward the soft, crackling tones, which seem to spill sporadically from Mirabella's room.

After long, straining strides, I gain the room's threshold and stumble in upon nothing I know, or recognize. Francesca, barefoot, is wearing a white T-shirt and faded, paint-spattered overalls. A cigarette droops from her lip. She's staring at a blank canvas. Layered around the room are dozens of paintings in various stages of completion. Tubes of paint, brushes, solvents, are scattered and littered here and there. The entire floor is covered in a thick, industrial canvas, which, like Francesca's overalls, is spattered chaotically with paint. A small black radio warbles incongruous crumbs of music from a corner.

Unsteadily, I walk to the only familiar item in the room, a fat, orange cat sleeping in a stained blue window bed. Francesca says nothing, is still pondering the canvas, as I look out the window at the colorful shed and garden below.

"Where," I ask unsteadily, as Tyler, eyes closed and as understanding as Buddha, pushes his head into the palm of my hand, "are Mirabella and Zeus?"

I don't turn around as Francesca stands and drowns her cigarette in a half-full cup of cold coffee. The hiss of the dying cigarette is an odd, warning laugh.

"Why, George? Why do you think we have this child? And this Zeus?"

Maybe it's the residual smoke clinging to her throat, but she sounds tired, very tired. Almost as if she's said the exact same thing a thousand times a day for a thousand consecutive years.

I turn slowly around to stare at her, only to discover her eyes are as tired as her voice. Tyler is still insistently pushing his head into my palm. Francesca glances quickly around the room and back to me and my oddly frightened, disbelieving face. She stomps immediately out of the room and into the thick air of downstairs, while I wonder who painted the shed and tended the vegetables.

When I do wake, it takes many, many minutes to fully realize exactly where I am—on a plane thousands of feet above the Atlantic, hurtling forward at hundreds of miles an hour. Even with this realization, it's difficult to distinguish this as reality instead of a dream.

Now, pressing a cold, damp cloth into the dry folds of my face, I think I finally understand why June's eyes are the color they are.

∞

Frankfurt, like Portland, is caught beneath cold, gray, wet clouds. We have only a forty-minute layover. It's barely enough time to wander off the plane, use the restroom, and go in desperate search of aspirin, or Vicodin, or Ambien, or Zoloft, or chewable kid's vitamins—anything for the hot poker being rammed, over and over, deep into my shoulder.

∞

Frau Gertrude von Grumpy, the retired weightlifter turned airport cashier, stares with absolute disdain at my hundred dollar bill and the €8.50 bottle of pills. I assume—hope—based on the symbol on the pale blue bottle's label, they are some form of Teutonic aspirin.

"Bitte?" I ask.

"Ja," she replies, and inexplicably accepts the bill and, for change, hands me a twisted mélange of Euro-script.

∞

In the airport's shiny, expansive restroom, I cram a half-dozen of the light green pills down my throat. The pills providing a certain courage, I sneak a peek at my screaming, swollen shoulder. It seems, to my untrained eye, a small portion of bone fragment has attempted to shove itself through the skin. Blood, collected and congealed, stains the skin's surface around the wound. Also, the disconcerting discoloration of a deep bruise, deep purple and toxic red, is spreading concentrically outward from the wound. If I hadn't expected worse, I'm sure I would have been sick.

Looking up from the morbid wound, I catch a businessman's appraising eye in the mirror.

"Das ist nicht gut," he comments, as if prophesizing the end of the world. However, it must not be imminent, as he has time to finish washing his hands and adjust his tie. Before he leaves he gives one last glance back, shaking his head, clicking his tongue in derision. Again he says, "Das ist nicht gut." I look back at my shoulder. I have to agree with him, it doesn't look good. Even the bag of ice, now filled with pale, sallow water, is useless. Without hope, I leave it by the sink and follow the man into the crowded concourse.

Before wandering back to the plane, I purchase another pale blue container of green pills. I suppose I should've verified with the stout and solid cashier that they were aspirin. Maybe next time. Maybe next life.

∞

From Frankfurt to Barcelona there are fewer passengers. During take off, the announcement for my apprehension is once again neglected. Nor is there a cataclysmic explosion. My disappointment, though not obvious, grows.

For company, besides my disappointment, there's the shuddering of the plane resonating into my shoulder. In a vain attempt to ignore the pain, I stare out the window and wonder.

∞

From Frankfurt to Barcelona nothing happens. Nothing. At least not on the plane.

I believe, however, everything is happening below us. It's like being in suspended animation. Catching brief glimpses of the Alps, the Central Massifs, and the Pyrenees passing beneath us, I realize an entire planet and its incalculable forces are furiously caught in the grip and throes of existence. People fighting, dying, loving, laughing, hating, crying, starving, hunting, running, driving, swimming. Animals stalking and fleeing. Forest fires and earthquakes. A planet living, while I? I simply sip another glass of red, take a pill or two, and pretend my shoulder isn't a sweltering volcano of pain. I guess, though, and it's a matter of perspective, some would say it's the same thing down there, up here.

Below, nearly on the other side of the blue-green orb, Joseph, Naomi, Judge Maundy, Jessica, Leslie, Margarita, ██████, the detectives—everyone—now knows I won't be arriving at the courthouse. I think the term on everyone's lips will be "skipped town." Once this is understood, the words will change from disbelief to: "I knew that bastard did it." "Guilty. Obviously." "Prison would be too good for him." "Bamboo beneath the fingernails!" "Shards of glass between the toes!" "Carnivorous beetles in the ear!"

There is a modicum of curiosity in me that wishes to know what Joseph and the prosecuting attorney's final arguments would've been. But, alas, maybe next time.

My delirium deepens. There's a portion of me that thinks about having another glass of wine, a few more pills, but an echo reaches me through the dark water of my mind. It sounds, curiously, like Francesca and Mirabella. They seem to be discussing something. Instead of the obvious—my short-comings as a father, a husband, et cetera—they, of all things, are discussing...I don't know what.

"Mamma, I like it."

"Sweetie, you don't need one."

"No. But I like it."

"Put it back, and let's go get some vegetables for dinner."

"Here's one for you. Put it on."

"Mirabella we don't have the time."

"Please?" They fade away as the darkness finally invades my consciousness.

∞

I'm woken by the gentle nudge of Eliza. She's still here? She's suggesting I sit up, place my tray and seat in an upright position, and make sure my seatbelt is buckled—all in preparation for our final descent into Barcelona International Airport.

Groggily, I agree. Once the tasks are completed I return to my dark, happy delirium, but not before taking another little green pill. If they're not aspirin, they're better, and I love them.

∞

Barcelona itself is caught in a low-slung sea of clouds. And landing is a curious affair. We descend for many long minutes through a thick bank of clouds. Outside everyone's window is a wispy white wall. After a few minutes, a sense of apprehension begins to pervade the plane. All the passengers are expectantly looking for land. However, there's only the thick wall of cloud. We wait and wait. Surely we've gone past the airport's landing strip and have entered the earth's crust. I wonder if everyone else thinks it's odd the earth, like the sky, is filled with wispy clouds. There's no one to ask, though. Everyone is gazing nervously out their own little portholes.

Moments before the apprehension swells into panic, the brown and gray hues of land loom suddenly up, only a few hundred meters beneath us. We let out a collective sigh of surprise and relief. The galvanizing force of imminent death having dissipated, everyone reverts back to perfect and absolute strangers.

The landing is uneventful, and the next thing I know I'm stepping off into another country, another time. Again surrounded by the unknown and exotic—though oddly familiar—I begin (again) to know exactly what June meant. There are dreams. There are visits. Sometimes, she said, it takes a lifetime to differentiate one from the other. I begin to think I'm getting closer and closer to doing just that.

$$\infty$$

Standing, swaying, in the middle of the crowded concourse with nowhere to go, nothing to do, except ignore the throb-throb-throbbing of my shoulder, I again decide to be the reed on the water's surface. Take me back, take me forth, take me to the truth.

Not surprisingly, minutes pass and people casually slip by me.

A new world, a new universe, begins to rise up and swirl around me. I close my eyes to listen. I know very little Spanish, but I catch a familiar word or two every so often. A musky sweat permeates the air. Somewhere music plays. There is the sound of a child crying. Men laughing. I keep my eyes closed and slowly let this new world, new universe, flow into me. Time will tell if it washes me away, or if I drown.

The subtle fragrance of a woman's perfume catches my nose and, with eyes still closed, I take a few steps in an attempt to follow. Quickly I lose the subtle trail. I open my eyes in hope of seeing where the woman was, where she was going, but in the milling throng it's impossible.

Again I close my eyes. A few more minutes pass, though it could've been hours, or days, when the mild and soft scent of talcum powder floats by. I don't know if it's from an elderly person, a diapered child, or a very clean ghost, but I follow it regardless. I lose it quickly and once again find myself waiting, with eyes closed.

Finally the curdled stench of a workingman lumbers past me. I follow as far as I can. I bump into a few people, my shoulder shooting sparks of searing pain back and forth and around my mind. Eventually I lose the salient trail. But something else takes its place. Something just as thick and acrid as the man's stench, but far more recognizable and frightening— smoke from a cigarette.

The smoke, after the woman's perfume, is all too easy to follow. Five, six, seven, eight steps, and I'm at the threshold. Both nose and ears are assaulted. One by smoke, two by chaotic voices, chatter, and laughter.

Opening my eyes, I smile at the discovery of a life buoy attached to a passing ship—a bar.

It's crowded, noisy, and smoky; I take the last seat at the bar. The lone bartender, a gentleman who looks—oddly enough— Japanese, with gray at his temples and a penchant for giving a slight bow after people have ordered or paid, is initially too busy to notice me. I close my eyes and wait.

Somehow I think I hear Francesca laughing. I think I hear Mirabella asking about butterflies. Then there is Zeus barking at Tyler, and Tyler's hiss and spit. There is also a lawnmower and a crow cawing. Then a man's voice, "Senhor? Qué paso?"

I smile sadly. I believe, after Francesca was done explaining butterflies to Mirabella, she was going to tell me how and where to find her. As it is, in weak, pathetic Spanish I order a beer and a sandwich from the bartender. He gives a slight bow and dashes off to get my beer and my ham and cheese sandwich.

No matter how long, how frequently, I close my eyes, I don't hear Francesca, or Mirabella, Zeus, or Tyler again. All is silence inside, chaos all around.

The sandwich and a second beer are nearly gone when I take three more of the German pills. I no longer feel the dull throb of my shoulder. In fact, I barely feel the dull throb of my entire body. Even my heart seems to have stopped.

I smile at the miracle. The miracle of medicine. The miracle of air travel. The miracle of sipping Belgian beer served by a Japanese man in the Barcelona International Airport bar as John Cougar Mellencamp plays over the stereo, while my life continues unraveling back in Portland is, to me, astounding. Amazing. Miraculous. It's like being in love. Well, almost.

Part of the unraveling, I should think, would include a warrant for my arrest. Maybe the FBI has been notified? Perhaps Margarita has banded together a vigilante mob and is stalking the streets in search of me? Perhaps ▬▬▬ is realizing I loved not her, but only Francesca? Perhaps I'll find Francesca and Mirabella before I die? Perhaps I'll realize.... Then a bottle behind the bar catches my eye.

I squint, and I'm almost sure it's the same bottle. I call the bartender over and point to the bottle. I nod as he points to it. He extends it at arm's length toward me.

Yes, it's the same brand the elderly woman with the birth date of August, 1942, was enjoying back at *The 715 Inn*. I can tell by the sparse line drawings on the label.

The bartender inquires if I would like a glass. I have never had Madeira. And on a stomach full of boeuf du jour, wine, pills, beer, ham and cheese sandwich, melancholy, pills, fractured collar bone, and second-hand smoke I probably shouldn't, but.. I'm in Spain, while my life is in Portland, unraveling.

I agree.

The liquid is dark amber, and smells beautiful. Occasionally, when Francesca and I were first together, on a Saturday, or Sunday, I would sleep in and she would get up early and putter in the yard. After digging in the dirt, she'd take a hot shower and return beneath the covers. It would be the smell of Francesca's skin that would eventually wake me. The earthy smell of dirt, perspiration, and grass slightly hidden by soap and shampoo. Her skin smelled exactly like the Madeira, beautiful.

And suddenly I know where I'm going—besides insane.

Hastily I pay the bill, leaving the Madeira untouched.

∞

My interpretation of what the ticket agent is saying is that the only seat left is in first class. With the memory of the Madeira, of Francesca's skin, still lingering in my mind, I can only agree.

My hand shakes as I hand the ticket agent my credit card. It has survived this far, but at some juncture I think it would, should, be canceled. Nervously, I wait and wait. I smile nervously. Sweat drips nervously down my back, under my arms. I'm beginning to smell myself rising off of my body. And it's not a pleasant odor.

Inexplicably, the machine prints up a slip. Hastily I sign it. She hands me the ticket, and points to where the gate is, and says, sincerely, "Muchas gracias, señor."

"Thank you," I reply, hurrying to the gate and the awaiting plane for one last flight, for one last push upstream to that clear mountain lake.

∞

Once I'm onboard, I discover Flight 759 will take longer than expected, four hours and thirty-five minutes, to reach its destination. However, here in first class I have many distractions, like wine and movies and plenty of legroom. I ask the flight attendant for a glass of Rioja (I pretend I'm alleviating the pain in my shoulder, but I know I'm actually attempting to drown my fear).

On my own private monitor, I select for my viewing pleasure *Elf* over a curious Hal Hartley film titled *No Such Thing*. Mirabella and I saw *Elf* when it was first released. She and I had so much fun we took Francesca the next day. I know by seeing this again I'm attempting to capture something already lost, but I can't help that, can I?

Thankfully, I know what to expect, and so I don't make a fool of myself laughing like an idiot all alone. However, I sit bolt upright twice during the movie. Each time causes great searing waves of pain to wash over me. Each time I take a pill, or two, and attempt to settle back down with a mouthful of red wine.

Each time I try to ignore the significance.

First, Buddy, the elf, played by Will Ferrell, is hit by a taxi while crossing a street. The number of the taxi which collides into him is 4 x 27! Second, the number on the door of the apartment where Buddy's long-lost father (played by James Caan) lives is 402!

Each time, unable to hold back my surprise, I sit quickly up, sending my shoulder into agony. Then I follow the pain with pills and wine. Then, at the end of the movie? Tears.

I don't know where they come from. Maybe it's remorse. Maybe it's fear. Maybe it's simple fatigue. Regardless of the cause, I cry, which I think disturbs the other passengers more than if during the movie I'd laughed hysterically. For many minutes tears slide down my cheeks and fall onto my lap. My head rests on the window and, outside, the blue Atlantic slips away beneath us. I cry and watch the sea slip quietly by.

A flight attendant stops by and places a warm cloth next to me. I don't thank her, I'm too busy crying, too busy being remorseful, or afraid, or tired, or.. and then, I see something off in the distance. Something green and glimmering on the sparkling ocean.. an island.

The island, the greenest island I've ever seen, seems to be floating on the bluest waves. Above the greenest island, floating on the bluest ocean, are the whitest clouds floating on the bluest sky.

Cruising at five hundred and thirty miles per hour, we get closer and closer. The impending arrival upon that strange fact-fiction island is, like death and taxes, inevitable. It's simultaneously exhilarating and frightening, frightening and exhilarating.

I never finished the story I'd tell Mirabella about the island and the Unicorn who learned to fly. Or, more correctly, she never heard the end. Inevitably, she would fall asleep somewhere between the Unicorn befriending the Farting Dog and the Laughing Cat and the three of them defeating the bloody Wolf-Dragon of Rance. I, too, would snooze for a while, cramped on Mirabella's bed. Then I would wake and trudge off to sleep. On my short trek down the hall from Mirabella's room to Francesca, I would quickly finish the tale.

Once the Wolf-Dragon was dead and the Unicorn covered in blood, they would discover a portal to a meadow where a path led to the High Cliff of Flight. The Unicorn would step through and the portal would instantly close behind. Sir Dog and Squire Cat would never know if the Unicorn took the path to the cliff, or not.

Squire Cat would argue, "No." Sir Dog, vehemently, "Yes." Pessimist. Optimist. The lines had been drawn. The battle would rage long and hard into their later years.

For me, tragedy is the true story of life. Regardless of how much hope and promise one has, or discovers, or shares, death waits for all.. even so for the Universe, in time. Therefore I don't believe there is any question—the Unicorn took the path and stepped off the cliff. Now, as to whether the Unicorn flew or not...that's sheer speculation.

∞

I stumble off the plane and through customs, making a beeline for another bottle of aspirin, or what I hope are aspirin. These, though, are a soft, milky shade of yellow. I take two, not even worrying about water (or wine) to help swallow them.

I'm outside, swaying at the edge of the curb; the sunshine is brilliant, and lazy clouds pass lazily overhead.

As the gentle breeze nudges me back and forth, a short, grizzled man with a cloudy left eye arrives and stands beside me. He joins me in my appreciation of the clouds overhead.

After a cloud that looks remarkably like Fidel Castro—or a penguin—passes by, I ask, "Do you think it odd the town of Timber is on the island of Wood, which is relatively barren of trees?" Honestly, I'm not expecting an answer. I'm actually expecting him to ask for a few escudos, or euros, for a shave or maybe a six-pack, but definitely not to answer me. And not, as he does, in the impeccable tones of the Queen's English.

"Life is peculiar, my friend. Perhaps it's only those words that keep this island afloat. Funchal. Madeira." I turn and stare at him, confused. The short, grizzled man with the cloudy left eye then asks, increasing my confusion, "So, my friend, what is it you need?"

We watch a few indistinct clouds drift by as I think about his question. Finally I answer, "Need? Need is an interesting term." I want, or need, to tell him that I need my wife and child back. I need my dog and cat back. I need my life back. I need a little understanding into what the hell I'm doing on this island, on this little planet, in this little solar system at the edge of a little, nowhere galaxy, spinning, spinning crazily through a vast universe filled with billions and billions of other galaxies.

I remain silent and we watch another cloud pass. This one is less like a battleship, more like a reclining Buddha. Another cloud and another, each a cocker spaniel, pass languidly by. The short, grizzled man with the cloudy left eye bides his time. He knows, instinctively, I'll eventually answer.

When I do answer, "It's too late for need—I require," he nods appreciatively.

However, irony fills his voice as he subsequently asks, "So, my friend, what do you *require*?" He scratches his chin. It sounds like sandpaper cleaning a chalkboard. "A woman? A girl, perhaps? Drugs? Or something, shall we say, more exotic?"

Ignoring the unnerving scratching noise, I answer, "Truth and understanding. Nothing else will do. Nothing. I mean it." The man, thankfully, stops scratching and smiles, genuinely, as if he understands.

"Well, my friend, you've come to the right place."

"Oh, have I?"

Ignoring my sarcasm, he says, "Oh, yes. Though the island is beautiful and filled with happy people, it was built on pain and fire. Fire and pain. That is why it, as you said, is so barren of trees." We watch a coiled snake on a bike float by. "The first explorers to land, over six hundred years ago, were unable to traverse the island. The trees were so thick and had grown so close together no one could pass between them. So, what did these explorers do?" This, I know—because I've recently asked one—is a rhetorical question. I shrug my one good shoulder and watch a juggling triceratops float by. "They, in their infinite wisdom, set the island on fire. It burned, out of control, for seven years. When sailing at night, you could see the burning island from hundreds of kilometers away. Once the island was finished burning, they returned." The grizzled man takes a silver flask out of his dirty, sweat-stained jacket, and sips appreciatively. He offers me the flask, which I, less appreciatively, also sip from, as he adds, "There is a local legend that claims the reason the crops grow so abundantly is not because of the fertile ash left over from the fire, but because of the mythical creatures that died in the fire. The souls of these creatures, say the locals, inhabit the food and wine, even seep into the sea, causing the fish to be delicately tainted, too." Taking another swallow from the flask, I know all too well the Unicorn who couldn't fly died here.

"Thank you," I say, handing him back the flask. I don't comment, but the liquid in the flask tastes surprisingly and precisely like water.

"You're most welcome," he replies, raising a hand and calling a taxi over. "If you find what you require, let me know." He tucks the flask back inside his jacket and brings out a badge. "It's probably illegal."

The dusty white taxi lurches toward us in a cloud of diesel. As it screeches to a halt, I'm forced to ignore the curious fact the phone number for the taxi service, stenciled everywhere in green is **291 336 873**. This, I attempt to convince myself, means nothing to me. $(2+9+1+3+3+6+8+7+3=42)$. It means nothing. It's simply numbers, inevitably lined up in the inevitable way they should be.

"Enjoy your stay in Madeira, Mr. Olson," the grizzled detective says, while opening the door for me. He then brusquely walks away, leaving me to climb into the taxi, accompanied only by the invisible gorilla of my confusion.

The driver looks remarkably like Zeus; he even has the little scar on his lip where Tyler once scratched him.

Looking at me in the rearview mirror, the driver asks, "Onde?"

I look back, bewildered.

He offers, "Wo? Oú? Dove? Waar?" Something seems to click, and finally he asks, unsteadily, "Where?"

"Oh. Uh…." My mind and tongue stumble for an answer. "I…I don't know."

He smiles and takes off in a cloud of blue-white smoke as if he knows exactly where that is.

Breakneck speed is achieved. Outside, the pristine scenery is nothing more than streaks, splatters, and blurs of color—a Pollock canvas.

I pull myself to a sitting position. The driver inquires, "You American? Yes? You hungry? Yes?"

Considering I had only the Rioja on the flight over, and the ham and cheese sandwich is now nearly five hours past, I agree. "Yes. I'm hungry."

"Brunette or blonde?" he laughs. "You betcha!" he throws a thumbs-up at me. "Sim! Rápido! Rápido!" and he stomps the accelerator down farther, which I'd hoped was impossible.

We fly past a dabble of gray and brown. It seems to be a cart filled with what looks like mounds and mounds of wicker items being pulled by a tired burro, which is led by an elderly man who seems more tired, if possible, than the burro. The driver honks and screams and thrusts a flailing fist out the window. I'm tossed against the door and my shoulder, so recently in dormancy, now reignites. Hot venom begins oozing from the wound's cracked dome and stains my shirt.

"No. No," I hiss through the smoldering steam clouds of pain.

"Pescado. Fish." Somehow the idea of eating fish tainted with the souls of mythical creatures intrigues me. Inexplicably, it almost makes me hopeful.

"Pescado?" He's mystified, and seems slightly offended.

"Yes. Sí. Uh, fish. Pescado. And vinho," I reply, fumbling to take the pill container out of my shirt pocket. Then I realize—not Spanish, Portuguese. I don't know any Portuguese. I repeat, "Pescado," and move my hand in what I hope looks something remotely like a fish.

"Ah," lightning strikes, "peixe?! Vinho?! Restaurante?! Sim?!" Both his hands are off the wheel, mimicking my fishy hand.

"Yes-yes-yes-yes." I say quickly, in hope he will return his hands to the steering wheel.

"I know place," he says, tapping his temple with one hand, the other still weaving, fish like, "Um restaurante boa. Sim. Peixe delicioso."

"Uh, bueno, bueno, bueno, bueno," I reply as we skip across a bevy of potholes.

Desiring something to focus on, besides our impending doom, I attempt to take the lid off the aspirin container. We take a shortcut straight through a curve, and narrowly swerve back into our lane to avoid colliding with a local bus. The pill container leaps from my hand and sallow yellow pills spill over the seat and into the footwell. The driver hurls the identical profanities and gestures at the bus and its driver as he had at the old man and the burro. The bus driver does the same. It must be a local custom.

Hastily, furtively, I fumble for a few of the spilled pills.

As I'm groping through sticky nuggets and dry crumbs, the driver slams us through blind corners, I attempt to recall a prayer, any prayer. Unfortunately, nothing comes to mind, and we hurtle on sans assistance.

The driver, smiling mischievously, turns around. I fear he'll begin to assist with my search. Instead he asks, "O Presidente?" I assume he's referring to the grizzled police detective with the cloudy eye, "He tell story? Story, sim?" He turns around in time to whisk the wheel and keep us from colliding with a crazy, European, concrete telephone pole.

Steering us back into oncoming traffic he asks, "Eh, story about amantes?" He then wraps both hands around his back and makes kissing noises. We drift back into the relative safety of our lane. He continues fondling his back, continues making the kissing noises. Disturbingly, it looks as if he's being mauled by someone with large knuckles and hairy hands. It's anything but a pretty picture.

Shaking my head free from the vision, I interpret amantes for him. "Lovers?"

"Sim! Sim! Lovers, or...or exploradores?" He salutes and strikes a stiff, solemn military pose. Again, both hands are far from the steering wheel. We're now veering toward a balsawood guardrail overlooking the sea and a plethora of jagged rocks.

My scavenging hand can retrieve only four pills. Each is covered in dark dust and brittle hair.

Before we collide with the guardrail, he drops his saluting hand and guides us back onto a relatively straight course.

After a succession of potholes, one after another after another after another and another, I curiously find myself in a sitting position.

However, the cracks in the caldera of my shoulder are beginning to grow and glow with pain. Noxious gases spew into the charged atmosphere. My brain sends a futile air raid warning to the rest of the body: "Evacuate! Evacuate! Evacuate!" It's repeated over and over. Over and over.

Straddling the yellow line, the driver careens us around another blind corner. A woman sweeping the front porch of her whitewashed house shakes her broom at us as we fly past.

The driver yells back, shaking his fist vehemently at her.

"Me sister," he explains, checking in the rearview mirror to see what I'm doing with the four sad pills in my palm.

"Explorers," I finally answer, attempting to remove the debris and detritus from the sad, sallow pills. "He told a story about the island's explorers."

"Ah, of course. Of course, exploradores."

We near the town proper, but the driver doesn't seem to notice or care. I lean forward to look at his license, so I can later give him a piece of my mind about his driving, whether that be in heaven or hell. The photo, disconcertingly, is of a man that is not driving the cab. I assume the name on the license is also not the person driving the cab: Juan Jésus Véspera. ($J + J + V = 10 + 10 + 22 = 42$). If you believe, if you follow the trail, inevitably you will be led to the path of Truth, which, ultimately, leads to the Cliff of Flight.

Even though our speed is inexplicably increasing, the speedometer rhythmically wiggles at a sedate forty kilometers per hour. The city begins to fold and wrap around us. Houses, pedestrians, and parked cars, fly past in a sickening blur. The first pill is adequately cleaned and thrown down my throat.

"You want hear story? About amantes? About lovers?" I'm unable to answer, for fear and pain have taken my tongue hostage. The driver who isn't Juan Jésus Véspera turns completely around. "It good story. You want hear?"

Frantically I nod and concentrate on scouring the remaining encrusted pills clean as we quickly near a red light. Cross traffic moves steadily by. Pedestrians cross. We shall all die. However, the driver, disgusted with my addiction, turns around in time to slam the brakes on. We squeal to a stop inches from a grandmother and her grandchild, who is dressed in the uniform of a private school.

The blue-white rubber cloud of the tires envelops us.

The grandmother smacks the hood with her cane, and walks on. The little girl and I stare at one another as if we've met before, as if this has happened, once, twice, a thousand times before.

The driver honks and yells into the ceiling of the car, "Lovers lost and bound to time wander the world!" The burnt stench of tire enters the cab, drifts across the intersection. The little girl looks back once more before she's dragged out of sight by the grandmother.

"Is that Shakespeare, or Rimbaud?" I ask sarcastically, attempting to ignore the deep fissures growing deeper in my shoulder. Quickly, I throw another pill into my mouth and swallow. Grudgingly, it tumbles down my throat.

"Ah, meu amigo." The light turns green and we are immediately back to forty kilometers per hour, which distinctly feels like two hundred. "É vida. É Miguel Ignacio Torres." ($M + I + T = 13 + 9 + 20 = 42$). Miguel Torres? I ignore the reference and the unsettling feeling crawling up my spine that I've been here before, done this before. I even attempt ignoring the suspicion the cabbie won't get out of the way of the clattering dump truck rumbling down upon us.

"Something to do with the—?" As we dodge at the last second out of the path of the dump truck, a small dip in the pavement sends us into the air. We land solidly; sparks fly out from beneath the cab and from my shoulder. "Les amantes?"

I ask in pain, with scalding magma dripping, oozing, from the wound and down my chest. My breathing has shortened, and I feel as if I sound like a cornered animal. A few strands of hair and other miscellany still cling to the two remaining pills. I don't care. I swallow them like Christmas candy as a snow-white wall looms a few hundred meters in front of us.

The cabbie takes the blind S-curve between two, large, whitewashed buildings like he's Mario Andretti. "Sim! Torres was poor poeta," he shouts, as surprised as I we didn't catch a corner and tumble to our deaths in a disintegrating ball of steel. Instead we skid, side to side for a moment, thin tires wailing like banshees, straighten, and continue headlong down the dark road.

"Aren't all poets poor?" I scream as we miss a hewn-stone retaining wall, and shoot past colorful corner stalls and out-raged vendors into the town central.

"Torres felled in love with, jovem Condessa, bonita. Condessa felled in love with him. Poor, poor amantes." He shakes his head sorrowfully as we pass, swerve, and curve around busses, cars, and burros escorted by old, gray-clad men. Miraculously, we only hit potholes and curbs. Over and over again. And again.

"I suppose," I speculate to the swaying wooden rosary wrapped tightly around the rearview mirror, "they died alone and apart, lamenting a love never consecrated or consummated?"

A moment passes where we catch one another's eyes in the mirror. We are somehow afraid of, though intrigued, by the other. Quickly it passes as we nearly sideswipe a couple of slow-moving tourists on blue Vespas.

"Ah, no, no," he says, wagging a finger at me as a flower cart from an alley marches sideways in front of us. He, instinctively, dodges us into oncoming traffic. Miraculously, we swerve safely back into the lane in front of an old, red, rusted Audi. The old Audi gives a long, lugubrious honk, which is nearly impossible to discern at our speed.

The anonymous cabbie, unfazed and seemingly unconcerned with minor margins of error or our lives, continues, "Torres and Condessa have três crianças, happy, happy, many, many years. Torres, though," the cabbie shakes his head, makes a click-clicking noise with his tongue, "never write one word more. Until—" He snaps his fingers and throws us around a sharp right turn; a handful of pedestrians scatter and barely escape. We shoot down a narrow, shadowy alley, the side mirrors occasionally screaming against the walls. As we fly down the alley, he's laughing and honking crazily. And seconds before I join his crazed chorus, we suddenly shoot into the town's sun-drenched main square. At one end is a church, at the other is us, skidding to a shuddering and thankful stop.

The few pedestrians who narrowly escape pound briefly and emphatically on the roof and hood in protest. The driver, still unconcerned, taps the fare meter. It reads 24.41. He taps it again. And then again. It stumbles over, dead at 24.42. Satisfied, he takes from his pocket a pouch and paper, and begins rolling a cigarette.

But what do I care of the fare? It's trivial. It's simply a precursor to the inevitable. Numbers in a series inevitably line up, one after the other, for centuries past and centuries to come. It's more difficult to boil water than it is for me to finish this, my life.

With my one good hand, I sift through the convoluted pile of miscellaneous currency crowding my pocket and ask, "Until?"

"Until?" The driver, rolled cigarette drooping from his lip, stares at me in the mirror like I'm a grain of sand on a vast sandy beach. "Until?" He repeats it to himself and not to the sand.

Maybe he doesn't recognize the word through my accent? I don't know it in Spanish, or Portuguese, or any other language for that matter. Futilely I nod, and place a ten and a twenty euro bill on the front seat, and repeat, "Until?"

"Ah, *sim*," he replies lifting the bills to his nose and sniffing deeply, appreciatively, "Until."

The door is open, I'm halfway out and headed toward nowhere, when he, the bills securely wadded up and thrown into the glove box, answers. "Until Miguel Torres write 'Um Poema de Despedida,' or 'Um Poema dos Amantes.' Torres then walk para dois dias to a.. a penhasco." The cabbie makes a slow, flat motion with his hand, then sharply cuts it off. "Penhasco." He does it again, and repeats, "Penhasco."

"Cliff?" I offer.

"Sim, sim. Cliff. Cliff on far, far side of an Ilha de Madeira. Torres he walk para dois dias to cliff where he—" He moves his fingers like the legs of a person. He walks this hand person along the edge of the dashboard, where it leaps off and comes crashing down on the dusty stick shift. There, dramatically, his fingers twitch sporadically, and stop, dead. "Poor, poor poeta." He takes a contemplative drag on his cigarette and shakes his head sadly.

I throw another ten on the front seat as he adds, "Now, engraçado, it a peregrinação." This time his finger person marches over the cab's interior. "Peregrinação." He then, with the same hand, crosses himself. He performs this charade two more times. "Peregrinação."

"A...a pilgrimage?" I suggest.

"Sim, sim. Pilgrimage para the breaken-hearted. Oito, nove, por ano pilgrimage all way, and...não mais." Again his fingers make the trek along the dashboard, jump off, twitch, and die.

This is all something I've heard before, but it's nothing I understand.

"Yes, but *why*?" I ask. "Por qué?"

"Por que? Por que não? Amantes heart-breaken. Else why?" The cabbie inhales luxuriantly on his cigarette and exhales the smoke through his nose, satisfied with this answer.

"No. No," I say desperately. "Why did Miguel Torres?"

"Ah, that very good question, senhor. Very good." He ponders, playing idly with the matchbook in his palm. He is thinking very hard. Attempting to remember all the rumors and stories he's heard over the years in bars, bistros, and pubs. Finally, he answers, unsatisfactorily, "Não saber." He's as disappointed as I. "Não saber."

I look at him, before I shut the door, and see a man of nearly eighty leading a tired donkey, pulling a cart filled with wicker odds and ends down a street toward nowhere.

"Nenhum problema. Obrigado, amigo."

The last thing he suggests, his hands swimming like a fish, before squealing out of the square and nearly running down a small group of German tourists huddled around a map, is "Restaurante Jango, 166 Rua de Santa Maria. Peixe great! Peixe great! Sim! Sim!" He shoots off like a bullet from a short barrel, waving and shouting a jubilant good-bye, "Vá se foder! Vá...Se...Foder!"

I wave, and can only muster a half-hearted, "Hasta mañana," as exhaust and tire smoke swirl around me.

Confused, unsure of what to do next, I gaze around the white-tiled square through a hazy-blue cloud. Tourists and locals alike lounge on the church's steps, mill around a few vendors' stalls, while a handful of couples, sitting at an open air café, sip sophisticatedly quaint drinks. Curiously, everyone is staring at me.

As innocuously as possible, I slink off down a side alley and attempt disappearing.

A block or two later, I ask a woman dragging a silver cart stuffed with vegetables and paper-wrapped meats, "Donde Restauranto Jango, por favor?" Me and my pathetic Spanish are just going to have to suffice.

The woman, suspicious, glances around. How far is help? How close is the killer?

"Por favor?"

She, now noticing my state of decline, takes pity on me, turns forty-five degrees, and points to a red door not more than ten feet away. It seems I've become more stupid than I look. The medal is in the mail.

"Ah, sí, sí. Of course. Gracias, señora." I attempt to play it off. But to no avail—stupid, blind, and dumb am I. Particularly speaking Spanish to a Portuguese woman.

She gives a nod melded with a derisive smirk and totters off. Her basket, crooked-wheeled, weaves drunkenly behind her.

Restaurante Jango is a hole in the wall, and, unfortunately, it's closed at this time of the languid afternoon. Though famished, I do not wait. I wander. I will wander until I find this path of Miguel Ignacio Torres's. Two days and a night? That's a cakewalk compared to the crazy-blind summer in the snow globe I've just survived. Believe you me, that cliff might as well be around the corner.

Instead, to my disappointment, around the next corner is the Mercado dos Lavadores, the Farmers' Market. Instead of solitude and sky, there is chatter and haggling and chaos. On the threshold I stare, bewildered and perplexed. Behind me the open square, and at the other end the austere church. Reluctantly I choose fruit and vegetables over salvation and divinity.

Colorful stalls of various fruits and vegetables crowd the market. Elderly women with sagging, drooping breasts wander purposefully, though seemingly aimlessly, around. They jam their purchases into large woven purses and carry them like heavy children. One woman, surely a professional, squeezes a red fruit until it practically cries and calls out for forgiveness. The woman puts it down and stalks away, disappointed. Fruit, it seems, needs to be hearty, capable of suffering and pain.

Standing, swaying, on the edge of the market, I notice the pleasant fact pomegranates are 4.2 euros a kilogram, blood oranges 2.4. If I weren't so tired, so drugged and drunk, so broken, I might flee screaming, the flames eating and chewing the air and me. Instead I sway and smile. Smile at a child, or is it an old man? It depends on how the sun illuminates him, how the shadow of the building hides him. I smile because he wears a faded, torn, wrinkled Miami Dolphins jersey. The jersey, of course, is Paul Warfield's, number forty-two. The old-child, child-ancient man with his begging cup squats near a stall selling peppers. The pepper seller has eight different varieties.

Turning here, I find another coincidence; turning there, I discover another proof of fate, of destiny. I turn again and again. Around and around, everywhere, is a reminder I've seen this before, done this before. I don't know where, but I've seen this before, done this before, lived this before.

In the spinning interim, remembering something completely new and forgetting the immediate past, an old plan strikes me. Strikes me like an iceberg, truth and conviction crashing in and flooding everywhere.

Then the plan for the rest of my life coalesces inside me. Stupid as it is, it makes sense. I will have a last meal. I will wander for two days and a night. I will find the cliff and become the Unicorn Who Couldn't Fly. I will redeem myself in my death. In that mystery my failure as a husband, as a father, will become obsolete. Death shall set me free. Shall burn and purify my poor personal island of regret, of disappointment, of remorse. I shall, hopefully, provide an adequate starting point for a new life in the next life.

That is what coincidence and circumstance have done, brought me to the foothills of my impending doom.

There will be an impeccable mystery wrapped and shrouded around me. Cabbies, judges, and old, gray women will tell the tale: "He left on a stormy night, jagged with lightning. Magically he eluded a dragnet of police officers and FBI agents. Was attacked and broke his shoulder in the struggle to slay the giant beast. Over thousands and thousands of miles he roamed and searched for his family. He struggled through great trials and tribulations. Suffered and survived. Eventually, bewildered by exotic lands and islands, he floundered in melancholy and remorse. Still he struggled on, hopeful to the sad and bitter end. Finally, the end of his travails near at hand, he discovered the mythical Cliff of Flight. For weeks he tottered on the edge, staring the Gods and the Fates in the eye, demanding they answer his pleas. But to no avail. Only the sad, sorrowful sigh of the wind answered him."

Why hadn't I thought of this sooner? Or had I? In another life? Another visit? This is perfect. It's simple and appropriate. A perfect plan. Perhaps the first true plan I've ever had in my life. There was no plan in studying English and Comparative Literature. No plan in going to Europe just for enjoyment, just for getting away, running away. No plan in meeting and marrying Francesca. Just love—as if that somehow was enough. No plan with the job, the house, Mirabella, Zeus, Tyler, everything. Things, life, simply happened—a personal evolution. Adjusting and reacting to one circumstance led to another, then another and another. Eventually, in the end, like having an opposable thumb and walking upright, there was Francesca, Mirabella, Zeus, Tyler, the house, the job, the car, the wine, the books, the life. Not anyone's fault, per se, only a gradual progression, something inevitable, like death and taxes—exactly like life.

Now, however, there's a plan. There is the last meal. There is the long walk to the cliff. There is the impractical art of learning to fly.

Therefore, the meal should be gradual, slow, articulate, and subtle. It, of course, should absolutely include "peixe! Peixe great! Sim! Sim!"

Therefore, I wait for Restaurante Jango to open.

∞

For the few hours before Jango opens, I wander aimlessly around the alleys and through the miscellaneous shops. I look at the local handicrafts, the wine, the wicker, the woven goods. My shoulder, surprisingly, has fallen into a sullen and despondent dormancy. Maybe it too is taken with the unique beauty of everything that is the island of Madeira?

I find a corner against a building and sit, eyes shut, in the sun. Gradually, the backs of my eyelids begin to glow sunset orange. My warming skin, in a mellow Buddha chant, asks, "Why? Why? Why? Why?" Not even attempting to conjure an answer, because one has already been supplied by the heavens,

I unbutton my shirt, exposing the well-traveled, well-soiled T-shirt beneath. As best as I can, I roll my sleeves up, never once opening my eyes. Everything I do now is going to be done with blind conviction. I sit back and let the hot, heavy rays of the sun bake truth and understanding into me and my bones.

∞

Immediately, or forever later, the scalding heat ushers me roughly up and into the cool solitude of a nearby building.

It takes a moment for my eyes, heart, and soul to adjust to the light, the solemnity, the cold air of the building. Which, after far too many minutes staring into the dusty expanse of the nave, I realize is due to the building being a church.

My stomach, caught in its own existential dilemma, growls demandingly, "Peixe. Vinho. Peixe. Vinho. Peixe. Vinho."

Instead of immediately acquiring sustenance and solace, I meander, clockwise, around the perimeter of the nave. In alcoves, beneath brilliant stained glass windows, men I know nothing about lie entombed in dusty marble sarcophagi.

Midway through my circuit, I notice another dusty marble sarcophagus in the cool shadows. This one is larger, more ornate. Atop it lies the marble effigy of a man and, for company, a sword. Beside the sarcophagus is a large bronze plaque.

I make my way to the plaque.

It tells, in Portuguese, with corresponding translations in Spanish, French, German, and English, the story of a man caught between the First and Second World Wars. It tells of his brief rule, his abdication, and his exile to the island of Madeira. The man was Karl I, Charles Francis Joseph, the last Austro-Hungarian emperor. He died on the island in 1922. A footnote by the date refers me to the fact, curiously and coincidentally, that same year Miguel Ignacio Torres wrote his "Um Poema de Despedida" and made his long, solemn trek to a cliff on the northern side of the isle.

This cliff, tragically, is where a few heartbroken lovers leap every year to their deaths. Unfortunately the footnote doesn't give a map, or directions, to the trailhead. Quests are never as easy as they should be.

I read the plaque, once, twice, and again—there's nothing else to do. After a moment I find a comfortable pew, and sit, and wait. Wait for what? I simply wait for time to pass. I wait for my hunger to become more acute. I wait for nothing more than Restaurante Jango to open.

∞

Eventually, above me, bells ring. A short smile wakes itself on my face as I stand and leave the cool, comfortable confines of the church.

∞

Restaurante Jango smells of olive oil, fish, and black pepper. I'm the first patron of the night, and I'm given a window table overlooking the alley where I was once lost.

From the Bela Lugosi-faced waiter I order a bottle of what I hope is red wine.

Thankfully it is. It's tannic, full-bodied, and bold. It's exactly what I need.

Halfway through the second glass, I decide on the most expensive item on the menu. I don't know what it is, but I order it anyway.

I offer the waiter a glass of the wine. He nods appreciatively and pours a healthy amount into his decidedly dirty, well-used glass, which he takes back to the empty bar, his office.

My meal is a conglomeration of seafood, sausages, and what I think is chicken, in a deep, bubbling, and spicy sauce of red. It's served with heavy hunks of bread which I use in an attempt to quell the subtle fire flaring from the sauce. Remarkably, it accompanies the wine perfectly. It's almost as if I knew what I was doing.

∞

The server, standing appraisingly above me, his cheeks slightly flushed from the glass of wine, nods approvingly at my empty plates and distended belly. He nods even more approvingly as I order a glass of Madeira and what I hope is dessert. It only seems fitting. Considering this is my last meal and all.

Again that short smile is waking itself on my face. It's as if my body knows something I don't.

It's also fitting that my tab is forty-two euros. Without batting an eye I hand him my credit card, savoring the culminated flavors of the Madeira.

Reluctantly, sadly, the server returns with melancholy eyes and hands me my card.

"No, senhor. I sorry. No." He shakes his head steadily, as rhythmically as a metronome.

It, like everything, was only a matter of time. They, the dirty, conniving FBI bastards, now have an electronic transaction trail from PDX to Restaurante Jango. A five-lane, newly paved freeway compared to the piecemeal, goat trail I followed to get here. Regardless, they won't catch me. It will be far too late. Far, far too late.

I hand the waiter my last hundred-dollar bill. He walks to the bar, where he does some calculations on a small calculator. He returns with a receipt longer than his arm and fifteen pounds of change.

I nod, agreeing to and accepting the burden. After a moment, savoring the final drops of Madeira, I stand and leave everything for him, once again, to sort out.

Stepping outside into the soft crimson light of a sun just setting, it feels like... it feels like a bedroom. A bedroom where a little girl can't sleep and a father lingers to tell a story in an attempt to make his life meaningful: "And as Unicorn, Sir Dog Fart-A-Lot, and Squire Laugh-Cat turn a corner and exit the dank bog, a giant castle looms over them on the near horizon. This, they know, is the lair of the evil, bloody Wolf-Dragon of Rance.

"Squire Laugh-Cat hisses, sounding remarkably French, 'I hate dragons!'

"Sir Dog Fart-A-Lot agrees, 'Yeah, Cat, who doesn't hate dragons?'

"The Unicorn, though, simply stares, realizing something altogether less obvious, but far more tragic."

∞

I assume the path out of town is north, northwest through the market, past the scattered houses, into the hills and over the horizon.

Before I linger too long thinking about this and that, I take the first step. And then another. And another.

It's particularly easy if I don't think about it, if I simply put one foot in front of another, unconcerned where I'm going, though knowing all too well.

∞

Halfway through the Mercado dos Lavradores, past vendors staunchly closing and packing up their wares, I hear above the din something familiar, but not recognizable. Glancing around, though not glimpsing the noise's source, I notice the beggar with the Dolphins jersey. A few miscellaneous coins and bills remain in my pocket. Why not? What am I going to do with them? I make my way to him and the beaten brass cup nestled between his knotty knees, gnarled hands, and feet.

Passing a shop, a few feet from the beggar, I again hear the same something. This time I recognize it as a laugh. Familiar, high-pitched, joyful, like a covey of quail skittering through damp, morning sage.

Immediately my eyes follow, attempt to peer into the dull gloom of the shop.

Three dark figures stand stiff with what I interpret as unease. I must look horrific, like a living corpse, a zombie. That or I've caught them doing something clandestine and evil. My interpretation could also be affected by their masks.

The stout, rotund one wears a mask of bright colors with a big nose, a toucan or other exotic parrot. The tallest wears a simple, flat, gold-enameled face. It's reminiscent of Greece and antiquity. Somber and slightly austere. The shortest one's is a fanciful affair—a white feathered mane encircles a soft purple face accented by ruby eyebrows, nose and lips, while a swirled, black horn juts, dagger dangerous, from the forehead.

My confusion dissipates as I notice the shop is a mask shop. A menagerie of faces, colorful heads with horns and feathers, wings and fangs, adorn the walls. Tigers, lions, and bears. Zebras, sharks, and eagles. The entire collection is gathered, is staring expectantly.

The stout, rotund one removes his mask to expose an elderly, mustached gentleman. He, I assume the proprietor, asks in crisp, accented English, "Might I help you, good sir?"

I shake my head. The empty eyes gazing intently from the walls cause a sharp paralysis deep within me.

Among the elephants, giraffes, and wolves are faces of more obscure, mythical creatures. These, of course, are the creatures that once inhabited this isle. They remain baffled and horrified by the unknown, yellow-orange monster which so swiftly claimed them. Everything is staring, is waiting, is watching.

Nervous, I play haphazardly with a few coins that whisper dully in my pocket.

The other two, patrons, I think, though perhaps they are mannequins, don't move, don't breathe, don't do anything.

They are perfect statues. If I'm a zombie, they indeed are concrete effigies. Their dark, unblinking eyes stare intently—black holes devouring matter and light. Devouring everything, including me.

Before discovering my profile is also hanging on the wall, or being pulled into dark oblivion, I turn back to the beggar and his cup.

The beggar's ragged head is downcast and deep in shadow. However, down the alley, just over his shoulder, the last rays of the day transfix the few clouds into a perfect oil painting. Behind me the slow disassembling of the market progresses in the muted tones of the tired.

I fish out the last coins and bills from my pocket and drop them into the beggar's cup. The coins sound as if they're heavy stones dropped from a great height. I also seem to hear the quick slap-slap of sandals behind me. Though it could be the beating of the carrion crow's wings, come to follow me.

The beggar looks up. He seems to hear them, too. Where his eyes should be, there are only scarred, empty sockets. The crows, it would seem, have been here before. A distinct sign I'm on the right path.

The blind beggar says, through a mouth barb-wired with stained, crooked teeth, "Obrigado, senhor. Muito obrigado."

Another disjointed series of sandals slap-slap-slapping seemingly brings one pair closer and another out into the fading light sifting into the marketplace.

The beggar adjusts his head once, twice, to the closing sound of the sandals.

I steady myself. The crows surely can't be strong enough to carry me off. Can they? Mustn't they wait until I've completely collapsed on the battlefield? Expired and grown cold. Carrion for the crow. A feast for the Devil's minions.

The sound of their breathing is hurried, expectant, and shallow. Maybe it's mine? The beggar's head twitches and rotates nervously. After a short moment it stops as if finding what it's been searching for.

Slowly I turn around. Instead of a murder of carnivorous crows I discover the two statues from the mask shop. Curiously, they both still wear their masks. Again they're more statues than living people.

Apprehensive, I look from one to the other to the other.

And back again. I wonder which eats my brains, which sucks the marrow from my bones? We wait and stare.

Perhaps, frozen with fear, they're speculating whether *I* eat brains and suck marrow? I resemble a brain-eating, marrow-sucking zombie much more than they.

We stare back and forth, one to the other, attempting to discern something. Something impossible, but distinctly probable.

No one asks. Not even for help.

The round, mustached man, now with a fez adorning his head, arrives and fills the shop's door. Initially he's puzzled by the scene. It seems, though, he's witnessed worse; he calls commandingly, "Ladies, your masks, if you please," and thrusts his pale palms out expectantly.

Neither moves. They continue to stare. The shop owner looks at me. I look at him. Both of us look back to the two masked statues.

After a long, long moment of everyone listening to everyone breathe, the blind beggar shakes his cup. The coins echo like bones.

The tenuous spell having been suddenly broken, the shop owner requests, "Ladies. Please. The masks." Then he realizes, "Unless, of course, you'd care to purchase them?"

Before another taut moment passes, the blind beggar, with his rattling cup, stands and limps off in the general direction of sunset. The sound of his hand, the steadying cup scraping along the rough wall slowly fades into the distance.

"Ladies?" the shop owner insists.

Then one speaks, the little mythic one, "Momma?"

Another spell is broken. In response a cool breeze bellows lightly through the vacant square. Leftover debris blows, dances, tumbles here and there. The breeze also brings an answer—the tall one nods her gold, gleaming head. It's a gesture of agreement, of abdication, of surrender.

The little one relinquishes first. She and the shop owner are overtly careful of the long, black horn. I don't know if it's the muted light from the setting sun, or my general state of drugged intoxication, but this little creature seems remarkably familiar.

The taller one deftly removes her glittering face. She shakes her head; long raven-winged hair falls down on her shoulders. It must be the muted light. Though it could also be the pills, the wine, the fatigue, the jet lag, and the impending doom, because she too seems familiar.

The shop owner gives a slight, courteous bow and immediately exits, clattering the door to the shop shut and locking it behind him.

Now left alone, we again find ourselves awkwardly staring back and forth, from one to the other, to the other.

Utterly stupefied, I can't help but stare and stare and stare at this strange woman, who is all too, too familiar. And she at me. The little one glances between her and me, then repeats again a word I've heard at least once before. "Momma?"

This, I slowly begin to realize, is the woman from my visit. Or was that my life? Regardless of whether my life is a visit, or vice versa, it seems I know her. Know her, because it feels as if we've done this once, before. Is that right? Only once? It feels like forever. Like forever is the most perfect thing.

"George?"

I know it's difficult—there's no way I'd recognize myself either—but inexplicably she knows my name.

Tentatively, I agree. "Y-yes."

There's another short silence as we find ourselves attempting to grapple with the ramifications of this answer. None of the questions seem to be adequate, and the little one, as if as a last resort, calls out, "Papa," and dashes toward me.

I can feel the disbelieving emotions melt and wrestle themselves deep into the muscles of my face, grotesquely twisting it into a look of horrible confusion.

Immediately the little girl stops in her tracks. Her ponytail flops over her head and slaps her in the face. Aggravated, she adopts an exceedingly cute pout, as she flips her hair away with the back of a hand, and stares at me in sullen silence.

"Mir-Mirabella?" My voice sounds dry and strangled. Automatically her mother places a protective hand on her shoulder. I don't blame her. I'm tempted to do the same for myself, but recognize it's far too late.

My face still feels as if it's contorted into a grimace of horrible confusion. Before the increasing wind blows me out of town, dust swirling past my ankles, I ask, "What.. what are you doing here?"

The familiar woman remains mute, simply shakes her head. I nod as if I understand. I only wish I did.

Long moments pass. Scraps of debris from the grocery stalls swirl and circle around the square. Time slows, stops.

I'm reminded of a last gunfight scene in a spaghetti Western.

The first stars slowly wake overhead. Our breathing seems to stop. Everything is happening around us as we wait and wait.

Somewhere a dog barks. Still we don't move. We clench, un-clench our fists. We lick our lips. We wait. An alley cat cries forlornly. Still, curiously, the gunslingers don't move. A lone crow calls over the rooftops. Its voice is shrill and demanding. The woman makes a decision.

My hand moves to an invisible gun, but instead she leans over and whispers something in the little girl's ear. The little girl looks at the confused man, me. She's about to argue some point of subtle contention, but the woman whispers some-thing else. The little girl, in anger mixed with frustration, turns and runs off in the opposite direction. Beneath each footfall a slight gasp of dust rises as her sandals hit the pave-ment, echoes of my descending heart. She turns a corner and my heart immediately stops.

The woman slowly straightens, her eyes intent on me. She sways slightly on the balls of her feet, settles herself in preparation. The camera concentrates on the twitching hands, the squinting, in-tent eyes. It moves back and forth between our eyes.

I hear knuckles crack, and see something shiny and glisten-ing at her waist.

The dog, the cat, the crow and wind are replaced by crick-ets. First a lone one, but gradually the entire square, town, and island are engulfed in their mesmeric cadence.

The duelists stare and wait.

Again I ask, desperation in my voice, "What.. what are you doing here?"

Even the crickets are shaken by the question and briefly fall silent. The woman takes a step back, as if she too is prepared to flee. Shooting people in the back is against the code; I'm forced to step forward. She takes another step back. Sadly I smile. This cat-and-mouse will never work.

Slowly, instead of a silver Colt .45, I take a very wrinkled and creased note out of a sweaty pocket. She edges slightly away. Nodding, inviting, I extend the note as if offering a scrap to a stray.

I attempt to make it very clear I mean no harm. I'll not shoot. It's exactly like the first week we had Zeus. Every movement, every gesture, needed to be obvious and apparent lest he react—run away, bite, snarl, whatever. In time he learned. Learned we meant him only love, only understanding, only the things he'd dreamt about while caged.

It takes a few minutes, the note clattering against my fingers in the wind, but eventually the woman takes the tentative steps and cautiously plucks it from my fingers.

I don't wait to see if she reads it. How can I? The note shouldn't exist in the first place. I shouldn't be here, nor should she. And yet, we are. I turn and walk away. Somewhere a cliff waits for me. Somewhere I need to discover if I can fly.

Behind me, barely above the crickets, I hear her fight the wind for the slip of paper.

In my mind she reads one side and then, of course, the other. After a few heartbeats of confusion the woman asks, "This? This means what?"

The wind has stolen her intonation and I don't know if it's a threat, a promise, or a realization tainting her voice. Perhaps it's nothing. Perhaps it's everything.

Turning around, only a few steps from the alley the blind man took, I reply, inadequately, "I don't know."

The woman shakes her head as if the wind and crickets are causing her pain. This I understand more than threats, promises, or realizations. "But how? How did you find us? How?"

I smile. The only answer I have, I use again. I believe, regardless of what she or anyone would ask, it would be the same. "Forty-two."

She can't accept it. Honestly, nor can I, though somehow it sounds correct.

"*How?*" Even in this thin light we can see our eyes are filled with incomprehension. She asks less emphatically, hoping the repetition will help, "How?"

I stare at the woman. The woman stares at me, dubious. Is it tears, or the growing cold that causes us to shimmer?

She says, "You look tired. And...broken."

My smile grows, and I answer, "I am."

Awkwardly we stare at each other, back and forth. Each shimmering and glistening in the wind. I feel as if we could do this for a million years. I feel as if we've already done so. I turn to where the sun is now only a ruddy glow on the horizon.

Somehow, seemingly miles away, the distance beginning to stretch out, I hear the soft wrinkle of the note being read again, turned over, again. The note, in the woman's regal handwriting, reads...

Sweetheart— If you can find me...you can have me...
...until...La Fin Du Temps.

"George?" I take a step. I'm almost there. The sun is now a blue memory on the horizon. "George?"

"Yes," I confess to the darkness.

"Where are you going?"

Over my broken, shattered shoulder and the remains of my life I answer, honestly and without hesitation, "Where you can find me."

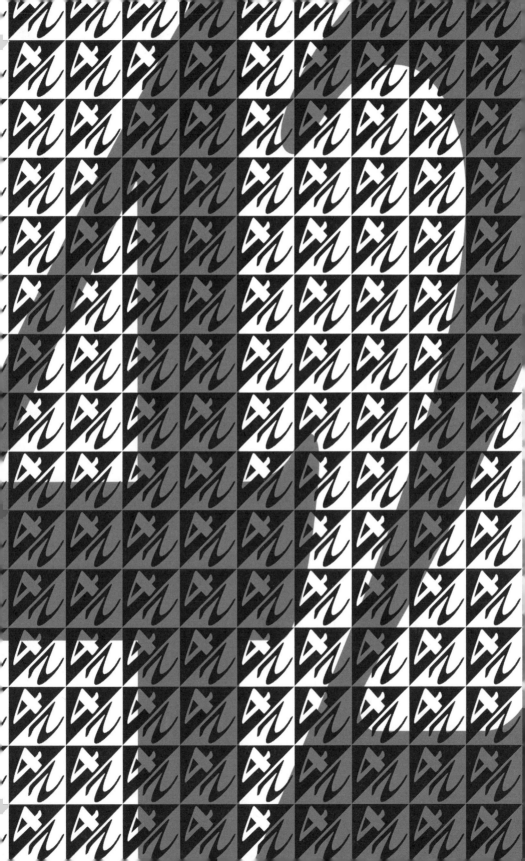

Epilogue

Through a mouthful of ovos com lingüiça I attempt to explain that I'm writing. To prove my point I wave my pen emphatically around.

"Besides," I mumble, "I'm two cups shy of being awake and chivalrous enough to escort anyone anywhere." But the morning Sirens, Francesca and Mirabella, don't want to hear it. Don't want to hear anything. They sing an argument. I add, "Regardless how beautiful. How mesmerizing."

They're unconcerned with my lamentations, my arguments. They're giddy with excitement about something. Maybe it's the impending flamenco lessons. Or, maybe, just life. Either way, it's slightly annoying. Particularly considering the time and the lack of caffeine.

Francesca continually asks how I found them.

I, as a friendly, gentle rebuttal, occasionally ask how they disappeared. And, of course, why.

At a small café, over our usual afternoon espresso and biscotti, Francesca and I again find ourselves at an uneasy armistice.

"Please, my love, tell me how and why you disappeared?"

Francesca smiles, sips the dark liquid from the white cup.

"How? Why?"

I know she knows I know how she'd grown tired. Tired of the perfect boredom and ennui only suburbia can provide. Tired of my neglect. Tired of being tired. She also knows you don't confess fear to friends. Because friends will tell you it will get better, it will be alright. And, before you know it, another year or five will have disappeared beneath the tires of boredom and ennui. So, I know why—all too well. And the how? The how is the easy part. Once there's a why the how is simple—is a matter of fate, of destiny, of time.

Redundantly, because I'd like to hear her say it, I ask again, "How? Why?"

Francesca, of course, replies cryptically. "You know, George, answers to difficult questions are not given easily. You also know those who ask are occasionally unprepared for the answer." She takes another sip and places the cup back in its saucer. "Perhaps," she asks, going on the offensive, "you can tell me how you found us? Doesn't that seem far less likely?" Again she smiles. This time, though, her smile is a cat-o'-nine-tails. It chews flesh, bites bone. I have no will, no choice—I acquiesce.

In my confession I describe how I journeyed on a dark and stormy night. How daggers of lightning exploded everywhere as I deftly eluded a dragnet of officers and agents. Was attacked by a hideous beast, and broke my collarbone in the struggle to slay its vileness. How, over thousands and thousands of miles, I flew in search of her and Mirabella. Struggled through great trials, turmoils, and tribulations. Suffered and survived. Eventually, bewildered by exotic lands and fantastic foes, I stumbled on the sacred shores of a mysterious and magical island.

"Yes, so you say." She glares, she smiles, she asks, "But how?"

We both hate my answer, "—forty-two." Unfortunately, though, that's all I have—the truth. "Forty-two."

Our cups are empty, only a few biscotti crumbs remain on the bone-white plates, the café receipt is held down in the gentle breeze by a few coins. We silently stand and walk home, unsatisfied, bewildered, but happy.

∞

"And the note?" she asks as we undress. We both remember tearing it, eating the halves in Paris, ages ago, lives ago. We can even describe the dry, sour taste of the hotel's stationary, the gagging taste of the thick ink.

Nestling beneath thin sheets, I attempt another explanation. This time, though, I sound like June. I feel my eyes become colder, bluer, which is odd, because they're green. "Just because we remember something doesn't mean it happened in this life, in this universe."

Francesca glares, then she smiles, and then we make love, slowly, perfectly. After, curled like kittens, we fall asleep— satiated, but not satisfied.

∞

Mirabella, of course, has her questions too. And, as usual, hers are more difficult to answer.

"Papa," she asks, doodling on a stray sheet of Francesca's sketch pad, "where are Zeus and Tyler?"

Francesca, reading in the other room, a glass of Alsatian pinot gris at her elbow, glances at me, concerned.

I begin, "Usually you have to lose something to gain something..." but Mirabella's eyes stop me.

Do you explain the transitory nature of Life, of everything? Even the Universe, someday, will cease. Why? Because Time and Eternity are bastards; they are the true Gods. Do you explain this to an eight-year-old? Could you?

I can't.

Instead, I ponder defining blood sacrifices, curious rituals, strange, twisted necromancers, but even I don't believe that.

So I say, "Sweetheart, Zeus and Tyler-kitty are on the most remarkable adventure ever."

Francesca smiles and returns to the world of her book as Mirabella's red, swirling pencil stops and she leans intently forward, "Yes, Papa?"

I sigh and reply, hoping she'll believe and that I, for a change, will be convincing. "They've gone questing for the three-headed squirrel's treasure, which, legend claims, is hidden beneath the last rainbow in the dark land of Burbia."

From that moment the story simply grows and grows, becomes beautiful and true.

∞

Tonight, like most, our whitewashed cottage is wrapped beneath a dark and comfortable blanket. The multitude of hovering stars, glimpsed out the window, seem to inhale, with perfect rhythm, the sighing sea. The handful of candles also inhale, exhale, the mysteries of the waves. The waves whisper cryptically back, and I smile at the cadence of the language, not knowing the meaning or implication.

Those that could interpret this for me, Francesca and Mirabella, are rocking quietly asleep.

When I'm done with this last entry I'll lie with Francesca and, again, cry myself eventually to sleep. It's something I do every night. Silently, so I hope and pray, to myself.

When Francesca reads this, she'll ask, "George, why in the world would you write so many lies?"

I'll reply, "Because there are so few truths," and sidle up next to her, kissing her just beneath the ear, causing her to giggle.

Gently pushing me away she'll claim, "You are an ass," and quickly pull me back into her arms.

Now, though, there are only stars, waves, wind, and words for company. And, honestly, I don't have many words left.

It's taken a long time to write this, to live this. Can you tell? I can.

Perhaps, though, for you, it's been a month or two sneaking a few pages during a lunch break, a chapter on the subway or bus? Maybe it's only been a week, a simple, little distraction during an hour after dinner, or before going to bed? Or perhaps it was devoured over a three-day weekend at the beach?

But, regardless of how long it's been, because we know time, we should finish and be on our way. Quickly, for I have a wife, a daughter, and a life to return to. And you? You have what you have. Is it enough? Is it? I hope so. I honestly do.

So, next time you turn the handle, and water flares from the nozzle, and steam rises like smoke, and you stand there, awkward but exhilarated at the impending sacrifice, attempt to journey to a mirror. Once you've arrived, voyage out of sight of land and look for a dark spot on the horizon. Find the island and spend a moment cast away. Disengage from the clutter and the chaos. Disengage from the scrubbing and the picking up of shit. Attempt the trek through the thick, thick trees to that high promontory far, far from your life. Attempt the trek with the fewest things you know and hold dear. Notice how her lips press to the glass, curling in anticipation of the cold, clear, golden wine. Notice the furrowed brow of concentration as the little one focuses on the red curl the pencil makes into a cat, a dog, a dragon, a unicorn. Eventually, if you can stay long enough, everything becomes noticeable, significant.

And, from such a vantage point, perhaps you'll notice another ship landing on the opposite shore. The crew, like dark ants, disembark. Quickly they become frustrated at being unable to find a path. As their frustration transforms to anger, little diamonds ignite and are thrown into the thick, thick trees.

Watching the flames grow, realizing it's too late to return or learn to fly, that's when the tincture of love, and appreciation for this life, stains your bones, seeps irrevocably into your marrow. When you realize what you need isn't so far away but right in front of you. That's also when the experience of reading a word, traveling across a sentence, a paragraph, venturing the turn of a page is elevated. Elevated to a breath, a heartbeat, a life. And when you close the book you can't help but wonder if it were fact, or fiction, my life or yours.

Ooligan Press Publishing Students
Responsible for This Book

Acquisitions

Lead Acquisitions Editor
Katrina Hill

Acquisitions Editor
Karli Clift

Design

Cover Design
Rachel S. Tobie

Interior Design
Cliff N. Hansen

Design Proof
Tim Harnett

Translation

Translation Coordinator
Kari Smit

Portuguese
Kari Smit

Spanish
Stephanie Kreutter

French
Aimee Rasmussen

Marketing

Marketing Managers
Bradi Grebien-Samkow
Jenn Lawrence

Publicity Lead
Amanda Taylor

Managing Editors

Haili Graff
Joanna Schmidt

Editing

Senior Editor
Kylin Larsson

Copyeditors
Robin Allred Jennings
Kate Willms

Additional Editing
Dan Bostian
Elizabeth Buelow
Emilee Newman Bowles
Rebecca Daniels
Chris Huff
Pamela Ivey
Professor Karen Kirtley
Blue Muni
Cassie Richoux
Lauren Shapiro
Jessica Tyner

Additional Help

Abbey Gaterud
Michael Hirte
Amanda Johnson
Bo Björn Johnson
Malini Kochhar
Sean Cunnison Scott

Colophon

Cover design by Rachel S. Tobie using **Goudy** and Goudy Modern Mt.

Interior design by Cliff N. Hansen using Gentium, Lucida Sans Unicode, **Arno Pro**, *Freestyle Script*, Jerry's Handwriting, *Lucida Handwriting*, Wingdings, *Pristina*, **GlooGun**, **Gill Sans Ultra Bold**, *Felt Pen*, Journal, *Monotype Corsiva*, aaaiight!, STENCIL FRA VENDOR CÔCO, Grimmace, and *Rebecca*.

Ordering Information

Ooligan Press titles are distributed to the book trade by Graphic Arts Center Publishing Company (www.gacpc.com) and are available at all major national and regional whole- salers. For ordering information, please call 800.452.3032 or use the instructions from the Graphic Arts Center catalog. To request a catalog, please phone 800.84.BOOKS.

Our books also may be purchased directly from the press by phone, fax, post, or e-mail. Educators, please contact us for a special discount on classroom sets.

Ooligan Press
P.O. Box 751
Portland, OR 97207-0751
www.ooliganpress.pdx.edu
503.725.9410
ooligan@pdx.edu

42